The Risk of Being
Ridiculous

A HISTORICAL NOVEL OF
LOVE AND REVOLUTION

HELLGATE PRES

Published by Hellgate Press/Fiction
(An imprint of L&R Publishing, LLC)

Hellgate Press Fiction
PO Box 3531
Ashland, OR 97520
www.hellgatepress.com

Editing: Harley B. Patrick

Cover design: Corey Maynard

Cover collaborators: Blair Saxon-Hill, John Crocker, Dahna Solar, Teryl Saxon-Hill,
Marlitt Dellabough, Harley B. Patrick, Shelley Maynard, Guy Maynard. Peace sign
drawn by Scott Stephen (1950-2001). *Cover contributors*: Craig Stephen,
Michael Lindner, Karen Klimax, Jeanne Maasch, Trish Martin.

Library of Congress Cataloging-in-Publication Data
Maynard, Guy, 1950-
The risk of being ridiculous : a historical novel of love and revolution / Guy
Maynard. -- 1st ed.
p. cm.
ISBN 978-1-55571-671-4
1. Young adults--Fiction. 2. Hippies--Fiction. 3. Boston (Mass.)--Fiction. 4.
United States--Social life and customs--20th century--Fiction. 5. Love stories.
gsafd I. Title.
PS3613.A957R57 2010
813'.6--dc22
2010028823

Printed and bound in the United States of America
First edition 10 9 8 7 6 5 4 3 2 1

The Risk of Being
Ridiculous

May the passion, the experience, and even the faults of my fighting generation have some small power to illumine the way forward.

—Victor Serge, *Memoirs of a Revolutionary*

For all of us. You know who you are.

THE ROCK FELT GOOD IN MY HAND. *Smooth. Fit easily in my closed fist. As the cops started moving slowly down the street, their steps in time, their clubs up, I rolled it in my hand like a baseball pitcher looking for the right grip. I didn't know where Mike and most of the other guys were, but now it didn't matter. Patrick and hundreds of other freaks were beside me and this was as good a place as any to make a stand. We held our ground as the rhythmic marching, the ringing thud of boots against the street, slowly closed the ground between them and us.*

The whole swirling world narrowed with the shrinking space between their straight blue line and our ragged and fluid throng. It came into focus, clear and certain. It was all right here and I knew what I had to do...

CHAPTER ONE

December 27-28, 1969

I-74 BOLTS EAST OUT OF CHAMPAIGN-URBANA. Straight and flat through the browned dead cornfields of Ogden and Tilton and then a quick hump over wooded hills past Lake Vermillion and right on through Danville to the Indiana line. Point and go. Me, Barry, and Stu flying on hash and wine and beer and the high-octane impulse to go, Barry's beige VW bug eating the throbbing white lines that dance in the spot light glow of our headlights, as Champaign-Urbana becomes a smaller and smaller dot behind us. Home, shit. Moving from here to there is the only place I know to be anymore. Has to be the right direction.

Barry's driving. Stu is sprawled across the back seat. I'm in shotgun trying to keep the pipe lit and the radio tuned. We talk. We laugh. We know we have eighteen hours in this tin can car, and we grab the rushing energy of the blur we are painting to speed us along our way across this flattened landscape. And in that blur, I float.

I was a stranger in my own hometown. Lost on streets I'd traveled hundreds, thousands, of times before on foot, on bikes, in cars riding and driving, with my parents, friends, sisters, band mates, girl friends, cops, alone, giddy with a kid's excitement, heavy with an adolescent's dread, strong with a young man's certainty, stoned, feverishly alert, as a thief, as a young Republican, as a rebel, drunk, daydreaming, scheming, tripping, depressed, joyous, jealous, in love, skipping school, going to work, going nowhere, wet, sweaty, scared, freezing my ass off, totally oblivious to everything but the wild thoughts in my head, at every hour of the day and night. Those were the paths that led from my parents' house out into my teenage world. I knew them so well that I stopped knowing them as anything outside of myself. They were still all there, exactly the same but strange now, and distant.

Flickering thoughts, shitty radio. Hard to find a static-free station, never mind a decent song. "Come On Down to My Boat." Bubblegum bullshit. I-74 veers to the southeast toward Indianapolis, and we fly through the sudden day-like brightness of the Crawfordsville Lights—a bank of powerful yellow-glowing towers that mark a point of passage on the Champaign-Boston run. Underway: cruising altitude and a sudden shift in reality. We weren't there anymore.

They were my friends, always my friends: Scotty and Alexander and Robin and Mitch and, even, Mary. But, man, I just didn't know how to make it real for them, to get them to take me seriously, to take the revolution seriously. "King protester," shit, that's what Scotty called me. Like it was some game. They are all against the war, for sure, done everything you can imagine to stay out of the army. Even more, they were against the lives we were supposed to be leading: high school, college, jobs, marriage, kids, debt, cocktails, and TV, and quiet compliance to the insanity. But it was more than just not fighting in the war or refusing to live phony lives. There was a battle to be fought, a revolution, a fucking world that had to be changed so there would be no more wars to fight and better lives were possible. It was more than just saying no to all the bullshit, we had to find something, build something, to say yes to—and then fight to make it real. That time was coming. Fucking serious shit—our lives, man, all of our lives.

The radio sucks. "I Think We're Alone Now." Hardly any cars on the road. Flat, dark farmland turns to bright light city as we curl around a sleeping Indianapolis. We are a small ball tumbling free through these wide quiet lanes. We pick up I-70 on the other side of Indianapolis, now pointing straight east again.

And my parents, shit, what was I supposed to tell them? My mother was so sad when I said goodbye to her, as my father slept, numb from whatever combination of drink and pills he'd chosen last night. "Your father really was hoping to have more of a chance to talk to you," she said. My father and I had shouted our way through my week home, but he still held out some hope that he was one good talk away from straightening me out. "We worry about you so," my mother said. "Don't, I'm OK," I said. "I wish I could believe that," she said. She *knew,* but what was I supposed to say? "You're right. There's some serious shit ahead, and I plan to be in the middle of it. There's almost no chance I'll ever be anything you want me to be." Shit.

My parents, each in their own way, had been proud of the idealism that I'd gravitated toward since I was just a little kid: the American Revolution and the dreams of liberty and real democracy that grew out of the same New England soil that we came from, the rugged individualist conservatism of Barry Goldwater, the nonviolent protest for civil rights and against the Vietnam War. After winning my class presidency as a high school sophomore on a platform of longer lunch hours, I had lost the same office—by three votes—as a senior, after delivering a speech assailing racism and other intolerances. That speech stunned the auditorium full of my classmates who were used to skits and frivolities at the class election assembly and who, after what seemed like a long silence when I finished, slowly rose as one and, with the teachers joining in, gave me an extended standing ovation, also unheard of at that event. Of course, I lost to the kid named Campbell who had dancing soup cans as the highlight of his assembly presentation. But my parents had been so proud when word filtered back to them through teachers and other parents about my speech and its reception.

But my idealism was no longer the fuzzy, cute stuff of a kid playing with big ideas. Reality was now fighting back and it was getting fucking heavy.

Indiana rushes by. Greenfield. Cambridge City. Richmond. Bright beacons of exits that glow for miles as we approach, then are suddenly gone, behind us. And here's Ohio. Lewisburg. Brookville. Vandalia. Springfield. Columbus. We grab Interstate 71, heading northeast toward Cleveland. The bubblegum just won't stop: "Sugar and Spice."

Shit. But it keeps away the silence of this no-time zone between late night and early morning, gives a beat to the jam inside my head.

And Mary, sweet Mary, shouting in my ear at the Red Lion, while a band of old friends played tinny loud versions of "Light My Fire" and "Sunshine of Your Love" and I was surrounded by a blur of familiar faces of people I didn't know anymore. I want too much. I give too much. I wouldn't know what to do if it was easy. That's what Mary, an old love who was never quite my girl friend, had said when I told her about Sarah. I didn't ask what she meant by that. She acted like I should know. When I was flailing around trying to win Mary's heart, she and Scotty, I found out later, were just casually fucking. Shit, I couldn't blame her— Scotty was so many things that I wasn't, tall and cool, and he knew how to let things come to him. Man, I'd love it to be easy. I just don't know how to make it easy, because it's always so fucking hard. How do you know how much to want? How much to give? How can you tell how much some other person wants and how much they want to give? Or how much they want you to want or give. Shit. It's just not easy. Not for me.

The radio crackles as I search for a clear signal. The reward is clear crap: "I'm Henry the Eighth, I Am." Mount Vernon. Mansfield. Wadsworth. There is a roll to the road now, like we are riding great swells on a vast sea.

The first time I saw this part of the country was in 1963 driving with my father in his flag blue Buick LeSabre. We were moving from New

Bedford, Massachusetts, where I'd lived my whole life, where all my friends were, where everything I knew and wanted was, to the desolate frontier of Urbana, Illinois. My mother and sisters flew. The boys drove. On a hot late August day, as my Dad and I moved west across Ohio and watched the landscape shift from the rounded hills of the East to the stretched flat horizons of the Midwest, we listened to a speech that a southern preacher gave to a rally in Washington. I got chills when I heard him talk about a dream he had for our country. He made me feel proud to be an American because, like him, I believed his dream could come true in America. Then, I could balance the American Revolution and Barry Goldwater and civil rights in my head because they all were part of this great American promise that I cherished. Even my dad believed in that dream, I think, in 1963. I was thirteen.

We had a good time on that trip, eating ham and cheese sandwiches and following our progress on a Triple A TripTik. I didn't understand why we were moving, but I knew my parents were troubled. And as it turned out, all the things they had tried to leave behind in New Bedford—my father's drinking and pervasive sense of failure, my mother's anger and sadness at the life she'd been dealt—followed us and kept eating away at our family. Conservative individualism got lost in racism and war. And the dream that Martin Luther King had inspired us with turned out to be no more realistic than my parents' hope of a new place bringing a new life.

We sail onto I-90, past the stink and lights of Cleveland, and reach to the East through Mentor, Painesville, Ashtabula. Finally, a decent song. At least top forty radio had to play the Beatles every once in a while.

Hey, Jude, don't make it bad, take a sad song and make it better.

The fucking Beatles. Thank god for the Beatles. Here we are on this deserted highway where Ohio starts to meld into Pennsylvania, picking up some Podunk station out of Nowhere, Ohioania, and the fucking

Beatles are singing for us. *Hey, Jude, don't let me down, you have found her now go out and get her.* How do they know?

I remembered Mike and me, in the early days at Mountfort Street, listening to *Abbey Road* for the first time, high on mescaline. The first side was full of great Beatles songs, but, shit, when we flipped it over, we flipped out, our eyes locked into each others, getting wider and wider, fucking speechless, as one riff flew into another, reaching deep down into our consciousness, plucking our strings, beating our skins, singing our souls: Soaring guitars: "Here Comes the Sun." A wall of harmony: "Because." A muffled, joyous voice: "You Never Give Me Your Money." Sad solo voice: "Golden Slumbers." Just rolling, couldn't tell where one song stopped and the next started. It was all one song, one jumbled, flying, floating, roaring, funny, sad, glorious fucking song: *And in the end, the love you take is equal to the love you make.* Man, Mike and me went insane. The Beatles singing, playing what philosophers had written big thick books about: existentialism or whatever the fuck you want to call it and the Golden Rule all wrapped up on one side of a rock and roll record. It was all there in some great fucking music—in a way that bypassed the cold analysis of the brain, the dry collection of words on paper—vibrations and sounds that made it all absolutely clear. And the thing that blew our minds was: Here were the Beatles, the group, who somehow fed off each other, fed off this great collective consciousness that was spreading over the world to create this incredible music. It wasn't like Dostoevsky or Hesse or Nietzche or Van Gogh or even fucking Marx, in some lonely room, staring at the wall, a prisoner of their consciousness, alone because of their consciousness, creating their art to avoid the madness that the weight of their consciousness drove them towards. The Beatles were a group, creating, learning, fighting the madness together. Like us. Like we wanted to be. Mike and Stu and Brian and Sarah and me and all the other kids in Boston and even the kids in Champaign, Barry and Scotty and all of them. Shit, kids everywhere were doing it. Berkeley, Prague, Paris—probably even in Conneaut, Ohio, which just went flying by—everywhere, man. And the Beatles were just riding that energy, focusing it, putting it into a form we could sing along with. *And in the end, the love you take is equal to the love you make.* Man, I hope that's true.

> *Hey Jude, don't make it bad. Take a sad song and make it better. Remember to let her under your skin. Then you begin to make it better—better better better better.*

Better. Better. Better. Better. Sarah. Sarah. Sarah. Sarah. Man, in three days, we'd be together and…. And what? I was supposed to know what by now. Supposed to know what the next step was. But I didn't, only that I couldn't wait to take it.

"Great song," I say into this new softer spell we have drifted into as the darkness that has enfolded us begins to break with the first hints of daylight.

"Yeah, great song," I hear from Barry's tired voice and a mumbled agreement from Stu in the back. It's time for a shift. We pull into a Sunoco station. Refuel. Grab Pepsis and Paydays. I get behind the wheel. Stu moves to shotgun. Barry curls up across the back seat. We get back onto I-90.

Gentle hills roll into the red dawn. A hazy and chilled whiteness wakes slowly as we whisper past exits counting down the miles to Erie, the next waypoint, and then Buffalo and Syracuse and Albany. It's a new day. Boston waits at the end of it. *Nah, nah, nah, nah, nah, nahnahnahnahnah.*

CHAPTER TWO

December 28

THE DOOR WAS UNLOCKED. OF COURSE. The door was always unlocked. Somebody must have the key. Probably Stu had it stashed somewhere in his room, but it'd been so long since anybody used it, the four of us who (usually) paid the rent and all the others who lived there from time to time never even thought about carrying a key. The glowing blue paint on the white chipped door said "Welcome ALL." And we meant it. Stoned, wired, rejoicing in no longer being crammed in that tiny car, I felt good pushing open the door and smelling home: old dope smoke, forgotten cat litter, leaking upholstered furniture: the distinct and familiar stink that reminded me that this is where it was all happening. And the wall…

As we filed into the apartment, we were met by a swirl of colors and words, a blur of blobs and lines, explosions and expressions, a collapsed rainbow of politics and art and stoned kids having fun. In playful pinks, letters almost smiling: "Distrust sad people, the revolution is joy." In a shiny bold blue counterclockwise circle: "In a time of revolution, no bystanders are innocent." Wild thick red strokes: "Be realistic, demand the impossible!" Sinister black in stenciled seriousness: "KILL YOUR

PARENTS." An intricate Escher-like drawing, hair thin lines intersecting and closing in on themselves to form a tower that spiraled and corkscrewed into the wall, disappearing in a vast imagined distance. Rolling script, green and neat, following an unseen line: "You never know what is enough unless you know what is more than enough.—William Blake." A multihued day-glo peace sign. A recipe for Mary Jane Superweed Candy, lined up just like it came from a cookbook, with flour and caramels and walnuts and "clean and sifted marijuana" and an option (to be used with "discretion") to psychedelicize with DMT or LSD. "LOVE" spelled with flower letters with petals and blossoms of yellow and orange and purple. Small red letters in a tight little square: "Political power grows out of the barrel of a gun: Chairman Mao." A damn good Mr. Natural on a scooter, saying, "Don't mean sheet." A skillfully drawn female nude beneath a hastily scribbled quote from Dylan: "He not busy being born is busy dying." And more and more, notes inside of letters, colors on top of colors, *Mad Magazine*-like doodles sneaking into every margin and blank spot. And down in the lower corner, closest to our front door, where the plastered painted wall met the wooden wainscoting, a small awkward-looking heart with the barely legible legend inside of it: "BT X SS." Guess who did that?

The wall had been decorated during a party we'd thrown on Thanksgiving, the Beggar's Banquet we'd called it after the Stones' great album. We had a turkey and everything. But the boys from New York showed up with some fine LSD and killer opium. And I found myself looking at the cooked turkey, admiring its golden, crisp skin and its full rich aroma and wondering how anybody could possibly eat it. I don't know if anybody did. The only other clear memory I have of that party was suddenly missing Sarah so much that everything, the music and the talking and the collage of people's faces, rolled together to form a blurry wall of noise that was keeping me away from her and I had to call her. I tried. I somehow got her on the phone, but I couldn't get my thoughts from my brain to my mouth. I don't know what she thought, but just hearing her voice, hearing her laugh as I struggled to make sense, made me feel better. I must have drawn that heart sometime after that, though I don't exactly remember doing it.

Stu and I shared Apartment 9 at 64 Mountfort Street with Mike and Brian and whoever else felt like staying there. We were all more or less students at Boston University. Mostly less. Stu had just dropped out. Mike and I were barely hanging on in school, but not quite ready to let go. Brian...? It was hard to tell about Brian. The four of us had met the year before when we all lived in a three-building dorm complex and ended up at the same parties or concerts or demonstrations often enough that we became friends and then more than friends, part of a tribe of radical, stoned-out, rock-and-roll-loving freaks. We'd been in this apartment since September, when Stu and Mike and I started our sophomore years and Brian, who came in at the last minute because the guy we expected backed out, was a junior.

The colors and wisdom of the wall rolled and flowed on both sides of the hall from the door until just around the bend, where Lenny was sleeping on the couch.

"Hey Lenny," I shouted, giddy with the homecoming high, feeling good about bringing Barry, a piece of my Illinois life, into our little den of insanity.

Lenny rolled over and squinted and softly replied, "Hey Tucker, what's happening?" Lenny was in the Coast Guard. He'd gone a semester or two to BU with us before he dropped or flunked out. And the Coast Guard, which was not fighting in Vietnam, was a better option than the always looming draft—if you could get in. But Lenny had figured out a way and whenever he got leave, he showed up at Mountfort Street and he always ended up stretched out on the first couch in the hall, his long legs hanging comfortably over the fraying edges. The hall had two couches on either side of the door into Brian's room. They were prime crashing spots and Lenny always made sure to claim his.

"Not much, man, we just cruised in from Illinois. So we're kinda flying now."

We filed past him: me, Stu, and Barry, each of us nodding, and Lenny nodding back.

The apartment was quiet. Strangely quiet. But shit, Stu and I had been gone. Who knew where Brian was? A lot of our other friends were probably still home for Christmas vacation. Some restrained bluesy music was coming from Mike's room.

I tossed my bag into my room—the first door on the left, across from Brian's door and Lenny's couch—which was as big a fucking mess as I had left it: papers and books and magazines and album covers spread all over the floor and creeping up onto the two mattresses which formed an L along the walls. Brown burlap curtains hung unevenly over the two tall windows that looked out onto Boston's back alleys. And a crooked Che Guevera looked down from the wall, smiling righteously above his bold red quote: "Let me say at the risk of seeming ridiculous that the true revolutionary is guided by great feelings of love." Next to him hung a Boston Tea Party poster advertising a bill of the Kinks, Traffic, and Boz Scaggs—what a show that had been. In the far corner of the room, under the window in the space between the end of the mattress and the wall, Tavola was curled in a ball, partially hidden by the heap of an old blue sweater. She looked up at me like she didn't give a shit that I was back. I walked over and stroked her soft black fur. She stretched her neck and rolled her head to meet my touch. It was good to be home.

"This your room, Tucker?" Barry laughed, hanging in the doorway.

"Yeah, man, the suite." My whole room had been furnished by one night's expedition down the alleys and back streets of our Back Bay neighborhood. Boards and concrete blocks for bookshelves, a funky small wooden desk with two drawers, and two fine mattresses. You wouldn't believe the shit people throw away. "Don't laugh at it, you'll be fighting for a spot in it before long."

"Hey, I ain't laughing. I just could tell it was yours." He really was laughing. Barry was my oldest friend from Illinois—the kind of friend that his parents thought I was a bad influence on him and my parents were convinced he was a bad influence on me. They were both right.

"And I'm proud of it." I was laughing, too, but I *was* proud of my room.

Stu had disappeared into his room, which was to the right at the end of the hall and the least public of the four bedrooms. He had a nice stereo and just seemed to need to be alone more than the rest of us. My room was the most public—the all-night lounge, the never-full motel. Mike's room, on the other side of the bathroom and kitchen from Stu's, fell somewhere in between—that's where Barry and I headed, following the sweet pleas of B.B. King's guitar.

The only light came from a small reading lamp that shined directly over Mike's shoulder to the thick book he held close to his eyes. He sat in a straight-back armchair (no alley find, he'd brought that from home). Mike's room had a single bed on a simple frame. A table-high bookcase along the opposite wall with his stereo across the top. Neatly arranged books on the middle shelf. His albums on the bottom shelf. Speakers on either side of the bookshelf. His reading chair and lamp were set in the far corner next to the bed and that's usually where you found him.

Mike slowly pulled his eyes from his book and looked me over. Only a hint of a smile came over his face, "Hey, Tucker," then seeing Barry behind me, he was a little more expressive: "Barry. What's happening?" Barry and Mike had gotten to know each other in three outrageous days at the Newport Jazz Festival the summer before.

I answered: "Man, we just cruised from Illinois in his goddamn little VW bug. Shit, it was cramped, but we had a hell of a time. We partied last night and when we were done partying we jumped in his car and just flew here. Man, it's good to be here. You're looking awful damn mellow."

"Well it was nice and peaceful until you fuckers showed up," Now his smile was big. "Where's Stu?"

"Stu's dropping his shit in his room. What's happening here? Where's Brian?"

"Still in New Jersey. Don't know when he'll be back. I've only been here a couple of days. Nothing's going on here that I know of. Doing lots of reading." Mike looked at me, then at Barry, then back at me with an expectant smile. "You guys got any dope or what? What the hell you waiting for?"

"Good to see you, too, Mike." Barry laughed, sat against the head of Mike's bed, and pulled out his pipe and tin of hash.

"Shit, I'm always happy to see a brother from Champaign, 'specially when he's packing hash," his laugh was a throaty, rolling jive, and his exaggerated grin showed the big gap in his front teeth. Mike was a bear of a kid, big and bulky, wild, curly bark brown hair thrown out from his head in all directions, a full man's beard framing his face along with thick black-framed glasses which magnified his deep-set eyes. He always wore his glasses, except, I guess, when he slept, or sometimes when he took them off just to freak us out. Mike was an intimidating-looking guy with his glasses on—he was like some kind of alien without them, especially when you were really stoned and he'd suddenly jam his distorted face right into yours. Mike was also the smartest person I knew.

His laughter and the fresh smell of hash smoke brought Stu and Lenny into the room.

"I recognize that smell," Stu said as he sat next to me at the foot of the bed and took the pipe. "We smoked a bit of this in the last week. Too bad you couldn't have been with us, Mike. Good times. Lots of partying."

Stu had gone home to Illinois with me for part of Christmas vacation. A slouchy five ten or so, Stu had a mass of thick black hair that rolled from a part on the right side of his head and mounded across the top. That and his shaggy, full black mustache set against the soft features of his face gave him kind of a stoned-out walrus look. Stu was always backslapping friendly and had a ringing wit that rode on the hard edges and soft r's of his Worcester accent, sometimes sounding a lot like his older neighbor, Abbie Hoffman, a hero to us all.

Stu gave his rundown of our week in Champaign-Urbana. Heavy drinking. My crazy family, though Stu was too nice to put it that way. Lots of hash, thanks to Barry, and rock and roll. He told Mike how I almost blew a free meal when I told Norman, one of my old band managers who was buying a bunch of us a Chinese dinner, that rock and roll stars don't deserve to be rich and we got into a hell of a shouting match.

Stu spread his arms out wide, stretched his eyes open, tilted his head toward Mike, like a wise parent moaning about a silly kid: "I told him he should've waited until after the guy picked up the tab to call him a capitalist pig."

I looked to Mike, not sorry, "And I told him what Marx said, 'The last capitalist will sell us the rope we hang him with.'"

Barry had the same reaction he'd had when Stu and I went through this routine in Illinois. "Shit, Ben, Norman's just a little punk from Danville. Marx? Shit!"

Mike laughed, letting this one go without taking sides. He got up to change the record. More B.B. "Every Day I Have the Blues."

Mike filled us in on his time at home in Springfield, his old man giving him a hard time, his mother freaking out. Sounded familiar. What saved him was getting together with his old buddy JT and getting high every night.

The pipe came round to Mike. He took a deep pull on it, then passed it to Lenny, who was sitting on the floor next to Mike's chair. Lenny smiled big as he took the pipe and sucked in the sweet smoke, and then started giggling as he tried to hold it in and it trickled out in spurts and coughs. He handed the pipe to Stu. Lenny was a tall lean black guy, whose Afro had been lost to the Coast Guard. He always showed up in a navy blue stocking cap and a navy blue pea coat with a six pack under his arm and never said much. Stu took his turn on the pipe and passed it to me.

I took a long hit on the pipe and clamped my mouth and eyes shut and held the smoke as long as I could. When I finally released the smoke and opened my eyes, the room was brighter and sharper. Stoned again.

Things were quiet around town, Mike said. He hadn't seen any of our other friends since he got back. He had run into a few Weathermen in Kenmore Square. Luke wasn't with them, but they all knew Mike and said they wanted to come over and talk to us about running with them in some of the upcoming actions.

"Let me know when they're coming," said Stu, from his perch beside me on the bed, as he took the pipe again, "and I'll be someplace else." He put the pipe to his mouth.

"They ain't gonna shoot you, Stuey," Mike said. Smoke filtered the room's dim light to ripples of gray. Mike looked at me with a knowing grin as he talked to Stu. "They're just assholes like you and me."

"No, I think they're a different kind of asshole," Stu said, his voice squeaky as exhaled.

"Crazy motherfuckers," Lenny piped in as he offered his lighter to Barry who packed a fresh bowl of hash.

"I think they are, too," I said. "They got that look in their eyes like the Meher Baba freaks or the Hare Krishnas. Shit, you know, like they *believe*. But they got guts and I think a lot of their analysis is right on."

The Boston area leader of the Weathermen—one of the factions that had come out of the crazy SDS convention last summer—was Luke, kind of a friend of ours, who'd been the leader of the anti-military campaign at BU the year before, a campaign that Mike and Lenny and Sarah and I had all been active in. Luke was older, a full-time organizer for SDS, a kind of charismatic guy who was tall with wavy ink-black hair and a granite face, a great speaker—and he usually made a lot of sense.

"But I don't know if I want to hang out with them. They're so fucking serious," I said looking at Mike, who shrugged again. "I mean, I like Luke. I guess we can talk to them, figure out some way to work together. I guess we're on the same side."

"Sure," Mike said, and took the pipe from Barry. None of us were really part of SDS. I signed up for membership once to help the BU delegation get more votes at the national convention—which turned out to be the one where it split into all the factions. I'm not sure which faction my vote went to. And my SDS "membership" didn't help much when BU decided to include me in an injunction against real SDS members—and members of the straightest faction, the worker-student alliance folks, at that. We—mostly Mike and me—worked with all the various factions on a lot of stuff and we'd always end up at demonstrations together. But we had our own little faction that didn't have an official organization or name. Some reporter once called us "hippie militants," which described us as well as any label, I guess. It was fittingly contradictory. Our faction stretched all the way from Stu to Mike, from rock and roll to revolution. The Weathermen were among the first politicos outside of Abbie and the Yippies and the White Panthers in Michigan to recognize the power of the cultural revolutions—the youth movement, the women's movement, and sex, drugs, and rock and roll, and all that.

"Anyway," Mike said to me. "I told them you were out of town and that we should get together sometime after you got back. You don't have to be here, Stu. You can go bury your head in the sand somewhere," Mike said, grinning at me, as he got up to flip the record over.

"You bet your ass I don't," Stu was smiling. He knew Mike's game—most of the time. "And for another thing." He paused and glared at Mike, then me. "Don't call me to bail your asses out."

"Ah, Stu, we know we can always count on you," I said.

"Count on this," he said as he raised his middle finger to me, and got up off the bed. "I'm going to bed and dream of a world without room-mates who try to drive me crazy."

"Hey, Stu," I said as he headed out the door. "It was fun having you go home with me."

"Yeah, sure, but I'm still not bailing your ass out of jail."

Lenny followed Stu out of the room to reclaim his spot on the couch. Barry and Mike and I took another round on the pipe.

"Shit, Weathermen? What the fuck are you guys into?" Barry asked, looking at Mike.

"Didn't Tucker tell you? We are the revolution, man, pig-offing, state-smashing, government-overthrowing motherfucking revolutionaries." Mike's grin was truly shit-eating now. And you could tell how stoned he was because his magnified eyeballs were now squinting little peas. "Shit, Tucker, I'm surprised you didn't tell our brother he was coming into a major cell of the international people's liberation movement."

"Tucker talks so much shit I don't know what to think about it," Barry looked at me and laughed. "He's been doing it for years. As long as I've known him. Except it used to be for Goldwater. Now it's Lenin and Weathermen. Shit, why should I start taking him serious now?"

"You got that right at least," Mike said. "Shit, man, I don't know what we're into," his voice tailed off now, almost quiet. "What are we into, Tucker?" He wasn't expecting an answer. "I'm into feeling pretty fucking stoned right now. That's some good hashish you got there." The pipe was out. B.B. pulled some heartache out of his guitar strings, his voice sharp through the smoky gray haze that had settled around us.

"So what happening with you, Barry?" Mike asked.

"Mainly I'm trying to figure out how to stay out of the goddamn army." Barry got the worst number of anybody I knew—five—in the draft lottery that had happened a few weeks before. Shit, what a crazy day that was, like some kind of government-sponsored Russian roulette, except the government was the one who loaded the gun and had their finger on the trigger—and pointed it at our fucking heads. Even if you got a good number—which I did (225)—you couldn't feel too fucking good because there was someone in the same room or someone back home—like Barry—who got a low number. Barry had just flunked out of school, which meant his student deferment was gone. He could basically get an induction notice any day. The fucking draft, man. Screwing up everybody's life. That was just one of the reasons we had to stop the fucking war.

"What are you going to do?" Mike asked. The jive was all gone now.

"I'm not going in the fucking army," Barry pulled a Marlboro out of his pack and lit it. I reached out my hand and he handed me one, too.

"Of course not, but what are you going to do?" Mike asked. Barry and I had had this conversation many times.

Barry told him about his bad knee from his days as a halfback for the Urbana Junior High School football team, and his redneck doctor who wouldn't sign the 4-F forms because he thought anyone with two legs should go in the fucking army. Barry held his cigarette in his mouth, little puffs of smoke shooting out as he talked. "So I'm going to a different doctor. If that doesn't work, I don't know what I'm going to do."

"You know we know people who can help you."

"Yeah, Tucker's told me all that shit." Many times. "I just don't want to do that unless I have to. I mean if it comes down to the army or Canada, shit I'm gone, but I am going to try everything else first."

"That's cool, man." Mike said. "Just so you know where to come if you need help."

"I do." Now it got real quiet. What else was there to say? Barry took a long drag from his cigarette and pulled it from his mouth as he exhaled. "Shit, man, I'm tired. I'm going to get my shit out of the car and hit the sack. In your room, Tucker?"

"Yeah, the suite—take the mattress under the window I'll be in there in a little bit. "

Mike and I watched him go. B.B was still wailing to "Help the Poor."

We talked about Barry. I just knew Barry would find a way out of the draft. All the time, we were growing up, Barry got away with incredible stuff. One time, we burned this car—a big old boat of an Oldsmobile— his dad had bought for him. Somebody dropped a cigarette into the back seat upholstery and it turned into a fucking smoldering smoking mess. But he came up with this story about somebody stealing it and us finding it—this incredible line of bullshit that his father actually bought—and we came out looking like heroes. I knew he was going to find a way out of the draft. He was going back the next day and seeing some new doctor later in the week. Still, it was a pain in the ass.

Mike and I talked about our trips home—how hard it was with family and old friends. He'd gone through a lot of the same stuff I had. Neither of us exactly said how good it felt just to be back, hanging out in *our* apartment—like home, but a kind of home we'd never known before, our home—but, man, that's what I was thinking sitting there with Mike as the hours and the miles and all the smoke and drink I'd taken in over the last day and a half piled down on me to make me achingly tired, a good ache, a full ache.

I told Mike about Sarah coming, how cool that was going to be. He was heading to Amherst for a big New Year's Eve party at JT's, and he was planning to see his old girl friend Pauline.

"I think she's going to come live with me after the break," he said.

That roused me. "No shit! That's great." Man, Mike had a way of dumping heavy shit like he was talking about a bus schedule. We'd had plenty of girls crash at Mountfort Street or spend the night. Brian had frequent and changing and often strange female guests. Sarah had been up for a few weekends. But we never had a girl live there before. And who would have thought it would be Mike to be the first. In the year and a half I'd known him, he'd never had a girl friend that I knew of. I'd never met Pauline—Paulie is what people usually called her. She'd been Mike's high school sweetheart and I guess they'd been on and off since, but he didn't talk about her much. It was like this whole other side of him that he kept hidden in some secret place. I liked when he let me in there—even for just a glimpse.

"I guess. We'll see." It was a trip just to see Mike show even a little bit of uncertainty. "It should be cool."

"Shit yeah, should be fine," I said. Of course, what popped into my mind was Sarah: maybe Paulie being here would help convince her that she should be here, too. "Man, wouldn't it be cool if Sarah would decide to stay here, too."

"Sure, man, that'd be great," he said without much emotion. He was as flat about my love life as he was about his own.

But, man, that would be cool.

CHAPTER THREE

December 30

ALL NIGHT, AS I TRIED TO CLEAN MY ROOM, I kept rethinking the schedule. Her plane gets in at quarter of ten. If I hit all the trains just right—don't have to wait long at Kenmore, smooth transfer at Park Street—it takes a little less than half an hour to get to the airport subway stop. You never can tell about those buses to the terminal, usually you wait no more than five minutes, but, shit, sometimes it's been as much as twenty. OK, so allow fifteen minutes waiting for the bus. And another ten to get to the Allegheny terminal. That makes fifty-five minutes from Kenmore to the terminal, if everything goes smooth. Take me five minutes to walk to Kenmore. Five minutes to find out where her gate is—and since it's always way the hell over the other side of the terminal—call it ten minutes to the gate. What's that now? An hour and fifteen minutes from Mountfort Street to her gate—if things go pretty smooth. Better allow an hour and forty-five minutes. So I'll leave at 8 o'clock.

I ached to see her, an ache that started at the tips of my fingers and penetrated through every layer of me to some deep place—my soul, maybe, shit I don't know. It'd been so long since we'd been together. So much had happened. I wanted to hold her and kiss her, to feel her softness nestled into me, to have her in my bed, my funky mattress on the floor, to go to sleep to her breathing and to wake beside her warmth. Yes, I wanted, longed, couldn't wait for all that closeness and touching and kissing, but this ache went deeper.

I wanted Sarah to be a part of it—my world, our world, this wild world that was changing every day. I wanted her next to me when we shook our fists at the deans or the cops or the multitude of students who didn't give a shit. I wanted her arm in mine when we formed a human chain to lock out the workers at MIT who were designing the latest and greatest U.S. missiles, and then to run—giddy and powerful—next to me through the streets of Cambridge after we'd made a righteous stand against the blue-helmeted baton-flailing cops, and to dance in celebration with me when the brothers and sisters who did get arrested snuck out a window of the bus that was supposed to take them to jail. I wanted to move with her, shaking and twisting, hot and high, to Johnny Winter or Lee Michaels or the Illinois Speed Press at the Tea Party or the Common or Sargent Gym. I wanted her by my side when we met with Boston Black Panthers after the Chicago cops had murdered Fred Hampton and Mark Clark, to fathom their dark, focused eyes, which were fixed on a revolution that was still an abstraction to most of us, eyes that had stared straight into the full wrath of the most powerful state the world had ever known and not blinked. I wanted to pass her the joint as we got high and talked white kids revolution at Mountfort Street. I wanted to hold her hand through the meetings and rallies and parties that shaped this Movement that pulled and pushed us as we pushed and pulled each other. I wanted her there for the constant, movable rap session with ever changing participants and *Arthur* or the Airplane or the Allman Brothers in the background, often stoned but not always, sometimes dead serious, sometimes insanely hysterical, always circling around mounds of bullshit but always, always, coming back to one basic question: With all we knew and all we'd seen, how the fuck were we supposed to make any sense of our lives?

Not that she was a stranger to that world. She'd been there the spring before when we took over the administration building at BU during the anti-military campaign—the first night we ever slept together was on the floor of Dean Dexter's office crowded together between Lenny and

Mike, fully clothed but connected by all kinds of passion. She'd been with us at Boston English when the kids turned on us and the smelly heat of sudden violence and the paralysis of fear made me useless, while she kept her head and calmed me down until everybody got out of there. She'd been at the Newport Jazz Festival—a *rock* festival this year—when, not able to get tickets for the final session, hundreds of us went over the fence as Led Zeppelin hit the opening chords of "Good Times, Bad Times." Just two months before, we'd met in DC for the Moratorium and stood arm in arm outside the stone-faced, red-paint-splattered Justice Department, shouting "Free Bobby Seale," and when the capitol cops had launched their barrage of tear gas, my gentle Sarah, her crooked nose and soft lips covered by a red checkered bandanna, had whispered in my ear: "Fucking pigs!"

But this year, Sarah was living at home in Philadelphia. Her parents had decided one year at Boston University was enough. The rap—one that Sarah even pretended to believe—was that it was the money. BU was an expensive school, but I never believed that. I had seen the look in her father's eye when Sarah and I had kissed goodbye outside her dorm at the end of our freshman year. I was blonde, long-haired—and definitely not Jewish. That was scary enough. But what was more frightening to him, what bristled through his look that darted between bewilderment and anger, was how different the girl I was kissing was from the one he'd dropped off at the beginning of the year. She had let her long, dark chestnut hair become its frizzed-out curly self. She had traded in her matching Villager skirt and sweater outfits for fading and ragged bell-bottom jeans and tee-shirts. She smoked cigarettes—the idea that she smoked dope, too, was still a little beyond the realm of what he could allow himself to believe. And she cared enough to march and shout about things like the Vietnam War and racism.

Her parents were convinced that some combination of Boston and me had made this new person out of their daughter, and they didn't like it. And they liked it even less after Sarah and I got more intense when we saw each other during the summer. The first time was on my way from Illinois to Boston to deal with charges the BU administration had filed against me and twenty other kids for our takeover of the dean's office. I was happy when I got the letter telling me I was charged because it gave me an excuse to call Sarah—and to see her, to cut through the awkward distance that summer vacation had shoved between us and our budding romance. Cruising in Barry's VW, we stopped in Philadelphia coming and going. And when Sarah and I saw each other again—making that uncertain end-of-school-year promise we'd left each other with come true in touches and kisses and dreamy smiles—the passion between us jumped to a whole new level, a passion so obvious that her parents freaked out and tried to keep me away from her, forbidding me from being in their house, not giving her messages when I called. She had to lie to her parents to meet me at Newport, where we slept huddled close in a sleeping bag on a grassy parking lot among thousands of freaks— now a couple, crazy in love.

But as summer moved closer to fall, her parents opposition seem to wear her down. They told her she couldn't go back to Boston. And I pushed her to fight them. In fact, I even wrote her parents a long letter telling them just how wrong they were to oppose our love, to try to stop this new woman Sarah was becoming. Sarah dug the letter, but still she acted like she'd almost given up—like if her parents said she couldn't go to Boston, there was nothing she could do about it.

Then we had a bummer at Woodstock. I was coming from Boston and got there a day before her. I waited with Stu at the spot we were supposed to meet—the ticket booth that had shut down when the massive numbers had turned the festival into a free concert. We waited, got rained on, got soaked, covered in mud, got rained on again, heard all the freeways were closed. Sure that there was no way Sarah could ever get there, I packed it in. Stu and I left, hitchhiked back to Boston without hearing any music. She arrived just hours after we'd left to find the note I'd written on the crowded message board—"I'm here, I'll check back every hour"—and hadn't crossed out. She waited two days for me to check back, then gave up to finally go see some of the show. On the way, her best friend Sally, tripping, fell into a lagoon of shit that ringed a bank of outhouses. They freaked and headed back to their car. She never heard any music either. The mud and shit and missed connection at Woodstock—which most people were saying was the greatest fucking thing to ever happen for our generation—broke the magic spell of our fairy tale romance. Shook her faith in me, for sure. Made me push harder. We'd come close to packing it in as the summer ended.

I couldn't believe she didn't just come to Boston on her own. I pressured her to make a choice, her parents or me. I had convinced myself that she loved me and that the attraction of me and Boston was stronger than the resistance of her parents and Philadelphia, but now I had some doubts, maybe I was fooling myself again that somebody could actually love me as much as I loved them. So I backed away from my ultimatum when I sensed I would lose—and I just might lose her forever. I couldn't, wouldn't, take that chance. I hitchhiked to Philly and, seeing her, feeling that pumping surge in my heart, that love that just overwhelmed me, I knew—and I think she felt the same—we just had to figure out some way to keep it going. Me sneaking around Philly; her convincing her parents that she was going to see her girl friends in Boston and absolutely positively would not see me. By any means necessary. Eventually—I think they all went to some shrink or something—her parents came to a grudging acceptance of our relationship. I'm sure they thought it might dull Sarah's attraction to me if I was no longer the forbidden Romeo. But that was no more successful for them than an ultimatum had been for me.

So through the fall, Sarah and I found ways to keep our love alive via five state turnpikes and youth-fare plane trips. That love even seemed to grow stronger, but it was obvious to anybody, especially the two of us, that our lives were drifting further and further apart.

We talked on the phone a lot. So much that we got the phone disconnected at Mountfort Street because we couldn't pay the bill, which pissed Stu off. So then we talked phone booth to phone booth using a phony credit card number from a code published in the *Old Mole*—free unlimited calling (Power to the People!). And we wrote three or four times a week. I wrote long rambling letters that drifted from poetry to serious political discussions to the playfulness of a kid crazed with love. I wrote one with eight different colored pens, changing colors with every letter. She wrote tighter, smoother letters full of love and silliness on thick, colored paper. She signed them "Yom Gumbo Caracha,"—"I love you" in her own private language—"Zelda Farkward." But her letters were full of loneliness and distance, too, the drag of her daily life marking time at her parents' house in the suburbs, going to school at Temple during the days, spending the nights with the older sister of one of her best friends who was at BU (Leslie, who lived around the corner from Mountfort Street at 858 Beacon Street), watching old movies till the little hours of the morning. Philadelphia was an obligation she had not yet figured a way out of. Boston was where the life she should be leading was going on, without her. She was stuck waiting, always waiting, it seemed. Waiting for the next weekend, or the next letter, or the next phone call. Waiting for the end of this year in limbo, when something had to change. Waiting until something happened, in her, in me, in the world, so we could be together all the time. And I was waiting for her, too, though I knew the swirling world around me wasn't waiting for anything. "Waiting," I wrote to her, quoting William Carlos Williams, "that's the worst word in the language."

As fall turned into winter, my letters grew more and more strident and intense: "Imperialism is like a big word for the forces of death," I wrote in thick black strokes. "The fight in the world is between the forces of life (third-world people, blacks, young people) and the forces of death. It's impossible to really be alive in this culture unless you are constantly struggling against it—and if you are struggling against it, you are living at such a high level of intensity that you are prepared to go to jail and die."

And hers became more and more cautious: "I just got another letter from you and I'm scared," she replied in looping blue letters, neat as a school teacher's. "Maybe we really are far apart. I'm suddenly beginning to feel we are living two completely different lives. I don't feel that I fit in to yours as much anymore. You're into things so much different than I am. I can't see a violent revolution with people killing each other in the streets or whatever and I have the feeling that maybe you're beginning to be able to rationalize the whole thing, and I'm scared."

Her caution scared me as much as my intensity seemed to scare her. It was no time for caution.

And that's why I ached for her to be there with me—to conspire, to breathe together the same sharp December air that carried exhilaration and audacity like so many incredibly hardy seeds that had taken root in me and our friends and freaks all over Boston, filling us with that outrageous and frightening belief that we could be—shit, that we had to be—part of a monumental Movement that could finally force some sense into the world. And that if we didn't, if we couldn't…this sputtering monster machine that was destroying Vietnam and killing black people and contorting every last aspect of being human would just grind us into so many piles of shit-meal. I could try to tell Sarah all this stuff, the passion and love and belief and anger and fear and doubts that were churning around in me, making me a dedicated revolutionary one minute and a scared kid the next. I could tell her about the total uncertainty and aliveness that I woke up with every morning. But I couldn't—at 300-miles distance—make her know it, make it real in a way that could heat her blood so she would feel that wicked and scary rush that came with living on the edge of something motherfucking big. In Boston, you could taste the quickening pace of change, the rapid rising of the stakes, in the bite of the winter air. See it in the warm eyes of other freaks when you met them on the streets. Feel it in the slow, frosty stare of the cops when they checked you out.

I was going somewhere fast—somewhere as exciting as it was frightening—and there was no way I could slow it down, even if I wanted to, but one of the few things that was absolutely clear to me was that I wanted her there with me.

CHAPTER FOUR

December 31 (morning)

I LEFT MOUNTFORT STREET AT SEVEN-THIRTY. Just jumped out of bed and threw some clothes on and headed out the door. It was rush hour. Anything could happen with those damn subways. And I just didn't want her to get off that plane without me standing there. Mostly, I was just ready for the waiting to be over.

It was cold, bitter fucking cold, in the early gray light, as I made my way down past Sergeant Pepper's Pizza and on to Beacon Street toward Kenmore Square, crossing the bridge over the Mass Pike. Man, I loved living in the middle of the city. Walk out the door and there's a circus going on all around you, people just being people. But people just being people can be damned amusing. In the residential neighborhoods where I grew up, streets of single-family houses, it was rare to see people that I didn't know walking down my street. I saw such a small, constrained part of the world when I walked out the front door: the Carters or the Ericksons or the Slifes mowing their lawns or unloading groceries. Here, outside my front door was a torrent of cars and lights and sounds. And people. All kinds of people: A couple huddling on the corner near the pizza parlor, the hoods of their heavy jackets meeting to form a kind of common tent, shelter while they kissed or argued or just figured out their next move. An old man, with a pock-marked face and navy blue knit cap askew on his crew-cut head whistling some pub tune, smiling for all the world and for nobody but himself, smiling because right now, whether it was the beginning or the end of his day, he was feeling pretty damn good. Two little black kids, in thick brown coats and red ear muffs and yellow calf-high boots, awkward bundles running past me, playing a kind of relay tag as their laughter rang out against the roar of the raging cars below, their mother, I guess, trudging dutifully behind, shopping bags on each arm, every once in awhile yelling into the noise of the city for them to slow down or watch where they're going. I didn't know any of them, but that didn't matter, they were all part of my world, and it thrilled me to belong among them. The sting of the cold was a rush, too. But I was flipping out mostly because I knew that when I came back this way, Sarah would be beside me, here, in this world, one of us, again.

The trip to the airport was smooth as could be. The bus to the terminal was waiting when I got off the subway and, though the gate was at the far end of the terminal, I got there at twenty of nine, more than an hour early. Just a little more waiting. Shit.

I didn't like hanging out in airports, especially Logan. Cops seemed to cruise Logan just looking for freaks to hassle. And I was alone. Not a good idea. Damn. Things were so quiet around Mountfort Street, and I was so absorbed in getting ready for Sarah, that I hadn't thought about that I was venturing into enemy territory.

I bought a *Record American* newspaper—Wretched American is what we called it—and found a corner in an empty seating area near the gate to hide in. I preferred the *Record American*'s tabloid sensationalism to the *Globe*'s supposed sophisticated journalism. They both told the same lies but the Wretched American was more entertaining with their silent majority rah-rah Americanism than the Globe with their objective liberal bullshit. And the tall broad pages of the tabloid were easier to hide behind. I scanned the sports page in the back. The Celtics had beaten the Knicks the night before, always a cause for celebration in Boston, even though the Celtics were dominating the league. Since we were at the end of a decade most of the rest of the sports section was given over to the kind of retrospective that are always everywhere around those milestones. The top sports stories of the decade were the Celtics' run of championships, the Red Sox Impossible Dream Year pennant in 1967, Ted Williams hitting a home run in his last at-bat in 1961, the Patriots AFL Championship in 1965.

I remembered listening to Williams' home run when I was a kid in New Bedford. A chilled fall day, just home from school, a transistor radio to my ear. I flipped out when I heard Curt Gowdy call the home run, "going, going, gone..." and started running around my back yard, like I was Williams circling the bases, screaming over fences and through yards to my friends: "He did it! Williams did it!" How could a person be as cool as Ted Williams? After all the shit he took from the writers and a lot of the fans—me and my father always loved him—last time up in his career, he hits the damn ball out of the park, then circles the bases like he's got a million better things to do and just keeps running into the dugout, never looking up, never tipping his hat or anything to acknowledge the incredible exclamation point he just put on his career. And fuck you, too!, he said, to everyone who expected him to be something other than he was. Shit, he was the best hitter who ever lived, what more did they want from him? I dug him just the way he was. God, that was a long time ago. Now, I lived just three blocks from Fenway Park—maybe, I thought, we can get to a couple of games in the spring. Maybe Stu would go with me.

The headline on the Wretched American's front page said "Happy New Year, VC: Yanks Dump 800 Tons on Enemy Positions." Motherfuckers. It was the heaviest bombing in South Vietnam in five months. All concentrated on a couple of villages near the Cambodian borders. What does eight hundred tons of bombs look like? What's left standing after you drop eight hundred tons of bombs on a couple of jungle villages? There was another story that Vice President Agnew, visiting the Philippines, said that the "pacification" of Vietnam was going well—

ninety percent of the countryside and ninety percent of the population was secured. Fucking liar. Where were we dropping all these bombs if ninety percent of the country was "secure"?

I knew—we knew—it was an act of desperation. The U.S. was losing—losing in Vietnam and starting to lose at home. But for all its failings and clumsiness, the U.S. empire packed a lot of fire power and could do a lot of damage. There and here. Bombs in Vietnam and murder in Chicago. Beatings, arrests, injunctions. All part of the same deal. A decaying empire fighting for its life. But the people in Vietnam were paying the biggest price—along with the kids our government had sent to do their dirty work.

There was a big picture of Agnew in Manila inside the newspaper. Down in the corner of the same page was a small box that said "Vietnam Casualties: Killed in Action: Army: FLYNN, Douglas B., Specialist, Boston; GILMORE, Timothy R., Pfc., Malden, Mass.; LEBLANC, Marc J., Sgt., Manchester, N.H.; ROBINSON, Willie T., Second Lieut, Roxbury, Mass.; Navy: TALIAFERRO, Anthony, Lieut., South Boston." Kids my age, little older, maybe, or maybe even a little younger. Fucking government. Now they were routinely killing black militants in the U.S. They still weren't ready to kill white freaks and revolutionaries but they were coming at us harder on the streets and in the courts.

Out of the corner of my eye, I saw two Boston cops strolling the walkway between the seating areas for the gates. Shit. I buried my nose in a story about some alderman in Braintree running off with the mayor's wife, which would have been on the front page if the Wretched American wasn't even more excited about escalated bombing than politicized adultery. The cops passed by me. I took a deep breath. My heart pounded like Keith Moon kicking the shit out of his bass drum. Damn, why do I let them do that to me? Pigs.

The clock on the wall said quarter after nine, still half an hour to go. I put the paper down. Other people were starting to fill in the seats around me, and the cops probably wouldn't be back for awhile. God, I couldn't wait to see Sarah. The longer we were apart, the more the insanity of us even thinking about having any kind of long-term relationship seeped into our heads. She was from a big extended family, aunts and uncles and cousins around every corner in Philadelphia, it seemed, and she lived an ideal childhood. Her mother loved being a mom and a housewife, threw big birthday parties and made homemade Halloween costumes for her kids every year. Her dad worked hard but was devoted to his family. Didn't drink hardly. Didn't smoke. Home for supper every night, met at the door by his loving family. That's not what my family was like.

Sarah was a straight suburban chick. She straightened her hair, went to her prom, never got in any kind of trouble. If we'd met in high school, we wouldn't have had anything to do with each other. But we'd met instead about halfway through our freshman year at Boston University. We lived in adjacent dorms called West Campus. One night in February—shit, not even a year ago—driven by a serious case of the stoned munchies, I went to the snack bar on the ground level of the girls' dorm for a cream cheese and jelly bagel. I must have staggered out of some friend's smoke-filled room, but I'm pretty sure I was alone when I went to the cafeteria. The lights were too bright and all the other people who were laughing and flirting and making a fucking federal case over whether to get a chocolate or a strawberry milk shake were just blurry hassles, obstacles in my way. I just wanted to get my bagel and get the fuck out of there. Then this smile emerged from the blur.

That's what I saw first—her smile. Her pale red lips, rounded up, relaxed and easy. Warm, welcoming, real in some way that stopped and stunned me. She wasn't flirting with me. I don't think she had any idea who I was or any particular interest in me. She just smiled as she passed me. And in the cheap buzzing fluorescent brightness, for an instant, everything and everyone else faded, and her smile gave true light to her face, which, I noticed only in a second flash, was strikingly pretty—sharp angles surrounding deep brown eyes, framed by thick dark hair. She smiled, and then she was gone. I hope I smiled back. Shit, I wished I'd said something—like "Hi." Who was she? Where had she come from?

How had we lived in connected buildings without me ever noticing her before? I don't know if it was love at first sight, but suddenly I couldn't think about much of anything else.

She was Sarah Stein and she was friends with people I was friends with. And soon, we became friends. Good friends. Buddies. Confidants. Comrades. But from that first time I saw her in that cafeteria, I wanted to be more than friends. She didn't—for a long time. But when the school year was almost over, things took a turn. We had a couple of weeks of sorta being boyfriend and girlfriend before summer vacation sent us our separate ways. We hadn't lived in the same city since. Now, once her plane touched down, we would have ten days not just in the same city, but in the same apartment, the same room, the same bed. We'd been waiting a long time to be together like this.

Twenty to ten and the other folks waiting at the gate were starting to stir. Three freaks came laughing loudly down the walkway. One of them with dark curly hair reaching wildly to the top of his shoulders saw me looking their way. He smiled and flashed me the peace sign. I returned the salute. It was far out to see some friendly faces, even though I didn't know any of them. I stood up and stretched. Ran my hands through my hair to kind of brush it in place. Checked my fingernails. Clean enough, I guess. Pulled my pack of cigarettes out of my pants pockets, found one that wasn't crushed too bad and lit it. Took a deep drag. Man, I hope this is good. I hope this is good.

Passengers started coming off the plane. I put out my cigarette and walked over near the door, so I'd see her sooner. Streams of people came off the plane, their eyes searching the waiting crowd for a friendly face. To me they were all only not-Sarah. And then she was there. Her long, raucous, shimmering brown hair rolled down her neck and across the shoulders of her pea coat, flowing down and resting, in wispy curly-cue's, on the rise of her breasts, which bounced in the flimsy covering of a red gauze, Indian shirt with little round mirrors that sparkled in the harsh airport light. Her piercing brown eyes found mine and her steps quickened. And she was in my arms, crashing into me, lips pressed hard into mine, the pressure of longing deferred too long. I drank in the taste and the smell of her—ivory soap and cigarettes and Prell and sweat and whatever else it was that was her—ripened by the crush of the crowded airplane. I breathed it deep.

"I can't believe I'm finally here," she said.

"Me neither," I answered. And we kissed again. Softer, this time, lips sinking gently into lips, yielding, savoring, lingering. Knowing that, at last, we had time, sweet time.

Reluctantly pulling back—we were in the middle of a crowd of people under the bright plastic lights of Logan Airport—I put my arm around her shoulder, she put hers around my waist and we pulled hard into each other and began ambling through the milling crowd, a dazed three-legged creature, all smiles. We passed the group of freaks, who were still waiting for their arriving party, and the wild-haired guy who had flashed me the peace sign got a big old grin on his face when he saw us coming.

"Right on, brother," he said to me. And then to Sarah, "Welcome to Boston, sister."

I could only answer with a smile—he dug it—and to try to pull her closer in to me.

"Gee," Sarah said quietly into my ear. "You think he could tell we're in love?" And she kissed my jaw, the breath from her nose tickling my ear and sending shivers all over my body. The melded being we had become was now moving very slowly, reeling awkwardly among the people hurrying around us, toting luggage and urgent places to be.

"You two want to watch where you're going," it was a stern, cold voice. I turned toward it, and my heart rate shifted gears. A uniformed Boston cop was glaring down at us. His partner was taking a drag on a cigarette a couple of paces behind him. "There's a lot of people here and you two are all over each other in the middle of the damn aisle."

"Don't think we were hurting anybody," I said, trying not to let my pounding heart make my voice sound nervous.

"Listen buddy, I just told you to watch where you're going." He was thick as well as tall and he spit his words at us. "It's a public airport and decent people don't want to see you two pawing each other."

"We weren't doing anything," Sarah shot back.

The cop measured Sarah with a long slow look. "Sure, honey. Look you two want a problem, we'll give you a problem. Otherwise, just watch where you're going and keep your hands off each other while you're in this airport." He turned to his buddy, who chuckled as he blew out a cloud of smoke, and they walked away

I grabbed Sarah's hand and squeezed tight as we headed—now ahead of the pace of the moving crowd around us—toward the baggage claim area.

"I can't believe that," she said, angry and hard now. "Pigs."

"Welcome to Boston," I said, squeezing her hand a little tighter.

CHAPTER FIVE

December 31 (afternoon)

SARAH NOTICED THAT I'D MADE THE BEDS. My clothes and papers were all in neat piles, and the floor between the mattresses was clear, as together as that room ever got. She gave me a long slow kiss as she dropped her bag on the floor, then pulled away when she saw Tavola stretch in the corner of the mattress by the window. She went over and picked up the cat and sat down with her on her lap, stroking her thick black fur with long smooth motions. Tavola purred loudly. After a while, Sarah looked up at me, with an easy smile. This was right, man, this was just right.

Stu wandered in and we shot the shit with him for a while. Stu and Sarah always got along good. He gave Sarah his rap about our trip to Illinois—man those guys drink a lot, Tucker's sisters are cool, his parents aren't bad, either, but that's easy for me to say, cause they're his parents, shit, man, he almost cost us a free Chinese dinner. Stu got on a roll and Sarah and I were doing lots of laughing. Sarah chimed in every once in awhile with a comment or a question, but I didn't say much of anything, just digging Stu and Sarah hanging out.

Finally sometime in mid-afternoon, we bundled up—Sarah in her pea coat and a crocheted green scarf, me in my trusty thick beige sweater

and my well-worn brown sports coat—and wandered out of our apartment. A frozen gray haze hung over the city, but still it felt bright to our
eyes after the murk of my room. We bounced up the cracking sidewalks
of Mountfort Street, the jolt of the cold and the rush of being out in the
world, together, making us a little silly. We paid homage to the phone
booth—a block and a half up the street by a car repair garage—where I
spent hours talking to her. She insisted that I sit in it and pick up the
receiver and put it to my ear, just like I'd do when I talked to her—just,
she said, so she would have a picture in her mind to think of when she
talked to me. I felt foolish, but I did it. She studied me from all angles
like some kind of painter as I carried on an animated conversation with
the dial tone. Then she opened the red-and-white folding door, kissed
me on the forehead, slammed the door tight, and ran away up the street
and disappeared. Surprised by her sneak attack, I waited a beat or two
before pulling the door open and following after, taking my time, knowing she'd let me find her, knowing that was the game.

The hum from the Turnpike vibrated in the chill, resonating through
the St. Mary's Street Bridge, a low rumbling rhythm that seemed to lay
a bottom for the frantic melody of the city. I could pull a song out of it
if I listened just right: *It's all too much for me to take, the love that's shining
all around you.* I waited for the light to change before crossing the street
to the bridge, something I'd never do—shit, nobody in Boston obeys
traffic signals—except it was a way of forcing myself to slow down, to
keep her waiting in her hiding spot just a little longer. Finally, I crossed
to the bridge with a strutting nonchalance, whistling to this tune that
now swirled around me—*it's all too much*—and she leaped out at me from
behind a concrete post that anchored the railing along the bridge.

"What took you so long?" she asked, laughing big, throwing her arms
dramatically around me.

"Somebody shut me in a phone booth."

"Who would do something like that?" And we kissed, the wet coolness
of her lips and the warmth of her breath thrilling in the dry chill of the
day. She stopped the kiss abruptly and grabbed my hand, leading me, al-

most dancing, across the bridge. *The more I learn the less I know, but what I do is all too much.*

The bridge took us toward BU and Commonwealth Avenue, that river of a city boulevard that flowed from our freshman-year dorms to the central campus of BU and out to the world of Boston: apartments and concerts and demonstrations and other campuses. BU sprawled out like a flat-faced fortress on the other side of the mighty Avenue, one cold stone box next to another. The only break in the façade was Marsh Chapel, an island of softening shapes and human scale, set back from the street by an open courtyard. Its weathered stone was as cold as the rest of the buildings, but the place was warmed by memory. For five days in October 1968, just a month into our college lives, as many as a thousand kids crammed into its pews and sprawled over its altar in the belief—or maybe just the hope—that we could provide sanctuary for an eighteen-year-old kid named Joe Brook who deserted from the army because he just couldn't handle going to Vietnam. It was an incredible instant community, full of songs and hugs and meaningful discourse and lofty ideals. Sarah and I were both there, though we didn't know each other then. I was with Mike a lot of the time, but Stu was there, too, and Brian—shit most everybody we ended up being friends with was there. It was like some kind of initiation or something. And we all lived up to the Sanctuary commitment to not resist when the FBI came for Joe Brook one morning at 5:30. We hummed "We shall overcome" as a mob of feds in black suit jackets and open white shirts grabbed his arms and legs and stretched him around like a human pretzel as they dragged him through the crowd to a flat black sedan that took him to the stockade at the nearest army base. We all left Marsh Chapel—the building's name now carrying all the emotions and memories of those five intense days— feeling good about ourselves. I don't know how good Joe Brook felt, suddenly alone in some cold army cell.

Hand-in-hand, but drifting in our own separate memories as we entered this familiar territory, Sarah and I crossed over the MTA tracks that divided Comm Ave. I kicked up some rocks from the track bed.

"Hey, this is where I got my ammunition to throw at that cop car." Grinning wide, I let go of her hand and stopped to take aim on a particular rock, like a soccer player, and kicked it all the way to the curb on the other side of the street. I smiled proudly at Sarah.

"Ben," she said, as she let out a heavy breath, and looked away.

"What?"

We were waiting for the traffic to clear, so we could cross the outbound side of the street. She looked up at me, sort of serious. "Ben, you act like it's some kind of game to you, but it's scary to me—throwing rocks at cop cars."

"Shit, I was pissed. They deserved it." The cops came to break up a worker-student alliance—straight commies—demonstration supporting GE strikers. Me and Mike were hanging on the fringes of the protest, and the demonstrators were just yelling and harassing a GE recruiter. Then a bunch of cops stormed in and shoved all of us out of the student union. Somehow, I ended up on the MTA tracks as the last cop car was pulling away, so I grabbed a rock and heaved it. I heard it hit the back window, but I don't know how much damage it did.

"I'm sure they did," Sarah said, looking over at me as we crossed the street. "But I don't care about them, I'm worried about you. I think they arrest people for throwing rocks at cop cars."

"I know, I know," I said, looking back at her, trying to smile without smirking. "I can't help it, Sarah. Shit's happening, heavy shit, and I'm in it…I want to be in it. I don't want to go to jail or anything, but…I don't know…You'd understand better if you were here."

We stopped on the sidewalk in front of Marsh Chapel. We were going to hitchhike to Allston but we weren't quite ready to stick out our thumbs yet. "Ben, I understand, or I think I understand," she said. "I just want you to be careful." Now she smiled, soft again. "You're too cute for prison stripes." She took my hand and kind of shook it to declare a stop to this sudden shift to seriousness. She was right. It wasn't the time for that. Not yet.

The fourth or fifth car stopped—hitchhiking was almost automatic on Comm Ave, like a people's mass transit—a freak in a rusted old station wagon. He was bundled up, heavy leather jacket, big thick scarf, and knit cap that draped awkwardly over his mountain of hair. His heater didn't work. But his radio did—BCN playing the Airplane:

> *Consider how small you are, compared to your scream,*
> *the human dream doesn't mean shit to a tree.*

He took us all the way to Harvard Avenue and got us stoned in the process. Decent enough pot, too, a rare thing since fucking Nixon started screwing up the crops in Mexico. As Sarah passed the joint to me, we cruised by West Campus, the dorm where we'd live the year before. From my seat in the back, I watched Sarah, riding in the front, check it out as we rolled past, her head slowly turning to keep it in sight until it was completely out of view. Then she turned all the way around and smiled at me.

Just up Harvard Avenue, we found the funky fish store where we wanted to buy clams. The place smelled like low-tide and the floors were wet. It was almost as cold inside as it was outside. And it was crowded and loud, a show: the rough chorus of fish men yelling out orders for "cahd" and "floundah" and "sahd fish" on top of each other with echoes ricocheting off the heavy coolers and the crude choreography of customers pointing and paying and fish men offering and fetching and wrapping. Sarah and I stood there for awhile, digging it—amazed by it. But we were right in the middle of everything and seemingly suddenly we looked up and a counter man with red-brown smears all over his worn hands and once-white apron was looking right at us. "Can I help you folks with something?" Sounded sort of like an accusation.

Sarah and I looked at each other in a kind of silent eye debate over who would speak. She lost, mainly because I had forgotten why we were there. That pot *was* pretty good. "Clams," she finally said. "We want clams."

"Good," the counter man said, talking to Sarah but looking at me out of the corner of his eyes, talking slow as though we might have trouble understanding English. "We got clams. We got razor clams, we got cherry stone clams, we got quahogs, we got steamer clams, we got chowder clams. What kind of clams is it that you wanted?"

"Steamer clams," Sarah said. That was easy. I could've answered that.

"Good," said the counter man. He was short and wiry, had brown hair that was rolled roughly back off his brow, and looked older than he probably was. "And how many pounds of steamers would you like?"

Sarah looked at me. I looked at the clams in their thin-ridged gray-brown shells piled high in the battered display case. I looked at the counter man, and finally spoke. "I don't know, what do you think?"

Now he started drumming his fingers impatiently on the top of the display case: "How am I supposed to know? Depends how many people, whatcha gonna do with them, how hungry you are, how much you like clams, two pounds? ten pounds? I don't know what to tell ya."

We really weren't sure of the answers to any of those questions. The volume in the store got louder. The crowd seemed to swell around us. Sarah and I locked eyes again and found ourselves somewhere between panic and hysterics. We pulled a number out of the air—five pounds?—I think I finally said it—and the counter man laid an old newspaper (Wretched American no doubt) on the scale and with a great clattering shoveled clams until the arm of the scale just reached five. In an instant they were wrapped and he was handing them to me: "Anything else?" he asked as he looked to the people waiting not so patiently behind us. Sarah gave him his money and we hustled out of the store, not looking at each other—because as soon as we did, after we were outside and out of his sight, we started laughing hysterically, falling, together, against the outside wall of the building.

"I have no idea how many clams we just bought," Sarah said when she could finally speak.

"I hope it's enough," I said, "cause I ain't going back in there."

"No way I'm going back there," she said as she caught her breath and slipped her arm around my waist. We started moving slowly down the street, me proudly cradling the bag of clams in one arm, the other arm draped around her shoulders.

We laughed our way up one side of Harvard Avenue and down the other back toward Comm Ave. We got more than a few dirty looks—because we were laughing so much? because we were freaks? Shit, who knew? Who cared? Fuck 'em. Sarah checked every window and pulled me to a stop when she saw something we might need if we were a married couple with an apartment just up the street in Allston: a beaten old gray trunk, a set of painted china dishes, an antique pine dresser. Finally, we found ourselves in the bakery around the corner on Comm Ave and, after much indecision—though this time with sugary smells and a welcoming vibe—bought a couple of chocolate chip cookies for immediate consumption and a long loaf of French bread to eat with our clams.

The haze over the city was turning dark. We crossed Comm Ave to find a market, where we could buy butter and lemon and garlic and some sodas. What joy: walking the winter streets together, hand in hand, little kisses when lights or traffic slowed us, shopping, an adventure into mysterious territories, pursuing simple tasks, mundane tasks for most of the people we passed on the street or waited behind in line, but like a dream for us, kids playing house, like we were a couple and this was our life: checking our list and counting out change and lugging grocery bags homeward as dusk settled over the streets crowded with cars and trolleys taking people home from work to families and suppers and New Year's Eve.

CHAPTER SIX

December 31 (night)

BACK AT MOUNTFORT STREET, I PUT the Kinks on Mike's turntable and Sarah and I shoveled out the debris of weeks of inactivity in the kitchen just to find the stove and a pot to boil water.

We steamed the clams and broiled the bread, which we painted with butter and garlic, filling the apartment with unfamiliar warmth and smells. We even cleared the piles of papers that covered the table that sat almost forgotten at the end of the hall between the kitchen and the bathroom, stole chairs from the desks in my room and Mike's, shut the bathroom door tight to block out as much of the kitty-litter smell as we could, and had a sit-down dinner, with bowls of melted butter to dip the clams in and a gaboon—a word my family made up, I guess, Sarah never heard of it—for the empty shells. A feast.

Turns out we bought too much. After we'd stuffed ourselves, almost half of them were uneaten. Stu shuffled around us, expressed his shock and admiration at this outbreak of domestic life in our little crash pad, and grabbed a hunk of bread to gnaw on. We couldn't persuade him to help us with our pile of clams. So Sarah and I sat alone together—in our island of order within the chaos of the apartment—eating too much, laughing about the fish man, how much he scared us, how funny he was, how we couldn't stop laughing—thrilled by this monumentally simple thing we had done together.

As we were cleaning up—itself a revolutionary act at Mountfort Street—and looking for some place to dump our clam shells, Stu asked if we had big New Year's Eve plans.

"New Year's Eve? Shit, man, where's the party?" I asked Stu.

"Someplace we don't know with people we never met—and, besides that, we're not invited," Stu said. It was strange with most of our friends home for the vacation, not having any place to go hang out.

"Ah, I don't think we'd like them anyway," I said, as I dumped the clam shells back on the newspaper they'd come in and tried to wrap it shut—but not nearly as smoothly as the fish man.

"Well, so we'll just have to make our own party," Sarah said, smiling and rubbing her hand gently down my back.

Stu was going to the Tea Party to catch the Grateful Dead and he invited us to go with him. I dug the Dead. I'd never seen them, but their latest album, a live one, really rocked. But I couldn't think of a way I'd rather spend New Year's Eve than hanging out alone in my apartment with Sarah.

I looked over to Sarah, who shrugged, which I took to mean we were thinking the same thing: "You scope it out for us, Stu, and if they're worthy of our presence, maybe we'll go tomorrow night." Sarah nodded her approval. Stu was our scout. Bands came to the Tea Party for three days and Stu always went on the first night—usually a Thursday—then would tell us whether we should all go. Most of the time it was "yes"—the Tea Party was having a run of great bands—and we'd head over as a group on Saturday night.

It got really quiet when Stu left. I put *Surrealistic Pillow* on, which seemed like the right blend of energy and mellowness. When I went back into my room, Sarah was sitting on the mattress, leaning against the wall with Tavola on her lap. I sat down facing her from the other end of the mattress. She smiled sweetly.

"Our first New Year's Eve," she said as she pet Tavola with long slow strokes.

"Yeah, that's right," I said. "Can you believe we didn't even know each other a year ago?" I got up and grabbed my pipe off the desk and pulled the tin of hash Barry had left me out of the drawer. "Wanna smoke a little hash?"

"Sure," she said. "What were you doing a year ago?"

I filled the pipe and tried to remember. "I was in Illinois." I lit a match and took a long pull, held it for a little while as I passed the pipe to Sarah, then coughed it out. "Oh yeah, that's right, I took acid with some friends in Champaign, my first trip—it was New Year's Eve—wow, that was great." Sarah sucked on the pipe, her eyes all scrunched up trying to focus on the glow of the hash. She coughed it up right away.

"You all right?" I asked. She nodded as she handed the pipe back to me and tried to catch her breath.

"Yeah, that was quite a trip," I laughed, remembering how amazed I was by how different the world looked with a little LSD. "I watched flowers in the wallpaper grow. I loved it." I lit the pipe again, and, as I was inhaling, managed to ask, "How about you?"

"I guess I was with David"—her old Philly boy friend. "We went to a movie or something. We probably watched the ball drop back at my house. Nothing too memorable. Didn't see any flowers growing out of wallpaper," she smiled as she took the pipe back from me.

Man, she could smile, lips just parted, in an easy, slightly crooked curl that spread all over her face, up to the softness in her eyes.

"Too bad, it was a gas," I said. She took a little hit this time and held it for a couple of seconds and exhaled—and the smoke went right into Tavola's face. Tavola raised her head suddenly, like she was startled, and then nestled back down into Sarah's lap.

"I think she liked that," I said. I took another long hit and held it as long as I could, and then blew it out toward Tavola. She curled her head in the direction of the smoke and then rolled over on her back and stretched her legs up toward Sarah's chest.

"I think she's stoned," Sarah said as she held up her hand to let me know she didn't want the pipe back. "I know I am. That's good hash."

I set the pipe on the floor next to the bed. "Yeah, it is. You can count on Barry," I said. Sarah was playing with Tavola, wiggling her fingers in front of the cat's face until she swatted at them and Sarah jerked them just out of reach, laughing.

She was beautiful in a way I never imagined before I knew her. There was something exotic and foreign about her, dark and angled and full, raw and tactile—from her hair flowing in glorious chaos down her long thin neck, over her shoulders, flipping across her back and bouncing on her breasts, to her laugh which rippled through her, loud and ragged, unpracticed, straight from her gut and soul, a voice of the passion that sparkled her eyes and shined through that goddess smile. She was lit by something that pulled at a deep part of me, making me weak, making me strong, sending me reeling into the unknown, taking me back to someplace long forgotten. She was a dream that smelled of garlic bread and hashish and talked in silly phrases to a stoned black cat and was glad to be sitting beside me on my bed. What kind of year had taken her from David and the movies to be stoned on this mattress beside me?

"Yeah, New Year's Eves are always kind of strange," I said, remembering suddenly what we were talking about. "Usually too much alcohol, I guess."

Sarah looked up from Tavola, and over at me. "Alcohol never was a problem for me. I've never gotten drunk on New Year's Eve," she looked down and started playing with Tavola again, circling a finger and moving it toward her. Tavola would wait until the finger was almost on her and then grab at it with both front paws. About half the time, she'd nab it and then hold Sarah's finger and bring her head up to nibble on it. Then she'd let go to let the game begin again. "I just think people expect too much from New Year's Eve, so they're always disappointed."

Man, we did come from different places. I was probably fifteen the last time I wasn't screwed up one way or another on New Year's Eve.

"I guess that's true," I said. "But part of what most people expect—or most people I know anyway—is to get drunk, and then…I don't know… then there's no telling what might happen."

"Like what?" she said. "Like what kind of things have happened to you?" Sometimes it seemed like we were exchange students from countries on opposite sides of the world, trying to get some insight into the bizarre customs of the other's culture.

Weirdo's party. I let out a deep breath and thought about how I could explain Weirdo's party.

"A couple of years ago—during my junior year in high school, so I would've been sixteen—shit, just three years ago—Weirdo, the guy who managed our band, threw a New Year's Eve party." I reached out and touched Sarah's hand, which was now again methodically petting Tavola, who was back into her sonic purr. I took a breath and grabbed for a cigarette. "It was a strange mix of people. Mostly Weirdo's friends from college, a lot of frat rat types and a bunch of people from the band scene, most of them were college age, too—and really pretty straight. And then there were some of us long-haired creeps—that's what we called ourselves after somebody called us that to insult us—guys from local teen bands. Bizarre scene. The house was packed and there was a shitload of champagne, which I freely helped myself to. And I was pissed off about something. Might have been that I'd just found out my girl friend had cheated on me, which is probably why we weren't together on New Year's Eve. And all these frat rats and sorority girls were treating me like some cute kid, the young rock and roller, and I was strutting and letting everybody know my opinion about just about everything—or something, I don't know. And I drank a lot…" I lit my cigarette and took a long drag. "…A lot. Maybe I tried to make it with one of the college girls or something—and obviously didn't get anywhere. Shit, I don't remember exactly what happened but it must have been close to midnight, and I kind of found a spot right in the middle of everything and started screaming and taking my clothes off. No shit. Ripping my fucking clothes off and screaming: 'You inhibited assholes, what's the matter with you? Are you scared of your bodies? What the fuck are you afraid of? Lose your inhibitions! Rip away your fucking hangups.'"

I stopped to take another drag. Just telling the story, I could feel the intensity of my drunken rage coming back. Sarah was staring straight down at Tavola, petting her slower and slower. I couldn't stop now.

"I don't remember exactly what I yelled, but something like that—and I took off all my clothes. Stone cold naked. Weirdo was laughing and trying to calm me down, but that just made me madder and louder. And the rest of the people were just kind of laughing at me but suddenly it got really quiet and they stopped laughing and were just staring at me like I was some kind of fucking baboon in the zoo. Those looks, man, I remember those fucking looks. Shit." I took another long pull. Sarah looked up and reached her hand for me to give her the cigarette. She took a drag and then just kind of let it dangle in her fingers. "Then suddenly I had nothing more to say and all the anger was gone and I just felt naked and cold and alone…And then—I don't know—Scotty or Barry or somebody must have pulled me out of there and got me to another room and wrapped me in some blankets and I must have just passed out there."

Sarah handed the cigarette back to me and looked back down at Tavola, taking her head in her hands and stroking her ears with her thumbs.

I let out a deep breath and put a hand on Sarah's shoulder. She looked up with a half smile. "I'm sorry," I said. "I hadn't thought about that in a long time. It all just kind of came rushing back."

She reached over and put a hand on my leg. "It's OK, Ben." She smiled, but now it was a different kind of smile. "Sometimes, it's just hard for me to connect the you that I know with the you that I hear stories about—this kid who gets drunk and does crazy stuff, this troubled kid from a screwed up family, the drunken father, the mother who didn't like you. The bad kid." She turned her whole body towards me, curling her legs together, as Tavola grudgingly gave up her spot on Sarah's lap.

"It's all me," I said. "I think I've changed some. I sure don't drink as much as I did in Champaign. And our friends and the Movement, something's happening that I feel part of and means something big, I think. And you…you know my luck's never been all that great with the girls…" I took a drag. "Until now. Until you." I scanned her face for a reaction, but her look was more question than statement. "But I don't know, that shit must all still be in there somewhere."

"I guess," she said, her eyes telling me that she was looking for a way to say something she'd been thinking about. "It's strange Ben, I know this smart and idealistic and funny and kind and self-confident—and very cute—boy who's opened new worlds to me, who's taught me things I never thought of before, who's helped me to grow up in a way I never even thought about, never would have thought that I wanted. Helped me to think about myself in a whole different way. I love that boy, even though sometimes he's impatient and self-righteous and does things that I think are silly or even stupid." She flashed a quick smile and took the cigarette back. "But Ben, there's another boy, too. Also very cute, but scared. Not bad, just really scared. I don't know what he's scared of exactly, but he needs to be held and hugged and loved and told that everything's going to be all right. He's a good hider, but every once in a while, I see him in your eyes. I saw him just now." She gave me a serious look and took a long drag on the cigarette. "I don't know that boy very well, but I think I love him, too. But he scares me, Ben, like you did just now."

Whoa. Our eyes locked for a second and it was like she was looking right through me and pulling me into her all at the same time. I must have looked worried.

"Don't worry, Ben, both those boys are you," she said. She laughed.

"I kind of figured that," and I laughed too, but I was still stunned. "I don't know what to say, Sarah. I can't explain me. Shit, I'm a mess, I know that, but I'm not so bad a mess when I'm with you." I let out a long full sigh. "If I can figure out some way not to screw this up . . . "

She scowled at me, "Ben!"

"Sorry...I didn't mean to get so heavy." She drew her face close to mine and kissed me a long slow kiss. When we stopped, I told her I loved her.

"I love you, too," she said, "but I bet I can whip you at 500 rummy."

I took that challenge and we played for the Championship of the World, smoking cigarettes, giving each other shit, having a good time. She did whip me good.

As she was gloating over her victory, it was probably getting close to midnight—no clocks in the apartment were set to the right time. I went into Mike's room and put the Allman Brothers on and turned up the speakers in my room just a bit. I floated with the dreamy organ and bouncy bongo beat back into my room and shut the door. Sarah was laying down, her head on the pillow, smiling invitingly at me.

We kissed: Kisses that had waited all day to be kissed, impatient kisses, greedy kisses, kisses reaching beyond lips to taste that moist tonguey flavor that drowns the superficialities of breath like cigarettes and hash and lingering garlic. I loved that taste of her.

We'd kissed first on a fresh April night, a couple of months after our brief encounter in the cafeteria. Those months had been filled with testing and trying, the two of us in this intricate dance of intimate friendship that tiptoed along the boundaries to love and romance or whatever you want to call it. My attraction to her was so strong that I tried hard to endure just being the friend, the nice guy who'd listen to her problems with other guys and her ambivalence about the life she seemed resigned to: a nice Jewish husband, life in the suburbs, shit, her parents life lived over again, a life that certainly had no place for me. I was willing to wait—well, not exactly willing, it actually drove me fucking crazy—but I knew that my only chance was to wait, that Sarah just didn't feel for me what I felt for her, and I could only hope that if we hung out enough together that maybe she would start to.

This dance took us from parties to demonstrations to long talk-filled walks along the Charles to blowing bubbles in dorm lobbies to exactly one official date (to see Norman Mailer's *Deer Park* of all things)—like some kids ballroom dancing, learning the box step, stiff and distant at first, and slowly yielding and softening and pulling closer. But I tried not to pull too hard, afraid of her resistance that would only increase the distance between us. But that April night, we left the usual crowd and partying, and wandered down to the Astroturf football field, which filled an oval bowl that our dorms towered over, and we led ourselves to a pile of chopped-up foam, the pit where high-jumpers and pole-vaulters landed. We talked soft talk and looked up to the hazy stars strong enough to shine through the lights of the city, which hovered over us, leaving us in this subterranean pool of darkness. Man, she was beautiful that night. She was wearing just a thin red tee shirt and worn bell-bottom jeans, and I watched her watch the blurry sky: her heart-shaped face nestled in the flowing pillow of her hair, the long sharp line of her nose an accent mark giving depth to her wide searching eyes and extra emphasis to the crooked puff of her lips. I eased my arm around her shoulders and I knew that I had to try to kiss her then, that it was goddamn time for us to kiss, that if we didn't kiss then, in that dark, soft pit on a spring night that could have been written by Wordsworth (if Wordsworth knew of Astroturf and pits o' foam and the haze of city night skies), we might never kiss, and finally, at last, I was more scared of never knowing if she might love me than I was of finding out that she didn't, that she wouldn't.

But her lips were soft and welcoming in the high-jump pit and we kissed and we stepped lightly across that line to something more than friendship in the short time—less than two weeks—we had left in the school year. The night before she went home to Philadelphia for the summer, I gave her a poem that I had stayed up the whole night before to write:

To Sarah
The golden tentacles of the
         swirling sweat-stained summer
slowly rip us away
                 from this one year world
         of existential terror
Your smile met me marching
         slowly down the road to nowhere
   and bade me to return
         to the world of the living
         invited me to crawl from my dream-proof hole
   and taste once more
         the sweetness of the ambrosia of life

But what was is gone
        and what is seems to be slipping away
    tomorrow lurks ahead
        uncertain and inevitable
    and spring rain sadness
        lingers over
            the ever sweet sorrow of parting

The days have run out
    the summer's knock
grows louder and impatient
        leave me with a smile,
    a laugh, and one more chance
        to taste the tender passion
            of your parted lips

As she read that on the last night of our freshman year in my dorm room, I could see her eyes slowly moisten. She finished and she let the beige sheets of paper with the soft blue ink float to the floor. There were tears now and she reached for me and pulled me close into her. "Thank you," she said, and it was love I heard in her voice. We kissed and danced our last dance of the year on the tiny mattress hanging from the wall. And we made love in every sense, except we didn't make love.

And it was never that easy to be together again. In the two hundred forty-nine days between our last night in the dorms and when Sarah's plane landed at Logan, we had been together a total of twenty-nine days. Spring to summer, summer to fall, fall to winter, it was a constant hassle to find ways to be together, to find places for our love. But each meeting was a joyful reunion, a proof of the old absence and fond heart thing. Whenever we could steal time alone, we kissed and touched and reveled in each other's lips and exploring the in and outs and softs and hards of each other's bodies. We'd kiss and play for hours once we had the sanctuary of my very own bedroom at Mountfort Street to frolic in—too rare a delight. After one Boston visit, I wrote her a poem called "The Weekend of 3,750 Kisses." Dreamy kisses. Long kisses. Silly kisses. We were incredibly physically passionate. But we hadn't made love.

It wasn't like it was a conscious plan. Sure as shit didn't have anything to do with waiting until we got married—marriage wasn't something we talked about—or anything like that. And it wasn't like it was a problem between us, like I wanted it and she didn't or vice-versa, as far as I knew. Or that we even talked about it. It wasn't ever that I didn't want it, I know that, but I didn't want it to be something that would come between us. In some ways, it was like the first kiss. As bad as I wanted it to happened—for all kinds of different reasons: because she really turned me on, because it was a kind of question mark hanging between us, because of what it would mean about our love—I didn't want it bad enough to screw up our trip.

Shit, man, I don't know. The thing was I was a virgin—an amazing feat for an almost twenty-year-old boy/man who played the role of rock and roll star for a couple of years, who talked and wrote about fucking as something we'd do a lot more of after the revolution, and who didn't believe in God or any of the bourgeois moral bullshit about sex and marriage. I had tried. The girl I dated longest in high school was a good Catholic girl who loved for me to slip my finger inside her underpants while we parked on quiet dirt cornfield roads, but wasn't going all the way until we got married, which, fortunately for both of us, was never going to happen. And, man, there were girls who followed the band and once I had enough beer in me, I'd make out with them and feel them up and shit. I don't know, maybe they would have let me fuck them. Came close with one. A girl a couple of years older than me from this small town in Indiana who seemed to really like me—almost fucked on the floor in one of the bedrooms of Weirdo's house after a long night of drinking and smoking hash. But we didn't—and I think it was me more than her. I was a little scared or something. I didn't love her or anything. Shit I didn't even really like her that much. I was afraid, I guess, that she'd think I did if we fucked. I know that all my friends were fucking girls, and a part of me just wanted to do it, find someone who would let me do it, but it just didn't happen. And Sarah wasn't just someone. Maybe there was something wrong with me. I didn't know if Sarah was a virgin. She probably wasn't. Nobody was, I don't think, except me. I sure as hell wasn't proud of it.

We wrestled with the clumped up green sheets and the crumpled pillows to clear a space to lay together. Finding our spot, alone finally in our celebration of out with the old, in with the new and, maybe, the end of this long beginning, and the beginning of something entirely new, something that we couldn't even really imagine, but that we knew had to be different and more: We kissed a long, wavy kiss, our lips rolling to a liquid rhythm, a give and take and push and yield that felt full of meaning, like a vow or a pledge—something solemn and deep. And when we finally had to pull back and breathe, I saw all that meaning glistening in the tender focus of her eyes. It was love, pure and simple. Love like I'd never seen it before, even from Sarah. There'd been love there, for sure, but it was like there was always something just over my shoulder that stole a piece of her look, that made me wonder just where and what she was looking at.

But now she filled me with this love that wasn't looking anywhere else but deep into me. This me. Clumsy and sloppy and confused and demanding and the most awkward suitor-boy friend-lover ever. Me. She loved me, she wanted me. Holy shit.

"I love you," she said. I believed her.

"I love you," I said. She knew that.

We kissed more and slid and yanked and eased out of our clothes. And she swept me away with this love that had no doubts and no fears, that took me in and nestled me against her smoothness and softness and fullness. Offered herself to my touch, to my lips. Radiant with the power and the pleasure of love, she glowed and raked my hair with her fingernails as I stroked and kissed the wonders of her smooth white skin—the rise of her breasts, the easy roll of her shoulders, the startling dip and curl of her long back into the rounding of her hips. I felt like I'd been admitted to a secret garden with flowers too beautiful for anyone to see every day.

Colors too deep and true. Smells too pure and sweet. Petals so smooth they seemed to melt when I touched them. A beauty that was really beyond my comprehension, but that became so real as my fingers felt the tiny bumps of excitement rising from the silk of her skin, as I smelled the blending fragrance of our heat and tender friction, as I tasted all the wonderful flavors of her. I was lost in this land of most delightful wonder.

I was surely lost and she led me to this place where love is made without power or guilt or deceit or fear or obligation. Love. Making love. Not some drunken fuck or some manly conquest. Love. Connecting. Her opening. Me filling. Us together. And the music—*Sometimes I feel... Sometimes I feel...Like I've been tied to the whipping post*—is pulsing to this amazing ascending crescendo of searing, soaring stretched and screaming guitar strings—and we are dancing this wonderful connected dance to it, embracing as completely as it is possible for two humans to embrace, lost in each other, moving as one, not able to, in the flashing heat that overtakes us, to remember exactly where I stop and she begins, until we explode together, exchanging precious pieces of ourselves, flowing and mixing and filling and emptying. Wow.

The record stopped. The apartment was quiet. Don't know if Stu was home or not. The new year, the new decade had surely come by now. We lay still and silent. My arm around her, not wanting to let go, my heart still pumping hard, my mind floating in a dreamy pond of ecstasy, Sarah's steady breathing took on the heaviness of sleep, a little rumble escaping her slightly open, slightly smiling mouth. I took a deep but easy breath, hoping to slow my heart without rippling the water I floated on, then timed my breathing to hers: slow now, in and out, in and out, and I could feel our bodies fill and empty together, in and out, in and out, easy now, her and me, in and out, in and out, in and out....

CHAPTER SEVEN

January 1, 1970

A SOULFUL BASS AND DRUM LINE CUT through the buzz of our anticipation. Then, one by one the guitars and then the organ joined in,
boogeying around the building rhythm, and pulling closer and closer,
until they all pounded on the beat together in a climbing crescendo of
chords that raised everything to another level.

Well I was feeling so bad
I asked my family doctor about what I had
I said doctor, doctor, Mr. M.D. (doctor)
Can you tell me (doctor)
what's ailing me?(doctor)

He said yeah, yeah, yeah, yeah, yeah (yes he did)
Yeah, yeah, yeah, yeah, yeah
All I need
All I need

(Good love)
All I need is love

(Good love)
Early in the morning baby
(Good love)
Late in the evening sometimes too
(Good love)

And the guitars took off in a rhythmic romp that forced a smile on my face and made my whole body roll with it. Sarah and Stu had the same smile and bounce and everyone around us did too.

C'mon baby
Squeeze me tight
Don't you want your Daddy
Just to be all right
I said baby, (baby)
Now it's for sure
I got the fever (baby)
And you got the cure (baby)

He said yeah, yeah, yeah, yeah, yeah (yes he did)
Yeah, yeah, yeah, yeah, yeah
All I need
All I need

(Good love)
All I need is love
(Good love)
Early in the morning sometime
(Good love)
Late in the evening and the afternoon
(Good love)

Everything slowed for a second, as Garcia looked down and started an easy picking of his strings that let loose this lilting flow of mellow notes, smoother and faster than seemed possible with the almost imperceptible movement of his fingers. The rest of the band hung back, giving him a beat and a melody to come back to, and he did, every once in a while—with a sudden flash of chords in perfect synch—but mostly he was dancing all around and through and over them—with this Pied Piper–like force that reached in to some nerve that made you smile and made you dance in a way that seemed absolutely basic, like breathing, this bodily reflex that had been waiting for this music to turn it on.

Everyone in the Tea Party—a bunch of milling little separate groups a couple of minutes ago—was now enveloped by this ecstatic music, a shining, fluid, charged organism that lifted us off the floor in full motion and shimmering colors, and turned this warehouse-like building into a psychedelic revival tent. We were all believers now as Garcia found new and startling notes somewhere on the neck of that guitar, raising the top of our heads with the sweet sharp trilling of his strings, tones that moved with the grace of a drifting cloud but then struck with the force of a lightening flash.

I looked over at Sarah, shining as her head rolled and her body swayed to the music. She was into it. We were into it. On the crowded floor, with everybody moving, she and I rubbed together, flowing with the music that swept us into each other—my hand grazing her ass, her breast pushing against my arm, our legs meeting mid beat. We weren't doing any kind of dance, really, no steps, but we were dancing, connected—the two of us together and then the two of us with Stu, who was bopping back and forth without much grace but with a lot of feeling, on the other side of Sarah. He shot me a quick smile as Garcia set off on another soaring lick. And we were dancing with the freak next to me, who seemed to be by himself, but was grooving with his eyes shut and his hands floating rhythmically in front of him. Shit, we were dancing with everybody in the place, all of us connected—the music driving us, us driving the music, all united by the rhythm, excited by the melodies, electrified by the energy that all of us created together.

Good loving
Give me lovin baby
Good lovin
All I need is loving
Good loving
Got to have lovin
Good loving

That was just the first song…and then they just kept going. They played and played. And we danced till our legs were soggy and our feet were melting into the floor and our heads swirled like the tumbling colors of a kaleidoscope. And the joints flowed and the smiles reigned and we wanted more and more and more. And they just kept giving it, continually taking us to new impossible heights, the room brightening as they shifted gears and textures. Brighter and brighter, higher and higher, then brighter and higher still. They played for hours and hours, hours that seemed timeless and instant, stretched long and pulled tight. How can they play so long? How can they ever stop?

We overflowed with a joyous pulsing energy, strengthened by its power but weakened from its abundance, its demands, when the Dead finally romped through "Going Down the Road Feeling Bad" and steamed into a pounding Bo-Diddly beat: Bomp diddabomp bomp bomp:

I'm going to tell you how it's going to be
You're going to give your love to me
I want to love you night and day
Love that's love and not fade away.
Love is real and not fade away
Not fade away

And there was no more left. No one could want more. With just enough energy to keep beatific smiles afloat on our faces, Stu and Sarah and I staggered the five blocks back to Mountfort Street, oblivious to the biting cold and the gray city that surrounded us.

~CHAPTER EIGHT~

January 2

I WOKE UP BEFORE SARAH, BUT I JUST lay there and stared at her, not wanting to wake her, but wanting to be there when she woke up. It was hard not to move. I was jammed against the wall—there just wasn't a hell of a lot of room with the two of us on my single mattress. But I kept as still as I could and watched her easy breathing, with her eyes shut and a few squiggly strands of hair floating across her soft blank face. Sarah sleeping, just her, plain and open, unguarded, next to me. Man, what a trip. I waited and watched her wake up, slowly open her eyes, and see me and remember where she was, watched the smile rise across her face when it dawned on her that it was real.

The apartment was completely quiet. No one else around. We lay there, talking softly, snuggling close, playful kissing, quick and silly. She wore just a tee-shirt and I wasn't wearing anything. Tavola climbed over us, straddling our two nestled bodies from heads to feet. Sarah laughed. I covered her giggles with my lips, and the vibration tickled my mouth and sent ricochets of chills all over me. She laughed all the way through the kiss and as she eased her mouth away from mine, her eyes sparkled with joy and I had to kiss her again and again and again and we just glided into sweet morning love.

We took our time getting it together, but we finally set off for Harvard Square to cruise around and get some muffins at Pewter Pot. It was motherfucking cold out, so we bundled up as best we could, and decided to take the MTA rather than hitchhike.

We almost never took the subway—the MTA goes underground at Kenmore Square, where we got on—except to the airport. Riding it to Cambridge was an adventure in itself, traveling through the other Boston, the straight Boston, people going to and from jobs or shopping or whatever it was they did with their days. It was early afternoon, so it was easy to find seats together near the front of the car. The subway mixes everybody all up, all kinds of people sharing space but carefully avoiding any other sort of connection. I checked out our temporary comrades. I couldn't help staring at a kid about my age, sitting opposite us, reading the *Record American* sports section. He had short blond hair and was wearing a worn white shirt and pressed black slacks. Where was he going? Where had he come from? What was his draft lottery number? What was his day going to be like? Was he in love? Did he have crazy thoughts? Where will he be when the revolution comes? In some life, maybe we would have known each other, maybe if we'd never moved to Illinois that could be me, my alternate life playing out in the workaday world of Boston.

Sarah nuzzled up to my ear and whispered, "It's not nice to stare," and pulled me back out of my wonderings. I put my arm around her and drew her close. She smiled up at me. Man, whatever it was that got me in this spot and not sitting by myself across the way, it was all right with me.

When we came up from the subway in Harvard Square, we were back in our world. The newsstand island buzzed with freaks and bearded professors and tourist hippies. Harvard Square was where kids from out of town would first go to see the freaks, to get a taste of the scene. The place was hopping, even though school was out.

As we surveyed the scene to get our bearing, we saw a familiar face across the way in front of the coop bookstore—Luke with a couple other people passing out leaflets. It was hard to miss Luke, not just because he was tall—he just carried himself like he was a big fucking deal.

Luke saw us and smiled big. He liked Sarah and me. I think part of that was politics. From the anti-military campaign at BU the previous spring—Luke led that as one of those famous outside agitators the media loved to talk about—he knew we were more into action than a lot of student radicals who could get lost in hours and hours of bullshit meetings and deep philosophical discussions. But I think he liked us as friends, too. He hadn't seen Sarah since then. Sarah hadn't seen him since he'd become a Weatherman. We headed toward him.

We clasped hands and patted each other on the back.

"It's good to see you guys," he said, looking back and forth from Sarah to me. "What's going on?"

"Sarah's up from Philadelphia," I said. "We're just cruising. Pretty quiet around here."

"That's cool," he said. He looked at Sarah. "What's going on in Philly, sister?"

"I'm going to school, not much else," Sarah said. "It's so good to see you." She looked at him with a lot of admiration, or something. I always thought Sarah dug Luke in ways that made me a little nervous. Shit, I couldn't really blame her if she did. He just exuded charisma and strength.

And in what had turned out to be a pivotal moment for him, it was Sarah who was by his side and me who was on the sidelines.

During the anti-military campaign, some of the activists went to local high schools to try to explain to the kids what it was all about—trying to stop the ways BU supported the military with things like ROTC and allowing military recruiters on campus. We were well received at the middle class schools—the kids seemed to dig rapping with real-live campus radicals. But when Luke and Sarah and me and this other guy, Johnny, went to Boston English High School, things were different. It was a tough motherfucking school—all boys who were on the low end of the Boston tracking system, Vietnam and factory fodder. Shit, the school looked like a factory—or a prison: a big block of brick surrounded by a five-foot high black wrought iron fence.

That morning at Boston English, the kids turned on us. After a short time of them curiously taking our leaflets and some mild, almost good-natured taunting, they formed a screaming mob around us, yelling "SDS go home." Then, just as we were trying to calm them down long enough for Luke to make a graceful exit speech—"we know you don't like us, but we're really on your side and we'll be back"—a short, fat, greasy-haired kid broke into the invisible circle around us and yelled at Luke, "I'm tired of your fucking shit. How would you like a knife in your belly?" And suddenly they were coming at us, pushing and shoving and kicking and punching: a mad scene, raw with the smell of skin against skin, hot with anger and fear. I covered myself as best I could and tried to bob and weave my way through the throbbing mob to find Sarah and get the hell out of there. We broke out of the crowd—they were focused on Luke, who stood out because he was taller than the rest of us and clearly the leader. But as we looked back, we saw Johnny trip and fall as he reached the fringe of the crowd. Kids swarmed on him, beating him and smashing his glasses, which had fallen in the street. I went back to try to help him and one of the kids broke a low-hanging branch off a nearby elm tree and started swinging it at me. I backed off and then he started beating Johnny with the branch. Other kids broke off branches and joined in. Shit, I felt helpless—and scared, goddammit. So I'd run back at the kids and they'd come after me and let up on Johnny for a moment, and he staggered slowly up the street—shit, he couldn't see where he was going. Then I'd retreat and they'd go back at Johnny. After a few repetitions of this brutal street dance, Johnny got far enough up the block, far enough away from the school, that the kids finally just threw their sticks at him and ran back to rejoin the bigger mob. Johnny's face was bloodied, his shirt ripped, his glasses twisted and hopeless. He was humiliated and pissed: "Motherfuckers," was all he said as Sarah and I helped him to the soft grass across Longfellow Avenue on the campus of Harvard Medical School—a block and a world away from Boston English.

Luke was still in the middle of the mob. Johnny was out of action. Sarah convinced me that I could never make it close enough to help Luke—the kids would pounce on me as soon as they saw me and they were less likely to attack a girl. So she tried to disguise herself by taking off her coat and putting her hair up in a red bandana that she had been wearing around her neck. I wanted to follow her, to keep a close eye on her, but she told me to keep my distance so I wouldn't give her away. I walked with her to the top of the block then stopped and watched her make her way down the street until she was out of sight. Shit, man, then I really felt helpless. I paced at the top of the street listening to the vague rumblings of the mob, trying to figure out what they meant. But it wasn't long before Luke and Sarah came walking up the street, almost casually. Luke was smiling. He had the beginnings of a shiner around his right eye and other scratches and bruises on his face. I think he saw the confusion and worry in my eyes because he smiled at me and patted me on the shoulder and said: "Hey, man, I fought back. And it felt good."

Luke got punched some and eventually got wrestled to the ground but the crowd was so packed in around him that nobody could get any real good swings. Johnny got fucked because he was isolated on the edge of the mob. But the amazing thing was that while Luke was trying to single-handedly fight off one hundred fifty crazed and pissed proletarian kids, a group of black kids came to his aid. They just smoothly and powerfully formed a circle around him, allowed him to say his parting words, and escorted him out of the mob, where Sarah-in-disguise was waiting for him. And, for Luke, some elemental part of what would become the Weatherman philosophy was born or clarified that day. I don't even know how influential Luke was on the national Weatherman scene. Maybe this same kind of scene had played out wherever the other leaders came from. But it was obvious as we walked back to BU that day that something basic had been revealed to Luke when he swung back at those kids.

Me? Shit, I felt like a coward, that I didn't do enough to help Johnny, especially. And Sarah had been the one to keep her head in the chaos, to go back to make sure Luke got out of there. Sarah and I were still dancing on the edge of romance then and I felt like I'd failed some fundamental test. As we walked the twenty or so blocks back to BU on that beautiful late April morning, she and Luke seemed to share some kind of triumph, Johnny was righteously angry, and I felt alone, submerged in confusion and doubt.

Things had changed a lot in the nine months since Boston English.

After all the actions that spring, when SDS really did play a critical role in getting a lot of students involved in protests at campuses all over the country, they had this crazy national convention where they split into a confusing bunch of factions. Basically, one side thought building alliances with American workers was the most important step toward the revolution while the other said that the role of young white revolutionaries was to support the Vietnamese revolution—the NLF—and the black revolution in the U.S., mainly the Panthers. Then it really gets confusing. The Revolutionary Youth Movement, the second of those two factions, split into two more factions: RYM I and RYM II. I'm not sure which was which, or who got to pick who was I and who was II, but one of the RYM groups was the Weathermen, after the line from Dylan's "Subterranean Homesick Blues": *You don't need a weatherman to know which way the wind blows.* In other words, you don't need a lot of fancy Marxist analysis to see that the Vietnamese and blacks were the vanguard, and that our most important job was to support them. I could dig that.

But where the Weathermen made a lot of Movement people—including me—uncomfortable is that they were into fighting, the pigs in particular. Not just fighting back or defending themselves, fucking attacking the cops. In October during their "Days of Rage," they went into the streets of Chicago and fucking picked fights with the cops with their fists and sticks and shit. Luke had even taken a group of Weathermen back to Boston English, where they took positions on the steps, held up their fists, and challenged the kids to fight—to show them how tough they were. It seemed crazy to a lot of us, but they were making us all think about what it really takes to make a revolution and if we were ready to do that.

Luke was way into it, but for a moment there in Harvard Square, he was just an old friend.

"Yeah," Luke said. "It's good to see you, too. Hey, these are my friends, Marsha and Steve." I'd met Steve before when we painted up some buildings the night after Black Panthers Mark Clark and Fred Hampton were killed by the cops. "These are some crazy motherfuckers from BU,"

Luke said to them, "Ben and Sarah." Sarah and I exchanged a quick arched look reacting to Luke's description.

"Yeah, Steve and I did some painting together," I said. We all kind of nodded to each other. Marsha, a foot shorter than Luke, had clear blue eyes and some wisps of blond hair that hung out of the scarf and hat she was bundled in.

Then Luke got serious. He *was* a serious motherfucker. "We could sure use you guys helping us out with our Panther support and other stuff. The pigs are coming down pretty hard on us right now."

"Yeah," I said, "we heard about the Harvard thing." A few months before, a bunch of Weathermen—maybe twenty, including Luke—had gone to the Center for International Affairs at Harvard, which had produced a lot of the brainpower behind the Vietnam War—McGeorge Bundy and Walt Rostow, motherfuckers like that—and just started breaking shit. The cops said that they also attacked the secretaries and other people working there. Luke was facing felony assault charges for that action.

"Fuck that," he said. "I'm not worried about that. There's much bigger things going on, and we need to figure out how we can get all of us who support the Panthers and the Vietnamese and are willing to stand up to the pigs working together. We'd really like to get together with you and Mike and some of the other righteous folks from BU and see how we can help each other. Otherwise the pigs are just going to isolate us and try to crush us. If we're all off doing our own thing, we're not nearly as powerful as we can be if we work together."

"Sure," I said. It made sense to get together even if I didn't like everything they did. Besides, it was hard to say no to Luke. "There's a lot of shit going on at BU, too. They're fucking with us with injunctions and hanging suspended sentences over people for the GE actions. People are feeling pretty beaten down right now."

"We can't let them do that to us," Luke was heating up. "Think about what the Panthers and the Vietnamese are facing—this is silly-ass shit compared to that. That's why we've got to work together, so we don't get beaten down."

"Yeah, right," I said. "I think Mike and Steve talked about getting together already." Steve nodded. "Mike's out of town now. When everybody's back, we'll do it."

"Cool," Luke said. "Glad we ran into you guys." He smiled and gave Sarah a big hug. I clasped hands with him, then Steve and Marsha. They went back to handing out their leaflets, and Sarah and I headed down Brattle Street toward Pewter Pot.

It was warm and sweet smelling in the restaurant. That was a rush in itself. A waitress dressed like someone out of a Shakespeare play, with a bright red vest laced up the front over a frilly white blouse, showed us to a booth in the corner.

We checked out the menus.

"Luke's pretty intense," Sarah said.

"Luke's always been pretty intense," I said, "but he's definitely at a different level now. Shit's getting heavy. No way around that."

The waitress brought us a steaming pot of coffee and filled our cups. It smelled great. I poured a bunch of cream and sugar in and took a quick sip that burned my tongue.

"I know," Sarah said. "But it's different. There's an edge that I never saw in him last year."

"Things are different than last year. A lot different." I blew on my coffee and took a big sip. Incredible.

"You keep telling me that. I'm not sure I like it so much. What do you think he wants to do with you guys?"

"I don't know." The waitress came ready to take our order. She had a long, thin face and wispy cardboard-brown hair pulled back in a ponytail. Tapping her pen on her order pad, she forced a smile. Sarah finally ordered a chocolate chip muffin and I got a blueberry corn muffin.

"I don't know," I said again. "They do crazy shit, no doubt about it. But how do we deal with what the government is doing to the Panthers who are just trying to set up schools and breakfast programs and teach black people to defend themselves against the pigs, and all the bombs they're dropping on Vietnam—shit, what they're doing to us at BU?"

Sarah didn't say anything. The restaurant was loud. Her eyes kind of wondered around, checking out other people.

"The Weathermen are intense," I said, "and they turn a lot of people off, but…I don't know. A lot of what they say is right, but then they do shit like beat up, or at least scare the shit out of, secretaries at Harvard."

"That doesn't seem so revolutionary to me," Sarah said, still not looking at me.

"Me neither," I said. "But we can't just hang out and get stoned and hope the pigs leave us alone. It just seems like people are either packing it in or getting ready to fight. And if we still want to fight, does that mean fighting the way the Weathermen want us to fight? Shit, I don't know."

Sarah looked back at me. "I can't see you doing that, Ben. Or maybe, I just hope you wouldn't."

The waitress set our muffins in front of us, along with a little pewter bucket full of butter. I cut my muffin in half, slathered it with butter, and took a big bite. Sarah broke a corner off hers and nibbled at it. She smiled.

"I know," I said between bites. "We'll talk to them. Maybe we'll do some stuff with them. I don't see us joining up anytime soon."

"Good," she said, and looked straight at me with a subject-changing smile. "Isn't this muffin the best muffin you ever had?"

"Yeah," mine was mostly gone. "The coffee, too." I used my fingers to sweep up all the crumbs on my plate. "Really good."

I reached across the table and took her hand and rubbed it slowly. Our eyes met and locked for a second or two. She put her other hand on top of mine, got a serious look that slowly turned into a kind of am-bivalent smile.

I squeezed her hand.

The waitress brought us the bill. We bundled up for the venture back out into the bleak cold. Sarah left first. I waited a bit until there was a crowd at the cashier's stand, jammed the bill into my pants pocket, and cruised on out of the restaurant. It was too easy.

We walked up Massachusetts Avenue, stopping at shops along the way: a great bookstore, a funky record store, a place with cool imported stuff—weird little trinkets and big-stoned jewelry, and brightly colored clothes that we oogled over—and a hip clothing store where Sarah lingered longer than I would have liked. But I did dig imagining her in some of those frilly freaky clothes that she held up against her as she looked in the mirror. We didn't have hardly any money, so we couldn't buy anything anyway.

By the time we got to the Orson Welles Cinema, we were ready to head back to Mountfort Street. We were in between subway stops, so we just stuck out our thumbs and got a ride in no time—from a couple of freaks in a beat-up old Corvair.

We climbed in the back. Sarah and the girl in the passenger seat started shooting the shit about the clothes store we were just in, how it had cool stuff but was insanely expensive. Sarah told her about the time she sort of accidently stole a necklace from there. She just tried it on and nobody paid attention to her as she wondered around the store looking at other things, so she just left and that was that.

Sarah could be outrageous like that—stealing shit or going back into the mob at Boston English or dashing from Pewter Pot without a second thought, for that matter. She could be gutsy and tough, but I know seeing Luke freaked her out. All the shit I'd been telling her about things getting heavy got a little more real to her with Luke's intensity. But shit, it freaked me out some too. Luke had crossed a line that I still straddled. I still didn't know how you made a joyful revolution with violence. I felt the anger and understood the analysis that says we have to fight back against a system that will do anything to prevent real change. But I couldn't quite picture who or what I had to become to fight like that. Like Luke? Like the Weathermen? Was that the only way there was to go? Sometimes I wondered who I was really trying to convince about the revolution—Sarah or me.

The folks who gave us a ride were so cool that they took us all the way to Mountfort Street, so I invited them up to smoke a couple bowls of the hash Barry had left me.

CHAPTER NINE

January 3

THE DAY WAS BRIGHT WITH A SPARKLING CHILL. We got quick rides but short ones. Four rides and an hour and a half barely got us out of Boston. But just outside of Natick, a guy picked us up who said he could get us to Worcester, almost half way to Amherst. He was a freak—long brown hair in a ponytail and a neatly trimmed beard—but a little older than us, driving a fairly new Buick or Oldsmobile. Must have been his parents'. He told us he was some kind of graduate student, home for the holidays from Berkeley, California.

"Berkeley, man," I said, "heavy shit going on there."

Berkeley was like a war zone, he said—the kids and the cops going at each other all the time, and the Panthers raising hell next door in Oakland. I got the feeling that he wasn't right in the middle of it, but he said you couldn't help being drawn into it one way or another. He was glad to be away from all that, to be hanging out for awhile with his parents in quiet Auburn. I told him it was getting pretty heavy in Boston, too, even though things had mellowed out a bit over the holidays. Sarah talked about being in Philly, where lots of shit was happening but just because of the nature of her situation—living with her parents in the suburbs—she felt disconnected from it all. We decided it'd be cool to have regular exchanges so people in the midst of the heavy shit could mellow out once in awhile and the people removed from the action could get a taste of it now and then

Amherst was kind of like that for us Boston kids, I guess—a sort of retreat. This was my first trip, but Mike said there wasn't too much political stuff going on there, just a lot of serious partying. Mike was the connection. He grew up in Springfield, not far from Amherst, and a lot of his high school buddies, including his girlfriend Paulie and his good friend JT, were at UMass. JT had been to Mountfort Street a few times and had hung out with us—Mike, Stu, Sarah, Barry, Scott, and bunch of others, a great collection of Boston, Illinois, Philly, and Amherst folks—at the Newport Jazz Festival the summer before. Amherst was a place where we could forget about the pigs and injunctions and the worker-student alliance versus the revolutionary youth movement for a few days.

The grad student dropped us off where Route 12 toward Auburn split off from Route 9 toward Amherst. It was mid-afternoon, and the day's brightness was starting to dull, turning toward a hazy gray. It was still fucking cold. Worcester was a solid gray city—old and tired. The remnants from its days as a manufacturing center were abandoned old brick factories with broken windows and empty loading docks where hobos had set up camp—and a lingering penetrating stink that smelled like traces of burning rubber blended with raw sewage. Old tires and car parts and just plain fucking trash lined the grimy roadway in what used to be an industrial area and now was more like an urban ghost town. And we had a shitty spot to hitchhike—the traffic going through on Route 9 didn't stop and had to take a left fork, which meant there was no good place to pull over and no good place for us to stand. We ended up just on the other side of the fork—it was worse further ahead where the road narrowed to dip under a railroad bridge. And even though Worcester was the birthplace of Abbie Hoffman and Stu Martin, it wasn't exactly a bastion of hipness. Steely looks from passing motorists matched the hardness of the place.

No quick ride this time. We started getting cold. And maybe a little scared. I watched Sarah stick her thumb out, with a determined look— even occasionally sticking her leg out and slowly pulling her pant leg up in mock titillation, mostly to make me laugh, I think. I was kind of up- tight—this whole thing, hitchhiking to Amherst, was my idea, and get- ting stuck in the pits of Worcester would be a real fucking bummer.

Half an hour, forty-five minutes, shit maybe even an hour, went by. Time was hard to get a hold of standing there in the grime and the cold and the breeze of car after car not stopping for us. Sarah decided it was time for the song. I don't know where the song came from. I guess she learned it at camp when she was a kid. And I can't remember when we— she—decided it was a lucky hitchhiking song, a magnet for rides. But we needed something, so she started singing:

Were you ever in Quebec
stowing timber on the deck…

"Come on," she said, her voice loud and exuberant against the hostile roar of traffic buzzing by us in the grit of the city afternoon. "You gotta sing, too, or it's not going to work." Her smile was shining: with the cold creeping through our outer layers and us totally at the mercy of the strangers speeding by us, she just lit up with this radiance that cast a spell on me. Silly as it was, silly as I felt, I couldn't say no. She started again:

Were you ever in Quebec
stowing timber on the deck

I joined in. Hesitant, quiet, a little embarrassed at first (oh dear, what will all these straight people who won't pick us up because they think we're hippie commie drug fiends think of me?).

Where there's a king with a golden crown
riding on a donkey

On the chorus, though, I got loud, her infectious silliness carrying me along. We were swaying, now, for warmth and in some kind of rhythm, our thumbs sweeping with each car as it passed then springing back to follow the next one.

Hey ho away we go
Donkey riding, donkey riding
Hey ho away we go,
a-riding on a donkey

We were laughing as we sang. It didn't matter now that cars were going by us, that we might never get a ride, that there were a million things that could happen to us: cops, freak-haters, or just being totally ignored until dark and cold closed in on us—it was great to be there with her, for us to be there together, in that dirty, grimy hopeless spot, singing a silly song, and believing that somehow we'd be all right: We'd get where we were going—or we wouldn't, and that would be all right, too.

Were you ever off the Horn
where it's always fine and warm.
See the lion and the unicorn
riding on a donkey

Hey ho away we go
Donkey riding, donkey riding
Hey ho away we go,
riding on a donkey

Of course, just as we finished the second chorus, a car stopped, a bright green Plymouth Valiant—like the one that Scott's parents used to have—pulling onto the shoulder as far as it could, and we hustled to jump in before traffic started backing up. As we ran, Sarah looked back at me a with a quick raised eyebrow: her shiny eyes saying, "See!"

The guy who picked us up looked to be in his thirties, shaggy short hair. Straight, but sympathetic. He was going to Belchertown, almost to Amherst. Outasight. He was a school teacher, first and second grade kids. He'd gone to school at Boston College. As we left the bricks and broken windows of Worcester and settled into rolling hilly farm land dusted with snow, he said it looked to him like things were getting pretty crazy in Boston.

"None of that stuff was going on when I was there," he said. "A few people were making noise about the House Un-American Activities Committee, and a few priests and students were starting to get involved with the civil rights movement. But things were pretty quiet. I don't know what I'd do if I was there now," he said in a way that made it seem like he was asking me a question.

"Most of the time, it's great," I answered. "I think we're really lucky to be in college, in Boston, now. There's just this energy…Sometimes it's heavy, but it makes you feel so alive, like we're doing something important."

"Well. I'm glad you guys are there and raising hell. Somebody's got to do it. Can't do much with my first graders in Belchertown."

"I think you could do a lot," Sarah said, from her spot between us in the front seat. "Teach them to ask questions, teach them to respect all kinds of people, teach them to…."

"Yeah, man," I jumped in, "you can plant the subversive seeds, so by the time they get to high school, they'll be ready to join us."

The teacher laughed. "It's hard to be too subversive with Dick and Jane," he said. "Besides, I've got to be careful. They're still not crazy about pinkos at Belchertown Elementary."

"Sure," I said, "but just treating them like human beings and telling them the truth is a revolutionary thing in itself."

"Being a teacher in a small town like that seems like it would be a good life," Sarah said. She looked over at me, a little embarrassed or something. I don't know why. Shit, if she wanted to be a teacher in a small New England town, it sounded fine to me. Beat the hell out of being anything in Philadelphia. I was digging just being with her in that warm car, almost sure to reach our destination soon. We were driving through picturesque and soothing country, stone walls and long-settled fields broken by silvery stands of bare trees. Picture postcard, Americana shit, and I dug it. It all seemed so real and solid, connected to something lasting. The teacher only had an AM radio, but today the music was sweet.

What goes up must come down, spinning wheel, spinning round...

"Small towns are quaint and quiet," the teacher said. "But they are small, which sometimes means small minded. If you're not one of them," he said, grinning as he looked over the two of us, "they can make it awful rough on you."

"I don't know. It's just a thought," Sarah said, looking at me again. "Seems like you really can make a difference in people's lives, make a real difference." She looked back at the teacher, "I think it's cool that you're doing it—and that you're a freak on the inside." I could tell he liked it when she said that.

Dusk was starting to settle in as we neared Belchertown and the snow was now a thick pad over the countryside, so the teacher offered to get us into Amherst—an extra ten miles for him. Really nice guy. I don't know if he wished he had been born a little later and could have been part of what was happening now or if he was content to root for us from the quiet sidelines of Belchertown. I sensed a calm satisfaction with who he was and what he was doing, but that something in our fight attracted him. Either way, there was no doubt that cat was a brother. It was good to know that people like him—living straight lives in the straight world—were behind us.

He dropped us at the first phone booth we saw once we got into Amherst. I called Gray Street and talked to somebody who found JT, who said he'd come to get us, though it took us a while to figure out and explain to him exactly where we were. About ten minutes later he pulled up in his green Mustang.

JT was a trip. Fire plug short, his hair looked like fine, frizzled bronze threads that rose from his head like flames from a burning house in a cartoon. He had a hose of a nose and flashing green eyes, and a speedy energy that always seemed to be looking for some kind of blaze. Quick talking, quick acting, whether he was rolling a joint or whipping up something to eat—both of which he was known to do a lot. And he was solid, man. He always seemed to show up in Boston when things were heavy and we were down and he'd bring us a box of incredible munchies from Mike's dad's bakery in Springfield—bagels and rye breads and pumpernickel loaves and halvah—and he always had pot.

It was good to see him. Bundled in a gray-black sweater coat, he blended perfectly into this suddenly far-north feeling landscape. He told us things were pretty raucous at Gray Street. Of course, Mike was there, that's a good start on raucousness. And most of the Amherst kids lived near by—unlike our Boston friends—so they were at full strength.

"But don't worry," he said. "You guys can take my room."

JT. Solid. We said all the right things: No man, we couldn't do that, we don't care where we sleep. But there was no way to talk him out of it, even if we really wanted to. That was perfect. A bed and a room of our own. Far fucking out.

Gray Street—the house—was at the end of a dead-end street in what looked like a quiet and normal residential neighborhood for a small Yankee college town. The white shingled three-story house rose from the snow-lined street like a big drift. Our friends had the top two floors. JT led the way up a central stairway, and as we went up, the quiet rapidly vanished as strains of The Band's "Across the Great Divide" reached out to greet us and, when he opened the door, normal disappeared, too, like we had just stepped through some looking glass and popped up in a stoned-out wonderland. The sound was deafening and the room we entered was a collage of couches and stereo speakers. Serious fucking speakers: huge horns hanging in the corners, painted in swirls of oranges and purples and reptilian iridescent greens, and enormous wide-mouth floor speakers that doubled as tables to hold newspapers, comic books, beer cans, and overflowing ash trays. Where there weren't speakers, couches and sections of couches sprawled in an upholstered mosaic of browns and grays and faded yellows. The living room. Dim light and people spread all over the place. And, from the dusky smelly smoke hanging in the air, I figured they might have been smoking a little dope.

We were warmly greeted. Hugs and introductions. Dicky, Liz, DEJ, Weird Jojo, Jellyhead, Lefcowitz, and more, too many to remember. Mike pulled himself out of a chair long enough to say hello and, with a flat voice and not much enthusiasm, introduced us to Paulie. She was different than I'd expected—though I don't know exactly what I expected except that I just figured Mike's girlfriend had to be insane in some way. Maybe I expected a female version of Mike—though that was entirely too freaky to even imagine. Paulie sure wasn't that. She was small and simple looking. Straight, short brown hair, quiet brown eyes, with a squareness to her face and a droop to her stance. But she had an open kindness in her smile, an innocent sweetness about her that was about as far from anything you'd think about Mike as you could get.

Mike handed me a joint. I took a long hard toke and passed it to Sarah. And like passing through a decompression chamber, our eyes and our ears and our heads began adjusting and we found our way to a spot on a couch and slipped—easily, happily, gracefully—from being strangers looking in to filling our own spots of color and brightness in this wildly vibrant and wholly welcoming tapestry.

There were joints—many many joints, fat joints, powerful joints. Bagels and breads from Mike's dad's place. A fridge full of beers and sodas. Loud music.

Short shouted conversations. About our trip. Worcester, man. Everybody shook their heads when we said we got stuck in Worcester for awhile. About upcoming concerts. Led Zeppelin was coming soon, and everyody was waiting for the Allman Brothers to come back. About school and how much we didn't care about it. About how heavy shit was getting in Boston: my injunction, our friends' arrests, people flipping out all over the place about all kinds of shit. About how we couldn't take this shit anymore. How we had to get somewhere, do something.

Sarah stopped taking hits on the joints and just passed them to me. She was already pretty stoned, her eyes heavy and clouded.

We'd had a long day. Shit, I was pretty stoned, too. The second or third joint had got me to hippie breakthrough—that leap when you shut your eyes after a good hit and you feel a harmonic vibration start at your eyeballs and then buzz to the back of your brain, all the sounds around you tumbling into the whoosh of a wind tunnel, and you disconnect from wherever it was you were and when you open your eyes you're on the other side of reality. And the joints just kept coming.

In a momentary quiet while Mike changed the record, JT looked at me with wide eyes and a luminous grin and said, "Hey, Ben, you want to drop some acid?"

I looked at Sarah, who just shook her head. Sarah didn't do acid—never had, never would as far as I could tell. Then I looked back at JT, who really was glowing: his smile was like the center of some kind of energy source, with a reddish, pulsing light emanating from it. "What do you got?" I asked "Is it any good?"

"It's blotter and I think it's pretty good," he said. "I dropped some just before I came to pick you up and I'm pretty fucking high now." He looked pretty fucking high.

I'd dropped acid somewhere around fifty times since my first trip last New Year's Eve in Illinois. I'd resisted it through the first semester at BU even though a lot of my friends like Mike and Stu and Brian were doing it. I was kind of scared of it. My head was fucked up enough without adding something that deliberately fucked it up more. But, man, once I did it, I loved it. A whole new part of my brain was open to me—an expansive, fun-loving, colorful part of my brain that goofed on me and allowed me to see the world in ways I couldn't even imagine. After that, I wasn't afraid of LSD anymore—though I did always respect its power and always tried to make sure that I only took it with people and in situations where I felt safe. Of course, that had come to include the ominous quiet of wandering the streets of Boston in the unclaimed hours between night and morning and the outrageous volume of some great rock and roll shows. I had tripped maybe four or five times when Sarah was around. Even though she didn't trip—something to do with not being willing to give up control of her head, which is exactly what I loved about it—she didn't seem to mind when I did. Sometimes she seemed to enjoy it, to goof on me, which is easy enough when I'm straight—when I was tripping I was totally defenseless. At the Newport Jazz Festival, she'd led me around, keeping a hold of me as she moved us closer to the stage. Sometimes, though, I think maybe it frustrated her when she'd talk to me and I'd have no idea what she was talking about or when I'd drift away to some other place.

"Would you mind?" I asked her now.

"No, go ahead," she said with a shrug. "I'm just really wiped out and tired. No way I'm staying up all night with you. But if that's what you want to do—have fun."

"Are you sure?"

"Yes, sure, go ahead," she said, not enthusiastic but not mad.

"Who else dropped?" I asked JT. I wanted to know who my companions would be after the pot and alcohol had put everyone else to sleep.

"Just me and Mike, I only had three hits and we saved one for you." I looked over at Mike, who was a couch and a half away from me, and he had that same pulsing smile that JT had. Looked like good acid indeed. And I liked the company. Mike and me had tripped together many times. And I'd tripped with JT at Newport, which was just a fucking gas.

"Sure, what the hell? I've never tripped in Amherst before."

"You've never *been* in Amherst before," Sarah was quick to add, the slightest of smiles forcing itself across her mouth.

JT reached into his pocket and pulled out a small folded piece of paper. He very carefully, very, very slowly—he was definitely tripping—unfolded it and held it out to me. In the middle was a smaller jaggedly ripped piece of paper with a purple dot in the middle of it, like one of those candy dots that come on strips of paper. I picked it up and put it on my tongue and washed it down with a chug of beer. As I did, Sarah flashed me a smile that was bigger than she really meant. Here we go.

The first rush from LSD comes when you drop it—even though it takes awhile to work its way into your system, especially when you've had seventeen joints and four beers. But as soon as I swallowed that little chunk of paper, I started feeling different because I knew that soon—thirty, forty minutes, an hour?—I would be where JT and Mike were. There was no turning back now, and I was roused by that rush of anticipation, waiting for that first twinge in my stomach, that first surge of psychedelic electricity in my brain.

But as I waited to get off, I also sensed a growing distance from Sarah. I think she was having a good time, but she really didn't know anybody there that well—except Mike. And Mike and her had a strange relationship. I think they liked each other. Mike always acted like he liked her when it was just him and me, but he was always a little cold to her when he was actually around her. So she thought he didn't like her and kind of hung back around him. Seemed like since Sarah and I became a couple, things were forced between them—like they had to be nice to each other because Mike was one of my best friends and now my roommate and Sarah was my girlfriend. No matter what, on this night, it wasn't going to be Mike to befriend Sarah while I tripped because Mike was already about an hour or so down the road that was stretching out between me and Sarah.

Sarah got along all right with the other women there who she'd just met: Liz and Paulie. I'd hoped she and Paulie would hit it off since my dream scheme was to have them both living at Mountfort Street before long. But Paulie was pretty quiet. She smiled and laughed as conversations went around, and a couple of times tried to shoot the shit with Sarah and me. But it was awkward—just a little off somehow, something we'd already talked about or had nothing to do with us. She really was like the opposite of Mike, whose machine gun style of rapping had earned the nickname—from Stu, of course—of Mikey the Mouth.

Sarah and Liz—a feisty woman who easily held her own with all these guys—actually seemed to connect more. They'd headed off to the kitchen together—I guess to take a break from the endless joints and the loud music—and came back later laughing about something.

But now, though Sarah was trying to be a good sport—every once in a while asking with genuine concern and interest, "How are you feeling?"—something was happening in both of us that pushed a peculiar and prickly tension into the usually comfortable space between us. Shit, acid really does disconnect you from routine relating with other people: every thought goes through a pin-ball maze, every syllable, every gesture becomes an absolutely conscious and singular act. So a strange brew of guilt (I knew she really didn't want me to take the acid) and being a little pissed about feeling that guilt (this is my life; she should get used to it) mixed with the LSD surging through my system to leave me at a total loss as to how to relate to her. And from her, I sensed a slow withdrawal of the openness we'd left Boston with not all that many hours before— to hitchhiking, to going to Amherst to be with people she didn't know, to joining in on my little adventure across the state.

After a series of automatic "fines," my answer to Sarah's question changed to "Great!" I felt it first in my stomach, a building and thrilling tension, like sparks on some psychic fuse. Then in my fingers, a current switched on, my pulse amplified and transmitting, so when I touched something—the arm of the couch, the cool metal of a beer can, the downy hair of Sarah's arm—I completed a circuit and a stirring tingling flow ran into and through me. Then slowly, through the fog of the dope and the alcohol, that current reached my head, my brain, not as a jolt, but as a vibrating wave that warmed and brightened me—like being awakened by the unfolding light of dawn. And then the full light hit me, and man, I was just there. And Great! Awake in a whole different way. Same room, same people, same sound, same light, same me. But everything was different.

When I said, "Great!" to Sarah, I saw the ridges of her lips, an asymmetrical patchwork landscape of soft oranges and pale reds, strain to contort themselves into a dry hard smile. Then she looked up and into, through, my eyes, and I could tell by the way her eyes searched, the way they fluttered and shifted, that she could tell just by looking how fucking high I was, which for some reason seemed to mellow her out. Her lips relaxed and regained a supple and liquid softness and a gentle upward curl. She laughed, sweet and naturally musical, like an echo in a tunnel of love, "Yeah, you look pretty great." I couldn't answer. I didn't know how to answer. I didn't really feel any need to answer. I tried to return a heartfelt smile—to thank her for her indulgence—but it was like I had to reduce the amount I was smiling to get to something that seemed sincere and was not just a chemical reaction. To find that point and hold it felt forced, so I just reached out and stroked the back of her hand, but my fingers felt like oversized gloves, clumsy and stumbling, bouncing awkwardly along her hand, instead of the smooth rub I intended. But I think she got the message, she took my hand in her two hands and squeezed it. Then let go.

JT and Mike, on the other hand, were grinning at me like fucking maniacs. "Hey, Ben, you're looking pretty fucked up," Mike said.

"If I look half as fucked up as you two, I'm in trouble," I answered.

JT let loose a howl. "Ben, you're in trouble."

Now it was the three of us, floating off somewhere together. Other people were still around, but now two entirely separate parties were going on. It was like we were on a stage with spotlights on the three of us and everyone else was in the shadows. We could hear things and see things that nobody else heard or saw, and we'd looked knowingly at each other, and the others would see us and say, oh those guys are just tripping. Sarah caught me a couple times exchanging those knowing looks and she'd say, "What?" And I'd look at her and try to explain, like "That organ solo, did you hear it? It was like, like somebody screaming, like somebody screaming cause they just saw something horrible, like…" but she had no idea what I was talking about and I could tell by the way she looked at me, with her eyebrows jumping to crinkle the skin on her forehead and her whole head rocking toward me: like "I'm really trying earnestly to pretend to try to understand what you're saying even though I know you're making absolutely no sense." So I just stopped. She figured that I was just hearing things or seeing things because I was tripping. I don't know that it ever crossed her mind that she was missing out on seeing and hearing things because she wasn't tripping. That organ was fucking screaming, and it was horrible, like someone was watching their best friend die. But a joy was buried inside that horror—and that was the overwhelming feeling that engulfed me—the intensity of that horror held in it the infiniteness of the love the screamer had for his friend. And I was moved almost to tears by the joy that filled me listening to that horrible screaming organ. Mike and JT heard it, too. But how could I tell Sarah that if she couldn't hear it. She didn't understand. She couldn't understand. She never would.

I sat stuck in that spot on that sofa for a while, who knows how long, more than fifteen minutes less than four hours, I'd guess. Time—I could see clearly—was a fucking liar that distorted our lives, like money. I had no desire to move, to go anywhere. Somebody kept putting great music on the stereo: Electric Flag, Country Joe and the Fish, Grateful Dead. There was an uninterrupted floor show: people talking, laughing, getting up and sitting down, changing places. Joints kept going around and I would pull deep on them because it felt good to feel the smoke tickle its way down my throat and into my lungs. The pot tasted like dirt, like rich, fertile dirt and I liked the feel of that earthy taste on my tongue. Exhaling was even more fun because I could play with the wispy smoke, make it dance, make it fly, make it a purposeful stream or a lazy drifting ring, watch it change colors as it drifted away from me: roasted marshmallow brown to puffy-cloud white to snow-cone blue. Sometimes the smoke mesmerized me so, I would forget that I still had the joint in my hand and Sarah would nudge me to pass it on, even though she wasn't taking anymore. I drank a beer—or several, I don't know—taking tiny sips cause the taste was hard and bitter, but I liked the chill slinking down to the pit of my stomach, which still had that nervous acid tingle.

I was like a spectator to this scene, even of myself, even of the inner workings of my body, but an intimate spectator. All my senses were inside the picture but the conglomerate me was outside of it. People seemed distant as though I was viewing them on a screen, but I felt like I could almost get inside them, too. The movement of their eyes or the quiver of their lips or the modulations of their voice told me things too intimate for me to know, especially since most of these people were strangers. It was easier, more rewarding to get into inanimate things. The arm of the sofa was amazing. Rich ribbings of luminous brown fabric, with a deep and mysterious texture that seemed to draw breath and exhale, to create this rolling flow of shifting tones from a sparkling tan to a thick chocolate, like a wheat field on a windy day. I reached down in awe to touch it and it was luscious and dense and, as I moved my palm slowly and softly across it, I could feel the rippling waves of grain, the little pricks of their sharp-tipped stalks stinging ever so slightly, an exquisite pain salved by the pillowy smooth plush of the hundred, thousands, millions of stalks flowing together. Had anything ever felt so good? Lost in the reverie with the sofa arm, which was starting to kind of turn me on, I felt a sharp poke in my shoulder. I must have jumped, startled, because Sarah sort of recoiled from me before she spoke.

"I'm ready to go to bed," she said.

"OK…OK," I said, not frantic—at least I don't think so, it was hard to know how what I did or what I meant to do, came out to other people—but disoriented. I had to try to refocus to make sense of what she just said. It was Sarah. We were at JT's place in Amherst. She wasn't tripping. She was tired. She wanted me to help her find where she was sleeping. JT had said we could sleep in his room. I had to get JT's attention and ask him to show us where to go.

I don't know how long that thought process took. Seconds? Minutes? It must have taken me awhile because Sarah was looking impatient when I finally called across the room to JT. Even then, it took me three or four tries to get the right volume—my first attempt I thought I was yelling but it came out barely above a whisper.

I did eventually get his attention, and, still grinning like a fucking maniac, he pulled himself out of his spot to lead us upstairs to his room. It was strange to stand up, feeling blood surge to my legs. I'd forgotten about my legs. And beyond that, I had totally lost track of the fact that there were other parts of the house besides the living room and the kitchen, which we had briefly visited when we first came in the house, and the bathroom, a closet of a room that I had visited just as I was getting off, where I'd stared into the medicine cabinet mirror and saw the face of a stranger.

JT's room was up some stairs just on the other side of the bathroom. We didn't say much on the way up. Sarah was wasted and both JT and

I were incapable of small talk. JT's room was cool. Amazingly neat, but really cool. Cut into the pitch of the roof, the ceiling sloped like a church steeple. The bed was raised like an altar beneath it. JT just kind of pointed to the bed and said, "here you go" to Sarah, who thanked him again. He said, "It's cool. I don't think I'm going to sleep much tonight" and he looked at me and giggled.

Sarah took off her jeans and climbed into the bed, didn't even bother taking her shirt off. I lay down next to her but on top of the thick white comforter that covered the bed. She just lay there and looked straight into me, now, not pissed or goofing on me, but she didn't look particularly happy either.

"How are you doing?" she asked

"I'm flying."

"I could tell," she said. Not judging, just saying.

"How are you doing?"

"I'm really tired and really stoned."

"Yeah, man, what a day, huh?" I said, really trying to make sense, to have a real conversation with her. But my words felt fuzzy, not the kind of solid things I was looking for. "Can you believe we left Boston this morning? Geez, do you remember singing in Worchester? Man, that seems like a million years ago."

"Sure does," she said, brightening just a little.

"I hope you had a good time."

"It was fine. I'm just really tired. And sometimes, it's hard . . ." Her voice trailed off.

"What's hard?"

"I don't know, Ben. I don't want to be a downer or anything, but sometimes it's hard to be with you when you're so fucked up. I mean, it's not like you're really even with me. And I don't really know anybody else here. I mean I'm not mad or anything—just kind of feel left alone or something."

Shit man, now I really had to try to make sense. It wasn't just the words she said. There was a sadness oozing out of her like a gray vapor that settled around my head. I reached out to touch her shoulder. It was cold and stiff.

"I'm sorry," I said, knowing that wasn't enough. But still it was like I was talking through a fuzz petal or a reverb chamber, the words came out sounding so strange, it was hard to concentrate on picking the ones with the right meanings. "I didn't really plan this. I asked you. You said go ahead."

"I know, still…"

"I love you," I said, grasping.

"I know," she said. Now her eyes were getting watery. Shit. She looked over at me and a sudden storm came over her face, dark and ominous, her mouth was tense, tears started rolling down her cheeks, her eyes like thunder clouds boring in on me—such a suddenly intense look of hurt and anger and accusation that my first instinct was to laugh. It was such an exaggerated preposterous pose that seemed to come out of nowhere. But I was tuned in enough to know that laughing would definitely make things worse, so I looked away before I did. "Maybe that's not enough," she said as I looked back to her.

Whoa. I was stunned to silence by this sudden blast. She glared. I withered.

"What?" finally I managed, though it came out as just a little more than desperately exhaling. "What does that mean?"

She held her glare and spoke firmly, "I don't know what that means, but I'm stoned and tired and you're so high you can hardly talk to me, and at least it seems to have gotten your attention for a second."

"Whoa, man. Sarah," something in her seriousness startled me into a surge of lucidity. Or, at least, I suddenly could put some sentences together. "I love you—really—and I'm really sorry you feel left out or whatever. But if you want to fuck with my head…I'm not very capable of defending myself at the moment. This may not be the best time to be discussing the future of our trip especially along the lines of what you just said." I actually had forgotten exactly what she had said, but I knew it was something I didn't want to be true.

Even before I spoke, the darkness around her had started to dissipate—like one of those classic Midwestern thunderstorms that raises hell than vanishes almost as quickly as it appears. She let out a long hot breath that warmed my face and tickled my eye brows, her face relaxed, her eyes still moist but now tender and sweet, and a little sad, but mostly just tired.

"I know Ben. I really don't want to bum you out or anything. I just…I don't know, Ben." She looked up and down my face and a smile slowly formed. "Man, you are fucked up." She let out a little laugh. "It just sometimes freaks me out how different we are…and that I love you so much."

No words came into my head, just waves of gushy feelings. Relief first, no damage, no long drawn-out battening down of any hatches. Then love, this deep, rich red glow, this full-body warmth, that I think was in my eyes as I looked at her, in my fingertips as I slowly stroked the course fabric of her shirt and felt her turn warm and giving. Words, fucking words, what useless little grunts. Time, words, money, how do we let these fucking illusions run our lives? This was real—these eyes, this touch, this now. How do we keep this? How do we stay here? She was the most beautiful thing I'd ever seen in this love that pushed through her sad, tired eyes, through all the darkness of her anger and hurt. I wanted to just hold on to that, to feel that easy roll of her shoulder, the warm veil of her breath on my face, to lay there beside her, wordless, timeless, free.

"I have to go to sleep, Ben." For all the love, Sarah was not where I was now.

"It's OK. I love you, Sarah, I mean I really love you," the only words that came close to meaning anything.

"I love you, too. Have fun. Be careful."

"OK," her words reminded me there was a world outside JT's bedroom. And somewhere in that world were JT and Mike, who were in the same place I was. I kissed Sarah, a soft squishy kiss that tasted good and could have easily led me in a whole different direction if Sarah hadn't pulled slowly away and said, "Goodnight."

"Goodnight," I said, savoring her wetness still on my lips.

CHAPTER TEN

January 4

AS I LEFT SARAH SLEEPING IN JT'S BED, my eyes were drawn to a flickering light that was escaping through a crack in the door at the opposite end of the hall. I hadn't noticed that on the way up. The light got brighter and more erratic as I got closer. I knocked softly on the door. No response, so I knocked a little louder. Still no response, so I pushed the door open, and I was knocked back by a throbbing light. A white, pure light, which filled the room then vanished faster than my eyes could blink. Light-dark, light-dark, light-dark, light-dark—fast and then faster. Like a hand-cranked movie, the frames flickering into one another unevenly, disjointedly, totally unreal, man. I was startled by it, stunned by this sudden assault of this throbbing light parade. But I couldn't look away, so I took a couple of steps into the room and shut the door. Only then did I notice—in the brief flashes of light—that a bright orange and green checkerboard surrounded me. I was inside it. The floors, the walls, the ceiling, orange and green squares shifting in the pulsing light. Holy shit. I was fucking high. I held out my hand in front of me and when the light shot on it, it was orange and green, too, squares tattooed to it by the beat of illumination. My checkerboard hand floated in the light, moving in sharp sensuous waves like some kind of exotic dancer before my eyes, swaying and swooping, out of my control, in and out of sight, as though it was slinking behind some deep black veil. Where had I wandered into? Outasight. Light-dark, light-dark, light-dark.

Somehow, I pulled myself out of there. The bedroom where Sarah slept was still there, at the other end of the hall, so I hadn't gone too far. I took a quick look at her. She was out, soft snores escaping her open mouth. Then I made my way down the narrow stairway in search of some reality check.

The living room scene had mellowed out some. The music was turned down a bit. The Dead doing "Dark Star."

Just a few people left—JT and Mike, of course, and the other guys who lived there, I guess, DEJ and Weird Jojo. I think they could tell I'd just had my mind blown.

"What's wrong with you?" Mike asked. "You look like you seen a fucking ghost or something."

"What's with that room, man?" I asked. "It's like I wandered into a fun house."

Mike grinned big. JT was laughing loud. The other two just looked at me like I was a tripping fool.

"What room are you talking about, man?" Mike looked at me, still grinning.

"The room at the other end of the hall from JT's with the lights and the fucking checker board." Mike was fucking with me.

"Lights? Checkerboard? Shit, Tucker you are fucked up." He looked around at the other guys as he talked to me, big smile, his right leg bouncing up and down. "You guys ever seen a room with lights? What kind of lights, Tucker? And a checkerboard? A checkerboard? Man, I think I'd like to see this room."

JT couldn't stop laughing. The other guys just let Mike play his game.

"Well, it's just right up the stairs, man. At least it was a few minutes ago. Something was there, and it was pretty damn pysch-E-delic. Whose room is that anyway?"

Weird Jojo cracked the slits that his eyes had become and kind of grumbled, "It's my room, man—got a strobe light going."

"Sheesh man, what a place to stumble into when you're tripping. The checkerboard?" I wasn't sure about the checkerboard.

"Yeah, I guess it's kind of a checkerboard. Squares of orange and green."

"Did you do that?"

"Yeah, what the fuck, I needed to paint the room. Seemed like as good a way as any."

"It was quite the rush, I'll tell you that."

JT stopped laughing long enough to talk. "We needed a roommate, so we put an ad in the paper, 'Freak Wanted.' Weird Jojo showed up."

"I think he qualified," I said, then looked at Mike. "Fuck you, Mike."

Mike just kept on smiling, "Hey, man. Just having some fun with you. I love that fucking room, man. I can just go and sit in there for hours. But aren't you glad you wandered onto it, not expecting it or anything? It's much better that way."

"Yeah, it was cool."

Weird Jojo and DEJ headed off to bed. I wondered if Weird Jojo slept with the strobe light on. Might make for interesting dreams. Waking up to that would also be freaky. Guess you don't get a name like Weird Jojo without earning it.

So now it was just the three of us. We turned the music down more so it was just kind of humming in the background.

> *Lay down my dear brother, lay down and take your rest.*
> *Won't you lay your head upon your savior's chest.*

We looked at each other and all started laughing at the same time.

"This is nice acid, JT. Thanks," I said.

"My pleasure, man. It's not often I get to trip with my brother from Boston."

"Hey, let's get out of here for awhile," Mike was standing, fidgety. "I feel like I've been sitting in this spot for a week."

Outside. Wow. I'd forgotten all about outside. The snow-lined dead-end street we'd come down some totally unknowable amount of hours before. Sure, outside would be interesting.

We staggered and stumbled our way down the stairs, opened the door, and stepped out into this big world, quiet houses lining the dark street, cars pulled up to the snow banks that marked the edge of the roadway, spots of moonlight that snuck through tree branches to plant golden patches on the blanket of snow that covered the yards. Big, fresh, quiet, and motherfucking cold. I took three steps down the porch stairs and froze, almost literally, in my tracks.

"Shit, man, I forgot my coat."

JT and Mike stopped, look back at me, in my sports coat and sweater and laughed. "Where the fuck do you think you are? Florida?" JT asked.

JT went back in with me to find my coat.

When we came back out, Mike was sitting on the porch stairs waiting for us. He looked a little dazed, as though he didn't even notice us at first. Then he looked up to the sky, that was clear and shiny, black with sparkling little pin pricks. "The stars, man," he said looking at me like I would know exactly what he meant. "The fucking stars." So we stopped and we looked. The stars were fucking amazing. Glowing, pulsing, glistening. So bright. And everywhere. You just got lost in the stars, the shimmering sheltering ceiling of the universe, so many and so much and so far, so all encompassing and enclosing, so huge you reveled in being a miniscule speck in the shadow of their brilliance. Time, money, words, girl friends, cops, even revolutions. Little dots on little drops compared to the stars.

"Yeah, man," I said to him, "the fucking stars."

We walked a few blocks past quiet houses. Seemed like we were making a racket just from the way our steps crunched the thin layers of icy snow that coated the sidewalks. We talked soft, though, not because we cared about the sleeping people all around us, but because that seemed like the right way to be under the stars and the slivery moon, passing through the whisper of darkness in the hush of snow. Sleeping people were just numbed and hidden away, they'd left this night to us and the luminous forces that surrounded us, that guided us, that gave sparkle and shine to the shadows just ahead of us. It was to them we gave respect and lowered voices.

"So is Sarah OK?" JT asked.

"Sure, I said, she's an angel. It's me that's fucked up."

That hung for awhile. I don't think he really knew what I meant. I guess I answered a question different from the one he asked. Crinkle, crunch, crunch, we walked on down the street. I had no idea where we were going, if we were going anywhere.

"So is she pissed at you?" He rephrased the question.

"Yes. No. She was. Then she wasn't. But I think she might be again when she wakes up in the morning."

"Chicks, man," Mike said. "They know how to fuck with your head."

We turned right on to a bigger street. I could see the lights of a couple of cars a few blocks away. Up ahead, I saw an open area.

"I don't think she tries to fuck with my head," I said. "She's just...I don't know...it's just..."

"See, man, she's got you all fucked up," Mike said. "I mean I dig Sarah. She's cool. She's pretty. She's smart. But man you just got it bad, you can't even think straight."

"Think straight?" I looked at Mike, his eyes glowing like something was burning inside him. "No, thinking straight is not something I'm doing too much of at the moment. I don't think I can blame Sarah for that. And you, how straight are you thinking?"

"No, man, you know what I mean. Not now, not this moment when we're both tripping our brains out. You know she's got you not knowing which way is up. But, hey man, it's cool, do what you gotta do."

We came to a park—a wide open space bright with gently drifted snow. Shoveled paths ran through it. Green benches lined the path. In the middle of the open space was a parking area with what looked like a police station next to it.

"What is that? Is that a police station?" I asked JT.

"Relax man," JT said. "This is the town green and, yeah, that's a police station, but don't worry about it. They're cool."

"What?" I looked at JT, then at Mike. Cops were not something I wanted to deal with.

"It's cool," Mike said.

"Really, Ben," JT said. "The worst that will happen is that they'll figure out we're tripping and come and try to goof on us."

Man, we were in the country. In Boston, I'd go ten blocks out of my way to avoid passing a police station when I was tripping. The worst vibrations possible. Oh, well, even if JT was a little small-town naive, I knew Mike wouldn't lead me into a dangerous situation with cops.

We found a bench that seemed like the right place to be—far enough from the cop station that I could almost forget about it. I dug my cigarettes out of my pocket and lit one. The warm smoke felt good sliding down my throat, but I held it a little too long—forgot it wasn't a joint—and had to cough it out. I was startled by the loudness of my cough resonating across the icy silence of the night.

"Speaking of chicks fucking with your head," I said to Mike. "What's happening with Paulie?"

"Not sure. I think she's still coming to Boston. We haven't talked about it much for awhile. See that's the difference between you and me. If it happens, it's cool. If it doesn't, that's cool, too. Either way, man, I'll go on breathing."

There were some other freaks hanging out on the green. A couple benches away, I could hear the murmur of low talk with occasional peels of soft laughter. Maybe they were tripping, too. Who else would be hanging out at whatever after-hours time it was in the cold of the village green?

Shit, Mike was right. I didn't know which way was up. Was Sarah right, too? Maybe love isn't enough? Man I was fucked up. How is it all supposed to fit together? What am I supposed to do? Not care as much?

Care more? I shut my eyes from the brightness of the moon and the stars and the shimmering snow, and the strobe from Weird Jojo's room was ricocheting around my brain and the checkerboard was there but each time the light flashed there'd be a different face in the squares: Sarah full of love on New Year's Eve, Mike laughing at me when I came down from Jojo's room, my father telling me to cut my hair and get a job, Stu saying he's not going to bail us out of jail, the cops at Logan, Barry laughing at me about Marx, my mother telling me how much they worry about me, Sarah singing and hitching, Mary telling me I want too much, Scotty calling me King Protestor, JT handing me the acid, Garcia whipping off another mind blowing riff, Luke saying we need to work together, Mike saying either way I'll go on breathing, Sarah saying maybe that's not enough—flickers and flashes, light-dark, light-dark, light-dark, light-dark, faster, and faster and faster and faster and faster....

"Ben, Ben...? Are you all right? Where'd you go, man?" JT's voice sounded like he was at the other end of a tunnel.

When I opened my eyes, it was cold again and moon-bright and quiet. Whew. Where did I go? I looked long and slow around me. Shit man, it just doesn't get any more serene than this. Fucking Norman Rockwell painting. New England village green covered in snow. The red glow of the sign from the police station a sharp spot of color in this black and white landscape. JT and Mike were smiling at me. I felt warm and safe next to them. "Yeah, yeah, I'm fine. I'm fine. It's just been a crazy fucking couple of weeks, man. Crazy, fucking...." I lit another cigarette, the texture of the smoke on my throat grounding me somehow—a familiar and undeniably real sensation.

We lingered on that bench until first the moon, then the stars disappeared, and the soft light of morning began sneaking over the horizon. We talked some and were quiet a lot, as comfortable with one as the other. True friends endure silence best. True friends. Words not spoken could be sweet next to the glow of smiling faces in the unsure light of dawn.

JT and Mike were crashing—having had a bit of a head start on me—so we loped backed to Gray Street, the crinkle and pop of our steps somehow quieter now than they had been in the black and shiny night when we ventured out. I was still pretty high, but I felt an incredible tiredness creeping through my body and into my head—little tinges of aches from my legs, hints of hunger in my stomach, a slowing of the stream of thoughts and images rippling through my head. Gray Street was quiet as we entered, everybody still sleeping, the living room a freeze frame of the scene we'd left however many hours before but illuminated now by the raw light of morning, overflowing ashtrays, beer cans on the speaker cabinets, a dope tray with a loose array of mostly seeds and sticks and an almost empty pack of Zig-Zags. It was really warm and it felt good to peel off the layers of jackets and sweaters I'd been wearing. JT managed to roll a joint out of what was left on the tray and we passed it around.

"A fine night," I said, as quiet as I could.

"Yeah," said JT, curling up on a couch, even as he took another hit on the joint.

"Yeah," said Mike, as he took off his glasses and rubbed his eyes with his knuckles. "I'm going to bed, man."

I finished off the joint with JT. I thanked him again for letting us use his room. "No problem," he said in a voice that was already half asleep.

I went upstairs, passing Mike, who had his own bed—his home away from home—in the hallway between JT's room and Weird Jojo's. The strobe was still throbbing, though dulled by the creeping dawn light. I whispered goodnight to Mike, but I think he was already out. Sarah was sleeping on her back, her face up, her mouth open just a little. Her deep breathing had just the faintest purr to it. I climbed on the bed next to her, my clothes still on, and lay on top of the covers looking at her. The ripple my weight sent through the mattress woke her for an instant. Her eyes opened, then focused, and then she smiled.

"Did you have a good time?" She said and reached out her right arm to pet my shoulder.

"Yeah," I said.

"Ooh, you're cold" she said.

"Yeah we walked to a park. A nice park," I said.

"That's nice. I'm glad you had a good time. I have to go back to sleep," she said.

"OK," I said. She shut her eyes, her arm still draped across me. She was lovely in the gray light coming through the arched window next to the bed. Lovely and still and innocent. How did I dare to love her? How did I dare to dream that she could love me, she would love me? Not just love me, but believe in me. Believe in me enough, enough to jump in with me and ride down this road that I had no fucking idea where it would lead—only that it would take us far away from the lives we had been shaped for.

Who was she? This calmly sleeping beauty with the crooked nose and the wild hair? Why was she here with me? Did she think I was somebody different? That she could make me somebody different? Did she have any idea what a mess I really was? Where was, what was, that piece of me that she saw that made her think I was somebody she could love? Me. What was that?

The swirl of my head slowed, and I was exhausted from the balls of my feet to the top of my scalp. I felt a soft and thorough ache in every muscle and joint in my body. My brain was spent. I took off my pants and crawled beneath the covers where it was warm from Sarah's heat and sweet with her smell.

CHAPTER ELEVEN

January 6

AFTER HANGING AROUND MOUNTFORT STREET all day—enjoying lingering in bed long into the afternoon and just being mellow—we decided to go see my sister in Cambridge, and Stu came with us.

Cary was one of my four sisters, two years older than me. I was in the middle: Teresa was four years older, Katherine, two years younger, and Kim, three years younger. Cary and I were the problem children in our problem family. While I was growing my hair and getting swept up in rock and roll, Cary was driving my parents crazy by dating a black guy. I was kind of an asshole—well, a racist asshole, actually—about her boyfriend at first. But as my own rebellion blossomed, we became allies, battling mostly our father together. Our mother, who'd been a bit of a rebel herself in her younger days, was sometimes our ally—maybe we were her surrogates in her own battle against our father and the life she ended up with. Our house was a stormy place in those years—my last couple of years in high school.

Cary and I also had common interests outside our household. We were active in the nonviolent draft resistance movement and marched together against the war and for civil rights in Champaign-Urbana, even had a brother-sister sit-in—along with about a hundred other people—when Dow Chemical had come to town to recruit people to make and sell napalm, which the U.S. government was using to incinerate the people and the countryside of Vietnam.

When her relationship with a different black guy, who she'd move to Ohio to live with, fell apart, she didn't want to go back to Illinois, so she came to Boston and actually stayed with us at Mountfort Street for a while. Now she had her own place with two other women and her own group of friends, but we kept in touch.

Cary was glad to see us. She hadn't seen Sarah since we were all getting tear-gassed by the DC cops in front of the Justice Department during the Moratorium in November. And she had gotten to be friendly with Stu while she was staying at our apartment. Shit, everybody liked Stu.

There was a small gathering happening at her apartment, a bunch of women hanging out, drinking wine, listening to some mellow jazz. I hadn't seen Cary since before I'd gone home for Christmas, so it was a chance to fill her in on the happenings with our family and mutual friends. Stu, Sarah, Cary, and I gathered in her room, which was just off a small living room and was sparsely furnished: a small dresser, some block-and-board bookshelves, and her mattress jammed under a bay window that hung over the sidewalk and looked out on the noisy, busy street. We had a small jug of red wine that we passed around as we lounged on her mattress, sharing blankets to stay warm against the cold air seeping in.

"So you met our family," Cary said to Stu. "So now do you understand why we're so fucked up?" Cary and I looked alike in some ways—lean and blond, blue-eyed. Brian had once said, after seeing a picture of me and my four sisters, that we were all variations on the same theme. But Cary's features were tighter and sharper, her hair, shorter than mine now, was curlier and a brighter yellow.

Stu returned a big-eyed winking smile to her. "That's a loaded question if I ever heard one. They treated me just fine. As for your and Tucker's fucked-upness: no comment."

"The parents were on their best behavior, I see. That's a good reason to take a guest home, Ben."

"Well, Stu's being diplomatic. We had a couple of bad nights of drunken arguments about the usual bullshit: hair, jobs, money, and the war and the Movement. But it wasn't all bad. It was great to see Kim and Katherine and Teresa—and even Ricky was good for a laugh. We all had a nice day on Christmas. We just can't talk about anything that means anything, especially after Daddy's had a couple of drinks."

"Sarah has yet to have the pleasure, huh?"

"I'm really looking forward to meeting the rest of your family," Sarah said, and she meant it. "Really, how can they be so bad and have you two come out of it."

Cary and I looked at each other and she started laughing, a kind of sudden, loud, wine-spitting laugh. I just looked at Sarah and smiled and shook my head in amused disbelief.

"I know I'm terrible," Cary said as she gathered herself. "I love them dearly and God knows they try, but I'm not buying any of this."

I filled her in on all the news I could think of. I still had a little of the hash that Barry had left us, so I asked her if she wanted to smoke some and I lit the pipe. As the sweet smell of burning hashish floated out of the room, accompanied by successive coughs as each of us tried to hold our hits, other folks drifted into the room. We all squeezed together to make room and passed the pipe to the growing circle. Introductions and pleasantries were exchanged in a kind of smoky low murmur that seemed to ride on the shifting intonations of the saxophone coming from the stereo in the living room. I was trying to explain to a woman I'd just met how Cary and I both ended up in Boston, when a sharp voice cut through the haze of conversations.

"So have you guys painted your wall yet?"

Stopped mid-sentence, I looked up to find the source. It was a friend of Cary's I'd met a couple of times, Holly. She'd been to Mountfort Street with Cary. We'd always been friendly enough, I guess. But now her eyes had a dagger-like intensity that was a little scary. Which became even more scary as I slowly came to realize she was looking at and talking to me.

"Have you? Have you painted your wall yet?"

I looked at Stu, at Sarah, at Cary, hoping for some help in figuring out just what I was supposed to say. Didn't get any. Looked back at Holly and her question was still hanging in the now quiet room.

"Ah…no," I said. "Were we s'pose to?"

"You should have."

"Why's that?"

"Because it's sexist and disgusting, that's why."

Wow. She was serious. Really serious. Fuck, man, I wasn't ready for this.

"How is it sexist and disgusting?" I looked at Stu, my roommate, fellow owner of the sexist and disgusting wall. He rolled his eyes and looked away, as if to say "this is your turf, man. Good luck."

"You've got a picture of a naked woman, you've got that incredibly chauvinistic quote up there. That's fucking sexist and disgusting."

Wow. The picture she was talking about was one of the drawings that people made during our Beggar's Banquet party, a black outline of a naked woman. It was a pretty good drawing, actually, drawn by an artist friend—a woman. The quote, Brian had painted over his door, from some old English poet: "To ye virgins, make the most of time." I'm not exactly sure when he did that. Brian thought of himself as a poet and was into sex in a sort of obsessed way, different, it seemed, than most of us (though I certainly didn't have a handle on what was a normal approach to sex). It was kind of his thing and he made a point of letting people know that. And one day he got particularly inspired (drunk? stoned? tripping?) and this quote appeared over his door. We hassled the shit out of him over it—especially Mike and me. He was chauvinistic in a lot of ways. I argued with him all the fucking time. But still he was Brian, our buddy, our roommate, and funnier than hell when he wasn't bumming out on acid.

"The picture was by a woman. It's art, you know. Brian's quote is Brian's quote. I can't really defend it, except that Brian is my brother and I know that he's not into hurting anybody." The room had become cold and clear.

The circle was broken as we each stiffened and drew in to our own spots. The haze was gone and instead everything came into an overly sharp focus—I could see the fine detail of a little brown hair that came out of a tiny black mole that was just to the side of Holly's mouth, which was now all twisted up in a hateful sneer. Cary stared hard, straight down. Sarah's soft brow tightened in confusion and concern. Stu was disgusted and pulling himself away—why do you even bother talking to these people? his eyes said to me. The rest of the room was aiming darts at me.

"It doesn't matter that the painting was drawn by a woman—it's sexist and demeaning. Your roommate is hurting people with his chauvinism and that disgusting quote is oppressive to any woman who goes into your apartment. And you're just as responsible as him because you don't do anything about it. And besides, at this point in history, women shouldn't have to explain anything to men. You need to accept that your own chauvinism blinds you to understanding what's oppressive to women. If I fucking tell you something is oppressive, you need to know it's oppressive and do something about it."

"You know, Holly, you don't even have to talk to me but if you're going to call me names, I'd just like to understand why." I wasn't going to win this argument. Maybe because I knew that in some ways she was right. Brian is a chauvinist. I live with Brian. Therefore I am a chauvinist. There was some kind of fucking logic principle that worked that way. The problem is that I knew that Brian was other things besides a chauvinist, but I could never convince her that those things were important enough to cut him any slack at all.

It's true that women's liberation was tough for me, even after I'd taken hard stands against the war and supporting black power. My "consciousness-raising" moment came during the MIT Sanctuary. In late October 1968—just a few weeks after the BU sanctuary at Marsh Chapel had ended with the FBI seizing Joe Brook—another Vietnam-bound soldier sought sanctuary across the Charles River at MIT. Activists took over the student union and it lasted six days before it kind of petered out. This time the feds waited for the crowds to wane before they captured the AWOL soldier. But Mike and I spent a lot of time there. The whole thing was kind of an extended teach-in, with a steady stream of speeches to the full group in the main hall and smaller groups meeting in rooms around the union. Somehow, I ended up in a women's liberation rap session. I probably thought it was a good place to meet girls, which I was kind of desperate for at the time. But it was a heavy scene in that room, and I couldn't get out once it started. And then they played the Rolling Stones' great song "Under My Thumb" as an example of the disgusting chauvinism of youth culture. I loved that song. My band in high school always did a kickass version of it, with Scott singing lead. You know, I thought, it was just a song. But after that session at MIT, I could never listen to that song the same way again.

That was a crack in my own male chauvinism, and intellectually I came to understand that liberating women from the roles they'd been stuck with was an important part of our Movement, not only from the political arguments but also by looking at the lives of my mother and my sisters and our friends—and Sarah. And in real life, I was trying, I thought. I tried not to say "chick," a word I know pissed them off. I tried to be respectful and supportive. But, shit, sometimes people like Holly made it hard.

"I'll send some men over to explain things to you," was Holly's reply when I asked for an explanation.

Shit, I gave up.

"Yeah, the quote is pretty disgusting," Sarah said, realizing I was out of arguments. "But if you knew Brian, you'd know it was more sad than offensive. He's just a needy guy, who plays the role of this big Romeo, and if you don't know him, he looks like a jerk. But he's not that bad if you get to know him."

Sarah had broken the stare down between Holly and me, now Cary joined the discussion. "But we need to show needy guys that they can't use women to make themselves feel good. The quote is objectively oppressive and he needs to know that. He needs to know the difference between being offensive and showing women some respect."

"Christ, he's just a kid and it's just some words," Stu just couldn't take it anymore. "He's not hurting anybody. Don't you people have more important battles to fight?"

"No," Holly said. "This is the battle. If people who consider themselves radical don't fight chauvinism wherever it is, how the fuck are we supposed to change society? If I were you, I'd paint that fucking wall or some people just might have to come over and do it for you."

"Shit, man, I gotta get out of here." Stu was up and headed for the door. "Happy fucking New Year."

Sarah and I moved to join him, but we were on the other side of the room. I looked to Cary, who gave me just a small hint of a sisterly smile. No other smiles for me in the room.

"You know, I think we're on the same side," I couldn't help myself, trying to get some small sign of solidarity. "We're going to have to figure out how to talk to each other some time."

"We're talking. You're just not listening." Holly had the last word, though Sarah and I both yelled "Happy New Year" back toward Cary's room we headed out the door.

Stu was waiting for us, leaning up against the outside of Cary's building, as traffic buzzed by, a loud and breezy parade of lights. He was pissed. I gave him a big old smile and lit a cigarette.

"Did I tell you I knew where to find the good times in this town?" I said.

He wasn't ready to laugh yet but he couldn't resist some kind of comeback as we started walking. "Next time, remind me just how full of shit you and all your politico friends are. Shit, man, I can't believe that."

"I know," I said as I handed the cigarette to Sarah. "They're just so far into what they're into they lose track of everything else. Holly's just a bitch. I think the rest of them are OK. Shit, Cary knows we're not the enemy. It's like in some kind of theoretical sense, Holly's right—chauvinism is bad, we should all fight it and fucking Brian is such an easy target—so nobody wants to tell her she's wrong to be so fucking vicious about it?"

"Have you ever asked him to paint it over?" Sarah asked. She took a deep drag on the cigarette then handed it back to me. "It really is obnoxious and if he's trying to attract women, that sure seems like the wrong way to go about it. Seems like a big turnoff to me."

"Mike and I talk to him about it a lot," I said, exhaling as I talked. "But I don't know if we ever actually asked him to paint it. It's hard to talk to Brian about shit like that. He thinks we're attacking him. He flips out and starts screaming…"

"Semantics! Semantics!" Stu finished the sentence for me, laughing at the scene we were both thinking of now: Mike and me trying to convince Brian that he was a male chauvinist—and that that was bad—and Brian insisting that the whole thing was a matter of the way we were using words until the discussion degenerated into Mike and me talking at the same time and Brian drowning us both out yelling, "Semantics, it's all fucking semantics."

"But Tucker, you gotta admit you do attack him," Stu was still grinning. "Shit, Mike's a big enough load by himself, but when you two gang up on him—and you gotta admit that you do—it's not a fair fight. Sorta like Holly and her flunkies ganging up on us just now. Brian's a good guy. He's got his hangups, but so do I and so do you and I bet all those chicks back there have their hangups too."

"Gee, I'm sorry I don't get to experience some of these exciting group dynamics when everybody is there at Mountfort Street," Sarah said, holding her hand out to me, signaling she wanted the cigarette back. "But I'll especially miss seeing Holly's painters come by. That'd be exciting, a happening. It'd be great to have a bunch of people there, getting stoned. You could give them helpful hints: 'Ooops! You missed a spot.' Or 'No…, no…, I don't think that color is quite right for this room.'" Sarah took a long drag and slowly looked up to Stu on her right and over at me on her left. We all laughed together. The growing distance from Cary's and our laughter as we passed the solid wood houses of a quiet Cambridge neighborhood had allowed us to see the threatened invasion of our apartment for what it was: another act—some Tom Sawyer-like scene with earnest folks and paint buckets—in the incredibly absurd drama we were living in and learning from. Shit, it just might be a goof.

The walk back was brisk and quick. We were fueled by the rush of the scene at Cary's and absorbed in filling the cold night air with dialogue balloons, as Stu would say. All anger was gone as we crossed the BU Bridge over the dark river back into Boston, the lights of the city's skyline shining like some other world off in the distance. No doubt, the three of us all had different hits about what happened at Cary's, about Brian— shit Sarah even had gone on a date, one date, with Brian during our freshman year—and on some deeper level, about how we change ourselves and others. But as we laughed and argued our way back to Mountfort Street we were reminded that something connected the three of us and our friends that was deep and strong—and fucking radical—even though we couldn't put it in terms as clear as Holly, or the Weathermen, or the Panthers for that matter. We were changing and growing together, trying to figure out how to be something that felt good, that felt right, that felt real, in a society that we had discovered to be a total fucking phony. The political struggle was important to me and Mike and some others, but Stu was more likely to get passionate about rock and roll and raising fucking chickens on some farm in the country. Sarah had her political side but wasn't into anything that came close to violence and smoked pot but wouldn't touch LSD. We'd argue—just like with Brian—but we always knew we were brothers and sisters, that we were trying to figure out the same shit, and sometimes our answers just came out different. But we were committed to each other, to our quest for a new way to live, which we were trying to stitch together based on what we learned everyday. Somehow, we knew, we would change the world. The power of our crazy-quilt collective was hard to explain to someone as sure of her rightness as Holly, but still warming on that freezing January night, and in that forty-five-minute walk from Cambridge to 64 Mountfort Street, Stu and Sarah and I reminded each other of all that we did have to celebrate, the beginnings of this something that was ours and was joyous and new.

CHAPTER TWELVE

January 8

"WHAT DO YOU WANT ME TO DO?"

"Stay here. Move here. Don't go back."

"I can't do that."

"Why not?"

"Because I can't?"

"Why not?"

"Because I can't, Ben."

"Why not, Sarah."

"Because I can't. I don't know why. What do you want me to say?"

"That you'll stay here."

"I can't, Ben. Not now. Why can't we just enjoy the time we have left."

"Because I'm sick of saying good-bye to you. Because I'm sick of missing you all the time. I want it to be like this all the time—I don't want to go back to you being there and us just talking about someday being together. This has been so good."

"So why do you have to spoil it?"

"Why do you have to leave?"

"Because I have to Ben."

"Why?"

"I don't know. God, Ben why do you have to do this? You know I can't stay here. You knew that when I came."

"Hasn't this been great? Don't you want to be here? Don't you want to be with me."

"Yes, it's been great. I want to be with you, Ben, but I just can't stay here. What would I do here?"

"You'd be here. You'd be with me, you'd be with us. Doing what we do. I don't know—we could figure it out if you wanted to. I mean what the hell are you doing in Philly? Going to a school that you hate, hanging out in your parents' house, watching bad movies all night long, wishing you were here. You don't have to do that. You can be here."

"I can't, Ben."

"Why?"

"I don't know. What do you want me to say? That I'm scared. That I don't really have my own life here anymore. That I don't want to just jump into your life, follow you around."

"I'm not asking you to do that. If you were here, it wouldn't be just my life anymore, it'd be our life—we'd make it our life. We could do it, we could figure it out if you wanted to. Shit, you wouldn't even have to live here if you didn't want to. You could stay with Leslie and Karen, they'd love to have you. At least we'd be in the same city. I just don't want you to go back to Philadelphia and be miserable. "

"I can't, Ben."

"Is it your parents?"

"I'm sure that's part of it. I am going to school. I do have some life there, as pathetic as you might think it is. And I do care about my parents. I'm sorry if that's too bourgeois for you."

"That's got nothing to do with it and you know it. Have I just imagined that you're miserable with your life in Philadelphia? Did I just make that up?"

"No, Ben. Why do you have to do this? Why do you have to make me justify myself. It's like you always have to test me, prove myself to you, prove my love to you. Well, I do love you, and I'm sorry if you can't believe that. And I can't move to Boston, now, and I'm sorry if you can't accept that. And I'm really sorry this is how we're spending our last night together."

"I love you, Sarah, and I do believe you love me. I just don't understand why you think you have to stay in Philadelphia. You don't have to. I'm sorry we're spending our last night like this, too, but I don't want it to be our last night."

"I don't either."

"Then why are you going back? Shit, we're talking about making a revolution in this country. We're talking about creating new lives, living new ways, and we can't even get to the point of living in the same city. And I just want you to help me understand why."

"When it's just you and me Ben, it's great, and even when it's just our friends, most of the time it's fine. But I don't know—who talks about revolution? You talk about revolution. Mike talks about revolution. Luke talks about revolution. I don't know that I want to come to Boston to fight the revolution with you and Mike and Luke. Or just get stoned all the time. Like in Amherst, when you took that LSD. How much fun do you think that was for me? A bunch of people I barely know and you're off on some trip where you can barely talk. I'm not telling you how to live your life, but I just don't know that I want to be part of all those parts of your life. What I am supposed to do when you're off fighting the revolution. Have supper waiting when you come home from your hard day on the barricades?"

"I don't know, Sarah. I hoped we'd be together on the barricades."

"Ben, maybe sometime I will be ready to be on the barricades with you. I'm not now. I just don't know what to say to you. I love you. I love being with you. I admire your ideals and your willingness to fight for them, but I'm scared about all this talk about violence. I'm not sure it's the right way to go to achieve what you want."

"Isn't it what we want?"

"I guess I'm not completely sure anymore."

"If you were here, it would all make so much more sense to you. You'd see the ways the pigs are coming after us, why we have to start fighting back."

"Then what, Ben? You talk about fighting the revolution, maybe going to jail, what kind of life is that for us? I could sit at home and crochet you prison sweaters. You used to talk about being a poet or a writer, living in a small New England town, where maybe I could be a teacher. You never talk about stuff like that anymore."

"I don't know, Sarah. You're right, I don't think about that anymore. Shit, I wish we could. I wish the world allowed us that luxury. But the reality is that U.S. bombers are blasting Vietnam off the map, the federal government is killing black people, and now they're declaring war on us—you and me and our friends. The injunction they've got against me is totally absurd—but they've marked me as their enemy and I'm kind of proud of that. They're screwing our friends who got busted at the GE strike rally. It's not like some distant thing we read about or watch on TV, it's happening to us now. If you were here, it would be so much more real to you."

"I'm sure you're right, Ben. I just don't know that that's the kind of life I want to live. I know I can't do it now."

"It's not like it's all battles and seriousness. We have a lot of fun. You and me had a lot of fun, didn't we? It's not just about smashing the state—it's about building our lives in some kind of liberated zone and I don't know exactly what that's going to mean. It'll be hard in some ways I'm sure, but it will also be fun and fucking exciting. The thing is, Sarah, I can't imagine doing that without you. Or I don't want to imagine doing it without you. You could still be a teacher. I'll still be a writer but it'll be different, different than we can even imagine now."

"In some ways, it sounds great. I'm just not where you are, now. I just feel like I'm getting pulled in so many directions; you're pulling me one way, my parents are pulling me another, sometimes I wonder if I can remember who I am without either you or my parents telling me who I should be. Sometimes I think I just need to get away from everybody for awhile, so I can try to remember who I am, and figure out what I want and not just how I'm going to react to what you want or my parents want. Maybe I should go to Europe this summer with Sally. I'd miss you. I'd really miss you. I love you Ben, but you're just so sure of what you want and how I fit into your plans, I just can't let myself follow along behind you until I'm sure for myself."

"I don't want you to just follow me. I want you to want to be with me enough to be with me—all the time. Shit, I'm not sure of much of anything except that I love you, that I want to be with you, and that in order to live our love in this fucking country we're going to have to fight somehow."

"I can't move to Boston now, Ben."

"OK."

Shit.

CHAPTER THIRTEEN

January 10

Dear Sarah,

After the revolution, you and I will live in a small house in a small town somewhere. Where? I don't know. You pick or we'll pick or we'll get blindfolded and point a finger at a map. It doesn't matter. Our friends will be around us in houses like ours and new friends will be there, too. Or a bunch of us could live together in one of those big houses where the rich people live now cause there won't be any rich people because there won't be any money because we won't need it, like Uncle Karl said, "from each according to his ability, to each according to his need." Stores will just be places of exchange, take what you need, no more, no less. If you're done with something or outgrow it or whatever and it's still got some life you just take it back to the community exchange. No one has jobs like people have now, where they hate what they do and somebody pays them less than they're worth so they can make a profit. People will spend half their days doing creative stuff—I could write poems and articles, you could macrame or do pottery or whatever the hell you want. The other half of the time we work for the community, whether it's in the garden or a factory or a school. According to our abil-

ity, we chip in where we can do the most good and nobody's competing with anybody, so we all just want to do the best we can to make our community stronger. Saturdays are celebration days, where we all get together and share our creative work, and sing and dance and make a huge community feast. Sundays we mellow out. And we aren't making a bunch of stupid things that people don't need and then bombarding them with advertising to convince them they do need them. And we aren't polluting the air and water because we know those are more valuable than any amount of money and nobody's thinking about money anymore, anyway. And there are no cops or jails. Everybody shares in the responsibility of keeping our communities safe. And for the inevitable assholes that can't quite figure out how to live in our utopia, we have islands or compounds where they all have to live together, but it's not prisons with guards and shit, just them kind of punishing each other until maybe it sinks into them that it's a lot better and a lot more fun getting along with everybody. No wars, no soldiers. We all defend our community together with the skills we learned in the revolution. No leaders. Teachers and organizers and coordinators, but nobody above anybody else. No one gets a privilege that everybody doesn't have. Health care and as much school as you want for everyone. Art is our most valued pursuit, and everybody does it. The old are respected. The young are listened to. Parents treat their kids like equals, teaching them without ruling over them. And people love however they want to love, couples or groups, or whatever. We don't need any legally sanctioned marriage deal, because people can define their trip however they want to.

You and me, in our small house, will wake up every morning together and ease into the day with kisses and laughter. We'll have cool and incredible kids and dogs and cats and a garden next to the house where we all will work together. We'll all be full of peace and purpose and bursting with love.

That doesn't sound bad does it?

Love,
Ben

CHAPTER FOURTEEN

January 12

I DIDN'T HAVE A WHITE SHIRT AND TIE to wear to court, so I just wore a sort of clean button-down blue shirt and the same old tweed sports coat I wore most every day and some brown bell-bottom cords that seemed decent enough. My lawyer, Harry Stone, was cool. He just asked me to get as cleaned up as I could. Shit, with my hair hanging down to my shoulders, it wasn't like the judge wasn't going to know I was a freak. Stu went with me because he didn't have anything better to do and he thought it might be entertaining. He wore his best flowered shirt and had tried to corral his mass of hair into some coherent shape. We rode the MTA down to Park Street and hoofed the few blocks from there to the court house, which was this massive flat block of granite that rose straight up from the street. Some geometric iron workings sat over the entrance and below a sculptural ornament of these three medieval-looking dudes and the slogan, "Justice for All." Ha! Was that ever true?

You couldn't just ease into the fucking place. The polished floors rang with each step you took, and the sound ricocheted off the tall, hard walls. Seemed like Stu and me made a racket as we looked for Harry, running the gauntlet of this lobby full of guys in suits and uniforms.

I was glad Harry was my lawyer. He wore a suit like the rest of them, but I could talk to him like a regular person. He had been one of the lawyers who'd helped us fight the disciplinary charges that BU had thrown at us for the occupation of the dean's office during the anti-military campaign the previous spring. Harry was a Movement lawyer, a member of the Lawyer's Guild. He worked for practically nothing on the disciplinary charges, something like ten bucks a head.

I'd looked at the charges from the anti-military campaign more as an honor and an opportunity than any kind of real threat. I got the officious letter on BU stationery telling me about the charges two weeks into summer vacation, about the same time I got a letter telling me I'd made the Dean's List for good grades. My parents didn't think that coincidence was as funny as I did. My first reaction was to be flattered that the BU administration thought I was enough of a leader or dangerous enough to be included as one of the BU 21. My immediate second thoughts were about Sarah and the chance that letter provided to call her. She didn't get charged. None of my best friends did, though Mike and Lenny and Sarah had all been there as much as I had. But that letter and that call changed everything for Sarah and me. They opened the crack I needed to get back in the here-and-now of her life and, holy shit, if that crack didn't blow open the door and turn our little freshman fling into this enthralling and potent stab at serious love. All Power to the BU 21!

The disciplinary trial, which finally happened at the beginning of the new school year, about four months before the injunction hearing, did turn out to be a joke. It was a great organizing tool to reestablish the Movement's momentum from the previous spring. Even a bunch of the faculty, led by Howard Zinn, supported us. Fucking administration liberals couldn't help themselves, couldn't avoid letting their belief in rules and process get in the way of their own best interest—so they gave us a stage and an audience for a showdown we couldn't lose: they find us guilty, kick us out, whatever, we rock the school; they let us off, no matter how or why, and we mock their authority and declare victory.

The room in the union where they held the hearing was too small for the hundred or so kids who turned out to support the BU 21. So the people who were shut out started raising hell, banging on the doors and coming in through the windows and shit. Total chaos. They had to call a recess and we demanded they put up speakers outside the room so everyone could hear—which they did.

The administration's case—presented by Dean Arnold Dexter, "Arnie" to his friends in the Movement—was feeble. They only had real evidence against six of us. One guy, Daniel Lucas—kind of a campus character—got charged only because he'd seen Dexter a couple of times during the summer and said, "Hey Arnie, when you gonna charge me?" A secretary from the dean's office testified that Matthew Wexler, one of the mellowest guys in the Movement, "terrorized her." Matthew was right on, but he had a little squeak to his voice and earnestness to his manner that made us all laugh when we tried to imagine him as a terrorist. He probably said something to the secretary like, "It could get pretty crazy in here, so maybe you ought to leave." I'm sure he said it with a smile.

Turned out they had some clear pictures of me, which Arnie presented. Three of the photos were from when we first took over the office and I was just part of the crowd (Harry thought my long, bright blond hair made me stand out) and one from a night when most people left the dean's office for a major strategy meeting in a bigger room downstairs, and Sarah and I and two others volunteered to stay to "hold" the office. We mainly didn't feel like going to the meeting. Sarah and I had posed for this photographer, who we thought was a freak. I was sitting in the dean's chair and Sarah was sitting on the desk beside me. It was a great picture. I thought of asking Arnie for a copy, but I didn't get a chance.

Our defense was going to be a series of political statements—mine was to be about the educational aspects of the anti-military campaign, how it made a valuable contribution to the intellectual climate of the university. I was ready. But the trial adjourned after the administration presented their feeble case and was supposed to continue the next week, but some wise administrator realized that there was absolutely no way they were going to gain anything by continuing, and they just kept post-poning the trial until it disappeared.

Shit had gotten a hell of a lot heavier in the time since we had shouted and laughed our way through that hearing, and the administration wasn't fucking around anymore with Mickey Mouse judicial committees. This was a real Commonwealth of Massachusetts court and this injunction was serious legal stuff, and my name was on it. Fighting it was going to cost me more than $10. Harry had said it could be $50—my entire monthly check from my old Champaign band, who were slowly paying me off for what I'd put into equipment—if it ended today, like it was supposed to.

We found the right courtroom and pulled open the heavy door. It was solemn and starkly lit, with polished wood railings and pew-like benches and a towering desk for the judge. This was definitely enemy territory. The two lawyers representing Boston University had precise haircuts and serious gray suits, more imposing foes than Arnie Dexter. Stu and I lin-gered awkwardly in the back, though the other defendants (or maybe "respondents," I think they called us), were already sitting at a table in front of the judge's throne. Harry finally showed up, smiling and reas-suring in his rumpled brown suit, his plain blue tie hanging off-center and loose under his collar.

The thing was, I shouldn't have even been there.

This hearing was about whether a restraining order that BU had ob-tained against eight of us should be extended into a temporary injunc-tion. I'm not sure exactly what that meant legally, what the difference was between the restraining order which said we weren't allowed to par-ticipate in demonstrations on BU property and could be held in con-tempt of court if we did and a temporary injunction that said we weren't allowed to participate in demonstrations on BU property and could be held in contempt of court if we did. It was part of a process, Harry ex-plained. You can get a restraining order pretty easily by showing there's a reasonable cause for it. The people being restrained aren't even part of that process. The next step—where we were now—was for the party seeking the injunction to ask a judge to extend it with the restrained parties also present. The judge is supposed to decide whether there is sufficient reason to continue to restrict the freedoms and constitutional rights of the people named in the injunction until a full-blown trial can be held on the details of the complaint to determine if the temporary injunction should become a permanent injunction. Shit, man, legal mumbo-jumbo.

But Harry told me I had nothing to worry about. He'd talked to one of BU's lawyers the day before, who told him that if I hadn't been involved in the demonstration that led to the injunction—and I wasn't—they were willing to drop my name.

The injunction was aimed at squelching a student movement to support workers striking against General Electric. That movement, which involved a series of demonstrations, was led by the worker-student alliance faction of SDS, which was kind of an arm of the Progressive Labor Party, which called itself Maoist. We just called them PL. It was the faction of SDS we had the least in common with. For one thing, they were straight. Not into pot or rock and roll. They scoffed at the concept of a revolutionary youth culture. They weren't any fun to hang out with. But more hard to handle, really, was their dogmatic and cold Marxism, which led them to believe that black power and women's liberation were counter-revolutionary because blacks and women were important to the revolution only as members of the proletariat, the legacy of four hundred years of racism and thousands of years of patriarchy didn't make them special cases. Besides that, they were reluctant to support the NLF in Vietnam because the Vietnamese revolutionaries were more closely aligned with the Soviet Union than the People's Republic of China. Shit like that.

So, though I supported the striking GE workers, I wasn't in the frontlines of that struggle. The first demonstration I didn't even know about. At the second one Mike and I and even Stu and others of our less political friends hung around the edges, as thirty or forty hard-core PL people chanted and generally harassed a GE recruiter who was set up in the student union. Suddenly, a whole bunch of cops showed up and herded everyone out of the union. We pushed back a little when they started shoving us, but we didn't have the numbers and weren't prepared to hold our ground or fight back. Me and my friends were just goofing on the whole scene anyway. The BU administration had been unpredictable about calling the cops in the past. During the antimilitary campaign, they called them right away at the first building we took over—the Office of Financial Aid—which we left immediately, but they never did when we held the dean's office for two days. Bringing cops in this quick for this small of a demonstration seemed like a real change in tactics—and that pissed us off. We hooted at the cops as they left the building and as they were pulling away down Comm Ave, I picked up a rock from trolley tracks and heaved it toward the back window of one of their cars, but I didn't think anybody saw me.

The cops' heavy-handed tactics at that demonstration fueled the movement to support the GE strikers, which was now coupled with keeping cops off campus—an issue that more people could get behind. At the next demonstration, a couple of weeks later, all hell broke loose. A whole shitload of cops charged into a crowd at the union. Lots of people got the shit beat out of them. Nine kids had to go to the hospital. Mike got maced when he freed some cat from a cop who was beating on him. Then Mike got his ass saved by Priscilla—an incredibly straight and dour-looking woman who was one of the PL leaders. She pulled Mike away from a cop who tried to grab him. Priscilla gave us shit all the time about our politics and cultural trip, but she had guts and solidarity. Neither Mike or Priscilla were among the twenty-nine people who got arrested that day, but our friend Christopher was—and he got the shit beat out of him in the process. The courts pulled a slick trick, by suspending all their trials to a later date, which meant they could hang all these charges over their heads, thinking that would discourage people from joining in future demonstrations. That police riot—which is exactly what it was—led BU to get the restraining order against eight people, including me, that led to this hearing. The thing was, I was on my way to Philadelphia to visit Sarah when all that shit went down. I wasn't even in the state.

Called out in the injunction besides me were seven PL people, including Priscilla. I went to a defense meeting with the PL folks, and they thought it was funny that I was on the list with them. They didn't take me particularly seriously. I was a curiosity—shit, man, a real live hippie militant. They wanted to mount a political defense, which was fine but I just didn't buy their politics. We agreed, eventually, in the friendliest terms, that it made sense for me to present my own case. I wouldn't oppose them in any way or do anything to weaken their argument; I'd just get my own lawyer. So I called Harry. Shit, I wasn't there, man. Those stupid BU administrators had got their radical files mixed up again.

So this hearing was supposed to be a formality for me. Harry said the BU lawyer had agreed that if I wasn't at the police riot—not his words—then it was a mistake for me to be listed on the injunction. Still, I got a chill when Stu and I walked toward the front of that austere and proper courtroom with Harry behind us. The BU lawyers looked serious. The PL people were relaxed. This was a great stage for them—shit, man, they were being persecuted by the government for supporting working people—and they were going to take full advantage. Stu took his seat in the peanut gallery, and Harry and me joined the PL folks at the defendants'—or whatever we were called, the people getting screwed—table.

The judge walked in. Briskly suddenly, with a kind of whoosh that shot around the courtroom as the bailiffs and clerks and lawyers—even Harry—stiffened to attention. All rise. Judge Hall was a dense small man with short brown, thinning hair a little askew on his head. His glasses hung on the end of his nose. He seemed to be in a hurry as the clerk read the injunction, then set it in front of him. He glanced at it impatiently and spoke.

"Do complainants wish to continue this restraint in the form of a temporary injunction?"

"We do, your honor. We continue to believe these respondents pose a threat to the safety and the ability of our clients to conduct their normal business operations," said one of the gray suits.

"And what say the respondents," said Judge Hall in a monotone without looking up.

The PL lawyer, Tom Radonski, spoke first. "Your honor, respondents are represented by separate counsel. I speak for respondents Baker, Bonini, Fleishman, Freuler, Lingo, Lundgren, and McInnis. Mr. Stone will speak for respondent Tucker."

"Fine, fine. Go ahead," said the judge.

"Your honor we believe this restraining order is an outrageous infringement of the constitutional rights of my clients and is a direct attack on the working people of this country."

"Mr. . . . ah, Radonski, is it?" The judge asked looking down his nose at the papers in front of him. "I trust you know that this is not the time or place to make those sorts of arguments. Do you challenge any of the facts in the complainants' document?"

"Your honor, we challenge their right to suppress legitimate political protest and the rights of working people to organize to improve their conditions."

"You can challenge that all you want, Mr. Radonski, but it doesn't mean anything in my courtroom. Mr. . . . ah, Stone, what have you got to say?"

Radonski didn't sit down, "Your honor, this is outrageous, " he said, his face reddening a bit.

"You're done, Mr. Radonski. Mr. Stone?"

Radonski sat. Harry stood up and smiled at the judge and at the gray suits at the next table. "Your honor, we believe that these orders amount to prior restraint in a delicate area of the law. They intimidate students holding lawful assemble. Contrary to the allegations of the complainants, my client and his fellow students have no plans to destroy the university." He was right. We had no specific plans.

"The actions alleged by the complainants would indicate otherwise," Mr. Stone," the judge said. "Do you dispute those facts?"

"The fact is, your honor, that this is a labor dispute, and the complainants are asking the court to support the side of General Electric and the university against the side of the workers and students."

"To save you the trouble of trying to make this argument in a future hearing, I rule here and now that this is not a labor dispute. One last chance, Mr. Stone, any challenges to the facts."

"Your honor, we stand by our constitutional arguments, but we also believe that respondent Tucker was mistakenly included in this action. Mr. Tucker was not present at the events of October 25, not a participant. Therefore, I move that his name be removed from the indictment."

"What do the complainants say to this?" The judge asked.

Without standing up, one of the gray suits said. "Your honor, we have no reason to believe this assertion. We oppose this motion."

Harry's demeanor switched from smooth and deferential to a little shaky and concerned. I looked back at Stu, who rolled his eyes and glared at the judge.

"Your honor, I spoke with Mr. Adams"—one of the gray suits, no doubt—"yesterday and he assured me that he would go along with this motion in regards to Mr. Tucker, who wasn't even in the city that day."

Adams spoke, "Mr. Stone must have misunderstood me, your honor. We believe that Mr. Tucker poses a threat to our client and is properly included in the injunction."

"No, your honor," Harry responded. He was pissed. "Mr. Adams was quite clear in his agreement to go along with removal of Mr. Tucker."

"Mr. Stone's characterization of our conversation is inaccurate, your honor." Adams spoke with a syrupy sureness. "I agreed to confer with my clients about Mr. Tucker. My clients believe he continues to pose a threat to them."

"He's a liar, your honor." Harry was red now.

"Sit down, Mr. Stone. And watch your language. Motion denied. We'll set a trial date for..."

"Your honor, every person at this table can testify that Mr. Tucker wasn't anywhere near…"

"Sit down, Mr. Stone or you could be looking at contempt yourself."

"Your honor…"

"Sit!" Judge Hall took off his glasses and stared at Harry. Harry sat, and lowered his head into his hand and rubbed his forehead furiously. The judge looked at the clerk, "Do you have a date for the trial?"

"February 12, your honor," the clerk replied.

"Does that work for complainants?" the judge asked.

"We'll make it work, your honor," said one of the gray suits.

"How about the respondents?" he asked.

"Yes, your honor," both Radonski and Harry replied.

"Very well, we'll see you then," said the judge and he was up and heading out of the courtroom. "I remind all of you that the terms of the restraining order remain in effect."

"All rise."

We did. All of us.

As the judge left the courtroom, it was like everybody let their breath out at same time. I was just stunned by the speed and brusqueness of the whole thing, let alone that reality seemed totally out of order, contemptible even, in this courtroom. The PL people were relaxed and joking, the proceedings had just confirmed their doctrine that the courts served the capitalist ruling class. I knew that, too, believed it, but I thought they at least had to make some show of playing by a reasonable set of rules.

"I'm sorry, Ben." Harry's easy smile was long gone. "The son of a bitch just lied to me. I don't know. Maybe he meant it when he said it, but the BU people wouldn't go for it. But he should have called me and told me that before now. I'm sure when we get to trial, they'll have no real case to keep you on there. They just want to try to keep you out of the action as long as possible. You just have to be careful for a few more weeks." He gave me a couple of soft pats on the back.

"Man, I just can't believe that judge. What an asshole." I said with my voice lowered as I looked at the emptying courtroom. I wasn't mad at Harry.

"Yeah, he was in a hurry. Must have had a date at the club. Don't worry, it's going to be all right. Just try to stay away from demonstrations at BU until the trial. If you can't stay away, wear some kind of disguise, dye your hair, or something." Now he was smiling again. "But really it'd be better if you kept a low profile for now. We just can't give them any more reasons to go after you."

Harry gathered his papers and we got up to leave. The gray suits had vanished. Maybe they were meeting the judge at the club. Stu met us in the aisle.

"What the fuck was that?" he asked. He didn't bother lowering his voice. "That was ridiculous."

"That was a railroad, my friend," Harry answered him, as we left the courtroom.

"Just your luck, Tucker," Stu said, "you got that asshole of a judge. What was his name? I want to remember it."

"Hall," I answered. "Judge Hall."

"Judge Hall. Shit, it should be Pre-Judge Hall as far as I'm concerned, that prick."

Stu's anger was righteous and real. Still though, when he said "Pre-Judge Hall," it made me laugh. And Harry, too.

"Yeah," I said, "Fucking Pre-Judge Hall." And we headed together out into the chill of the Boston afternoon.

We parted ways with Harry under the "justice for all" ornament. Shit. That's all it was, this justice—an ornament, a frill, a façade, an illusion that there were rules that protected the powerless from the powerful. "Who ever told you life was fair?" my mother had lectured when I pouted against the injustices of childhood and family dynamics. She'd been proven right too many times for me to hold on to that belief about my life, but as long as I could I'd clung to the belief that outside of my little world where things were crazy and unfair, was this noble place called America, with its Constitution and Bill of Rights, and its Thomas Jeffersons and Abraham Lincolns, and its celebration of liberty and freedom and justice, where there were things you could count on and believe in. How silly and naïve that all seemed now.

Justice for all? Not for Fred Hampton and Mark Clark, not for Christopher and the rest of the people arrested and beaten at the GE demonstration that happened when I was in Philadelphia, and today, not for me. I know now that justice in American had never been for all. Not for Indians or black people or poor people or women or anybody who stood up to the few that this ornamental justice serves. Justice that wasn't for all was no kind of justice at all, just another tool in the hands of the pigs who also held the cops (not to mention the fucking army) and the media and the money. Now, I was in their sights and my righteous intellectual realization of rampant injustice had turned into a twisting, tightening knot in the center of my gut.

What chance did we have? We lose trying to play by their rules, since they change them whenever they want. They had all the institutions, all the firepower. We had...each other, our brothers and sisters, and the unshakeable, if totally insane, belief that we had to stand up against them because there was no place for our lives in the world they had made.

CHAPTER FIFTEEN

January 13

MIKE AND I SAW A FAMILIAR GROUP huddled in the usual circle as we approached the four-story brick, concrete, and glass box of BU's College of Basic Studies. Timmy Brownlee and Rosie Brothers and Teddy Bowman and four or five others were laughing and talking loud and swaying and hopping to try to keep warm. When they saw us coming, they all turned to greet us, the vapor of their breath mixing with the denser smoke of the joint they were passing to form a wispy cloud that seemed to dissolve as we entered the circle. Rosie handed the joint to Mike. "Welcome back to school, man," she giggled.

The first day of the new semester. Mike and I were determined that this would be our last. We were both in CBS, which was like a junior college within the university, a two-year program to whip underachievers into shape to be proper college students. It was separated physically as well as academically from the rest of the university. Most of BU was in a continuous strip from the BU Bridge to Kenmore Square, mostly in solemn old stone buildings with all the stodgy seriousness that colleges try to show. CBS was on the other side of the BU Bridge, heading toward Allston, between a car lot and the National Guard Armory, in a building that looked like it belonged in a suburban industrial park next to a dozen other identical buildings with offices for the phone company or an insurance firm.

Just by its very nature, CBS attracted a lot of freaks and radicals—or kids who turned into freaks or radicals after about ten minutes exposure to the scene in Boston. Most of us couldn't get into any of the regular programs, but we'd somehow—good test scores, eloquent essays—convinced the admissions folks that we had enough potential that two years of CBS would make us worthy to transfer into one of the grown-up programs like the College of Liberal Arts or School of Public Communications. Mike and I had no plans of moving to the big school. I'm not even sure why we were still in school—parents, student loans, a good excuse to hang with lots of our friends and do a little rabble rousing? Stu, who had been in the communications school, was our vanguard—out of school and now working at a nearby hospital.

CBS was like high school. We were divided into sections of about twenty-five kids who had all their classes together and the subjects were simplistically general like "science" and "rhetoric" and "psychology" and "social studies." All the reading and tests were the same for all the sections, so it was pretty easy to do well without working too hard. You get four or five people together and divide up the work. Instead of teaching us to be good college students, CBS taught us how to beat the system by working together—a valuable lesson for sure, but I don't think that's what they intended to teach. And shit, man, the first year was so easy—I made Dean's List both semesters—that it wasn't even that much fun trying to play the game the second year. This year most of us were seeing how well we could do without doing any fucking work at all. First semester, I didn't make the Dean's List, but my B-minus average was still on the edge of being respectable.

Most of the classes were just a bore, though I did have a couple of decent teachers. My psychology teacher was cool—the class was a lot about existential psychologists like Erikson and Laing and Fromm and especially Maslow and his hierarchy of needs. That stuff made a lot of sense and our teacher, Dr. Lucchi, always tried to relate the theories to our lives. Shit, a lot of that humanistic psychology stuff was saying exactly the same kind of things that freaks were saying about society and how it distorted lives. Through serious research and intellectual investigation they'd developed this theory that was pretty much the same as we'd got to just by keeping our eyes and our minds open: this society pissed on the most essential things that give meaning and purpose to human existence: compassion, cooperation, community, art, love. And Maslow, shit man, his philosophy blended perfectly with Marcuse and Marx to make a revolutionary ideology that started with changes in each of us as individuals and extended to the whole world.

I also had a cool rhetoric teacher, Dr. Barrington, who was really a Beat poet disguised as a college professor. He encouraged me to write about what was happening in my life and in the Movement. In fact, spring semester of my freshman year, we had a joint assignment from his class and our social studies class to write about social change during the industrial revolution in England. But just as I was sort of starting my research on William Blake and a poet's view of that period ("How have you left the ancient love/That bards of old enjoyed in you!/The languid strings do scarcely move!/The sound is forced, the notes are few!"), the anti-military campaign got going and we took over the dean's office. So I wrote about that instead, "Social Change in the Twentieth Century at Boston University." It was a good paper, I think, sort of like Mailer's *Armies of the Night*—a personal perspective on political protest. I got an A from Barrington, and an F from my social studies teacher, who was—as Barrington called all the fuddy-duddy English teachers who try to make writing into just a bunch of rules—an old school marm who managed to make studying revolutions and social change tedious. This year, Dr. Barrington had picked me as one of only eight people to be in a special poetry workshop with him. That was outasight.

This first morning of the semester, we only had time for a couple of hits before we had to go to class. But I got a nice buzz. My first class was a science lecture in Jacob Sleeper Hall, which was well named because the seats in the big lecture hall were surprisingly comfortable (one of the few pluses in this dull building) and the lectures usually amazingly monotonous. I did manage to stay awake for most of that first lecture because the prof—a slick smooth talking dude named Barbieri—was trying to explain something called Avogadro's Number—something to do with gases and atoms and molecules and shit like that. I couldn't really make much sense of what he was saying, but I really got off on the name and everything related to it seemed insanely funny. As Barbieri rattled on, I'd look over at some of my friends and we'd have to hold our mouths to keep from laughing out loud. Barbieri would shoot us dirty looks but he just kept talking about old Avogadro and his number.

Mike and I made it through our first morning of classes, and headed back down Comm Ave toward the student union for burgers. Just as we turned into the plaza in front of the union, we saw Dean Dexter. I just kind of stared at him, but Mike started fucking yelling at him: "Hey, Arnie, if anything happens to my brother Tucker because of your silly-ass injunction, I'm coming after you personally." Dexter, a little balding man in a crisp dark suit, lifted his eyes and glanced quickly in our direction but acted like he didn't see us or hear Mike or have any idea who we were, and then he scampered off toward his office. Mike yelled after him, "Don't worry Arnie, I know exactly where to find you." Then Mike looked at me and grinned big so I saw the gap in his teeth and a shine in his magnified eyes: "What a fucking weasel," he said. I laughed. Shit, man, Mike. I'm glad he was on my side.

The union cafeteria was thick with the moist warm smell of institutional coffee and a roomful of bodies shedding the winter chill they left outside—and buzzing with excited conversations. It was lunchtime of the first day back. We saw a bunch of our friends—Christopher, Jeffrey, Ellen and Debby (you never saw Ellen without Debby and vice-versa, so it was always Ellen and Debby), Jerry, Dennis, Patrick—at a table just on the other side of the food area.

"What's happening?" echoed around the table as people kind of dosi-doed around each other to clasp hands and hug.

"Shit man here we go again," Mike said, still standing addressing the table as a whole. "I seem to remember seeing all you fuckers the last time I came in here."

"And we ain't moved since," Christopher said. "How the hell you guys been? I heard about your bullshit injunction hearing, Ben. Welcome to the club."

"Well, it was bullshit, but it's still nothing compared to what you had to deal with, just a fucking injunction." Christopher had been arrested, as well as getting the shit beat out of him, in the police riot that led to the injunction, the one where Mike and Priscilla had taken turns freeing people from the cops, the one that happened when I was on my way to Philadelphia. Christopher, an intense looking dude with jet black hair that was long but neat and a well-trimmed mustache, was charged with trespassing and rioting. Bullshit charges. He was a BU student in the student union so how the hell could he be trespassing? And the cops started the riot when they started trying to pull selected people out of the crowd—people fingered by Dexter and some of his administration henchmen. At their hearing, the judge had continued the cases for three months with the provision that if they stayed out of trouble, the charges—for which they had no fucking evidence to begin with—would be dropped. But if they did get in trouble again the state could just pile the old charges on top of whatever new ones they came up with. Like the injunction, it was a way to intimidate people from protesting. No matter how peaceful the demonstration was, the cops could attack and arrest you—which is exactly what had happened to Christopher—and you'd be screwed. It was just another way for the university and the cops to try to keep people from standing up to them.

"It's all the same shit, you know that," Christopher said.

"Yeah, man, I know." Mike and I grabbed some chairs and squeezed into the expanding circle. "Man, you guys should have seen Mike just now threatening Arnie Dexter. Arnie looked a little shaky."

Everyone laughed at the image of Mike shouting down Arnie. Mike could be really scary, come across like a hard motherfucker, especially if you didn't know him.

"And I meant it, too," Mike kept his tough-guy tone, but he couldn't keep a smile off his face because we were all laughing so hard. "That little weasel will think twice before he fucks with my brother Tucker."

"Thanks, man," I said. "I'm starving. Let's grab some burgers."

We left our books at the table and headed toward the big U-shaped area with cafeteria-style food service offering burgers, sandwiches, salads, deserts, and drinks. The burgers were wrapped in paper—yellow for the cheeseburgers and white for the plain ones—and stacked in piles under a heat lamp. I put a couple of cheeseburgers in one coat pocket and a third in another pocket. Mike did the same, or at least I think he got three, too. Shit, he might have gotten four. Then I walked over to the soda machine, got a coke and stood in the cashier line to give the student working there a quarter for my drink. Mike didn't even bother buying a drink. He just headed straight back to the table. But, shit, man, I was thirsty.

Taking burgers from the union didn't even seem like stealing. It was too easy. The cashiers were just students working there. If they knew we did it, they didn't give a shit. It was just part of the deal of going to school at BU. We hit the union cafeteria almost every day and loaded up on burgers. One time, Mike got one that wasn't done, so he took it back and they gave him a new one. Stealing burgers was vital to our survival since the dorm cafeterias were hard to sneak into and we just didn't cook. Whoever said there was no free lunch didn't hang out at Boston University's George Sherman Union.

Back at the table, we got caught up with our friends. Christopher and Dennis had an apartment on St. Botolph Street. Jeffrey was still at 1387 Comm Ave with Dale and Cheryl and Walter. Dale and Cheryl had both dropped out of school, but Walter and Jeffrey, another CBS kid, were hanging on. Ellen and Debby had moved into the apartment at 858 Beacon Street with Leslie, Sarah's friend from high school and also in CBS, and Karen, who'd been Sarah's roommate freshman year. Their apartment was right around the corner from Mountfort Street and was where I was hoping Sarah could live if she decided to come to Boston but wasn't quite ready for the full dive into Mountfort Street. Debby invited everyone to a house-warming party at their apartment that night. Jerry and Ronnie were still sharing a room at the Myles Standish dorm in Kenmore Square. Ronnie had been my roommate for part of freshman year and Jerry had the room next door. We hung out a lot at Myles Standish, which was in Kenmore Square, not far from Mountfort Street. You could always find somebody with some pot there. Patrick lived just down the hall from us at Mountfort Street. His roommates were pretty straight so we didn't spend too much time in his apartment, but they always had a full refrigerator—something we never had. So Patrick would come and hang with us at our apartment. We'd get him good and stoned and then talk him into raiding their refrigerator and scoring us some good munchies. It worked most of the time.

It was cool to sit around that overcrowded table in the steamy warmth of the union cafeteria, chairs angled every which way to keep squeezing people into our limitlessly expandable circle, Mike and me wolfing down our liberated burgers, the table a mess of coffee and soda cups and overflowing ash trays—to be a part of this laughter and these stories. Cozy and secure with these people, but more than that, connected to them and to whatever it was that all of us together added up to. That was it. This energy, this spirit, this defiance, this joy, this revolution that was only partly political. This was the core of our cell, our collective, our soviet, our cadre, our guerilla band—this gathering of boys and girls, men and women, who were figuring out how to say no to what stood in the way of lives that made some intrinsic sense to us and yes to whatever might lead us toward that sense. I wished Sarah was there now, because this was the life behind all the words I spouted, the reality behind all the theories I espoused: kids who should be planning their careers and figuring out how to get their piece of the incredible wealth that was waiting for them instead were trying to figure out how to fight war and racism, how to live decent lives in a world overloaded with valueless wealth and governed by worthless values, as well as trying to figure out how to get stoned that afternoon or to get some desired somebody into their life or their bed. And there were as many answers to try on as there were people at this table—more than that: multiply this table by other tables in this cafeteria and tables like these in Amherst and Champaign and around the world. Sarah had a place at this table, in this circle, here and now. Then it would make sense to her—that it wasn't just me, but me as part of this whole that she belonged to as sure as shit.

I was sitting next to Debby, whose curly, tousled light brown hair rested on the shoulders of her dark brown turtleneck. She asked about Sarah. I told her that she'd been up during the vacation but was back in Philly now. How great it was to have so much time together just the two of us.

"But man, I wish she was here now," I said, "sitting with us all, so she could see how easily she would fit right back into it. She'd know in half a second that she was still part of it."

"Oh, I know she would," Debby agreed. "God, being home in New Jersey for a month was just a drag, like I was completely alone and dis-connected from everything that meant anything to me." She looked around the table to her other half. "I had to call Ellen every day just to kind of remind myself that that wasn't really my life anymore, that we had a new life in Boston that would still be there at the end of the vaca-tion. I can't imagine what it must be like for Sarah. You know, I was really excited to see Leslie and Karen when I got to our new apartment, but it was even greater coming in here and seeing everybody hanging out— that was when I finally really felt at home again."

"Would you mind giving Sarah a call and telling her exactly what you just said to me?" I was only half-kidding. "Man, I know exactly what you're saying. It was like that for me in Illinois, except I took Stu with me and was only there for a week. When you get caught up in the old world, it's just so hard to remember the new one."

Jerry, who had very straight, very black hair that framed his long oval face, asked me about Stu from across the table. Everyone sort of cheered when I told him that Stu actually had dropped out of school, but that was quickly followed by a deep groan when I added that he'd already started a job and had to go to bed early every night and get up early every day. Shit, we even had to try to keep things quiet after about 11 o'clock at Mountfort Street so he could go to sleep. That was the problem with quitting school—you sort of lost your cover for fucking around most of the time. Work was definitely a scary alternative.

Just then Brian came up, a buzz of energy. I hadn't seen him since he'd been back from vacation. He must have gotten in after I'd gone to sleep the night before. I hadn't even noticed he was sleeping in his room as Mike and I rushed to get it together to get to our first class. As usual Brian had a surprise for us—he'd cut off all his hair. When he left he'd had a flowing mane of golden hair. Now he had a crew cut, though the earring in his left ear and his thick mutton chop sideburns left no doubt that he was still a freak. That was just like Brian. He'd been one of the first guys at BU to have really long hair. Now that lots of guys had long hair, he'd cut all his off, so we'd all say, "Fucking Brian, can you believe him?"

Brian was short, even shorter than me, about 5 foot 6, and the crew cut gave him kind of a tough guy image, a far cry from the pretty boy freak he'd been. He got a big smile on his face as he checked out the group huddling around this little table: "Shit, man, did you guys forget to send me an invitation?" Brian spoke with an accent that mixed New Joisey brash with hippie cool and had one of those voices that carried across a room, even when he thought he was talking soft. "What's happening?" he said as hand slaps and back pats went all the way around again and we squeezed out a place for him before he headed to the food area to get some lunch. Brian was an English major, an aspiring poet. And crazy, man.

He was a late addition as a Mountfort Street roommate. The guy who was supposed to be our fourth—another CBS kid named Sam—had decided to not come back to BU at the last minute, so we had to scramble to find somebody to fill his spot. Whatever other living arrangement Brian had, had fallen through, so it worked out well for all of us. He was tighter with Stu than with Mike or me, not too into politics, and we did get into some serious arguments about women's liberation and other political stuff. He just was really an individualist, I guess, saw himself as an artist and resisted being tied to a movement that in any way tried to shape his consciousness. He didn't want to have to explain himself. Sometimes he seemed like a bundle of impulses that would just explode in unpredictable directions. And man you didn't want to be around him when he took LSD. He never failed to freak out somewhere along the way. We tried to warn him every time he thought about taking it, but every time he swore it would be different. He'd always say his first hundred acid trips had been great. I guess I wasn't around for many of those and I think he was well into his second hundred trips and still trying. No doubt, Brian was a freak among freaks. He loved rock and roll and loved to get high and he was just funnier than hell. Shit, he had to be one of us. It was just impossible to imagine Brian as a straight person.

When he got back to the table, somebody asked him how his vacation was and he launched into a monologue.

"Have you been to Cranford, New Jersey, lately? That's how my vacation was. Stuck in Cranford Fucking New Jersey with my parents who still think that long hair means you're a sissy and that anybody against the war in Vietnam is communist," the volume of his voice was at least matched by the relentless speed of his speech, which rushed out of him like air out of a popped balloon. "Christ, my parents gave me a hard time about not going to church, not going to church for Christ sake, can you believe that shit; they're pretty sure I'm going to go to Hell; they're just not sure the MAIN reason—cause I'm a long haired faggot cause I don't want to go kill communists for my country or because I haven't taken communion in three years; I did go to church with them just because they hassled me so much; I pretended to take communion but what they don't know is that I didn't swallow, man, you know what I mean?" He laughed a loud, anxious laugh and looked around the table. Most everyone was smiling and chuckling. You could tell Brian hadn't had a receptive audience in a few weeks. He drew a quick breath and was off again.

"I wouldn't swallow that shit; it wasn't worth the hassle to tell them that I thought it was all bullshit, so I'd go through the whole thing and then on my way back to my seat I'd pretend to cough and take the wafer off my tongue and just hold it in my hand; the body of Christ, shit; it turned into just a gooey mess in my hand, like I'd just beaten off or something; now THERE's a good reason for going to Hell; sitting in church holding the fucking body of Christ, turning into this sticky blob in my hand and thinking about beating off; I bet that's a MAJOR mortal sin." I looked at Debby as Brian said that and she kind of rolled her eyes. Still, she was laughing with the rest of us. Brian was on.

"Christ, man, my parents think I'm going to Hell for what they know about my life; if they had any idea—ANY IDEA—what my life is like here, they'd probably turn me in directly to the Pope or something, for fucking immediate excommunication and direct shipment to Hell; just turning me into the cops or even forcing me to join the army wouldn't be punishment enough for my sins; Burning Hell is what I deserve; so everyday, I'd sleep til my old man left the house, then I'd get up and walk to this park down the street from my house and smoke a number; freeze my ass off and I was paranoid as shit, but man, I had to do it; I just couldn't take it; I met a couple of freaks there, who were pretty cool, but it was still Cranford, New Jersey, where they still think it's 1957; so we'd huddle in these bushes in the park and talk real soft as we smoked a joint and jump if we heard anything; then I'd go home and hope I'd smoked enough pot to be able to totally tune my parents out; but man, I don't think there's enough pot in the world for that; my old man just wouldn't quit about my fucking hair; you're a disgrace; what do you think people think of you? we're respectable people, you make us ashamed; what the hell are you ever going to do with your life? they just drove me fucking crazy. So one day, one of the freaks I'd met in the park gave me some acid." Mike and I looked at each other, sensing now where this story was going. "When I went home that day my old man started in with the same old shit and since I never said anything to them anyway, they had no idea that I was tripping my brains out; they probably figured that something was happening when I just kind of played with the pot roast my mother served—I usually at least had a good appetite when I came home stoned; my old man even bitched at me about THAT in between ragging on my hair; so finally I just stood up in the middle of dinner, walked into the bathroom, got my old man's clippers and just buzzed my hair off, then I walked back and sat back down at the table without saying a fucking word. And, man, did that shut him up. For the first time I can remember, he didn't say a fucking WORD to me the rest of the night. That was the highlight of my vacation. When I woke up the next morning and saw what I'd done, I totally freaked out. So I went and got my ear pierced—that was a trip, trying to get my ear pierced in Cranford, New Jersey—and when I showed up at dinner that night with an EAR-RING, that gave my old man a whole new thing to rag on me about." Fucking Brian, man. Just listening to him was exhausting. But it was good to see him, see that he was the same old Brian. By the time he was done, it was about time for afternoon classes to start.

Mike and Jeffrey and I after a brief discussion decided to head back to CBS for our afternoon classes. Shit, it was the first day of school—if we couldn't get through our classes that day we might as well just bag the whole thing then and there. On the way out of the cafeteria we saw other groups of people we knew—other cells in the BU revolutionary movement. The student leaders like Daniel Lucas and Matthew Wexler, who were freaks and friends but had titles like president of the student body and editor of the school newspaper. The PL gang who were sort of my buddies now that we'd been through the injunction hearing together—they smiled and waved at me. A group of the younger kids—freshmen—who lived in the dorms and would hang with us at demonstrations. Lots of clenched fists salutes and "right-ons."

Just as we were bundling up to head back out into the cold day, we ran into Larry Schleh, a grad student who'd been the resident assistant on my floor in the dorms the year before—and who let us get away with pretty much anything short of burning the fucking building down, and we hadn't really even tested him on that one. Schleh, who had wispy blond hair floating from his head and round wire-rimmed glasses, was your classic fucking liberal. We'd rap for hours with him about the inherent flaws of the system, how the very nature of the system prevented any meaningful change and he'd say yeah, yeah, you're right but unless you've got something better ready to put in its place, you've gotta keep working in the system. What the fuck was the point of working within to change a system that was set up to prevent any real change from taking place? So, we'd go round and round. But he was a good guy and let us smoke pot and have girls in our rooms.

"You guys doing anything Thursday night?" he asked.

"We got lots of studying to do," I answered. "You know how hard we hit the books—sure wouldn't want to get behind the first week of school. Why? What's going on?"

Schleh told us he was working with old people at the Brookline Jewish Community Center as part of his practicum for his master's degree. "We've been talking about current events," he said, "and I've got to tell you these people really aren't too crazy about what you hippie radicals are doing on campus. They think you're a bunch of crazy communists."

"So," Mike said, "did you tell them they were pretty much right?"

"No, come on you guys. I know you guys are smart and have put a lot of thought into your opposition to the war." We all laughed. "No really," Schleh was oozing sincerity. "I'd like you to try to talk to these folks, talk about why you're against the war, and why you're protesting on campus. I just think if they could meet real live anti-war students—thoughtful, intelligent guys like you—it would help overcome some of their stereotypes and might just make them think twice about supporting the war. Hey, I'm giving you guys a captive audience. Besides they'll be some good food there you can stock up on. Bring a friend or two if you want. Come on, it would help me out a lot, too."

"Wow, thoughtful, intelligent guys—you must be desperate," I said.

"Yeah, the speaker I had lined up just cancelled on me, but you guys would be great. I know it."

So we agreed, got all the details from Larry, then Mike, Jeffrey, and I headed off for another afternoon of higher education—thanks to the joint we shared on the way back to CBS.

CHAPTER SIXTEEN

January 14

Dear Dad,

Thanks for your letter. Yeah, I'm sorry, too, that our time together always seems to get lost in arguing. But I don't know when that's going to change as long as you're convinced that I'm just a mixed-up kid who is going to see the errors of my ways any day, as soon as I start listening to you. It's the things that bug you the most that are the core of who I am. I'm a long-haired freak. I smoke pot. I steal burgers from the student union. Me and my friends are trying in every way we can to undermine the system because the system is set up to destroy our humanity. I don't care very much about school because school tries to turn me into another cog in the machine and, with a few rare exceptions, isn't helping me to figure out how to live some kind of decent life in this corrupt and decadent society. I'm trying to get a job to support myself because I hate taking money from you, but I have no ambition to find a career and make a lot of money and chase that delusional thing this society calls success. I want to be with Sarah and my friends and do what we can to stand against this madness and build lives that make sense to us.

Until you can accept that's who I am, then it's hard to even begin a conversation--as we found out when I was home. I'm sorry--really-- that it's so hard for you. I'm the same kid who you were so proud of as a young Republican when I went to Washington with you and met all those congressmen or when I wrote the letter to the editor for Goldwater that all your friends congratulated you for. But you can see what's happened with the war and the draft, ongoing racism and attacks on black leaders and the student movement, too. Your man Nixon's only making everything worse. I know you have to see that, too.

So much that I believed in turned out to be a lie. I still believe in those principles of freedom and justice that we celebrated on Patriots Day in Lexington, those great days when I was a kid, but sadly I'm learning in all kinds of ways that this country is mostly on the wrong side of the struggle for freedom and justice.

I think I told you that we were expecting the BU lawyers would drop my name from the injunction because I wasn't at the demonstration that led to it. Well, they double-crossed us in court and the judge was an absolute pig and wouldn't listen to anything my lawyer said. Justice, man, what a sham. So, I'm still dealing with that.

It's sort of interesting that now you think nonviolent protest is a good thing and what I should be doing, even though you were dead against it a couple of years ago when Cary and I were doing that kind of stuff in Urbana. A lot of good nonviolence did Martin Luther King and all the black people still trapped in the ghettos and second-class citizenship by racism. The government loves protest that doesn't really challenge them, because the people blow off some steam and nothing changes.

I'm not saying I'm going to run out and start being violent, but I am saying we've got to do a lot more to challenge the system than signing petitions or carrying signs. Part of that is living lives that flaunt the system and attract others to join us, build alternatives to the dying ways of the old order. I'm not sure where I fit in the political movement anymore, a lot of people are getting apathetic--or scared--

and others are getting pretty intense. I'm not ready to give up, but I'm not sure what that means right now.

Sarah was up for awhile after I got back. We had a good time, but it ended and she's back in Philadelphia, which is never a good ending. I'm not sure what's going to happen with us either. Uncertainty all around.

Keep writing, maybe somehow we can figure out a way to make sense to each other.

Keep the faith.
Love,
Ben

CHAPTER SEVENTEEN

January 15

"DO YOU KNOW WHAT HO CHI MINH used as the first sentence of Vietnam's Declaration of Independence from the French in 1945?" I looked up from my scribbled notes and into the audience of about twenty-five people old enough to make my grandmother look young. Most of them were men and most of them were eyeing me like I smelled bad. I don't know if it was the way I looked or that Schleh had introduced me and Mike as activists from BU that had drawn this snarling scorn to their stubbled, sagging faces. Shit, maybe they were just pissed off because they were old and tired and I wasn't. The few women scattered in the crowd, who had used some lipstick and make-up to make themselves look a little more alive, seemed less hostile, a couple even offering matronly smiles. They were all bundled in sweaters and scarves, even though the small room seemed plenty warm to me, and they all looked uncomfortable in cheap folding chairs that were spread out a safe distance from where I spoke. Go ahead and talk, the scowling men seemed to challenge me, we ain't listening to you.

"'All men are created equal. They are endowed by their creator with certain inalienable rights, among these are life, liberty, and the pursuit of happiness.' That's how Ho Chi Minh started his Declaration of Independence, using the words from our Declaration of Independence because he was fighting for the same thing that we fought for in our Revolution—independence from a colonial power."

Schleh had set us up on a slightly raised platform in this low-ceilinged unevenly lit all-purpose rec room in the basement of the Brookline Jewish Community Center. He and Mike and I sat in chairs across the platform. When he introduced us, he told this gathering of the BJCC Golden Agers that this was their chance to try to understand the "younger generation"—shit, sounded like something out of *Life* magazine.

I was talking about why we were against what the U.S. was doing in Vietnam and then Mike would explain some of the recent actions and demonstrations that we'd been part of: the anti-military campaign the previous spring, the November actions that had tried to shut down missile laboratories at MIT, the local and national demonstrations of the Moratorium against the war.

"Ho Chi Minh was America's ally during the Second World War," I went on to this den of dirty looks. "He and his army helped us to defeat the Japanese in Indochina. Part of the understanding we had with him was that after the war, we would support his efforts to win independence for his country from France. But somehow President Truman forgot that understanding and allowed the French to reclaim their colony."

Stu and Lenny had come with us—I guess cause they had nothing better to do. And they thought it'd be funny to watch us try to explain ourselves in a way that a bunch of old straight people would understand. Besides, Schleh had promised us there would be some good refreshments—way more than the old folks could eat—and that we could eat as much as we wanted and then fill our pockets. Stu was bumming when we first got there because he realized he'd worn a coat with only two small pockets in it. But fortunately, Lenny wore a double layer of coats, which both had big deep pockets.

As I talked, I could smell a thick sweetness coming from a table across the back of the room, but that had to compete with the burnt tar smell of an oil furnace that occasionally let out a groan in a nearby room. A pretty unappetizing combination. But Stu and Lenny were definitely checking out that table in the back—instead of paying any attention to me—as they sat near the door in the front of the room, chairs up against the wall, trying to blend into the dusty fake pine paneling.

"So, the Vietnamese—led by Ho Chi Minh—had to fight for eight more years to win their independence from France," I went on. "Abandoned by the United States—which actually supported the French in their effort to maintain their colonial rule—they naturally turned to the Soviet Union for help."

"Naturally. They were communists," a man with three layers of chin and a thick accent shouted from the middle of the room. "That's why they got the help from Russia."

Schleh jumped in, "Why don't we let Ben finish, then you can ask him all the questions you want."

"It's all right," I said. At least somebody had heard something I'd said. "I don't mind. The most important thing is to try to explain and understand how we got to where we are today in the war. Yes, they were communists, but communists who were America's allies until we supported the French against them. Who knows what might have happened if we had supported an independent Vietnam after World War II. What's important to understand is that the Vietnamese have been fighting for their independence since World War II and that the war that is going on there now is just a continuation of that struggle. And the problem is that since World War II, the United States has been on the wrong side of that struggle."

"What do you mean the wrong side? We're fighting communists." This voice, raspy and mad, came from the back of the room, though I couldn't see who was speaking because he was blocked by two guys in front of him.

Schleh started to say something, but I motioned to him that I was all right. This was getting interesting.

"I guess I believe that if the Vietnamese want to be communist, they should be allowed to be communist."

Disgusted groans drowned out the struggling furnace. "Just like when the United States no longer wanted to be ruled by England, we chose the kind of government we wanted." The room was getting hot and everybody was sitting up a little straighter, even Stu and Lenny, who couldn't help but pay attention now. I was still convinced that anybody who really knew what was happening in Vietnam would be against the war.

"Let me just tell you a little more about the history, why I think the United States has been and is on the wrong side. The Vietnamese defeated the French in 1954 at the famous battle of Dien Bien Phu, winning independence. Those two countries signed the Geneva Accords, which called for Vietnam to be temporarily divided into two areas, north and south. Part of that deal was that elections would be held in 1956 to reunify the country. Vietnam was never supposed to be turned into two separate countries—that was a temporary, transitional arrangement. Vietnam is one country and that's what this war is all about.

"The thing is, everybody knew who would win the election in 1956. Ho Chi Minh was the most popular man in that country, the unquestioned leader, the 'George Washington of Vietnam,' somebody once called him. The Vietnamese agreed to the Geneva Accords, to the temporary division of their country, because they had been fighting for a long time—in World War II against the Japanese and eight years against the French. They were tired of fighting and they knew that Ho Chi Minh would win the election in 1956 and the country would be reunited under his leadership."

"And communist," said the triple-chinned man.

"Yes and communist," I took a deep breath. The scowls had hardened and I saw anger spark in some of these old and tired eyes. I looked to Schleh who just kind of shrugged and to Mike, who was working on a serious scowl of his own. I just wasn't getting through—even the matronly smiles were gone, replaced by a bewildered concern as the old women watched their men dig in for a fight. I didn't know what to do except try to go on.

"The United States knew, too, that Ho Chi Minh would win the election, so they decided they could not allow those elections to go on. So we created a country called South Vietnam and installed a pro-American, anticommunist government. For four years, from 1956 until 1960, those who supported a reunified and independent Vietnam tried to use peaceful means to win their country back, but they were faced with brutal repression from the government, which got a lot of help from the CIA. So in 1960, a broad coalition of communists, students, intellectuals, and even religious leaders formed the National Liberation Front to fight the U.S.-puppet government by both political and military means."

"Where do you get this communist propaganda?" It was a new voice from a thin, sharp-beaked man sitting right in front of us. "What are they teaching you in college these days?"

"You can get this information out of lots of books about Vietnam…"

"Try doing that in a communist country," the thin guy shot back.

"So are you saying that as long as we're fighting communists"—fuck the script; these people were assholes—"it doesn't matter if we break promises, rig elections, repress dissent, destroy a country, and send our young boys there to kill and die?"

I couldn't understand a single word of the collective roar of derision that came flying back at me. But their message was pretty clear. Some of the men had even risen to their feet and were emphatically jabbing their fingers at me.

Schleh stood and held his hands up to try the calm down all these angry old men. "Come on," he said, trying to speak gently. But he had to raise his voice to be heard. "The reason I invited these guys here was so you could try to understand them better. We can't understand anything if we don't listen." He gave me a look that carried a plea to try to avoid igniting any more explosions. I took another long breath and eyed the restless crowd. These guys were old, but they had us seriously outnumbered.

"You know I grew up as a great fan and admirer of the American Revolution," I said, trying to smooth the edges from my voice. "I still admire the Sons of Liberty and all the guys in the three-cornered hats who dared to stand up to England because they believed we should be an independent country. That's really what the war in Vietnam is—it's a war of independence. But the United States doesn't like the political system that most people in Vietnam seem to favor. I really don't think that's any of our business. Besides that, the U.S. has economic interests in Southeast Asia and it wants a government that will protect those interests." That brought another round of groans and dismissing hands waved in my direction. I glanced over at Stu and Lenny, who were pushing themselves as far back as they could against the wall, trying to disappear. I bet they were wondering if the rugalach and lemon cake waiting in the back of the room were worth being associated with a couple of commie agitators.

"I'm almost done with the history, then Mike's going to talk about what's going on now at BU and around the city. So the NLF, the coalition of groups opposed to the U.S.-installed government in the South, started a guerilla war against that government. No Russians, no Chinese. All Vietnamese. And they were winning. So the United States increased its military aid and sent troops, supposedly just to advise the South Vietnamese army. But the Vietnamese, the NLF Vietnamese, what our government calls the Viet Cong, were still winning. By 1963, things were so bad for the South Vietnamese government, that the U.S. government helped to overthrow and assassinate the leaders that they had put in there in the first place—and supported a new government backed by the military." That brought an ear-grating chorus of howls that rattled the cheap once-white ceiling tiles. I just kept talking.

"Really. I know this sounds crazy, it doesn't sound like the kind of thing our country would do, but it's true. That's why we're so upset. That's why we feel so strongly that we have to do everything we can to stop this war. After the U.S. overthrew the very government it put in place, things just kept getting worse, so in 1964, under President Lyndon Johnson, after the Vietnamese supposedly attacked some U.S. Navy ships, an attack most people now recognize didn't happen…"

"Most communists maybe…" it was the old triple-chin guy again. But I didn't even slow down now. I was just looking for a way to finish my rap and let Mike take over.

"…Congress passed a resolution, call the Gulf of Tonkin Resolution, which basically gave Johnson the power to escalate U.S. involvement to a full-scale war—what we have now. Since then, the U.S. has dropped thousands of tons of bombs on Vietnam and we now have more than half a million troops there. We've killed two million Vietnamese and lost almost 50,000 of our own soldiers. We believe that's wrong and a terrible waste. It's not good for our country and it's certainly not good for Vietnam." Period. I stopped. There was no applause, only an agitated silence as I nodded at Schleh to let him know I was done.

"Thanks, Ben. I'm sure there might be a few more questions for you later." Questions? Nobody was asking questions. These guys didn't believe a word I said and nothing was going to change that. Fucking Schleh, the always hopeful liberal. He was convinced that all we needed to do was to keep talking and eventually reason would set in. He nodded at Mike to begin.

"Yeah," Mike said as he shifted in his seat, pushed his glasses tight against his forehead, and glared back at the audience. "What you need to understand is that the reason you are having such a hard time believing and accepting what Ben just told you—which happens to be historical truth—is because the government systematically lies to you and the media repeats the lies so much that they start to seem like the truth. You may not like to hear that, but it happens to be true." Mike wasn't looking at any notes. He looked straight out at the guys who'd been hassling me and beat out the rhythm of his confident cadence with the thrust of his finger-pointing right hand.

"The anti-war Movement is trying to do two things. First, we're trying to get the truth out about the war. Since we don't have the same access to the media that the government does, the only way we can do that is through protest and demonstrations. And talking to people like you when we get a chance, but we don't get this chance very often. And because most of what you hear about what we're doing is also through the media, which tell lies about us, too, you start out not listening to what we say even before we start talking. What's happened here tonight is a perfect example of that. When we try to tell you the truth about Vietnam…"

"Your truth ain't *the* truth," yelled the guy in the back row, who I could see now and who rolled a stub of a cigar around in his mouth. "What made you kids think you're so damn smart?"

"...Just like that, you get mad and start yelling at us," Mike was lecturing, his voice assertive and sure, his stroking right hand now starting as a fist and opening for emphasis on the down beat. "Just because to accept the truth of what we're saying you have to question the legitimacy of the government itself and it's obvious you're not ready to do that. Unfortunately most Americans aren't ready to do that. So the other thing the anti-war Movement is trying to do is to make it more difficult for the government to keep fighting the war. By trying to stop ROTC and other ways colleges support the war, like research at MIT and BU and other places, by encouraging draft-age men to resist the draft, and GIs to desert or refuse to serve in Vietnam..."

"You're helping the enemy, that's what you're doing, you're helping communists who are killing American soldiers." It was the thin man in the front row again, taking Mike's challenge and throwing it back at him. "Are you proud of that?"

"Look, we're not happy about anybody being killed." Mike calmed his voice and stopped the jabbing of his hand, opening it toward the man who sat only about five feet away, in a kind of conciliatory gesture. "We're not against the American soldiers. We think they're being used by our government, put into a bad situation where they have to kill or be killed for reasons most of them either don't agree with or don't understand. We think the best thing we can do for the American soldiers is to stop the war and bring them home."

"But you wouldn't go there yourselves, you cowards!" It was the guy in the back, who was now standing and had pulled the cigar out of his mouth and was pointing it at Mike. "You're a bunch of spoiled kids, hiding in school..."

"Wait a second," Schleh tried to calm things down, but it was too far gone now.

"No, you wait a second," the guy in the back row took a couple of steps toward us. "What the hell are we listening to these cowards for? They don't want to fight for their country so they fight against their country and the brave boys who are fighting for them, for their freedom to sit here and spout all this crap. I've got a grandson over there and God knows I wish he didn't have to be there. But he's there doing his duty. It makes me sick to look at these ungrateful spoiled kids. Thank God we didn't have to count on these guys when we were fighting Hitler."

Mike was pissed now. He pointed his finger back at the cigar-toting guy, "Listen, man, do you have any idea what your government is doing to the Vietnamese. It would make Hitler proud."

I jumped in before the cigar-toting man, who was moving closer to the front of the room, could respond: "Honest, we really believe the best thing we can do for your grandson—the best you could do for your grandson and for all the soldiers—is to do everything we can to make the government stop the war. Now."

Half the men in the room were now standing and shouting. The man with the cigar pointed the stub at me as he kept coming toward us: "Don't," he said, his voice trembling with anger, "don't you even talk about my grandson, you don't deserve to even speak his name, you, you…"

"Can I say something?" It was Stu. The calm assertion of his voice— a new voice in the middle of this circus—brought a sudden silence to the room and kind of froze everybody, even the cigar man, who looked away from us and at Stu, who rose and leaned against the wall. I looked at Mike, surprised that Stu would venture into this heavy a political debate. Mike shrugged and both of us turned with the rest of the room toward Stu.

"I've been listening to all this, to you people yelling back and forth about politics and duty and country, and I feel my heart just get sicker and sicker and as hard as this is for me, I think I just have to tell you this story." I'd never seen Stu this somber, and I had no idea what story he was about to tell, but the urgent sincerity of his words had at least for the moment saved us from the prospect of having to fight our way out of an old-folks meeting.

"My father died when I was very young, but I had two brothers who were enough older than me that they became sort of like a couple of fathers for me. They took turns teaching me the things a father teaches a son. They taught me how to throw a baseball, how to shoot a basketball. They took me to baseball games at Fenway and basketball games at the Garden. They helped me with my Torah portion when I prepared for my Bar Mitzvah. They even tried to help me figure out girls when I got old enough for that, but, well, you know, there are some things even a father can't teach a son." For the first time in this tense evening, there was a trickle of laughter through the room. All the men who had been standing slowly settled back into their seats, including the man with the cigar, which was now back in his mouth and still.

"My oldest brother wanted to be a doctor. He was a good student and a good son. He always made my mother so proud. And, of course, he was the best brother a boy could ask for. And he was also a good American. When he finished college in 1965, the war in Vietnam was escalating, and as a good American, he believed what the government said, that Russians and communists were trying to take away the freedom of the people of Vietnam and that it was important for our country to stop that. So he decided, that before going to medical school, he would enlist in the army to serve his country. I remember how handsome and brave he looked in his uniform, how proud I was that he was my brother, how I couldn't wait until I was old enough to join the army, too.

"Six months after we said good-bye to him, waving small American flags as he boarded a plane at Logan Airport, an army officer showed up at our door to say he had been killed in action."

I looked at Mike and he looked back at me, as stunned and puzzled as I was. The room was dead silent. Stu gathered himself and went on.

"I remember how numb I was at his funeral. I just couldn't believe he was dead. But I did believe it when people told me he was a hero and I was really proud when the soldiers in their dress uniforms picked up his coffin, with the flag spread out over it, as the bugler played taps. And when I stopped being numb, I got mad. Mad at the communists for killing my oldest brother. So I completely understood when my other brother decided to drop out of college to join the army. I would have done it too if they would have let me, but I was only fifteen. My second brother was never quite the student my older brother was, but he had always been sort of artistic, so he was studying graphic arts in college. My mother, still mourning my oldest brother, tried to talk him out of joining the army. She told him there were other ways he could honor the memory of his brother. But he was determined to go and fight the communists who'd killed our brother.

"When another officer came a year later telling us that he, too, had been killed, my mother broke down. I was ready to do anything to get in the army to avenge my brothers, but she was so distraught, I had to agree when she begged me to swear that I would never do that. But, like some of you here tonight, I was mad when anybody said that what America was doing in Vietnam was wrong. To me, they were saying my brothers died for no reason. I got in lots of fights in high school with people who said the war was wrong or who said they would go to Canada before they'd serve their country in Vietnam.

"Then, as the war dragged on and more Americans died and more and more bombs got dropped on Vietnam, one day—a year or so after my second brother died—out of nowhere, my mother said to me, 'Do you think it was worth it? Do you think your brothers died for a good reason?' I was shocked that she asked me that question, but I couldn't get mad at her. She was still a wreck, still devastated by losing two sons. For the first time, I allowed that question into my head. I started listening to some of the critics of the war. Started reading some of the books that Ben talked about, about the history of Vietnam and the war. I became obsessed with the question my mother had asked me, 'Was it worth it?' I really wanted to believe that it was.

"But I have to tell you, as sad it makes me, that my answer is no. It's not worth it. What we're doing in Vietnam was not worth my brothers' lives, it's not worth your grandson's life. It's not worth one single more American or Vietnamese life. When I finally had to face that answer, I had to tell my mother, too. That was hard. Really hard. To tell my mother that her sons, my brothers, had died in a war that was unjust, that we shouldn't even be fighting. And do you know what my mother said?" Stu paused and looked slowly around the room, into all the eyes that were respectfully, almost reverentially, on him, including mine and Mike's and Schleh's. Lenny, sitting just to the side of where Stu stood, stared up at him, eyes wide, his mouth hanging open. The only sound in the room, besides the occasional groan from the furnace, was an involuntary wheeze of someone's breathing. But even that was measured and polite.

"My mother said, 'You must do whatever you can to stop that war. I'm too old, too tired to fight. But you and the other young people, you must make the government stop the war. For your brothers' sake, this is the best way for you to serve their memory, so other boys don't have to die, so other mothers don't have to mourn.'"

Stu looked once more into the crowd of Golden Agers, then up at us. Then he lowered his eyes and sat down. I could see some of the women put their hands to their face, to wipe away the beginnings of tears. The men, ready to fight a few minutes ago, sat back in their chairs, looking tired and a little confused. I looked at Schleh and Mike. There was, clearly, nothing more to say. Except Schleh had to end it somehow.

"Thanks, Stu, for that moving story, which does help us to put these issues into some kind of perspective. I'd like to thank our guests once again and remind everyone that there are refreshments in the back of the room." There was actually even a smattering of applause as he shook my hand and then Mike's.

As we stepped down from our platform, three of the women and a couple of the men who hadn't said anything walked over to Stu and somberly shook his hand or put a sympathetic arm around his shoulder, like they were at a funeral or something. The rabble-rousers left the room as fast as they could, avoiding even eye contact with Stu or any of us.

"Man, do you believe that?" I said to Mike. "Did you know that?"

"No, man," Mike answered. "I can't believe he never told us that before."

A few people came up and shook hands with Mike and me, thanked us for coming, but mostly we were ignored, which was just fine by me. We waited until all the old folks had made their way through the re-freshment line before we started in. Stu and Lenny had already been through the line as a couple of the sympathetic women had led Stu through, making sure his plate was full. Now Stu and Lenny were standing by the door, chowing down and waiting for us. I didn't have much of an appetite, but since this was the only thing we were going to get out of this evening, I wolfed down a piece of the lemon cake, which was kind of mealy and dry, and rolled a bunch of the rugalachs in a napkin and stuffed it in my pocket. I didn't even look to see if anybody was watching me. Shit, there was still a bunch of food there and Schleh had said we could take whatever we could carry.

When we finally got over to Stu and Lenny, I patted Stu on the back and said, "Man!" He just smiled at me as he popped a rugalach in his mouth.

The four of us filed into the hallway, which looked something like the entry to a bomb shelter, stark and colorless—and overheated from the noisy furnace. As we put on our coats and bundled up to head out into the cold night, Mike and Lenny and me all turned on Stu.

"Shit, man!" said Mike, grinning with disbelief.

"Holy shit, man!" said Lenny, shaking his head.

"I can't believe you never told us any of that," I said, concerned that we'd opened up this deep source of pain for Stu. "Why didn't you ever tell us before?"

Stu smiled again. "Because it's not true."

Now I was really confused, "What's not true?" I asked.

"None of it's true. I made it all up." He was really smiling now.

"You don't have brothers who went to Vietnam and got killed?"

"Nah, I have one older brother. He's selling insurance in Hartford."

We all just kind of looked at each other, silent, even more stunned now. The tragedy of his tale had blown us away, but, shit, man, it was an act. That totally blew our minds. "Man," I said, fumbling for words, "you...you were good."

"You fuckers needed help," he laughed. "You weren't getting anywhere with those folks. Good thing I came or the headline tomorrow would have been 'Anti-war Activists Mauled by Old Jews.' That would have been really embarrassing."

"You son of a bitch," Mike said with a proud grin so big it sparkled in the basement hallway's funky fluorescent lights. Then he let out a belly laugh that ricocheted against the hard walls and the low ceiling and enveloped us all: "You son of a bitch."

CHAPTER EIGHTEEN

January 17

I CALLED HER AT NINE O'CLOCK, ALWAYS NINE. I was anxious as I dialed—suppose she got hung up somewhere, suppose somebody else was using her phone booth, suppose the stupid fucking phone company had finally figured out that every freak in America knew their credit card system. Or maybe she just wouldn't show up. Or maybe a hundred other things—I never knew exactly what to expect.

I always called from the Mountfort Street phone booth, just up the street from our apartment building. Sarah had changed phone booths a couple of times. The first one was near a little corner store and she thought somebody might notice that she came there every few nights and talked for a long time. So she went to another on a dark corner by a closed gas station, but that was a little creepy. So she found another one on a busy street near office buildings that were closed at night. I'd never seen that phone booth, but from what she told me and the sounds I could hear in the background, I could see it in my head—a narrow and tall island of isolation rising from an old sidewalk where people didn't walk much anymore, in front of a closed real estate office, new and big cars whizzing past, her VW parked on the quiet street around the corner—and her, spotlighted by the booth's soft light, bundled in her pea coat, biting her lip, smoking a cigarette, waiting for the phone to ring. I hoped.

She was there and she answered, breathless and sounding as anxious as I felt: "This better be Ben."

Calling phone booth to phone booth, using a phony credit card number, we had unlimited free calling and the only way we could get busted was if they somehow caught us in the act. It was pretty damn foolproof.

"And what if it's not?"

"Or at least somebody almost as cute," I could hear the smile come over her face.

"And how would you know that over the phone?"

"Oh, I'd know."

"I'm sure you would….Hi, Sarah."

"Hi, Ben." Our mutual anxiety seemed to lift in a sudden rush, like the release after you've held a breath too long.

Man, I needed these calls. I wrote her something almost every day, though sometimes it took me two or three installments to finish a letter. And she wrote me almost as much. I loved getting those letters, felt a rush as soon as I saw the pastel envelopes that she always decorated with some kind of flourish to my name and address. But still, the letters in some ways made the distance between us more real—mine composed in late night loneliness, usually sitting on my bed, sometimes with voices and music ricocheting around the apartment and people running around outside my door. Having to sit there alone, scribbling all my passions on paper was a reminder of just how definitely not there she was. And in her letters, her loneliness, her boredom, the overwhelming sense of her resigned sadness just kind of sat there on the page like dried tears, mementos of a moment I wasn't there to hold her and tell her how much I loved her. But talking to her, for that hour or so every three or four days, made it feel like we had a relationship not just some paper fantasy. We could respond to each other, argue and make up in five minutes time, laugh at each other and hear the laughter, hear the full shape and roll of that love that sometimes seemed so awfully quiet, such a flat and far-away thing on those letter pages.

We caught up on stuff we'd been doing. She told me about her classes and some cool people she'd met at Temple, though one of them was some guy named Kevin—that was a little disturbing. But she said it so casually, and she'd even given him my name and address because he was coming to Boston soon and was looking for a place to stay. So maybe there wasn't anything to worry about. Really, I was glad—mostly glad—to hear she had met some people that could give her some life outside of her parents' house.

She told me about her Group Dynamics class where they divided up into groups and did these non-verbal interactions, playing with tinker toys and rubber bands. Sounded like a course that belonged at CBS. But she said it was cool and showed a lot about people even though nobody could say anything—how creative some people are, how methodical other people are, how easily some people can be influenced by the slightest indications of someone else's expectations or judgments of them. She said her group was going to do some kind of project where they'd faint in the street and see how people passing by reacted to them. That sounded kind of fun.

I told her about our adventure at the Jewish Community Center. She appreciated that story—her mother worked with old folks at a Philadelphia Jewish Community Center. I said maybe we could do an encore performance there since it'd gone so well here. She was surprised we'd do it, but laughed when I explained that a captive audience and free food was just a little too tempting for Mike and me to pass up. She was as amazed as we had been when I told about Stu's outrageous performance.

Then I told her about the party a couple of nights before at 858 Beacon Street—Leslie and Karen and Debby and Ellen's apartment—the first big party of the new semester. It was a good time. Brian scored some beer, so we had a little more alcohol than the usual Boston party. Karen, who was kind of an amateur photographer, showed me this magazine-size photo she'd taken of me during the middle of a lecture one day at CBS. She just turned around and suddenly was focusing her camera on me—so I gave her the finger, but not so much giving her the finger as giving the camera the finger. Kind of a cool shot. So she had this big picture of me and she said she was going to send it to Sarah, though she wanted to airbrush the finger out, so Sarah could put it up at her parents' house without having to explain. I wanted her to just give it to me, but she wouldn't. Then as we we're leaving, Leslie just kind of slipped me the picture and I tucked it under my coat and took it home. When I told Sarah all this, she kind of laughed, but I could tell it made her sad.

"What's the matter?" I asked.

"Nothing."

"Really? Suddenly you sound… I don't know, pissed or sad or something. The party was great. But still it was a drag for me that you weren't there. It was like 'what's missing from this picture?' Shit, Sarah, it's always like that. Everybody asked me about you. That's mostly what I talked about—was you. What am I supposed to do? Should I have not told you about the party?"

"No. It just makes me feel so…so out of it. You're hanging out with Leslie and Karen and talking about me, like I'm some poor sad, distant relative."

"Sarah…you know that's not how it is."

She didn't say anything. I could only hear the static of the traffic outside her phone booth. "Sarah," I said, "do you have any idea how much I miss you? How fast I'd trade a night alone with you for all the parties in Boston?"

"Ben, I know," I could hardly hear her, but her voice still creaked with sadness. "It's just…last night, it's like I almost had a nervous breakdown. I mean I didn't but…I was just going stir crazy in my room and I had to get out. So I got in my car and just drove around for an hour and a half, just talking to myself. I felt like I had to talk to someone but I couldn't call you, so I just drove and talked to myself. I couldn't think of anywhere to go, so I thought I'd go to that boy Kevin's house and talk to him. I pulled up outside his house and decided it was crazy. I mean I don't even really know him. So I drove away, but then I went back and even went up to the door and rang the bell—but then I suddenly changed my mind and ran back to my car."

"Sarah…" I don't know what was in my voice: jealousy, worry, love, anger?

"Ben, if anybody had been watching me, I would have been committed," her voice was energized now but also kind of desperate. "I finally just went home and just cried until I fell asleep…Ben, if he, that boy Kevin, ever comes to Boston don't ever tell him about any of this. He wouldn't understand my intentions. He doesn't know that I'm naturally crazy like you do."

"Sarah, what's going on?"

"I'm just flipping out…I don't know."

"What's with this guy Kevin?"

"Oh, Ben, don't worry—there's nothing going on with Kevin. He's just a nice boy I met. I've talked to him, like, twice. I just needed somebody to talk to and he was the only person I could think of."

"What do you need to talk about? Talk to me." Just then, I saw an old man with a thick black coat and one of those gray old-time hats, like my father used to wear to church when I was a kid, heading up Park Drive toward my phone booth. He didn't look like a phone company cop, but I wasn't sure until I saw a little white yappy dog at the end of a leash that dangled loosely from his folded arms. Phone company cops wouldn't be clever enough to come up with that kind of cover.

"It's the same thing, Ben. I can't be there and I just have a hard time being happy here. Nothing new for you."

Shit, what could I say? "I don't mind hearing it again. It just makes me sad that you're so lonely. "

"Then I had this dream—you're going to get it now—that you went to Temple and we had a lecture together. But I got my schedule all mixed up and I went to a drivers' ed class by mistake. Then I got into this car, but I couldn't reach the brakes, so I crashed. Then I went to find you to tell you about it and you were in the phone booth. But you wouldn't talk to me."

"Sarah…"

"It was a dream, but it was strange. It seemed so real. You wouldn't even look at me. I pounded on the glass and I was crying but you just kept on talking without even looking at me."

"Sarah…I'm in a phone booth. I'm talking to you. I wish you'd walk by right now and pound on the glass…Sarah, man…The last time I was sitting in this phone booth and you came up to it, you slammed the door on me and ran away. Do you remember that?"

"Yeah," she said with just a slice of a laugh.

"I don't know what's going on in your head, but you can't forget that I love you and I miss you and it drives me fucking crazy that you're there needing someone to talk to and you're driving around in the middle of the night to some guy's you hardly even know and I'm here just wanting nothing more than to talk to you."

"Ben, I know, I just…I just flip out being by myself so much."

"I need to get down there. Maybe I can get down there next weekend."

"Can you get a ride?"

"I don't care. I'll hitch. I need to see you and sounds like maybe you could use a little company."

"I'd love it. I'm sorry to be a downer. I just…"

"It's OK."

We talked a long while more. She was thinking about maybe trying to get a job, to get out of the house for one thing and to make some money for trips to Boston and for whatever she was going to be doing when school got out. I told her about my futile search for a job. Since we lost the Shawmut bank janitor job—a three-night-a-week job for three people that five of us shared—just before the Christmas break, I hadn't had any luck. Shit, I was trying. I had a few possibilities, but nothing had come through yet. The $50 a month from my old band just didn't go very far, and the only way it seemed like I could make any money was to write papers for people, but I'd only had a couple of customers so far this semester—and those guys paid me in dope.

She asked if I was worried about the injunction. I'd written her a long letter about the hearing. Not really, I said, but shit, you never knew where things would lead. I told her that Luke and some of the other Weathermen were finally going to come by Mountfort Street to talk about doing some things together. She wasn't too excited about that. Because of all the legal booby traps that had been set up, things were quiet at BU, but people were starting to talk about an action to protest a speech by S.I. Hayakawa—who had brutally put down a student strike when he was president of San Francisco State. He was speaking at Northeastern University in a couple of weeks.

"You aren't going to go to that, are you?" she said.

"I don't know. Maybe. I'm not under any injunction at Northeastern."

"It certainly wouldn't help your legal situation."

"I can't just stop everything because they come after with us this bullshit injunction."

"Maybe you could skip this one, not because of them," she said, making her voice sort of phony sweet, "but because of me."

I laughed at the silliness of her tone. "I don't know Sarah, I don't know what kind of thing it's going be or who's going or anything. We'll see. I'll try not to do anything stupid."

Sarah got tired of talking about Movement shit, so she asked about Tavola. I had an ongoing battle trying to keep track of her. She sometimes disappeared for days, though she was back now. I'd hear her soft paw rubbing against the window as she waited patiently on the fire escape for me to open the window and let her in. Then she'd curl up in a black fuzzy ball and sleep on my mattress for hours. Whenever she was awake, though, she had a frantic look in her eye and a pacing restlessness and before you knew it, she was gone again. Shit, I wasn't going to chain her to my desk. I was even afraid she might be pregnant. There was no reason why she wouldn't be. She was out running the streets and alleys of Boston most of the time. Sarah made me promise that if she had kittens that I'd save one for her. Kittens, man, that's just what I needed now.

Sarah talked about the next summer. She was hoping to go to Europe with her friend Sally. It sounded great, except it was a lot further from wherever I would be than even Philadelphia was. I had no idea where I would be, what I would do. I'd put in an application to work at the Cape Cod National Seashore, which was like a national park. That would be cool. But outside of that I didn't have any options. Stu had talked about heading to some farm in Ohio with some folks he met. Maybe I'd go there for a while. We'd also met these stoned out hippie types who put on this happening that just wandered down Comm Ave one day. They were part of a collective called the Hog Farm. They were buying a whole shitload of land in New Mexico and were basically inviting anyone who felt like it to join them. Maybe I'd go there. I knew I didn't want to go back to Champaign. And I didn't really want to work in the city in the summertime. Man, it seemed like forever away.

"I just wish we could be together, sometime, somewhere." I told Sarah.

"Why?" she asked.

"What?" I was kind of stunned. Her question came out of nowhere.

"I want you to give me reasons why we should be together." She was playing with me.

"So I don't have to spend so much time in this fucking freezing cold phone booth."

"That's not a very good reason."

"It's a pretty good reason to me. OK, so neither of us have to spend time in fucking freezing cold, or creepy, phone booths."

"Much better."

"OK, wait, here's another one. So you don't have to worry about carrying matches. You can always just light your cigarette off of mine."

"OK, yeah, that's better. Got anymore?"

"Hmm, I don't know…let me think…Oh, I think I've got another one… So we could kiss almost constantly."

"Ooooh, don't you think our lips would get sore?"

"No, I don't think so. I think we'd build up really good kissing muscles. It would be fun trying."

"OK, yeah, I'm into that."

"What about you? Don't you have some reasons?"

"Hmmm. Now I feel pressure…Um, I know, we'd save lots of money on stamps."

"Stamp money?"

"Yeah, and paper, too. We'd save a lot."

"OK, OK. What else?"

"I don't know. I bet I could come up with a hundred reasons."

"You think so?"

"Yeah, I'm going to go home as soon as we're done and start working on them. You have to, too."

"A hundred?"

"Yeah, a hundred. Don't think you can do it?"

"Oh, I can do it."

"OK then, it's a deal. I have to go, Ben. I've got a list to make."

"Sarah, I love you. That's why we should be together."

"OK that's one for you. I love you, too, Ben."

"I'm coming down next week."

"Can't wait."

"Please don't go to any strange boys' houses in the middle of the night."

"Don't worry, Ben. You be careful."

"OK? So we'll talk Tuesday, same time. I'll call. "

"Same time. I'll be here. Goodnight, Ben, think of me when you go to bed."

"Don't worry, Sarah."

CHAPTER NINETEEN

January 19

THE WEATHERMEN KNOCKED ON OUR DOOR. Nobody ever knocked. Everybody always just came in. There were four of them, and Luke wasn't with them, which was a surprise. The whole scene was kind of awkward anyway. We didn't have too many scheduled meetings at Mountfort Street—it was more like this rolling happening that every once in awhile turned into some kind of event like a party or a heavy rap. So they stood in the doorway for awhile and then we got all sort of tangled up as we nodded and smiled and exchanged names. As we began moving down the hallway, one of the women who I didn't know—she looked really young and kind of hard—nodded at the flow of drawings and words on the wall and said, "Cool wall, man."

I led them into my room. Stu and Brian had split, having no interest in this little get-together. But Patrick from the apartment down the hall was there along with Mike and me. Jerry, who lived in Myles Standish, a dorm at Kenmore Square, and who ran with us at demonstrations, said he'd be there but he hadn't shown up yet.

Steve and Marsha were with Luke when Sarah and I saw him at Harvard Square. I'd run with Steve one night not long ago—the night after the cops killed Chicago Black Panthers Fred Hampton and Mark Clark.

Three groups went out from Mountfort Street after midnight to paint slogans around town. Steve and I went with Patrick and Matthew Wexler, the BU student government leader who was kind of a freak who we hung out with a lot. We all piled into Matthew's VW, loaded up with red and black spray paint, and hit the big Sears store, which wasn't far from Mountfort Street where we painted slogans on a huge sign of Ted Williams advertising fishing equipment ("Sorry, Ted" I actually thought at the time), the National Guard armory, which was our main target and which we attacked like a guerilla band with whispering and signals and lookouts and shit like that, and West Campus, which was across the street from the armory and we included just for old times' sake. We painted things like "Power to the Panthers," "NLF is going to win," "Avenge Fred and Mark" and "Fuck the Pigs." It was a rush, felt very clandestine and subversive. And a lot of fun.

The two I hadn't seen before were introduced as Cindy, who dug our wall, and Anthony. I was surprised that Steve and Marsha had brought people we didn't know. These two didn't reek like feds, but their presence added some tension to the room. Anthony was young, like Cindy, and both of them kind of hung back as we spread out over the two mattresses and the floor in my room, forming a loose U-shape, everybody with their backs to a wall. The Stones were playing on Mike's stereo—I knew the Weathermen dug the Stones—with the speakers on in my room, but low enough that we could talk. I had to pick Tavola up from a corner of the mattress under the windows, where she'd been inert since she'd crawled back in off the fire escape a couple of hours before. She just kind of flopped into the corner on the floor, hardly opened her eyes. Then, as I was moving a pile of magazines and papers and shit out of the way to clear another spot for someone, I dropped a bag of dope I had stashed there when I was trying to get my room together just before they came. It fell on the floor and a little pot spilled out of the bag. I was embarrassed, but everyone laughed so I just picked it up and set it on my desk.

"So where's Luke?" Mike asked.

"Things were gettin' kind of hot, so we decided it would be best if he got out of town for awhile," Marsha answered. Her long, stringy blond hair hung straight down to her shoulders, and her wide blue eyes flashed with a piercing intensity. She wore a brown sweater that was fuzzy with little wool balls. "Before he left, he made sure to remind us about comin' over here and talkin' to you guys. He really thinks we need to do some things together. He thought it would be cool for us to come even without him. Is it cool with you guys?"

I asked if Luke's, uh, vacation had to do with the Harvard thing, the felony charges he was facing after the Weathermen went kind of crazy at the Center for International Affairs at Harvard.

"That and other stuff," Steve said. He had a long oval face that was framed by a scrawny chin beard and short dark hair with uneven bangs. He also wore a beat-up sweater—his was black—and jeans. "The pigs were really focusin' on Luke, so we just thought it better for everybody if he was out of sight for a while. He's fine, though. He's still fightin'. He talks a lot about you guys, about what you did last year at B.U., about how you guys were more into doing shit rather than just talking." All the Weathermen seemed to try to not sound as smart or as intellectual as most of them were, so they slurred their pronunciations and avoided big words at all cost.

Then Steve looked at me and said, "Luke talks a lot about when you guys went to Boston English last year"—when Sarah and I went with Luke to a high school during the antimilitary campaign and the kids turned on us. "That was a big day for him. We went back there a few weeks ago—man," he said, smiling at Marsha, "those are some tough motherfuckin' kids. But shit, man, we gave 'em a good fight for awhile."

One of the tactics the Weathermen used was to go to working class high schools and chant communist slogans and basically challenge the kids to fight. Working class kids were central to their revolutionary strategy. They figured most of the adult white proletariat was hopelessly co-opted by the privilege America's imperial status gave them and most middle-class white college kids would run home to Mommy and Daddy as soon as shit got heavy. Working class kids were tough, not yet co-opted, and the bodies the government was using to make war on the Vietnamese. That's where the Weathermen were looking to get the recruits for their People's Army that would fight alongside the black liberation fighters, who would be the vanguard of the revolution. First, though, they had to show these kids they weren't a bunch of sissy-ass college intellectuals. So they'd go pick fights with them.

"We didn't really go there looking to fight that day," I answered, with a little bit of a laugh. Maybe Luke had. I know he was invigorated by the violence—while I was just confused—and he had yelled at the mob as the black kids escorted him out of there that he'd come back.

Luke kept his promise and did go back to Boston English, with Steve and Marsha and seven or eight others. This time, though, the Weathermen just kind of lined up on the school steps and raised their fists and said, basically, "Come on, let's go." I didn't really get that either.

The Stones' "No Expectations" filled in an awkward gap in the conversation after I let Steve know that my Boston English experience was a little different from Luke's—and his. Finally, Mike broke it: "So what are you guys into? What do you want from us?"

"Luke was right, no bullshit from you," Marsha said with a smile. "We just think we could work with you guys more, do some things together. Shit's gettin' heavy, man. And the people who really want to make a revolution in this country have to start workin' together. Luke knows you guys are serious about your politics, that you support the Vietnamese and the Panthers, that you dig youth culture, and that you're not afraid of action. You're the kind of people we want to work with. And we need to work together because the pigs aren't fuckin' around anymore. I know the shit's coming at you guys at BU, too."

Just then, Jerry came in, looked around the room and did a double take because everybody looked so serious and official. He said a kind of timid hello and we went around with introductions, and he found a spot just to the right of the door, turning our U into something of a circle.

The Weathermen were taking a lot of heat. Their actions were so provocative and up-front—the Days of Rage in Chicago, the thing at Harvard, fighting it out with high school kids—that they got arrested all the time, so much that a lot of their leaders had to go underground, which was pretty clearly where Luke was, though no one was saying it in those words. They were trying to develop a broader base of support to start building their People's Army. Working class kids weren't exactly thronging to their collectives. The Weathermen had been down on most of the student movement, but it seems like they had determined that their best hope for short-term allies were the radical freaks, the hippie militants: those strange creatures whose political line was some imprecise mixture of loving rock-and-roll, supporting the NLF, smoking dope, fighting in the streets, hating racism, goofing on the straight left, believing in their friends, smashing the state by any means necessary, and equal helpings of Karl and Groucho Marx and Vladimir and John Lenin/Lennon. Us.

"What kind of stuff?" I asked.

"Well we gotta keep working on Panther support," Steve answered. "You guys have been solid there. But we gotta do more than pass out leaflets and paint slogans on buildings."

"So what can we do?" Patrick asked. Over the past few months, Patrick had spent more time in our apartment and less in his own. His roommates never came over. They were pretty straight. Patrick himself still had some remnants of his preppy past showing: his hair was safely long, his beard neatly trimmed. But he got stoned with us more and went into the streets with us.

"We just can't let the pigs get away with the kind of shit they're doin' to Bobby in Chicago"—talking about the gagging of Black Panther Bobby Seale during the Chicago Conspiracy Trail—"or what they did to Mark and Fred," Marsha said. "When they fuck with the Panthers, we've got to fuck with them."

We all nodded and kind of muttered "Right on."

Jerry looked slowly around the room and then asked, kind of softly, "What k-k-kind of things are you talking about?" Jerry, another CBS kid, sometimes seemed just a beat out of rhythm, but he was solid.

Marsha did her own sweep around the room, lips tight and eyes hard. She was picking her words carefully. Then she smiled. "Breakin' shit and hurtin' pigs. We obviously don't want to get too much into specific tactics here and now. It's good to know that you guys understand what's happening with the Panthers and the need for white radicals and revolutionaries to respond." She looked straight at Mike and then me. "And we do have an idea for a specific action where we can start working together. Where we can get a sense of how we work together in the streets." She nodded at Steve that he should pick up where she left off. The Weathermen were into this no-leaders thing. But there was no doubt Marsha was the leader of this group.

"Hayakawa—the pig president from San Francisco State—is comin' to speak in Boston at the end of next week," Steve said. "At Northeastern. He is a motherfucker. He crushed a student rebellion led by third-world students, called the pigs in and let them loose against the Chicano and black students who'd formed this far-out coalition."

"Yeah, we know who he is and what he did," Mike said, reminding Steve that we weren't some spaced-out runaways on the Boston Common, where, based on the silent Anthony and Cindy, it seemed like the Weathermen were doing a lot of their recruiting.

"OK. Sure." Steve looked to Marsha, who nodded, and then back to Mike. "Sure. So anyway, it's a perfect situation for an action. This motherfucker speakin' at the most working class college in Boston." Just then, I heard the record making that crackling sound of being stuck in the last groove of the side, so I got up to flip it over.

It was strange moving from my room full of people and heavy vibes out into the quiet hall and then into Mike's room, so neat and still. The voices coming from my room sounded far off, like they were drifting through a long tunnel from another world. I flipped the album over and wiped the top side with my sleeve and set it back down. I turned the volume up just a little before I gently lowered the needle into the opening groove of side two. The raucous opening chords of "Street Fighting Man" stopped all the talking for a moment.

When I went back into my room, everyone smiled at me. "Good song," Marsha said.

Steve seemed to pick up where the suddenly louder song had interrupted him. "So we don't think it's going to be anything too heavy or anything. Probably not that many people. But it's a good chance for us to bring home the oppression of third-world people by this society to kids from working class families. And it's a chance for you guys to be in an action together with us, not much risk, but a chance to get a feeling for how we work together, see if we can trust each other."

Mike looked at me, then at Patrick and Jerry, sort of gathering consent to speak for us. "We'll probably be there. The four of us—right, you guys?" We all nodded. "And probably a few more people. Cool people. People Luke knows. We can check out the scene and figure on hanging together, but I think we want to keep our own affinity group, the people we're used to having beside us in the streets. We don't know the rest of your people. We don't know Northeastern. We really won't know what the scene is going to be until we get there. So we'll show up. We'll find you and then we'll take it from there."

"That's cool," Marsha said. "The Northeastern SDS will get some people there, but they don't seem to know what they're going to do. Who gives a shit what they're going to do? Some other groups from around the city are going to show up, but I think it's going to be mostly folks who are into action. It should be interesting. Cool."

There was another lull in the conversation, the business they'd come for apparently taken care of. Anthony kind of wiggled in his spot and looked around the room and finally spoke, "Hey, man, do you think we could smoke a joint of that pot we saw." He looked at Marsha, who grinned approval.

We all laughed. Mike spoke—even though it was my dope. "Yeah, Tucker, where are your manners? Roll these folks a joint."

"Sure, Mike," I laughed. I grabbed the bag off my desk—payment for a paper on John Stuart Mill I'd whipped out for a dope-dealing friend. I crumbled up a couple of buds onto a magazine and used the top of the rolling papers to rake the flakes, so the seeds would roll out of the pile. I rolled a big fat one and lit it up. As I passed it to Cindy who sat, still quiet, to my left, I looked at Marsha and asked, as I blew out the smoke. "So what the hell happened in Flint?"

"What do you mean?" she asked. The Weathermen had had what they called a National War Council at the end of December in Flint, Michigan. It was supposed to be a happening where youth culture and armed struggle came together—music and celebration and kick-ass revolution. But the party that was supposed to go along with the politics fizzled, and the main thing we'd heard about it was that they were talking about digging Charles Manson, who led a gang of mostly women to kill seven people, including a Hollywood star named Sharon Tate—killed her and her guests, ate the dinner the victims were about to eat, and then stabbed Tate in her pregnant belly with a fork.

"What's with this Manson shit? We heard people were making fork signs and saying how cool Charlie Manson was. Where's that at?" I asked.

"He killed pigs, man. We're all going to have to kill pigs eventually," Steve said matter of factly as he took the joint from Patrick and took a long pull on it.

"Seems like a sick fucker to me," Patrick said as he exhaled. "I mean what's political about murdering some rich people? What good does that do the Vietnamese or the Panthers?"

"Killin' rich honkies is revolutionary," Marsha said. "Most white people are too fuckin' privileged to ever become revolutionary. They are the enemy. Anything that fucks them up or scares them or hurts them is right on. We're all still pretty timid about real violence—killin' people and shit. But man the revolution ain't going to be a fucking tea party, there's gonna be lots of white honky blood shed. Charlie Manson wasn't afraid of shedding some."

Whew. It was this kind of shit from the Weathermen that turned so many in the Movement off. I looked at Mike as he handed the joint to Marsha. His face straining a bit trying to hold his hit down, he kind of raised his eyebrows to me. Marsha held the joint to her mouth and focused her eyes on the glow of the tip, which brightened as she drew hard on it.

"Well, I don't think I dig him," I said. Jerry and Patrick nodded their agreement with me. Mike shrugged. Marsha slowly shook her head as she held her breath and passed the joint to Jerry. She giggled when she finally exhaled.

"Shit, man, I probably wouldn't dig him to hang out with," she said. "But I'm not going cry over rich white people gettin' killed in their mansions when our fuckin' government is massacrin' the Vietnamese and wagin' war on black people in this country."

"Fuck Charlie Manson," Mike said. "Who the fuck is Charlie Manson? He's some asshole charged with murder. Who knows what his trip is? He ain't my hero but I don't know enough to condemn him either. It's just kind of bullshit for you guys to make him some kind of people's hero just cause he offed some pigs. It just seems like cheap, showy bullshit. Fuck him. He ain't going to be at Northeastern or help Luke or any of the people who got busted at the GE riots. He's just part of some media circus. Fuck him."

Patrick laughed first, something about Mike's tone and the heaviness in the room, and we were all starting to feel stoned, as the joint made its way around the room for a second time. Pretty soon, everyone was laughing, so Mike felt the call for an encore. "What?" he said with a big grin. "I say FUCK him, man," he said with extra emphasis. "Fuck HIM."

The Weather people were all laughing really hard. Anthony was even a little out of control, had a hard time catching his breath. It's like they hadn't gotten stoned or laughed for a while, or both, and they kind of overdid it—sort of like their politics, I thought. Even Marsha was giggling, her eyes had softened up, her mouth relaxed as she wiped a speck of dope from her lips. For the first time, I noticed she was actually kind of pretty, sharp cheekbones and a long neck, and she was well-shaped beneath her ratty sweater.

The conversation rambled. It was almost like recess for the Weather people. Anthony came alive. When the Stones record ended, he asked if we had any Creedence, so I went into Mike's room and found *Willy and the Poor Boys*. A great album. I stuck it on the turntable and turned it way up. The funky beat of the title tune filled the apartment.

When I went back to my room, Marsha was standing up and dancing. She'd learned a step or two somewhere along the way. She gave me a big smile. I smiled back. Anthony was standing on my mattress and doing something sort of like dancing, bending at the knees, shaking his bowed head, and throwing his hands into the air. Steve and Cindy were just kind of grooving in place. Jerry and Patrick were laying back digging the music. Mike was moving his head in time with the music, eyes shut. I stood in the doorway for a while, chuckling to myself as I took this scene in: Some fierce People's Army we were putting together. Mike opened his eyes for a second and saw me checking him out. He raised his head and showed a visible laugh.

I watched Marsha dance. She moved with a fluid grace and a glow that told me she knew how good she looked in motion and that she liked that I was watching her, that I was digging the smooth roll of her hips and the flopping bounce of her breasts beneath her heavy sweater. And the light in her eyes. I wondered where she was a year ago or two years or four years ago, before the Days of Rage and the Weather world. A star student, serious and studious? Believed in Martin Luther King and the power of thoughtful, peaceful protest? Earnest? Concerned? Somebody's daughter? Somebody's girl friend? Liked the Fifth Dimension or The Supremes or the Association? Thought about being a doctor or a lawyer or a poet? About being a wife or a mother? About a future that had no idea about offing pigs and sticking forks in pregnant bellies?

I worked my way back into my spot on my mattress between dancing Anthony and Cindy. Marsha, opposite me, sat back down after the song ended, her cheeks bright red and shiny. There was a shyness to her smile now, like she'd shown something she hadn't meant to. She and Steve exchanged questioning looks. Just who was recruiting who—and to what—in this little get together? I wondered what it was like in their collective? How it was different from Mountfort Street. I mean, shit, I knew it was a totally different trip. Men and women living together for one thing. They condemned monogamy but dug sex. They practiced collective discipline but politically embraced "youth culture." So fucking different people in the collective, changing partners all the time, was part of their political trip, I guess. Shit, they talked about communist sexual relations. How did that work? From each according to his ability, to each according to his needs? Wow. How do you figure that? Was there a schedule? Did they rotate? Did all the women have to fuck all the men? Supposed they liked somebody best? Suppose they didn't like somebody? Did all the women want to sleep with Luke? Did all the men want Marsha? Who had Marsha slept with the night before? Who would she sleep with tonight? Fuck, man, it was hard to get a handle on how that would work. And the youth culture thing? It was like they took acid and dug rock and roll because their Marxist-Leninist analysis of current concrete conditions in latter day capitalist society told them that was the right political thing to do. Shit, man, we just did it.

Cindy pulled close to my ear and told me again how cool she thought our wall was. I laughed. I told her that some women's liberation folks thought it was chauvinist and counterrevolutionary and wanted to paint it over. She looked amazed. "Man, those sisters have got to lighten up," she said. "If they spent more time supporting the Vietnamese and black people instead of getting uptight about a little right-on artwork, they'd be better off." She'd learned the Weathermen line on woman's liberation well. Then her eyes brightened and she said, "Hey, man, do you still have any pens or paints? I'd like to add something to the wall if that'd be cool."

I dug around in my desk and finally came up with red and black magic markers and gave them to her. She giggled as she headed out to the hall. As I went to sit back down, Anthony extended his hand to me, we did a kind of thumb-lock handshake, and he said, "Man, thanks for the pot. This is the best pot I ever had, I think. Man, is it like Panama Red or Acapulco Gold or something?" His eyes were open wide, his pupils little bbs.

"It's cool, man," I said, digging just how stoned and silly he was. "Glad you like it. It's just some decent Mexican."

The room was now divided into little conversation groups, the rumble of talk and laughter rising to meet the volume of the music. Then the last song on the side ended and it was like we were all shouting. Everyone stopped talking at once, looked around the room for a beat or two, and, as if someone had given a signal, started laughing in unison. Just then, Stu popped his head in my doorway.

"Well, I see I'm just in time for the revolution. Where are the pigs? Let's get 'em," he said.

"Hey, man," I said. "You're just in time to flip the record over. Then it's time for the revolution."

"I'll do it for The People," he said looking around the room. "Not for you," he said smiling at me.

As Stu went to flip the record, I could hear Brian, who had come in with Stu, and Cindy talking in the hallway. Cindy showing Brian her favorite parts of the wall, Brian reacting enthusiastically and pointing out some of his favorites. It probably hadn't quite registered with Brian yet that she was a Weather person—a serious revolutionary—and I'm sure he was sizing her up, wondering what his prospects were. She was kind of cute, though a little on the skinny and young side.

The music came blasting through again—"Fortunate Son." When Stu reappeared in my doorway I signaled to him to turn it down a bit, so we could talk a little better. He gave me a disgusted look and then went and did it. I rolled another joint, as Anthony looked at me kind of amazed, as if to say—with a little bit of fear and some excitement, too—"another one?"

When Stu came back, I lit the joint and handed it to him. The smell of dope lured Brian from the hallway. Stu handed the joint to him. They sat on the floor in the middle of the circle and we did another round of introductions.

"So are these some of the guys who will be joining us at Northeastern?" Marsha asked.

Mike looked up, a shit-eating grin on his face. "Nah, Stuey and Brian won't be joining us at Northeastern. Will you, boys?"

Stu look straight-faced at Mike, "Who's playing at Northeastern?" Brian laughed.

"Nobody's playing, man," Mike said. "Just a little street action. A little rumble with the ruling class. You boys up for that?"

"Only if you promise I'll get to see my hero, Mikey, putting his money where his larger than life mouth is, kicking some piggy ass." Stu said.

Brian, pulling hard on the joint, had to laugh and cough out his lung-full of smoke. "Right on," he said and took another long hit.

"Hey, it's cool," Marsha said. "Just wondered."

"Yeah, my brother Stu is not into that kind of thing," Mike said, his eyes all scrunched up beneath his glasses, a mocking smile stretching his face. "He's into peace and love. Peace AND love. Right, man?"

"Hey, I'll give you a piece of my love if you keep up this shit," Stu said. Anthony was laughing now. This Laurel-and-Hardy-like exchange had pulled Cindy away from her drawing and she was standing in the door-way looking confused. Stu looked at Marsha and Steve and said, "You guys really take him seriously?"

Marsha couldn't help but laugh, the way Stu punctuated his question with a look of total disbelief. As the joint came around one more time, she held up her hand to say no. "I'm already plenty stoned," she said. "Can't you tell?"

"Too stoned, what's that?" Brian said, laughing as he said it. This was amazing, Brian getting stoned with Weathermen. And laughing. Steve wasn't taking any more hits either, but everybody else was.

Marsha forced a smile, and then she looked seriously over at Steve. "We probably ought to be going." Steve nodded. Anthony looked disappointed. Cindy hurried back into the hall to finish her drawing.

"So really what's going on at Northeastern?" Stu looked at me, not expecting to get a straight answer out of Mike.

"A pig named Hayakawa's going to speak. So some people are going to show up to let him know we think he's a fucking asshole. These folks are going," I said, nodding at Steve and Marsha. "And we're going to go and we'll see what happens. Sound like fun, Stu?"

"Nah, that's not my department. I'm better at scouting out the groups at the Tea Party." He looked at Marsha. "If you want to know if the Saturday show is worthwhile, then I'm your man." I'm not sure Marsha knew what he was talking about but she couldn't help but smile at him because that's just how Stu affected people. "Northeastern? Hayawhatshisfuck? Fighting pigs? Stick with Mikey Mouth and Tucker and these guys."

"Thanks, I'll remember that," Marsha said, laughing. "Glad we met you," she grinned at Stu and kind of nodded at Brian. Then she looked around the room at Jerry and Patrick and Mike and then me. Her look was kind of forced friendly now, she was back in her role. "It was good talkin' to you guys. Thanks for the high and the music. We'll see you at Northeastern. Right?"

"We'll find you," Mike said.

"If you talk to Luke, say hi for us," I said, immediately realizing that was a silly thing to say. Like a fucking high school kid talking to kids from a different high school.

"Right on," Steve said, smiling, humoring me. He still didn't quite get where we were coming from, so my juvenile comment must not have even struck him as odd.

They filed out almost as awkwardly as they had come in. Anthony, lagging behind, flashed a big old smile and a quick clenched fist. Cindy had to go around the others in the hall to poke her head in the doorway to say goodbye and that she hoped we liked her drawing.

As we heard them make their way down the hall and out the door, we all just sat there, suspended. When the door shut behind them, we all exhaled at the same time and exchanged smiles.

The record ended, but we all just sat there in the quiet for a few seconds until, not surprisingly, it was Brian who spoke. "Man, those dudes are a trip aren't they?" He said looking at me and then Mike and then to Stu, where he knew he had the best chance of getting agreement. "What was with this chick, here?" he said, pointing to where Marsha had been sitting. "She seemed pretty uptight, like she couldn't handle her weed or something."

"I think she liked me," Stu said and gave me a sly look.

"Shit, everybody loves you Stuey," Mike said. "Hey man, she was cool. She doesn't smoke a lot of dope. Obviously. Then you fuckers come in and she just couldn't figure what to make of you. I can understand that. I have that problem myself."

"Yeah, I thought she was really cool. She was definitely the most together one of them," Patrick said. "Except for the Manson thing. I just don't get that."

"Me neither," I said. Stu asked what we meant by the Manson thing and I told him what Steve and Marsha had said.

"Oooh, I don't know if I want her to like me now," Stu said.

"I liked her," I said.

"I think she liked you, too," Patrick said with a mischievous laugh.

"No, I don't mean anything like that," I said, not acknowledging any reality behind Patrick's little comment. That was one of those things that was there for a second, but that second was passed and whatever it held was gone, a possibility not pursued and now seeming nothing but absurd. "It's like with Luke. He's so smart and I agree with a lot of where they're at on an intellectual level—about capitalism and shit, and even revolution, and I like him, like I liked Marsha, but there's something that not quite real, not quite…I don't know."

"I know what you mean," Jerry said. "It's l-l-like the words coming out of her mouth don't match what she seems like as a person."

"That Cindy was pretty cute, I thought," Brian jumped in. "It's hard to imagine her offing pigs."

"Yeah I know what you mean, Jerry," I said. "It's like basing your life on your politics rather than your politics on your life, or something like that. It doesn't seem real that way. I mean you change your line and suddenly things that aren't cool—smoking dope, randomly killing rich people—become cool. You have a collective meeting to decide who you fuck or who fucks you. I just don't know about that."

"They have collective meetings to decide who fucks who?" Brian was in shock.

"I don't know exactly how it works," I said. "But I don't think they believe in good old fashion love and romance."

"Shit, now I really hope she didn't like me," Stu said. "But man if they think Charlie Manson is cool, than I think they're assholes."

"Of course they're assholes, Stuey, but so are you and so am I and so is everybody in this room," Mike said. "We're all assholes. It's just that it happens I like you and, I think, most of the time you like me. And of course what they say is bullshit. It's a little less bullshit than what PL says and a lot less bullshit than what the pigs say, but it's still bullshit. You know that. I know that. It's all bullshit, Stu. Everybody's an asshole and it's all bullshit. Sure communism makes more sense than capitalism but it's still bullshit for us to be sitting here in the middle of capitalist America in 1970 and talking about communism. We have no real idea what that means. It's bullshit for the Weathermen to talk about digging Charlie Manson because they want to make violence cool. It's bullshit for you to say you don't dig violence and go off to your rock and roll shows while the pigs are killing Panthers and Vietnamese and beating the shit out of our friends at demonstrations. It's bullshit for Tucker to make fun of the way the Weathermen treat sex just because he's gaga over some chick and can't fathom sharing her with his comrades. It's bullshit for Brian to be hitting on some little Weather chickie when he don't even know the first thing about her or them or anything. It's bullshit for me to tell you it's all bullshit. That's because I'm just as much an asshole as the rest of you."

"So what the hell are we supposed to do, Mike?" Brian asked, exasperated.

"You're asking me? I'll tell ya, but that's bullshit, too. What's real is the six of us sitting in this room, getting high, listening to music. Beyond that, it's a pisser. I mean we can't just crawl in a hole and let the world pass around us—as much as Stu might like that," he laughed. "But, shit, man, that wouldn't even be any fun. So you gotta pick what bullshit you want to believe, what assholes you want to hang with. I think we gotta fight the pigs. I think the pigs are fucking over way too many people. They're killing people, they're screwing up the world, they make beautiful shit ugly. Besides that, it makes me feel good to fight the pigs. I can quote you Marx and Marcuse all day long, give you intellectual justification for any fucking thing you want, but the truth is it makes me feel fucking alive to fuck with the pigs. When I'm in the streets next to Tucker and Patrick and Jerry, I know I'm on the right side. I also dig smoking pot and listening to rock and roll, so I do that. And I want to hang with you assholes. Don't ask me to explain that.

"The thing is, man, you've got to pick your bullshit. And I'm going to do everything I can to convince you that my bullshit is better than yours. But if you're being real to yourself, you take what you want out of that and leave the rest. That's why I can dig the Weathermen. That's why I can dig where Stu and you are coming from. I think you're totally wrong about some things, of course, but I know you're my brothers and you're being what you gotta be. Assholes." He smiled. "How about another fucking joint, Tucker?"

"Yeah, thanks Mike, that clears everything up." Stu said. "Oh and by the way: Fuck you, too." But I could hear admiration in his voice.

I rolled a joint, chuckling to myself. Fucking Mike, man. Stu got up to put some music on, mellowing things out a bit with Dylan's *John Wesley Harding*. Jerry was asking Mike about what he thought the Weatherman would want to do at Northeastern. Pick a fight, is what I thought I heard Mike say. Patrick and Brian were talking about some people Brian and Stu had run into while they were out. I lit the joint, handed it to Mike and stood up and stretched.

I really needed just to move around a bit, so I wandered into the hallway. As I did I remembered Cindy and her eagerness to add something to the collage on our wall. I scanned the wall trying to find it. It stood out in stark black and red surrounded by purples and pinks and oranges and greens, right between Mr. Natural saying, "Don't mean sheet" and the Firesign Theatre quote, "How can you be in two places at once, when you aren't anywhere at all?" It was a stick figure, straight black line going down, two arms going up, two legs spreading from the bottom of it. A black rectangle with a red star in the middle was hung like a shirt off the up-and-down line. A circle sat on top, the head, with thin black lines shooting out from it, the hair, I guessed, of a woman. One of the upright arms held a crude looking gun—an uneven triangle at one end for the butt, a line for the barrel with a semi-circle for the trigger. A dialogue balloon came from a little line in the middle of the head circle. Inside the balloon in all capital bold red letters, it said "OFF THE PIGS!!!." Below the figure, she'd signed her name in black, and dotted the i with a small red star.

CHAPTER TWENTY

January 21

THE NEPCO HOT DOG FACTORY WAS STUCK in the industrial hinterlands of Allston, so it was a long walk home and it was cold. But man, I just didn't feel like hitchhiking and I didn't have a quarter for the MTA. I didn't want to talk to anybody, didn't even want to have to look at anybody, or have to work hard not to talk to or look at somebody. I got out of that place and started walking, my head whirling but I didn't even want to try to slow it down to make any sense of anything. I kicked at whatever got in my way: candy wrappers, empty cigarette packs, the little milk cartons like they always used to give us in elementary school. Just kick 'em, let loose on 'em, and see where they'd go. My hands were shoved deep into my pockets, my shoulders pulled in tight, so I was a contained bundle, moving in my own world, past the cold fenced factories, the streets filling with workers heading home, darkness creeping over the city. "Fuck 'em," was the only thought I had that made any sense.

"Do you have any food processing experience?" the guy had asked me. Shit. I hated applying for jobs, filling out those applications in those little synthetic-feeling rooms, with thin veneer walls and flimsy doors, plastic chairs and cheap tables that wobbled underneath the forms. I had a hard enough time filling out the forms without them moving on me. Food processing experience? Shit man, I didn't have any experience that mattered to them. "Singer in a rock and roll band" was always good. Younger summers in the corn fields? A week and a half as a busboy at the Country Squire Steak House before I quit because they told me to cut my hair? Even the few weeks I'd spent cleaning the Shawmut Bank in Kenmore Square with Mike and Stu and Walter didn't count because it wasn't even really me who had that job. I was just filling in for Jeffrey, who quit because his back was bothering him. And references? Mike? Stu? My lawyer Harry? Dean Dexter? Prejudge Hall? Yeah, I had references. Shit. And the guy who interviewed me was always an incredibly straight person with a thin tie and worn white shirt, who hated me when I walked in the door, had already decided there was no way in hell he was going to give me this job, but he was going to let me fill out the forms so he could laugh at it before he rolled it up and threw it in the trash can as soon as I left. Food processing experience? Fuck 'em.

The Nepco job would have been a good one. Paid $3.90 an hour. Four to ten, five nights a week. Shit, man, I'd be rich. But it wasn't going to happen. The thing was if I got the job, I'd have to spend all my nights in a fucking factory making hot dogs. The thought of actually getting the job was even more depressing than the reality that I never had a chance of getting the job in the first place. It was a drag to have to pretend that I actually wanted to do that. But I hated asking my parents for money. I had a hard time stretching my band check—when they remembered to send it—and my paper writing only occasionally brought cash. I had to keep looking.

Walking and kicking felt good. Along Brighton Avenue, the dreary block-wide factories gave way to smaller shops and stores. Shit man, here I was—revolutionary, aspiring poet, legendary Eastern Central Illinois rock star—applying for a job in a hot dog factory. And bummed cause I wasn't going to get it. And at the same time happy as hell that I wasn't going to get it. I laughed. Fuck 'em.

Hitting the commotion of Comm Ave was like reentering my world, leaving the world of thin-tied straight people and impossible forms behind. And I laid my foot into a green and gold Narragansett Beer can that was teed up on the lip of the driveway to a closed furniture warehouse. "Hi neighbor, have a 'Gansett"—the refrain that popped up between the innings of the Red Sox games I'd listen to as a kid—I thought, as the can sailed into the frenzied flow of traffic that roared past me. I watched it bounce off the tire of one car, take a hop into the fender of another, and then disappear in the lights and the motion, crushed no doubt by some car driven by some guy who had no idea what he'd done, no idea that I was standing on the side of this bustling avenue watching this old empty beer can get swept away in this torrent, no idea that we were now connected and always would be.

I yanked my hands out of my coat pockets and dug through my pants pockets to find a cigarette. And dug some more to find some matches. That first long, deep draw filled me with a rippling gritty charge. Then with the long exhale, I felt my whole body let go of the armor of tightness I'd worn into my little skirmish with the straight world. Shit, man, what a day.

I'd woke up that morning to Stu screaming about his fucking cereal. Mike and I had stayed up late the night before getting high, rapping about all the heavy shit that was coming down, the injunction, the Weathermen—and Sarah, what was I going to say? What was I going to do when I got to Philly? I knew we were moving in different directions and that if that something didn't happen soon, the distance could just fucking overwhelm us. Mike wasn't much help with that—Paulie had decided not to move to Boston, after all, and Mike was back to his cynical view of romance. But he listened as I ranted.

Mike got a bad case of the munchies and the only thing to eat in the apartment were Stu's Frosted Flakes. Stu had to get up at 7 o'clock every morning to get to work by eight and had developed a ritual where he got the newspaper from the corner store and he'd read the sports section over his bowl of Frosted Flakes. That was about the only rule in Mountfort Street: hands off Stu's Frosted Flakes. I mean, shit, he had to go to work. The rest of us kind of ambled over to school or the union and could always find something to eat somewhere. So Stu's Frosted Flakes were sacred ground, off-limits. But Mike couldn't help himself. Stu was asleep.

We were stoned. Mike grabbed the cereal and just started taking handfuls. I had a little bit, but I told Mike to make sure that there was some left for Stu, not to eat it all. I'm sure he didn't really mean to, but all of a sudden the box was empty and he kind of looked at me with this sheepish expression and said, "Ooops." At the time, I couldn't help but laugh at him, but I knew Stu was going to be pissed.

So Stu woke up and freaked out. Started screaming at Mike. Mike always woke up grumpy. He couldn't fucking see anything for one thing, his eyes were all sort of clouded over. He was like a grotesque mole right out of his hole. So when Stu started screaming, he just yelled back at him: "Man if there's cereal in this apartment and I'm hungry, I'm going to eat it." Which only pissed Stu off more. I lay in bed and listened as long as I could, then got up to try to get them to calm down. But neither of them would listen to me and Stu took off for work, hungry and pissed.

Then at lunchtime over burgers, word spread that a coroner's jury in Chicago had ruled the killings of Fred Hampton and Mark Clark justifiable homicide. Motherfuckers. Justifiable homicide. An army of cops kicked in the door of the Panthers' apartment at 4:30 in the morning, shot Mark Clark in the chest at point-blank range. He was a seventeen-year-old kid who was sleeping on a couch in the living room—kind of like Lenny in our apartment. Fred Hampton—who was only twenty, basically my age—was killed in his bed. Four others Panthers were wounded. The Panthers were able to get off one shot in self-defense, and the survivors were charged with attempted murder. Justifiable fucking homicide. The pigs were out of control. The Chicago Conspiracy Trial was nearing a verdict and no matter what happened there, shit was going to fly. I thought about Luke and Marsha and the other Weathermen. Shit man, they were right to be so angry. I was angry, too. And then I had to try to get my shit together to act as straight as I could for some asshole at a hot dog factory.

After the long walk home from Nepco, I stumbled into our apartment, shed of the depression I left the job interview with, pissed about the Panthers, worrying about Sarah but anxious to get there and see her, wondering if Stu and Mike had worked out their trip yet. The apartment was quiet, surprising since we had eight people staying there at the time—the four regulars, plus Lenny who had a couple of weeks leave before having to go somewhere to do some heavy duty training, and the boys from New York (some freaks from the Bronx Stu and Mike had met at the Miami Pop Festival). Stu's door was closed but I could hear some music coming from his room. I went into Mike's room and he was in his chair reading. He grunted at me. I sat on his bed and told him about the hot dog factory. He nodded but he didn't really look very interested. Stu must have heard me because he came in, and I asked him about his day at work.

Mike looked up from his book when Stu said his day was OK for work, especially considering he'd had to start his day without any cereal.

"So you enjoy running a concentration camp for animals?" Mike said, in kind of a flat tone. Stu worked at Beth Israel Hospital in the research area. He took care of the animals who were used in experiments, fed them and cleaned their cages, stuff like that. Sometimes he'd come home and tell us about the rabbits or the mice. I think he actually liked the job for the most part—for a job.

Stu looked at Mike for a second, kind of flared his eyes and then looked back to me to continue our conversation.

"How many animals did you send to their death today, Stuey?" Mike was smiling but his voice was harsh. I laughed but tried to get Mike to stop. "C'mon Mike," I said.

"Fuck you, Mike." Stu glared.

"Fuzzy little rabbits?" Mike said, putting a little mock sweetness in his voice. "Cuddly little rats? Dogs? How about dogs, Stu? Did you kill any dogs today?"

"Fuck you," Stu said. "I didn't kill anything. You know, if your pecker was half as big as your mouth, you might get laid every once in awhile."

"No you don't kill anything. You just fatten them up and lull them into a sense of security before you send them to the ovens. Just like Eichmann."

"Mike," I said. "Come on."

"Hey Tucker it's not my fault that we have fucking Adolph Eichmann of the animal world living in our apartment. I'd think you'd be as shocked as I am at what Stu is doing to those animals."

"Fuck you, Mike," Stu turned to leave.

"How do you know what happens to the animals?" I asked Mike. "I'm sure Stu treats 'em good."

"Shit, Tucker, you sound just like the good Germans," Mike said. "They're just sending the Jews away for a little vacation. I'm sure the kind Nazis wouldn't do anything to hurt them." Then he looked at Stu: "Eichmann."

"Fuck you, Mike." Stu said and gave Mike the finger with both hands as he left the room."

"Eichmann," Mike yelled after him.

Mike looked at me and smiled and kind of chuckled.

"Shit man. It's really not funny, Mike," I said.

"Ah, I'm just busting his balls. He knows that."

"He might know it, but he doesn't seem to like it."

"It's cool man. Don't worry about it. Stu can take it." Mike stood up to put some music on. Just then, Stu came running back into the room. He had a small camping hatchet in his right hand and he leaped on Mike, jumped on his back, knocking him to the floor and riding him down. He swung the hatchet way back behind his head—as if he was going to crush Mike's skull.

"You've gone too far this time, you fucking asshole, why do you have to just keep sticking the needle in, deeper and deeper. This time, man, you really pissed me off and I'm going to make you sorry." Stu was flipping out, screaming.

Mike was trying to laugh, but Stu definitely had him in a tough spot. "Hey, man, fuck you, can't you take a joke? Get the fuck off me. Are you crazy? I was just kidding, man."

I jumped up from the bed and grabbed Stu's arm before he could swing it. I was freaking out: "Stu, come on man, it's just Mike's bullshit. He didn't mean anything. Mike, why don't you just shut up for a minute."

"Tucker, you know he's an asshole," Stu tried to lower his voice to sound more in control, but his eyes still were screaming like a maniac. "Let me just have a few whacks at him."

"Stu!?" I yelled.

"Oh, man, I'm really fucking scared," Mike said with his face into the floor. "You better fucking get some good whacks in because you know as soon as I get up off this floor, you're a dead man. Eichmann."

At that, Stu pulled his arm up suddenly to try to break my grip.

"You guys, shit!" I yelled. I was wedged in between them, trying to keep hold of Stu's arm so he couldn't swing it and my back was pushed against Mike's back, so I was helping to drive him into the floor. We were locked in that position when Brian walked in.

"What the hell are you guys doing?" Brian asked, surprised but laughing, too.

Stu turned his head slowly toward where Brian was standing, let up on the downward pressure of his arm, then smiled and said, "We're goofing on Tucker."

What he said didn't really register with me at first until Brian laughed and said, "Well you looked pretty convincing to me. I thought you guys were trying to kill each other."

"You assholes," I said, letting go of Stu's hand and rolling off Mike's back to sit on the floor. I rubbed my hands across my face to wipe away the sweat I'd work up trying to stop my two best friends from killing each other. "You assholes."

They were all laughing. Mike rolled over on his back, laughing hard and smiling big at me. Fucking proud of himself. I kicked at him. He stopped laughing. "Hey man," he said, "you've just been way too uptight lately. So me and Stu came up with our little plan to snap you out of it. Ain't that right, Stuey boy?"

"Yeah, man," Stu said when he stopped laughing long enough to talk. "I couldn't believe the look on your face when you came diving at me off the bed. Your eyes were like flying saucers."

"You assholes," I couldn't think of anything else to say. "You fucking assholes."

"Stu, you were maybe just a little too convincing," Mike said. "When you jumped on my back, man, I wasn't sure for a second whether you were really kidding or not."

"I must admit, Mikey, the thought did cross my mind of all the times you have been a true asshole and I was tempted just a little to get one good swing at you, but then I remembered the true target of our mission today."

"You assholes," I said. "I should have just let you kill each other. A long time ago."

"Hey Tucker," Brian said. "You've gotta admit they got you. Good. You looked pretty funny stuck in between them."

"Yeah, they got me, but they're still fucking assholes. And so are you for that matter." I got up and walked out of the room. It was quiet as I left, but by the time I got to my room I could hear them talking and laughing again. I went in and shut the door. I lay on my mattress, rubbed my hands against my face again, trying to kind of scrub away all the shit that had been thrown at me that day. "Fucking assholes," I thought. "Fuck 'em." Then I laughed quietly to myself as I remembered the crazed look on Stu's face as he came charging into Mike's room, hatchet high. I heard louder laughter and now music coming from Mike's room. Assholes, I thought again, but I smiled as I picked up a notebook lying on the floor next to my bed to start a letter to Sarah, even though I was going to see her in two days.

CHAPTER TWENTY-ONE

January 23

MY LAST RIDE—A COUPLE FREAKS DRIVING a beat-up old Ford van heading from New Brunswick, New Jersey, to Cincinnati—left me off at the Willow Grove exit. It was dark and fucking freezing as I walked up the long exit ramp, but I felt pretty damn good. I'd left Boston in mid-morning, later than I'd hoped, but I'd gotten good rides all the way: from the Mass Pike entrance to Sturbridge; from there all the way to the Tappan Zee Bridge with some crazy motherfuckers who were heading into the City. It took me a few short rides to get out of the shadow of New York. The worst wait was on the New Jersey Turnpike near New Brunswick. The New Jersey pigs were assholes about hitchhiking. Shit, I was standing about twenty feet in front of a sign that said "Hitchhiking Prohibited," looking out for cops in the oncoming traffic, when the Ford van picked me up and they told me they were going all the way past Philly. Cool. We even smoked a couple of joints along the way. I still had a decent buzz as I dug into my pockets for a dime to call Sarah from the phone booth by the truck stop at the top of the exit ramp.

Her father answered. Shit. We didn't even bother with any niceties. I asked to speak to Sarah—no doubt he knew who it was—and he told me, in a voice deflated with disgust, to hold on a minute. I think they were in the middle of dinner or something, which must have just pissed him off more. I could hear him say to Sarah, "It's for you" and I guess she could tell from his displeasure that it was me, because her voice was already celebrating when she got on the phone, "Ben!"

It took something like half an hour for her to get to me. I smoked a cigarette leaning up against a blank side wall of the truck stop, sucking in the smell of diesel and the warmth of dense fried foods floating out of the restaurant's overworked exhaust fans, digging the roar and darting lights of the turnpike traffic below. I was glad to be out of that maze, but thinking how cool it was that I'd stuck my thumb out in Boston that morning and here I was smoking a cigarette three hundred miles away in fucking Pennsylvania, waiting for Sarah.

I straightened up when I saw her little beige VW turn into the parking lot. She pulled up right next to me and suddenly all the distance that hung so heavy between us was gone. She jumped out, leaving the door hanging open, and she was warm and her lips were wet and we ground ourselves into each other to make sure, it seemed, that we really were real and there, together.

Man, she looked great. Her heavy coat hung loose over a thin white tee-shirt, a grab-and-run look that showed she hadn't wasted any time getting out the door. The image I carried around in my head was so pale and flat compared to this flushed-cheeked, soft and full woman with shining eyes. She held me tight against her. I lost myself in her, the just-sour tang of her lips, the faintly flowery smell of her hair, the smooth electric pulse of her skin that sent jolts running through me as our faces pressed against each other. The lingering sense of motion and uncertainty from my day on the road dissipated in the sureness of her arms.

The noise of the freeway and smells of the truck stop and the bite of the cold night air brought us back to the hard reality of the parking lot and we slowly pulled away from each other and climbed into the car. I was in Sarah's world now, as I watched her turn the key, hunch over the steering wheel, and smoothly shift the gears as she guided the car south

toward Melrose Park, the suburb where she lived. The road—state highway 611 tamed by the stop lights and speed limits of the outer edges of
a big city—curved through village centers and passed car lots and big
department stores and restaurants. The world smelled different here,
sharp and musty, bittersweet like the feelings this route from the turnpike
to Sarah's house triggered in me. I traveled it with such giddy excitement
last summer, coming and going from the meetings that took our love
from a freshman fling to an overpowering passion. But the trips since
then were heavy with anxiety—from dodging her parents, at first, and
lately and maybe harder, trying somehow to relate to them. And Sarah
was different here. She wore glasses to drive and seemed sharply focused.
She was trying to navigate the gulf between this old world of hers and
me, the awkward pirate from a seductive world of excitement and danger.
She carried that tension just beneath the surface whenever we were there.

"Where we going?" I asked as I began to recognize the surroundings
as being close to her house.

"Are you hungry? We could go to my house and you could get something to eat."

I was hungry. I hadn't really thought about eating, though. And I
couldn't handle seeing her parents quite yet.

"It'd just be for a little while. They wouldn't hassle you. Really."

"No, really, I'd just as soon grab a burger someplace, if that's OK. My
head's just not ready for that whole scene." I was still stoned and disoriented in Sarah's world.

"OK," she said. She was quiet for a minute, then looked over at me
with an easy smile and soft eyes, "My parents really aren't bad people,
you know. I think they're trying."

"Maybe they're not bad people. They just happen to hate me. At least
your father does. He can't hide it. I could tell from ten seconds on the
phone."

Sarah sighed. We pulled into a Ginos, and I got a couple of cheeseburgers and wolfed them down. She wasn't hungry. I told her about my
rides. Those guys heading into the City. They must have been speeding

or something. They never stopped talking. First they were going to go here and see those people and then over there and see these other people but then they would have to pick up some booze and those guys really liked rum so they'd also have to pick up some Coke somewhere cause they just couldn't drink straight rum the one time they'd tried that they ended up puking their guts out in Central Park during a great concert by the Fugs man the Fugs were so cool they'd have to get down to the Village sometime to see what was going on down there and then they'd have to go see these other people who always had great pot but they should stop at a bagel store before they go because they would definitely have the munchies there—and on like that for the forty-five minutes I was in the car. They never asked my name or where I was going. They told me where they were going and I told them where to let me out and they were off. They were probably still talking nonstop wherever they were.

Sarah laughed when I told the story, raucous and loud. I loved to make her laugh, to watch her eyes brighten and moisten, her mouth roll open and her chest heave free and loose. It was a kind of making love, I thought, to make her laugh. She opened up and let me in to this intimate part of her. Trying to be funny was as scary as anything with a girlfriend, that no-laugh silence almost worse than the unreturned touch. I wasn't afraid to risk being funny with Sarah, to be silly, that was part of why I loved her so fucking much.

After the burgers, we went to Sarah's aunt's house, where I was going to stay. Her cousin Jack, who was our age, was living there and going to Temple University like Sarah. He was a pretty cool guy. The house was a big old stone place, just one block from Sarah's. Her aunt was a painter, and the inside of the house had an artsy feel to it, lots of framed pictures and unusual colors. When we walked in, her aunt and uncle were watching TV. I'd met them before and they were cordial enough. We exchanged a little small talk about when I got in and how long I was staying and then they told us that Jack was upstairs, so we headed up there. The upstairs was cool. A big central room was painted bright yellow with a bold black stripe running horizontally all the way around and

Peanuts characters painted on the walls throughout the room: Charlie Brown, Snoopy, Linus, Lucy, Pigpen. Comfortable chairs, including one double-sized, curvy molded, bright yellow, plushy soft upholstered chair—almost sofa-size. Cool place to hang out. Jack was up there with a buddy of his. His room was off one end of the big room. His older sister, who Sarah was pretty tight with, had a room next to his, but she was going to school at Penn State. We shot the shit with Jack and his friend for a while. They were going out to meet up with some other folks and invited us to go along. But I was pretty wasted from my day on the road, so we declined.

When they left, Sarah turned on the TV. Shit, I hadn't even seen a TV since I'd been home at Christmas. She found some bad old movie about this beautiful young model who gets seduced by this whacked-out old millionaire. Sarah had become a bad old movie junkie since she'd been back in Philly. We pulled the double-sized chair around in front of the TV and curled up together. I put my arm around her. I tried to watch the movie—all this corny old-fashion New York high-society kind of talk: "By jove Gibson, who is this little vision of empyrean blue?" and shit like that. But I couldn't keep my eyes off Sarah and I softly rubbed her shoulder. I guess she could feel me looking at her, because she turned to me and said, "What?"

"I'm really glad to be here with you. Everything's so crazy in Boston, sometimes I just feel like I'm being pulled somewhere…"

"I'm glad you're here, too," she said and gave me a short sweet kiss and turned back to the television.

I rubbed harder on her shoulder. I felt the bump of her collarbone beneath the thin fabric of her tee-shirt, the dip of the soft well at the base of her throat. I reached across myself and put my other hand on the leg of her jeans, fraying and smooth from wear. She softly put her hand on top of mine and looked at me and smiled and kissed me again, but this was a purposely quick and punctuated one.

"My aunt and uncle are downstairs," she said as she looked back at the television.

"I don't care," I said, soft and dreamy as I kept staring at her sharp profile.

Her eyes were hard when she looked back at me, full of questions. She stared, unsmiling, deep into me. She moved her eyes slowly up and down my face, looking for something. I didn't know what. I couldn't say anything. I just wanted to kiss her for a long time. To feel her shoulder yield to my rubbing. To reach beneath the thin veil of her tee-shirt, the tightness of her jeans, to feel her hidden skin. To have her swallow me, to feel that wholeness that I only felt when Sarah and I went beyond who we were separately into that place where we were something entirely different together. I didn't know how to ask for that as our eyes locked and the television droned on in the background ("I say, man, are you mad?"). And then she took her hand off my hand and put it on my shoulder and pulled me gently towards her, her eyes and her mouth opening to welcome me in to her. We were quiet and smooth, creating barely a ripple in the night, as we let go of everything but the love that glided between us.

That night drifted away as we cuddled close and watched TV, grooving on just being in the same place and touching. Every now and then, I'd tell her about stuff going on in Boston, but with a kind of distance— like I was looking down from some high place on my life and I could talk about it without the swirling intensity and confusion I felt when I was in the middle of it. I'd gotten another letter from BU's lawyers just the day before expanding the injunction so now I wasn't allowed to impede, obstruct, disrupt, hinder, or otherwise interfere with any disciplinary hearings at BU. Sarah was quick to observe that still allowed me to mock them. She laughed when I told her about Stu and Mike goofing on me. She raised her eyebrows when I told her about the Weathermen and Marsha, how cool she was except for the whole Manson thing. Sarah couldn't understand how anyone could think Charlie Manson was cool. And she didn't think anyone who thought Charlie Manson was cool could possibly be cool. I couldn't really explain it very well and I wasn't trying to convince of her anything, just wanted to bring her into the

Boston life somehow. She was worried that Tavola was gone so much, but she made me promise again I'd save a kitten for her if she really was pregnant. She didn't have much to say about her life. School was OK but not too exciting, except it did get her out of her house for a few hours a day. I was glad not to hear anymore about that Kevin kid.

Jack wandered in sometime in the middle of the second movie we watched—this was Charlie Chan being chased by some gangsters at a wax museum, crazy shit—and laughed at the silly parts with us for awhile before finally saying goodnight and heading into his room. Sarah fell asleep in my arms. I was dog-assed tired but I was digging holding her, so I clung to a little ledge of consciousness. Finally the static of the end of the day's TV programming woke her, and she forced herself to stir and pulled herself away from me and said she had to go home. It was 1:30 or 2:00 in the morning. I offered to walk her home, but she said no. She was afraid I'd freak out her aunt and uncle when I came back—and it was just a block in a neighborhood she's lived in all her life. We kissed a long soft kiss and she was gone. I laid down, my clothes still on, on the cot in the corner of the big room under Pig Pen's cloud of dust, but I didn't go to sleep.

I thought. How did I get to this place, to be sleeping in this big stone house in this placid suburb? It was her world, that girl a block away, now climbing into the bed she's slept in since she was a little girl in the house she's always lived in. But it was a world that had no place for me and that I didn't want any part of—except Sarah. I was the enemy, an invading barbarian who wanted to rip the young beauty from the safety of her family and her village. And yet, here I lay, safe and warm in their midst. "I say, man, are you mad?"

CHAPTER TWENTY-TWO

January 24

I DID SLIDE OFF TO SLEEP EVENTUALLY and slept hard until Sarah woke me with a tickle to the nose and a big morning smile. She smelled like tooth paste and orange juice when she kissed me. Man, it was great waking up to her. The day was already bright outside, mid-morning I guessed.

"So what should we do today?" she asked.

"Hey, this is your town," I croaked, still trying to work the sleep out of my face and my voice. I reached into my coat, draped over a chair next to the cot, and grabbed a cigarette out of the pocket. I lit it up and took a deep drag and then let out a howl of coughs. Had to get the old lungs going.

"Well, we could go down to the art museum or maybe just go downtown for awhile. Sometime, maybe, I'd like to try to find a birthday present for my father. His birthday is this coming week."

I must have looked a little less than excited about shopping for her father's birthday, but I didn't say anything, just took another drag on the cigarette and blew the smoke out slowly in fat white rings.

"We don't have to," she said. "I'm just not going to have a lot of time during the week." Then she got a sweet old smile on her face and rubbed my shoulder tenderly and said, "Hey, Ben, maybe you could get him something. That would really surprise him."

"Yeah, I bet it would," I said and sat up. "You know I just don't know what the right gift is for someone who hates your guts and wishes you would just disappear and die."

"Bennnnnnn," she said, dragging out my name.

"Sarahhhhhhhhh," I said dragging her name out longer, and I jumped out of bed to go to the bathroom to wash my face and shovel my hair into place.

We headed into the city in her VW. She drove. I had never really learned how to drive a stick shift. Scott had tried to teach me once during high school in Illinois, but ended up laughing too hard at my clumsiness to finish the lesson—and got worried that I'd do permanent damage to his parents' trusty Valiant. Barry had made it easy for me to fake it—his VW had one of those automatic stick shifts that were really pretty cool. But I didn't mind being the passenger with Sarah driving. Gave me a better chance to check out Philly. We went through a hard-ass ghetto between the tree-lined tranquility of Melrose Park and downtown. This place needed a revolution, man. Houses that looked like they'd already been bombed. Streets crumbling. Businesses boarded. Fat, white cops arrogantly patrolling the streets like a fucking occupying army. Dirt and grime everywhere, people just milling around. It was scary driving down those streets. Those people should be pissed at the white people who passed through their neighborhood on their route between the commerce of the city and the comfort of the suburbs. Shit, that's what I was doing. How could they ever know that I was on their side. I was pissed, too, but I didn't have to live like this—and I was glad.

We went to the art museum, an enormous monumental building set in the middle of a grassy island surrounded by broad boulevards. The front was dominated by long, wide granite steps—like the Lincoln Memorial, but I think even more steps than that—which led up to a huge plaza surrounded by the U-shaped structure of the museum. The building was intimidating, like some kind of tomb. When we entered through the giant doors, I was subdued by this undertone of mumbled mutterings, the kind of reverent hush you hear when you're around something dead. Now I remembered why I didn't go to museums very often. Strange place to put art. But I guess it was something to do.

I followed Sarah. She knew a lot about this stuff. She could tell who painted a lot of the pictures without looking at the signs. I dug some of them. There were a couple of Van Gogh's that were really cool. I was amazed by the thickness of the paint on the canvas. When you got real close you could almost taste his intensity in the ridges of the stroke. But I got the feeling that you weren't supposed to get too close to the paintings for very long. There seemed to be a proper distance to stand and a right way to stand, too—head slightly tilted, hand to chin—to correctly appreciate the art. I tried to do that, too, but whenever I could, I snuck up close to see the cracks and lines and distinct colors. That gave me a feeling for the real people who had made these pictures, and I dug them a lot more.

There was a special exhibit by this photographer poet named Minor White. The photographs were black and white, simple scenes that kind of grabbed your attention and pulled you in. Mountains, oceans, frost on a window, paint peeling from a wall, light on a windowsill. They seemed so real, so focused and sharp—clearer than anything ever looked to my eyes—but there was also something surreal about them. And the deeper you went, the finer you followed the focus, the more surreal it got. Shit, who would have thought a picture of paint peeling would be art. I laughed when I first looked at it—shit, I could do that—but after I stared at it awhile, I realized it was just fucking incredible—movement and texture and lines and all that art shit that Sarah talked about, but it was more than just those concepts, it hit at something deep in me.

Sarah was moving faster through White's stuff than I was. I was stunned and mesmerized by it all. Mounted between the photos were some of his poems. Some of them seemed to have connections to the photographs, others didn't, not that I got anyway. I thought this was a pretty cool gig White had—photos and poetry. Maybe I should start taking pictures. Moving from one photo to the next, I looked to see where Sarah was. She was just finishing reading a poem and she looked up and saw me looking at her and gave me an odd half-smile that left me curious.

I eventually made my way to where she had been. There was a cool photo of the sun low in the sky over the Pacific Ocean. Crystal clear like all the rest of them, but a trippy swirl of light and blurry lines as the ocean blended into the sky. The poem next to it was short: "Is it you or I who says/ Out of my love for you/ I will give you back to yourself."

I read it again. Then looked to find Sarah, who was sitting on a bench, waiting for me, watching. I walked directly to her, skipping the last couple of photos. She smiled, a serious kind of smile.

"Are you OK?" I asked

"Yeah," she said. "Amazing stuff, huh?"

"Really amazing. Really, really amazing," I said. "Are you sure you're OK?

"Yeah," she said, taking my hand and squeezing it hard as she stood. "Ready to go?"

We spent the rest of the day wandering around downtown Philly. She bought her father a pair of dungarees for his birthday. Slightly subversive, I thought, and considerate at the same time. That Sarah. I just couldn't find the right thing to get him with the $4.37 I had in my pocket. It was dark by the time we headed back toward the suburbs. I was starving. Sarah tried to convince me to go to her parents' house to eat, said there was plenty of food there and they would have already eaten so we wouldn't have to sit down to dinner with them. I wasn't into it, so I talked her into stopping at a Roy Rogers hamburger joint on Broad Street. We were on the edge of the ghetto, but actually not all that far from her house. She pulled into a narrow parking place in the lot.

The restaurant was crowded and a little scary. We were the only white people there, though no one seemed to pay much attention to us. But there was no place to sit, so we grabbed the burgers and sat in the car and ate them. I treated and still had almost a dollar left. At least enough to buy cigarettes for the trip home the next day. We ate the burgers fast and Sarah turned the key to start the car. Nothing happened. She tried again. Nothing. She looked at me. Looking for an answer I didn't have. She tried again. Nothing. Again. Again nothing.

"What do you think could be wrong?" She asked me.

"I have no idea," I said. "Has it ever done anything like this before?"

"I don't think so." She tried again. Nothing.

"It's probably the battery or something," I said. "Maybe something to do with the ignition. Sorry, I just don't know much about cars."

She tried again. Nothing. We sat in the cold car. The traffic was loud from Broad Street. People were going into and coming out of the restaurant in a steady flow. We just sat there for a while, neither of us saying anything. Finally, she looked at me, a tense smile on her face, "What are we going to do."

I smiled back, probably just as tense. "I don't know," I said. "Try it one more time." Nothing. I got out. Walked to the front of the car to see if I could see a wire hanging loose or something else obvious. I was just about to reach down to open the hood when I remembered that what I was about to open was the trunk. Volkswagen engines were in the back of the car. I must have learned that sometime with Barry's car, but it escaped me under the pressure of the moment. I straightened up, smiled at Sarah, who had gotten out of the car and was standing leaning on the door, watching me. She was definitely looking tense now. I walked to the back as calmly as I could, as though there was some good reason for me to check the trunk first before looking at the engine, and opened the hood. I had no idea what I was doing. I couldn't even find the battery. But I shook and pushed on some wires the way I'd seen other people do when cars wouldn't start.

"OK," I said, as if I'd done something. "Try it again." She climbed back in the car sort of eagerly and turned the key. Not a damn thing. Shit.

"I don't have any idea what I'm looking at back here," I said. "Sorry"

"It's all right," she said.

"Maybe somebody has some jumper cables," I said, though I also had vague memory that there was something tricky about using jumper cables from a regular car to a VW. And I still hadn't found the battery.

"Maybe we should try popping the clutch. Do you know how to do that?"

"I don't know how to drive a stick," I said.

"Oh, yeah. I've seen people do it, but I don't know if I could do it here." The car was parked facing uphill up against a fence. Behind it, between the restaurant entrance and the parking spaces was just a narrow lane that led straight into busy Broad Street. It'd be a tricky maneuver for somebody who knew what they were doing.

Just then a young couple came out of the Roy Rogers, looked like they were heading to the car next to us. They eyed us sort of curiously and I must have looked desperate, because the man said to me, "You folks alright?"

"Car won't start," I said. "And we don't know why and I don't really know what I'm doing."

He smiled. "Hmmm. Well I could try pushing you, but you got a steep hill here and a busy street down there and if it doesn't work, you're worse off than you are now."

"Yeah, and I, uh, don't know how to use a stick."

"Hmmm," he said, "Well, that would be a problem then." He looked at Sarah.

"I can drive a stick," she said, "but I've never popped a clutch. I don't know. I could try."

"Yeah, well, I'd love to help you folks, but I think you might be best off calling a tow truck."

"Sure, OK, thanks," I said, and the couple wished us luck and got in their car and drove away.

Sarah looked around, saw a pay phone against the restaurant, took a deep breath and looked me hard in the eyes. "I think I have to call my father."

"Why? Isn't there someone else we could call? Anyone else."

"I can't think of anyone else. Ben, it's getting late. I'm cold. I just don't know what else to do. My father would be really pissed if we showed up being towed—which he'd end up paying for—without me calling him first."

202 *The Risk of Being Ridiculous*

"OK," I said. I had no other answer. It was her world. If we were in Boston we'd just walk home or hitch hike, then find someone who could help us fix the car. I don't think we could do that here. Shit. I followed her to the phone, leaned up against the building while she called, kicking my heel into the icy pavement as she talked to her mother then waited a while until her father came to the phone. Her side of the conversation was quick answers to the questions he must have been asking: "It just won't start." "I don't know." "At the Roy Rogers on Broad Street." And then she hung up. She smiled at me. My smile back was a pissed off smile. I wasn't pissed at her. I was just pissed.

We sat in the car quietly until he got there. Sarah told me he'd been asleep in front of the TV when she called. Her mother had to wake him. He drove up in a big old gray Oldsmobile. He pulled into a parking space a couple over from ours. We met halfway between the two cars. He was a little bit shorter than me and stocky, and he carried himself like he was used to being in charge. His hair, which was swept across his head, was standing up in a couple of places, the effect of sleeping on the couch. I said hello with a half-hearted smile—we hadn't seen each other since I'd been in Philadelphia. He nodded back and said a curt hello, his eyes looking past me to the Volkswagen and Sarah.

"Did you try to jump start it," he said kind of swinging his look back to me for a second.

"No, I…"

"OK. Well get in and I'll push it into position."

"I can't, uh, I don't know how to, um…drive a stick shift."

He looked at me for a split second with a kind of mocking disbelief, the crinkle of a smile started on his lips, then quickly shifted to straight-faced exasperation.

"OK. I'll drive. You push." He handed his keys to Sarah. "You watch for cars coming. If I get this started, I'm going to keep on going home. You drive my car home."

He got in the Volkswagen, which was parked at an angle, facing uphill. I was in the front ready to push. Sarah was in the back, off to the side.

Her dad let up on the parking brake and started rolling backwards. I pushed, but gravity did most of the work until he started to swing the rear end around so the car would be pointed straight down the hill toward Broad Street. I pushed hard then but after the car was just a few feet clear of the parking spot, and still shy of having a straight path downhill, I slipped and lost all the momentum. Sarah came to help, but her dad had hit the brakes to keep the car from starting down before he was ready. Sarah and I both put our shoulders into the front fender and were ready to push more when her dad yelled for us to get out of the way, that we weren't going to get that car any further uphill, and he thought he could make it from where it sat now. We stood up. He yelled for us to go watch Broad Street and signal him when it was clear. Sarah led the way. I was useless.

When Sarah gave him the sign, he let the VW roll down the hill and then with a sudden jerk the engine sputtered to life. He stopped before he actually entered Broad Street and gunned the engine and eventually the sputtering gave way to a loud purr. He looked back at us standing above him in the parking lot, to Sarah, then me, and after just the slightest raising of his thick eyebrows he looked back to the road before pulling away.

Sarah smiled at me as we turned toward the Oldsmobile. I didn't bother smiling back. We climbed into its dark poshness without saying a word. I hated the softness of it. The cleanliness of it. All the lights on the dashboards. The automatic windows. The stereo radio that was tuned to some easy listening station. The smell. Thick upholstery and plush carpet and a strong heater and him.

Sarah looked for a rock radio station. I didn't care. It wouldn't make it any better. I huddled close to the window, watching the street, as though if I could keep my focus outside this car, I would not be absorbed by it, not pulled into it.

"He was helping us," Sarah finally said.

"Yes, that's true." I said.

"What do you want from him?"

"Not a thing."

She exhaled loudly and turned the music up. Van Morrison singing "Brown Eyed Girl." I loved that song. But not that night.

I watched the streets of Philly—row houses and neighborhood shops and old stone churches and supermarkets with empty parking lots—go by. I watched the houses get bigger and the trees more frequent and the traffic lighter. I hated it all.

We pulled up in front of her parents' house, a gabled wood-framed house pleasantly set in a nicely landscaped corner lot that rose above the street. The Volkswagen was already parked. Sarah looked at me with a kind of grim smile as she got out of the car. I followed her into the house, which was warm and bright and thick with a lingering garlicky smell from the evening's dinner. Sarah's mother greeted us with a big smile and a little too much exuberance since everyone else in the house was pissed off one way or another at the moment. She offered me some left-over dinner, some kind of chicken something or other, but I politely declined, not pointing out the obvious fact that we had just been rescued from a fast food hamburger joint. She meant well.

Sarah's dad was already settled in front of the TV in the family room, which was a couple of steps down from the living room and kitchen area where we stood awkwardly with Sarah's mom. He didn't get up. Sarah finally walked over to the top of the steps and said thank you to him. I couldn't hear his response as Sarah's mother was chit-chatting asking about my trip in, how long I was staying, and that kind of stuff. Sarah disappeared down the steps leaving me alone with her mother. Shit, I felt stranded. I didn't want to follow Sarah down those steps and get trapped down there with her dad, but we were fast running out of small talk.

I hated standing here. It hurt like a deep muscle ache that no matter how you twist or turn won't go away. I just wanted to get the fuck out of that house. Time crawled until Sarah came back and asked me if I wanted to walk up to Jack's house to relax for a while. Escape. I poked my head in the doorway that led down to the family room and said a muffled thank you and good-bye to Sarah's dad. He looked up from the TV and nodded with a look we both understood perfectly.

It was cold and quiet outside. The silence between Sarah and me got heavier and the sounds of our feet hitting pavement got louder with each step we took.

She finally spoke, just before we got to Jack's house.

"Look, Ben, I don't know why you're mad at me. I didn't do anything wrong."

"I'm not mad at you. I'm just mad. Mad that we have to put up with this fucking bullshit."

"All he did was come and help us with the car. What else could we have done?"

"I don't know. But that's just the point. This is their fucking world. Man, I don't know how you can stand being here."

"It's my world, too, Ben."

"It's not my world. It's not our world. It's your world without me. Can't you see how much he hates me. He can't hardly look at me. And then... I can't drive a stick shift. What the hell good am I?"

"It's just hard for him. You're hard for him."

"Sorry, but I don't think that's my problem."

Now we were standing outside her aunt's house, not wanting to go in while we were in the middle of this. But it was fucking cold. I lit a cigarette and cupped it in my hands for a little warmth.

"Ben why do we always have to fight when we get near the end of our time together," Sarah asked.

"Because there always is an end to our time together."

Sarah was quiet. She held out her hand and I passed her my cigarette. She took a quick drag and handed it back to me.

"Sarah, I just don't feel like I can be myself here, that we can be ourselves. We lurk in the shadows and we cringe in front of your father. We kind of go into hiding..." I took a deep drag on the cigarette and looked up into the bare tree that hung over us.

"Shit's getting so heavy in Boston. And everywhere. Panthers getting killed. Cops getting away with it. Weatherman fighting cops. Luke underground. Fucking Nixon's going berserk. Our friends getting screwed. Even the stupid fucking injunction BU's got over me. Who knows what's going to happen at Northeastern next week. It's like things are going to explode any minute and we're cowering in front of your father in this uptight fucking suburb. Shit!"

She reached again for the cigarette and took a longer drag. I could see tears starting to trickle down her face. She handed the cigarette back and looked straight into me, a hard look.

"Ben, sometimes, I wonder…I wonder why…why we even try. We're so different. I love you Ben, I really really love you, but, shit, Ben, Weathermen and Nixon? What do they have to do with you and me and my father coming to help us because the car won't start? I'm sorry you don't like my parents. I'm sorry you don't like where I live. But this is who I am. Look at me. Look around you. This is who I am and if you can't accept that…" The tears were coming hard now. I reached to put my hand on her shoulder and she pulled back.

"Sarah," I said, softer now. I hated to see her cry, "we all came from some other place. We met, we fell in love, in a new place. Our place. I don't think this is you any more. I think this is who you used to be, who your parents want you to be. Injunctions and arrests and cops fucking with us is reality, that ghetto we drove through today is reality. This…" I said sweeping my arms around me, "this is hiding from reality.

"I don't know what's going to happen with all the shit in Boston. I wish I could tell you, I wish I knew. Sarah, I love you more than anything, but I know that if there is a future for us, it ain't here. And the sooner we recognize that one way or another, the better for both of us."

"What does that mean?"

"I don't know what it means…." A car went by us, getting louder until it passed us and then its sound disappeared slowly into the night. "Sarah, you know that thing in the museum today?"

"What thing?"

"That poem."

"What poem?"

"It said something about loving somebody enough to give them back to themselves."

"Yeah, what about it?

"I don't know. Is that us?"

"I don't know, Ben, I don't know what to think anymore."

"Sarah, I don't want to make you try to be something you're not. Really," I took a deep breath. "Really. It's just, I've seen what you are when you're let loose of what you think you're supposed to be. I've seen how happy you are, and how strong, and how great we are together. How much fun we have. How fucking right it feels. And then…I see you here…and it's just not…"

I couldn't finish that thought. Sarah took the cigarette again and took a drag. It was almost down to the filter now. She held on to it.

"Ben, I don't know that I'll ever be what you want me to be," she said. She'd stopped crying, her eyes looking into me were softer now. She took another drag. "Or maybe you're becoming something I don't want to be, that I can't handle.

"I can't believe you're even thinking about going to that Northeastern thing with all the shit you're dealing with." Now she looked intense again. "You're making choices that I just don't understand, that could ruin any chance we have. How can you do that?"

She handed the cigarette back to me. I took the last drag, tasted the bitter bite of the filter starting to burn, then crushed the remains into the icy sidewalk

I didn't know what to say. Is this how it was going to end? Because I couldn't drive a fucking stick? This is what Philadelphia did to her, made her think of all the reasons we couldn't work, shit, that we shouldn't even try. But as I looked into her eyes filling up with tears again, my anger was all gone, replaced by an immense sadness.

"We're both making choices that make it hard," I said softly, and I reached my arms around her and pulled her in close to me. She nuzzled her head into the crook of my shoulder. Her eyes were wet again, I could feel her tears on my chin. "I love you," I said.

"I love you, too," she said. We stood there holding each other for a while. Then Jack pulled up in his little MG sports car. Sarah and I grimly smiled at each other, took each other's hand and squeezed. We greeted Jack and headed inside for another night of hanging on to each other in front of the TV, not saying much, not looking much beyond that night and that upstairs room at Jack's house.

CHAPTER TWENTY-THREE

January 25

I RODE BACK TO BOSTON WITH SARAH'S friend from high school Wally, who was going to stay with us at Mountfort Street while he looked into art schools to attend the next year. He was a good guy. He had five joints of killer Jamaican for the trip, but he wanted to wait until we were well under way to smoke the first one. But almost as soon as we hit the New Jersey Turnpike, a state cop car started following us. Wally was driving really slow but the cops stayed on our tail. After about a mile, it was obvious we'd been targeted, so Wally slid the envelope he had the joints in across the seat to me. I leaned hard against the door and carefully, slowly opened the wing window on my side. I pulled the envelope slowly up to the window—in a way that couldn't be seen from behind us—and dropped it out of the car through the wing window. Both Wally and me were pretty uptight, but the cops didn't pull us over for another mile or two.

They were assholes. Gave me shit about my hair, calling me "pretty boy" and shit like that. Asked us if we had every drug that anybody had ever heard of, like they'd just had some kind of refresher course on drug busts: "Any dex-o-dreen? Any sil-o-sy-bin mushrooms? Any ell-ess-dee?" They must not have seen the envelope of joints fall out of the car because they started tearing the car apart looking for any remnants of drugs. We knew they couldn't bust us unless they planted something, which certainly was not out of the question. After they searched the whole car, they searched us. They made me empty my pockets on the hood of Wally's car. They got more than they bargained for: six or seven packs of matches, an almost full pack of Marlboros, two pens, a note that Sarah had written me right before we left, two wrappers from Mounds bars, about thirty-two cents in change, a scrap of paper with a bunch of phone numbers written on it (they checked that out for awhile), a stub from the ticket to the art museum, this cool little shiny rock I'd found when I was waiting for a ride on my way to Philly, and a whole bunch of other little shit. It almost covered the whole damn hood. Think it kind of blew the cops' minds how much shit I could carry in my pocket. Not a drug to be found. I dug that. Finally, they let us go, but they gave Wally a ticket for driving three miles an hour under the speed limit. Fucking assholes.

We felt relieved but bummed that we couldn't get high for the whole trip. In New Haven, we picked up three freaks from Baton Rogue, Louisiana. It was a trip hearing freaks with southern accents. They were cool. They'd been at a party, two nights before I guess—their sense of time seemed distorted—and the three of them decided they really, really wanted to see some snow. So they started hitchhiking. It was cold in New Haven, and they weren't dressed for it—but there was no snow on the ground. I told them I was pretty sure there was snow in Boston and they were welcome to stay with us, so they went all the way to Mountfort Street. It was dark, but there was snow on the ground. After Wally parked his car, the three of them burst out of the car and dove into the nearest snow bank they could find. The were laughing and hooting, rolling around in the snow, picking up handfuls and smashing them into their own and each other's faces. Wally and me just stood there watching, smiling, digging how much they were digging it. Man, it was good to be home.

CHAPTER TWENTY-FOUR

January 27

I DIDN'T MAKE IT TO SCHOOL. I only had one class and I slept too late to make that. So I just went to the union, copped some burgers and hung out there for awhile, then went back with Jerry to Myles Standish. We smoked some dope and listened to music. A couple of freshmen came by Jerry's room—Mac and Wes—and I told them about Northeastern and they said they were into it. I knew they were cool. They ran with us at MIT and some of the Moratorium stuff at BU.

I wandered home sometime in the late afternoon, Kenmore Square and Beacon Street clogged with people and cars, the gray haze of the day starting to darken. I dug the rush of leaving the warm, smoky, crowded dorm room and hitting the cold frantic scene on the streets, carrying my own personal little glow. The buzz of the city vibrated through me as "Bleed On Me," a Stones song we'd just listened to, bounced around in my head.

At the apartment, everybody was in Mike's room: Mike in his chair, Stu and Brian on the bed, Wally and Lenny on the floor and between them was this real young looking kid with straight, shiny brown hair that hung down to his shoulder. He was skinny and kind of hunched in on himself as he sat with his back against the foot of Mike's bed.

"Hey, Tucker, meet Eddie," Mike said with a big smile on his face. "He just escaped from the nut house."

The kid laughed, looking at Mike a little nervously, then looked at me and smiled. "Hi," he said extending his hand toward me. "Your name is Tucker?"

"Yeah, or Ben," I said shaking his hand. "Ben Tucker is my name."

"Benjamin Tucker the Third," Stu added, shooting a grin at me and then the kid.

"Fuck you, Stu," I said. "Call me whatever you want," I said to the kid. "And welcome."

"Thanks. And don't worry, man, I'm not really crazy," Eddie said. He seemed sharp and self-assured for someone so young—especially someone just plunked down in a funky apartment with a bunch of freaks he didn't know. "My parents just couldn't handle me, so they locked me up in a rich kid's loony bin."

"But he escaped man, ain't that cool?" Mike said. "This little fucker's only fifteen years old, but he tokes like an old pro. Ain't that right?"

"Like a grizzled veteran," Brian said as he lit up a joint and passed it around the room.

"Hey," Eddie said, "it's been three months since I had any weed. Makes you hungry." Fifteen, man? I hardly knew what pot was when I was fifteen, it was some exotic thing that beatniks and drug addicts used. At fifteen, me and Scott and Barry were the Urbana High long hairs because we had a few hairs over our ears.

"How'd you find us?" I asked Eddie.

"After I slipped away from the nurses in Harvard Square—they brought us into the city for an outing—I called Fred Niemann, who I knew from a camp I went to a few years ago. He picked me up, but he was paranoid that my parents would know to check at his place. So he brought me here."

Fred was a friend of ours from CBS, and he, like everyone, knew that the sign on our door—Welcome ALL—was no bullshit.

"And I said, 'hell, yes, he can stay here,'" Mike said, stoned to the point of shrinking eyeballs. "This is your next stop on the under-fucking-ground railroad. All aboooarrd."

Everyone was laughing.

"You just gotta fight for your spot," Brian said. "Lenny's pretty much planted on one of the couches." Lenny looked up with a stoned giggly grin and nodded to confirm his claim. "Wally's got Ben's extra mattress for now," Brian went on. "That means if you're lucky, you can grab couch number 2."

"Which ain't bad if you can work around that spring popping out of the middle of it," Stu added.

"You guys, I'm just glad you're letting me stay here," Eddie said. "Really, man. To be free. You guys can't imagine how good it feels to be out of that fucking place."

"Don't worry, you'll be safe here," I said. I looked around the room. Everyone was smiling. We were together on this. Little Eddie looked like he was starting to relax a little. Damn, it felt good to know that we were the refuge for this kid, the open door: Welcome ALL.

"Remember though," Mike said, looking suddenly kind of serious. "If you get any food or money or dope, it belongs to the people."

Eddie looked a little confused, "The people?"

Now Mike smiled big again and held his arms wide open as if to embrace all of us sitting there: "We are the people!"

Brian laughed loudest, but we all joined in. "Power to the people," Stu shouted above our laughter. "And speaking of food, let's introduce little Eddie to the girls at 858, maybe they'll be in a charitable mood."

CHAPTER TWENTY-FIVE

January 28

Dear Family,

There's a rock and roll song by a group called Steppenwolf called "Monster." The words are really good.

Once the religious, the hunted and weary
Chasing the promise of freedom and hope
Came to this country to build a new vision
Far from the reaches of kingdom and pope

Like good Christians some would burn the witches
Later some bought slaves to gather riches

But still from near and far to seek America
They came by the thousands to court the wild
And she just patiently smiled and bore a child
To be their spirit and guiding light

And once the ties with the crown had been broken
Westward in saddle and wagon it went
And 'til the railroad linked ocean to ocean
Many the lives which had come to an end

While we bullied, stole and bought our homeland
We began the slaughter of the red man

But still from near and far to seek America
They came by the thousands to court the wild
And she just patiently smiled and bore a child
To be their spirit and guiding light

The blue and the gray they stomped it
They kicked it just like a dog
And when the war was over
They stuffed it just like a hog

And though the past had its share of injustice
Kind was the spirit in many a way
But its protectors and friends have been sleeping
Now it's a monster that will not obey

The spirit was freedom and justice
And its keepers seemed generous and kind
Its leaders were supposed to serve the country
But now they won't pay it no mind
'Cause the people grew fat and got lazy
And now their vote is a meaningless joke
They babble about law and order
But it's just an echo of what they've been told
Yeah, there's a monster on the loose
It's got our head into a noose
And it just sits there watchin'

Our cities have turned into jungles
And corruption is stranglin' the land
The police force is watching the people
And the people just can't understand
We don't know how to mind our own business
'Cause the whole world has got to be just like us
Now we are fighting a war over there
No matter who's the winner
We can't pay the cost
'Cause there's a monster on the loose

It's got our head into a noose
And it just sits there watching

America where are you now?
Don't you care about your sons and daughters?
Don't you know we need you now?
We can't fight alone against the monster.

It says a lot. Thanks a lot for your letter Mum. Don't worry too much about not leaving us a viable heritage. It's kind of fun trying to make a new one. It's good to hear the news about Barry. I knew there was no way the army was going to get him. It's just a drag he had to go through all that.

School is now in its third week. I've been going most of the time. It isn't tremendously fantastic, but it's all right. This semester we're putting together this kind of colloquium on revolution as a historical process of change. It's no credit, no grade, it's for our personal knowledge. It's pretty good.

I've been looking for a job pretty unsuccessfully. I went to BU placement again, got three possibilities——one of which is still possible, at this rug place. I even did the want ads. So I'm still unemployed and poor. I do need money—rent is coming up—so if you could send me some I'd be very happy—if you don't, I'm in trouble. I'm sorry I haven't done very well as far as supporting myself goes. All I can say is that I'll keep trying to find a job so this won't happen next month.

Last weekend I was feeling very depressed and confused so I hitch-hiked to Philly to see Sarah. It was good to see her. We love each other a lot, but things are not looking good for us right now. Why is it so hard? A friend of hers gave me a ride home. We got stopped and searched by the New Jersey cops. Jefferson Airplane is right, America does think we're all outlaws.

I went and saw Cary a couple of weeks ago. She seems to be doing OK. But every time I go see her one of her roommates hassles me about our wall. We had a party and a bunch of people drew on our wall. One girl drew a profile of a nude girl. The politicos don't like it, they think it's antifeminist. It makes me mad. I'm growing less and less political and more and more revolutionary. Ideologies are traps for minds who are tired of not having answers. People who get into ideologies forget about people a lot. The only answer I know is that there is no answer and we gotta learn to love that and just live each day as best and as full as possible not hurting anybody unwarrantedly and helping people when you can. That's all I've come up with so far. I'll let you know when I get some more.

Hayakawa of San Francisco State is going to be at Northeastern to-morrow night—s'pose to be some sort of action against him. I'll probably go. There's no injunction against me at Northeastern.

Not much else to say. Hope things are going OK there.
Keep the faith.
Love,
Ben

CHAPTER TWENTY-SIX

January 29

STU TRIED TO TALK US OUT OF IT.

"Hayakawa. Who the fuck is Hayakawa? Is he worth your time? There's a much better show at the Tea Party tonight. Ten Years After and Mott the Hoople. They've got a much better sound than Hayakawa."

"Sure, Stuie, go have your fun at the rock and roll show," Mike said, a little smile peeking out from his beard. "We'll be out fighting for your rights to get high and enjoy music. Think of us out in the streets while you're in that warm safe concert."

"Oh, Mike," Brian was half-laughing. "What does Hayakawa have to do with getting high and listening to music? That's such bullshit."

"Everything, man," Mike said, lowering his bushy eyebrows. "Hayakawa has everything to do with getting high and listening to music. Am I right, Tucker?"

I laughed. Even though he was just busting their balls, Mike was right in some ways. It was all the same fight. The Chicano and black students at San Francisco State. Rock and roll. The commuter students at Northeastern. Our wall. The working class kids at Boston English. The lies of American history. The Black Panthers. Smoking dope. Lenny splitting his time between the Coast Guard and our couch. The GE strikers and our friends who got busted in demonstrations supporting them. The bullshit of the American Dream. The Vietnam War. Little Eddie escaping. Making love not war. Luke underground. The girls at 858. The GIs used by the government. The injunction against me. The draft. Television and art. Sarah and me trying to figure how to love in the middle of all this shit. Peace and love and revolution. Hayakawa and Ten Years After and Mott the Hoople. All one great big bundle—and we all knew that in our own way. We'd had this discussion a million times coming at it from a million different angles and we weren't going to get any closer to saying it the same way on this night as Mike and Patrick and I waited for the guys from Myles Standish—Jerry, Wes, and Mac—before heading out to the demonstration at Northeastern. We'd do our demonstrating and Stu and Brian would go to their show and Lenny would nurse his trusty six-pack, then we'd all meet back at Mountfort Street and get high and tell each other about what we'd done. And we'd never really know who'd changed what.

Call out the instigators because there's something in the air,
We've got to get together sooner or later...

"Yeah, man, you're absolutely right," I said. "I heard the first thing Hayakawa did at San Francisco State was ban rock and roll and crack down on pot smoking. Then he went after the militant third-world students." I grinned at both Brian and Stu, who shook his head with a smile. He knew we were going to Northeastern no matter what he said.

This little exchange loosened me up a bit. I was feeling kind of uptight. The Myles boys were late. I was going to miss my phone call to Sarah tonight. She was going out to dinner with her family to celebrate her father's birthday. Sure as hell she would have tried to talk me out of going to Northeastern.

I did have mixed feelings about going. But I knew that we had to go. We had to show the pigs that the crackdown at BU, the injunctions they were getting all over town—the Northeastern administration had a court order to try stop tonight's action (I wasn't named in that one)—the repression of the Panthers, and the crazy-ass conspiracy trial going on in Chicago weren't going to crush the Movement. The truth was, the pigs tactics were working. As the stakes were raised, fewer and fewer people were showing up for demonstrations, and militants were more and more isolated. I knew that we had to keep fighting, but sometimes I just wasn't sure what the Movement was anymore, exactly where it was moving us to. I couldn't really make sense of it in a way that went beyond this one decision in front of me, beyond this night and whatever was waiting for us at Northeastern. But somehow it made even less sense to me to not go, to join Stu and Brian at the Tea Party. I knew that would please Sarah, but not going to Northeastern was a kind of surrender that I wasn't ready to make.

…Cause you know that it's right. We have got to get it together.
We have got to get it together…now."

The Myles boys finally showed up and Mike and Patrick and I threw on our coats before heading out into the cold night.

"Everybody got a dime?" Patrick asked as the six of us filed out of Mountfort Street. Standard demonstration equipment—if you got busted the cops would give you one phone call, but you had to pay for it.

We decided to walk. It wasn't that far—maybe half-an-hour—if you cut through the Fens. The MTA would have taken almost as long. And the walk gave us a chance to talk and get our heads together. We told Wes and Mac about our meeting with the Weathermen and what they wanted to do. We were going to check them out when we got there, but probably still do our own thing. We knew that some Northeastern SDS folks got tickets to get into Hayakawa's speech. They were planning to disrupt it and demand that the demonstrators outside—people without tickets—be allowed in. Those of us on the outside would make noise and try to get in somehow. We expected maybe one hundred or one hundred fifty people, the usual crowd of action-oriented freaks who had tried to shut down the MIT missile labs the November before and had been in on Panther support stuff.

Our route took us down Jersey Street past Fenway Park, looming big and silent in its winter hibernation. Looking up at its tall brick walls, I lost track of the loud tactical discussion taking place around me and flashed back to the summer days and nights, when my dad and I walked this street—then full of people and anticipation, the smells of grilled onions and sausage and roasting peanuts—with tickets to another world, green and fresh and hopeful, in our hand. That seemed like a different lifetime, and I felt a tingle of that little kid's warm excitement as I drifted back to it for a second. Then I heard Mike asking me who else I thought might show up from BU. Brought back to January 1970, I saw this was just another city street with quiet taverns and closed souvenir shops and cars parked complacently along the side. No Red Sox–Yankees tonight. It was a different us against a different them.

"Matthew and those guys, I guess," I said, "but not a lot of others." Some of our friends who might be there couldn't because of the bullshit suspended trials hanging over their heads from the GE demonstrations.

We moved through a calm residential neighborhood, three and four story brick apartment buildings with names like The Summerset or The Hawthorne set in stately concrete letters above the doorway. It was dinnertime, not much of anybody else on the streets but us, and light slipped through draped windows to tint the chilled twilight with a silvery glow. As we headed down Queensberry toward the dark of the Fens, we laughed and talked, moving in an awkward pile of six guys on a narrow sidewalk, shuffling positions. If a guy in front turned around to talk to someone behind him, he had a good chance of getting bumped off the curb, then having to circle around to join the tail end of our little parade. We could've been going to a party or a concert, shit, maybe even a lecture by some noted linguist. Just six college kids rambling through Boston on a winter night.

When we crossed the bridge in the Fens, a tensing surged through us. We were getting close. Laughter got a little tighter, conversation a little stiffer. We started looking around, more aware of where we were and who else was around, who was watching us. We looked to each other. I caught Mike's eye and he nodded. "Here we go, man." To Patrick, to Jerry. To Mac and Wes. Smiles, hard smiles, ready smiles. I felt good with these guys.

As soon as we reached Huntington Avenue we knew something heavy was happening. We could hear it and feel it before we saw anything: the simmering hum of a lot of people waiting for an unknowable something they were sure was coming. Then the quadrangle outside the auditorium where Hayakawa was speaking came into view, and, holy shit, man, it was packed full of people—more than I'd seen at a demonstration in Boston in a long time.

We stopped for a second on the fringe of the scene to orient ourselves, to shake our shoulders, finish our cigarettes, and pat each other on the back. The sidewalks of Huntington Avenue were full of people drawn to the spectacle building across the street. The six of us took a collective deep breath—taking in the baked warm smell of a nearby pizza joint, where the patrons pressed tight to the window with a slice in one hand and mug of beer in the other, ready for the show—and headed into the action. "OK, we've really got to try to stay together," Mike reminded us as we stepped into the street.

We crossed the trolley tracks that ran down the middle of the avenue, heading toward the entrance to the quadrangle, and we saw a swarm of Red Squad pigs—undercover cops who specialized in working demonstrations, hassling radicals—a dozen or so of them. Shit, we knew who they were. We saw them all the time. They looked so obviously like they were trying not to look like cops. They were huddling in the back corner of the quadrangle. We were kind of late, so they must have thought all the usual militants were already up toward the front of the crowd. They checked us out as we checked them out. We were surprised, though, to see that a tall black guy was among what we had always thought was exclusively a white man's club. We waved and smiled: "Hey, Red Squad, What's happening?"

We moved into the crowd on the grass and began to work our way up toward the front. Shit there must have been a thousand people there, maybe more. We saw a few people we knew and greeted them with clenched-fist salutes or thumb-lock handshakes. But it was mostly people we didn't know. Lots of straight-looking people. Funny smells—perfume and hair spray and after-shave cologne mixed with an occasional whiff of pot and cigarettes. It was a weird scene. More the kind of a mixed crowd you'd expect at a Ten Years After/ Mott the Hoople concert than what we usually saw at actions in Boston recently. Shit, I thought, next thing you know, Brian and Stu will pop up.

Cops, about twenty altogether, formed an aisle for the people trying to get into the auditorium along the ten wide stone steps that led to the entrance. They were surrounded by demonstrators. We saw pockets of militants here and there with NLF flags and other banners. They were trying to get a chant going: "Pigs out, people in." We joined in, thrusting our clenched fists into the air as an accent, as we kept snaking toward the front.

Pigs out...people in
Pigs out...people in
Pigs out...people in
Pigs out...people in

But there wasn't much cohesion in the crowd. A lot of people were standing around looking at other people standing around. When we got close to the auditorium steps, we ran into Matthew and his friends from BU. He told us that the Northeastern authorities had freaked out and refused to let anyone into the auditorium who didn't have a Northeastern ID—even though they had sold tickets to non-Northeastern people at double the price they'd charged Northeastern students. They must have heard about the plans to infiltrate. Besides that, they had a bunch of security people at the entrance and if they didn't like the looks of someone with a ticket and the right ID—that is, if they were long-haired or black—they'd just take the ID and throw that person out. The people they did decide to let in had to have their picture taken and their seat number written down next to their names. So the authorities had managed to swell the crowd by turning ticket-carrying people away and had pissed off a whole bunch more people. The size of the crowd attracted more Northeastern students who'd never seen anything like this: one day only, fascism drops in on your campus. Check it out.

We saw the small Weatherman contingent under an NLF flag near the base of the steps. Making sure the six of us stayed together, we made our way to them. Marsha, wearing a black motorcycle helmet and a black leather jacket, saw us coming and smiled. She was still awful damn pretty even though she was trying to look tough, but I didn't see any of that girlish shine that had crept over her after a couple of tokes and some good rock and roll at our apartment. She wore the focused smile and the big eyes of a warrior ready for battle.

"Glad to see you guys made it," she had to shout over the noise of the crowd, which was like the rumble of early thunder, with shouts of "Let us in" and "Fuck Hayakawa" rising angrily above it. "Isn't this far out? The stupid fucking pigs have given us the dynamite, now we've just gotta light the fuse."

"I can't believe how stupid they are," I said looking around and seeing hard-eyed radicals and turtle-necked liberals and little packs of neatly dressed Northeastern kids, some carrying books and talking curiously into each other's ears. We had to huddle close together to hear each other. Mike and Marsha and I formed a little circle, with Patrick arching his head in to hear what was going on. Jerry and Wes and Mac formed a line behind us, their heads and eyes in constant motion, trying to take the whole scene in.

"Man, I can't believe how many people are here." I said. "The cops are pretty seriously outnumbered."

"Yeah and these people are pretty pissed, too," Marsha shouted. "This is great."

"What are you going to do?" Mike didn't have to shout much to be heard. His voice was naturally loud. "This place is crawling with the Red Squad."

"Yeah, our old buddies," Marsha said. "I know which ones to bum cig-arettes off, which ones smoke straights. Fuck 'em, though, what can they do in this kind of crowd. If we got you guys and another group or two, we could try to bust our way in. If we just get some of this crowd to fol-low us there's no way these cops can stop us."

"Then what?" Patrick asked, looking up the steps toward the entrance.

"Then we'll fucking shut down Hayakawa and there'll be a whole bunch more kids who know what it's like to fight cops and win," Marsha said, "even if it's only for a little while."

"Most of these people have never been to a demonstration before— let alone fight cops," I said.

"It's about time they did," Marsha said. "Man we can take them," she said looking back at the line of cops. She was probably right. The cops looked worried. The rest of the Weathermen—all twelve of them—stood close to the police line and shouted shit like: "Ever hear of Custer, pig? Well, get ready for your last stand." Marsha laughed. Then she shouted back at us, "But we have to move fast before they get any help. What do you think? Have you seen anybody else here who'd want to go with us?"

"We just saw some other BU folks," I said. "But I don't know if they'd want to be part of the attack." I looked at Mike and he shrugged. Shit, I didn't know if I wanted to be part of the attack. It was one thing to try to do something—shut down the missile labs at MIT, take over the BU dean's office, even try to get in here tonight—and force the pigs to try to stop us. But this, what Marsha was proposing, was different. This would be twenty or thirty people, if we could get that many, throwing them-selves at the police lines, going toe-to-toe with the cops—who did have clubs and guns. I think Marsha was right, if we had enough people we could take them, which would be cool, but still I wasn't feeling too good about it.

Shit, I flashed back to the counter-inauguration demonstrations in Washington when Nixon took office a year ago. I was with a bunch of hippie militants, a couple hundred of us, who surprised the very efficient DC cops, by suddenly leaving the inaugural parade route and running through the streets. For a few blocks we were totally loose. Some young black kids joined and showed us how to trash, breaking windows and scattering garbage cans and shit like that. It was cool for a while. Then we passed an intersection where there was a lone cop, stuck there directing traffic. He found himself surrounded by demonstrators feeling stoked by our surge through the streets. He foolishly tried to redirect us or slow us down or something. Then somebody pushed him. And somebody else pushed him from another side, and he went down. And then eight or ten people surrounded him, punching and kicking and taunting him. I stopped running and suddenly felt dazed and dizzy and sick to my stomach. Why were they doing that? He couldn't stop us. Soon the DC cops swooped in and reclaimed the streets with a dazzling display of force. I just watched it all as if I was out of my body, outside the whole experience—sort of like I felt when the kids attacked us at Boston English—and then just wandered the streets of Washington, alone and disoriented, for hours as the cops dispersed smaller and smaller groups of demonstrators, until I somehow found my way back to the church where the other folks from Boston were staying. The attack had ripped all the righteousness away from us and I didn't know how to cope with that. The idea of an attack that night at Northeastern made me uneasy, too.

It's not that I was against violence, but I had a hard time figuring out when I was for it, when I could actually throw a punch at somebody. And, shit, man, even with our numbers, it was still scary picking a fight with cops.

The Weathermen wouldn't get very far without some help from somebody, but I could tell looking at Mike and Patrick and the three guys standing behind us, who seemed to share my doubts about Marsha's plan, they probably weren't going to get it from us.

"It's one thing if you have a committed disciplined group—a big enough committed disciplined group," Mike started to explain to Marsha when a roar swept from the back of the quad toward us. Cries rang up behind us: "Off the pig!" "Get off our campus." Then we all turned and saw a column of TPF cops—the Tactical Police Force, Boston's biggest baddest pigs—clearing a path through the crowd to reinforce their beleaguered brethren in the front lines. Maybe a hundred of them. "Sieg Hiel," someone yelled. Then someone else, "Sieg Hiel." Then the crowd, in real unison for the first time, took it up:

Sieg...Hiel
Sieg...Hiel
Sieg...Hiel
Sieg...Hiel

And we joined in throwing our hands in the air in a mock Nazi salute,

Sieg...Hiel
Sieg...Hiel
Sieg...Hiel
Sieg...Hiel

filling the night with the chant which bounced off the auditorium and ricocheted around the tall buildings surrounding us, becoming an ominous echo of itself. The cop's reinforcements had brought the crowd together, but the chances of any successful people's offensive diminished quickly as the TPF cops moved into position.

As the "Sieg Hiel" chant slowly faded, Matthew joined our group, looking anxious. "Listen, man," he said loud, to me and Mike, especially, but kind of taking in Marsha out of the corner of his eye, "there's a lot of people here who have never been close to a confrontation with the cops, if the shit starts flying, it's just going to be chaos and a lot of people are going to get hurt. We've got to try to keep it from getting out of hand."

Marsha jumped in. "I thought that was the pigs' job."

"No, not tonight it's not," Matthew said, turning toward her, changing the tone in his voice to something like a plea in his squeaky earnest voice. "I think the pigs would love to attack. The Red Squad knows where you are. Where we are. It would just give them an excuse to pick us off and they could do it, cause everyone here is just going to scatter as soon as they attack. This isn't a good place to pick a fight."

Patrick and Jerry and Wes and Mac, now all part of our bigger circle all nodded. "Matthew's right," Mike said, looking at me and then Marsha. "We've got to try to keep people cool."

Marsha smiled, undefeated, as she started backing away from us. "That's not our style," she said. "But good luck to you." She raised her fist shoulder high, saying, "Power to the people," and she headed back to her group. They all gathered around her, and she must have explained what we had just said, because they all turned toward us, looking pissed or bummed or something. Then they turned back toward the cops and resumed their shouting and fist-shaking.

We walked with Matthew back toward the rest of his people and whenever we saw someone we knew we told them to yell and scream as much as they could and try to talk to the straight students, make it a political lesson, but to avoid giving the cops an excuse to attack. Most people were cool, saw that was the right thing to do.

We took a position in the middle of the crowd about twenty-five feet from the bottom of the steps. There were benches there we could stand on to get a better look at what was happening. The chants were getting louder:

Hey, hey, ho, ho, Hayakawa's got to go.
Hey, hey, ho, ho, Hayakawa's got to go.
Hey, hey, ho, ho, Hayakawa's got to go.
Hey, hey, ho, ho, Hayakawa's got to go.

The six of us were yelling as loud as anybody else but also keeping a close eye on what was happening around us.

The TPF pigs moved into position forming a long line across the top of the steps in front of three large glass entry doors and filling in the line that formed the corridor up the steps toward the middle door. They weren't wearing their usual riot helmets, just the soft regular cop caps. Seemed like nobody was ready for this to be what it was turning out to be, and the TPF must not have had time to don full riot gear before they hit the streets. As the cops one by one took their positions along the thick blue line, they came to attention, legs spread, their nightsticks held out in front of them, forming a combative diagonal from their chest to their shoulders, ready. Fucking pigs.

Ho, Ho, Ho Chi Minh, the NLF is gonna win.
Ho, Ho, Ho Chi Minh, the NLF is gonna win.
Ho, Ho, Ho Chi Minh, the NLF is gonna win.
Ho, Ho, Ho Chi Minh, the NLF is gonna win.

It was tense on the steps. Demonstrators were pressed against the line of cops, and when the TPF filled in that line they had to push the crowd back to make room. There was a lot of jostling as people reluctantly gave way to the pigs, who were none too gentle as they pushed back.

Then somebody reached across the line and knocked a cop's hat off. The crowd cheered. The cops started swinging. First just the few around the cop who lost his hat as six or seven of them rushed into the crowd after the kid who did it. Pushing, knocking, clubbing anyone in their way. The crowd booed and hooted. Then the whole blue line surged across the steps like a fucking mad dog suddenly let off its leash. The people on the steps fell back, some falling on top of each other, as they were caught in between the charging cops and the crowd behind them, which surged forward. The yelling came together as another booming, angry chant, much louder than before:

Sieg...Hiel
Sieg...Hiel

Sieg...Hiel
Sieg...Hiel

We held our ground and, waving our arms in the air, tried to get people around us to do the same—because moving forward only made it harder for the people on the steps to get away from the club-swinging cops. I was pissed and yelling, too. I felt my blood pounding in my chest. I took long deep breaths to try to keep it together.

Sieg...Hiel
Sieg...Hiel
Sieg...Hiel
Sieg...Hiel

It took the pigs only a few minutes to clear the steps. They formed two lines, one along the bottom of the steps, one along the top. Now they held their clubs shoulder high. Nobody was getting in the auditorium any more. Nobody who was in was getting out. A rush of righteous rage surged through the crowd. Nothing turns people into radicals faster than watching cops beating on people trying to get away from them. Our chants were now a fucking roar.

The steps belong to the people
The steps belong to the people
The steps belong to the people
The steps belong to the people

And people started throwing shit. Matthew was moving fast, looking worried and talking to everybody he knew. He shouted in my ear: "This is going to blow any second, try to keep people calm, get them to retreat slowly." I nodded and patted him on the back. He gave me a quick smile before he was off to tell someone else.

Just then I saw a freak standing on one of the benches near me throw something toward the auditorium, followed by the sound of glass breaking. A loud cheer went up from the crowd. I took a couple of steps toward the thrower and yelled: "Hey man, come on. You've gotta cool it." But he didn't hear me. He was smiling, fist raised in the air, proud of his hit.

Hey hey ho ho Hayakawa's got to go
Hey hey ho ho Hayakawa's got to go
Hey hey ho ho Hayakawa's got to go
Hey hey ho ho Hayakawa's got to go

I headed toward Mike, who was standing on another bench with Jerry. "What's happening?" I yelled up to them.

Mike looked down to me, eyes big, a kind of crazy smile on his face.

"People are throwing stuff, but it's all going over the cops—hitting the building—somebody busted one of the windows over the doors. Motherfucking cops are just aching to let loose."

Patrick had moved right next to me. Mac and Wes were on the other side of the bench. Matthew and his group were a few feet away from us, huddling. I heard more glass break. Then there was a commotion behind us, lots of yelling and people moving in that direction.

"Shit, man, they're busting people behind us," Mike shouted and jumped off the bench toward me.

Just like that, the six of us were together and moving toward the action behind us. Two plainclothes cops, Red Squad goons, were trying to arrest the kid I'd seen throw the rock. They were trying to pull him back out of the crowd, but demonstrators were pushing and shoving them, trying to help the freak get away. We moved in to help, too, and just then the kid broke free, and ran past us back into the thick of the crowd. The cops tried to follow but we cut them off, just got in their way. One of them ran hard into Mike, who greeted him with a raised forearm that sent him flying back. Mike turned to me with a righteous smile. Suddenly the plain clothes cops found themselves surrounded by demonstrators, and started slowly trying to back their way out, as they were showered with taunts: "motherfucking pigs," "shit-licking swine."

A breath-sucking gasp turned our heads back toward the steps. A lot of scared people were coming right at me. The pigs had attacked from the steps. I raised my arms to slow the tide down, but I was knocked back by people just trying to get away as fast as they could. I could hear Mike yelling, "Be cool, be cool, don't panic," but I couldn't see him. People weren't being cool. It was just fucking chaos as the hysterical retreat moved through us like a flash flood, spinning us around and splitting us up. Patrick was still in my sight and I could hear Matthew not far away still yelling for people to walk and stay together. I had no idea where everybody else was. At first, the charging cops were just glimpses of dark blue and swinging batons in motion, seen through the frenzied kaleidoscope of a panicked mob, but they moved quickly and soon their advancing line—now starkly clear in my sight and jagged and raw and wildly violent—was only about ten feet from me as I started my own retreat.

I kept Patrick in view and looked for the others as I tried to stay safely in front of the police line but not run, not panic. Shit, I was scared. They were mean-looking motherfuckers and they were definitely aching to kick some commie hippie ass. But there was something else happening. I don't know if it was adrenaline or just fucking anger or what. But goddammit, I wasn't going to run.

The bulk of the crowd had moved out of the quadrangle now and into the street. A lot of them just kept going, getting away from this scene as fast as they could. But a smaller group was beginning to mass on Huntington Avenue. With the thinner crowd in the quadrangle, the cops could zoom in on specific individuals and beat the shit out of them.

Patrick and I were making our way toward the wrought iron fence we'd have to go over to get to the street when I looked back and saw a tall thin girl in a dark blue pea coat fall down as she tried to retreat from the advancing pigs. Two cops immediately started wailing on her with their batons. I saw blood spurt from her head and they kept swinging. I went back toward her, yelling at the cops, "Goddammit, you motherfucking pigs stop it. Goddammit why are you doing that?" Other cops went past them and started heading toward me as I stood there screaming and shaking my fist. "Goddamn, motherfucking pigs, leave her alone."

Patrick came rushing back to me and grabbed my shoulder, "Ben, come on, you can't help her. They're coming after us now. We gotta find the others. Come on, let's get out of here."

He was right. Goddammit. Like fucking Boston English. Like the GE demonstrations. Like the Moratorium or Election Day 1968 or the counter-inauguration. Like Joe fucking Brook at Marsh Chapel. Like Chicago. Like Vietnam. Like the Panthers. Watch people get the shit beat out of them and shake my fists from a safe distance. Motherfuckers. I followed Patrick to the fence, took a look back, saw the bloodied girl being helped to her feet by some medics or other demonstrators who were seeing to the wounded the police had left in their wake. I shouted at the pigs one more time and leapt over the five-foot fence. Fuck it was easy. I was strong. I was mad. My head was absolutely clear. I wasn't scared anymore.

What was left of the demonstrators—two hundred or so of us, maybe—had massed on Huntington Avenue from one sidewalk to the other. No sign of the Weathermen. Before Patrick and I could enter the street, a Boston police paddy wagon tried to bull its way through the crowd, nudging the freaks who grudgingly gave way. Just as it hit an open path and began to speed up, it was showered with a barrage of rocks that cracked its window and dented its thick sides. It was almost musical, the percussion of shattering glass and the trilling melody of pounded metal. A jeering cheer went up from the street as it sped away.

Patrick and I moved across the street looking for our friends, stopping on the trolley tracks, where we both reached down and picked up rocks. The pigs, having cleared the quadrangle with a kind of frenzied furious attack, had regrouped to form a two-deep phalanx to try to clear the street. They knew most of the innocent bystanders were gone now, the demonstrators left would not be so easily routed.

The rock felt good in my hand. It had the flat smoothness of a good skipping stone, but with the heft to do some damage. It fit easily in my closed fist. As the cops got closer, I worked it into throwing position, my index and middle fingers forming a v around its broad side. We still hadn't found Mike and Jerry and Wes and Mac. But now it didn't matter. Patrick and a throng of freaks were beside me, and this did seem to be the place to make a stand. We held our ground as the pigs rhythmic marching, the ringing thud of boots against the street, slowly closed the ground between them and us.

As they moved toward us, their eyes came clearer into focus. Contempt. Hatred. Just fucking pissed-off straight-ass white-man anger. Shit man, I don't know exactly what it was, but I do know that each and every one of those cops wanted to mash my fucking skull with his club. Or Patrick's. Or the guy standing next to him. They wanted us. Bad. The cops approached a kid who looked liked a student sitting on a bench, waiting for the next trolley. Without warning two cops swung their clubs at him knocking him and his books to the ground. Another cop kicked him in the gut without hardly breaking the cadence of the march that was bringing them closer to us.

I wasn't really thinking anymore. I just did it. I had a clear shot at the front line of cops, and, finally finding the perfect grip, I drew my arm back and threw my rock. Hard and true. It knocked his hat off, some cop in the middle of the line, and must have got his head too because he dropped to his knees where he was helped by the cops around him. Everything else stopped for a millisecond and the world and all the shit flying around my head was reduced to me and that cop, with a red trail of blood starting to make its way around his eye and down his face. It felt right—that millisecond. Not good. Not victorious. Not sensible or reasoned or strategic. Just absolutely fucking right.

Patrick turned to me and cocked his eye in congratulations as he cradled his own rock. A freak about ten feet away caught my eye with a big old smile on his face and shouted, "Good shot, brother." As I returned his smile, I felt a hand underneath my elbow. I turned toward it and saw a black man, thin, tall, and very serious looking, moving right toward my face and reaching up, way up, under my arm as if to grab me. I was confused for an instant—why was this guy grabbing me?—but one look in his eyes told me he was not on our side.

I yanked my arm away from him, and sort of pushed Patrick between him and me, yelling, "He's a cop." Patrick's interference gained me a little time and I started running through the crowd, away from the front lines of the confrontation. As I was running I saw Mike and Jerry and ran toward them, sort of jumping on Mike's back, as I went by yelling "There's a cop. He's after me." And then kept running. But by the time Mike could react, the cop was by them, and I broke out of the crowd into the open of Huntington Avenue with him about twenty feet behind me. Shit, I was sure I could outrun him.

I turned into an alley about a half block down Huntington from the demonstration and for a second or two, it was just me in that alley, running hard and free. Then I heard the cop's voice for the first time, yelling: "Stop or I'll shoot."

CHAPTER TWENTY-SEVEN

January 29-30

I TURNED TO LOOK BACK. He was coming toward me fast. The pocket of his trench coat bulged.

"Stop or I'll blow your goddamn head off," he shouted.

I stopped. The alley was so dark in front of me, I couldn't see to the end of it. Next to where I stood was a pile of busted up cardboard boxes, smelling like rotten food.

"Put your hands up," he shouted. "Now!" He still had one hand in the pocket of his long, dark coat, and he was pointing something. I put my hands up. Could've been a gun. Shit, it could've been his finger.

"Turn around!" he said.

I turned around with my hands still in the air, looking into the darkness. Shit. Goddamn. Motherfucker. Those were my only thoughts. Shit. Goddamn. Motherfucker. He could've killed me right there or beat the shit out of me. It was just me and a Red Squad pig in a dark alley. Me with my back to him. Shit. Goddamn. Motherfucker.

"You just stand there and don't move a goddamn muscle. You got that."

"Yeah." Shit. Goddamn. Motherfucker.

He frisked me, patting me hard, starting under my arms and working down. Then he grabbed my right wrist and yanked it down and twisted it around and jammed it up against my back almost to my shoulder blades. "I think you're in some serious fucking trouble, my man. Some serious fucking trouble," he said as he ground my right hand into my back and whipped my left arm around into a matching position. He then held them both with one hand, with enough pressure to make me bend at the waist.

"Assaulting police officers is a very bad thing." He locked the handcuffs around one hand and then the other. "A very bad thing." He pulled straight back on the handcuffs, which doubled me over with my arms out straight behind me. "Let's go."

He turned me around so I was heading back toward Huntington Avenue. Then he kind of shoved me in the back, still holding the cuffs with one hand. "Walk!"

I didn't say a word. Shit. Goddamn. Motherfucker.

As we got close to Huntington Avenue, I heard the rumble of the crowd in the streets again. I could see groups of freaks moving away from the police lines. I wondered what was happening with Mike and Patrick and Jerry and Mac and Wes. How would they know what happened to me?

I saw a paddy wagon on Huntington Avenue, next to the alley. Six uniformed cops huddled next to it. When they saw us coming, two of them moved toward us, one moved to the back of the paddy wagon, and the rest surveyed the scene around them.

The Red Squad cop pushed me into the arms of the two uniformed cops without saying a word. Each took one of my arms with hard, tight grips. They moved fast, almost lifting me. My feet got tangled up in themselves trying to keep up with their pace so they just sort of dragged me for a few feet, before I could get my legs underneath me again. Just as we turned the corner around the back of the paddy wagon, where a cop was holding the door open, I saw Patrick and Mike moving away from us about twenty-five feet down Huntington Avenue. They saw me, too. We made no acknowledgment. They couldn't help me right then and I didn't want to draw attention to them. Our eyes locked for a second. Mine said, "Shit. Goddamn. Motherfucker." Other demonstrators were yelling at the cops—"Pigs." "Let him go." "Blue Meanies." The cops picked me up and drew back, like a baseball pitcher winding up, and threw me into the back of the paddy wagon and slammed the door.

I landed on my stomach. It was suddenly quiet. I was alone. I laid face down, right where they'd thrown me, for a while, stunned. I had to roll over on my side and draw my legs up, almost into a fetal position, and then push with them and my locked-together arms to get myself upright. Then I slithered my way up on one of the benches that ran along both sides. I sat on the edge of the bench because my hand-cuffed arms made it impossible to sit all the way back and the hard metal walls stung my hands with their cold if I leaned back against them. I couldn't see a fucking thing but I could smell piss and fear. Shit. Goddamn. Motherfucker.

I was screwed, no doubt about it. I knew that like I knew my name. But I couldn't even think about just how screwed I was. I didn't know how to figure that or deal with it if I could. I knew it would become all too clear, all too soon. What I had to do was to get through each minute as it came, without losing it, without freaking out. I couldn't afford to freak out. Holding it together right this very minute was going to take every bit of my energy and concentration. That was really all I could think about.

We just sat there for a while. I don't know how long. Time was no friend in this situation. Now was bad but whatever next thing was waiting would be at least as bad. And whatever place they'd take me was sure to be worse than this fucking dismal hunk of metal that held me. Outside kids were probably still running and yelling and hassling cops. Charged up and pissed, but moving from here to there, toward some kind of desired end. But I was somewhere else entirely, a prisoner.

Finally, we started moving slowly. I was still alone. Shit. Not that I wanted anybody else to get busted, but I knew that the pigs were busting other people. I was hoping somebody would share this dark cold place with me—someone to talk to, to compare stories with, to get some strength from. Just as we were getting started I heard a couple of quick thuds against the side of the paddy wagon. There were still kids out there fighting. I found that somehow reassuring, like the tap a prisoner hears in one of those old foreign legion prison movies—a sign of life outside. *La lutte continué.* Then the paddy wagon sped up and it was just me alone again, riding down streets I couldn't see toward a place I didn't know— but that I knew I didn't want to be.

All I heard was the rising grind and fall of the paddy wagon's engine. Each time it came to a stop or started moving again, I slid along the bench because I couldn't grab a hold of anything to anchor myself. I slid until I could brake the motion by scraping my shoes against the floor— the way I'd stopped my bike with no brakes when I was a kid.

For a second—just a second—I thought of Sarah and the bitter sweetness of the last kiss we shared in Philadelphia. Her tangy soft lips and watery eyes. The promises and questions that pulsed between us as we hugged, desperate not to let go, knowing we had to. Her brave tender smile when I looked back from Wally's car. I felt a drift to that warmth that Sarah lit in me. Then the paddy wagon hit a pothole that sent me flying off the bench, sprawling on my side on the frigid metal bed, stinging my knee which hit the floor first. Sarah?—the chilly thought crept over me—shit! What was I going to say to her? What would she say to me?

Stop it. Stop it. Stop it, I yelled at myself as I dug for the strength to right myself in the paddy wagon that was now speeding along. I absolutely couldn't even start to think about that. I moved forcefully now and quickly. I got back up on the bench and scooted on my ass all the way to the end by the door, which had a small indentation where I could lock my foot to keep from sliding.

We drove a long way, it seemed. Where the fuck were they taking me? I desperately wanted a cigarette, but there was no way I could get one out of my pocket. Shit. Goddamn. Motherfucker.

Finally, we slowed and then pulled into what seemed—from the sudden smooth glide of the tires below me—to be some sort of garage. A police station, I guessed, as we pulled to a stop. I slid just a little bit away from the door and braced myself for the encounter to come. Shit, at least I'd be able to smoke a cigarette—and start dealing with whatever tribulation was sure to come.

The doors flew open. Two uniformed cops stood there looking at me. One of them had blood on his face and was holding some kind of compress to his forehead. They studied me like I was a zoo animal, but nobody said a word. I sat there waiting for them to grab me or tell me what to do. I wasn't moving until somebody did something. Then the bloodied cop nodded to the other one, who slammed the door shut. The engine started, and we were moving again.

What the fuck was that? The bleeding cop might have been the one I hit. I couldn't tell. But why would they do that? At least they didn't set him loose on me. Shit, I still didn't have a cigarette, but I sure as hell wasn't going to ask those guys to help me get one. Since the Red Squad cop had turned me over to the uniform cops, nobody had said a word to me. Nobody had asked my name or read me my rights or told me what I'd been arrested for. They'd put me in a paddy wagon by myself, driven me to some place where some cops just looked at me, and now were taking me someplace else. I couldn't make any sense of it, but I also couldn't bother trying just then.

We stopped again. This time, the doors opened and the lights and sounds of a busy city street flooded in. Four uniformed cops were waiting for me.

"Let's go," one of the cops yelled at me. I stood up and moved to the door.

The driver came around and said to my escorts, "This is the cocksucker that hit Riley with a brick."

"Shit, he don't look that tough to me now," one of the two cops in front said as he and the guy next to him grabbed my thighs and yanked me out of the paddy wagon. "He looks like a fucking pussy to me," he said.

I had a strategy: not say a fucking word I didn't have to. Name, rank, and serial number. Try not to give them a clue I was scared shitless of them.

The two guys who pulled me out of the paddy wagon led me into the station, each holding an arm and forcing it back as hard they could, making this procedure as painful as possible, the other two followed close behind along with the driver, pushing me in the back every once in awhile. They were talking at me the whole time calling me a faggot, a cock-sucking scum, a worthless piece of shit. I just put a stone mask on, no expression, my eyes straight ahead. Fuck, man, as long as they weren't hitting me I could deal with this.

The station was hot as hell. The cops took me down a crowded hallway. The five of them towered over me. I was lost in the circle they formed around me. We filed into a small bright office crowded with cops at desks, some freaks sitting next to a few of them. Everyone in the room looked up as we came in. The two cops held their tight grip on me and pushed me through the room, with the paddy wagon driver right behind. The two cops who were my rearguard hung back in the doorway.

"This is the sonuvabitch that hit Riley with the brick," the driver announced to the room, with special attention to a cop who had an empty chair beside his desk, which is where I seemed to be heading.

"This little pansy ass?" The cop said as the two other cops shoved me into the chair. "I guess a big enough brick can make a man of anyone." He laughed and a few of the other cops around the room laughed, too. What the fuck? Why did they keep talking about a brick?

The driver whispered into the ear of the desk cop, who listened and nodded, looking at me the whole time. Then the driver walked around my back and yanked my arms way up, so my shoulder blades were completely twisted in on themselves, and he unlocked the handcuffs. As my arms fell suddenly, my hands hit the backside of the chair and I felt a surge of pain. But then it felt good to stretch out and sense my arms as separate things. I shook them to get some feeling back.

The desk cop, who had short buzzed-cut dark brown hair and a shirt that was a size or two too small for his healthy gut, was piling up some forms.

He put a wire basket on the table and told me to empty my pockets into it. I had actually cleaned out my pockets before heading out earlier that night—in that different lifetime—so it wasn't much. My cigarettes—a curled up half pack of Marlboros—some Matching Roommates matches, a flyer for some upcoming theater presentation that someone had handed me as we were arriving at Northeastern, my tattered wallet—and my dime. That was it. I kept my dime.

"Can I have a cigarette?" I asked.

"Sure, pal, of course," he said. "But not right now. We got some business we've got to take care of first."

He took out a card and read me my rights, in a thick Southy accent. "You have the right to remain silent…" and the rest of it. I'd heard them before, except with an Illinois twang.

"What's your name?"

"Ben Tucker."

"Let me see some ID?"

I pulled my wallet out of the basket and took out my BU ID and my Illinois driver's license and handed them to him.

"It says here your name is Benjamin R. Tucker the Third. What kind of fucking name is that? Is your daddy a banker?"

"No." Name, rank, serial number.

"Hey gents," he shouted to the room, "the brick-thrower's name is Benjamin R. Tucker the Third. Can you believe that?" Then he looked back at me. "So Benjamin R. Tucker the Third, what does the R stand for? Rockefeller?" A cop sitting at the next desk laughed.

"No. Rollins." Stone face.

"Where do you live, Mr. Benjamin Rollins Tucker the Third."

"64 Mountfort Street."

"And you are a student at Boston University?"

"Yes."

"So what were you doing at Northeastern tonight."

"Uh…I don't think I should answer any questions like that until I see a lawyer."

"You don't think you should?"

"I'm not going to answer any question like that until I talk to a lawyer."

"Is your daddy a lawyer?"

"No."

"Too bad because you're going to need a good fucking lawyer, Mr. Benjamin Rollins Tucker the Third. Do you know what you've been arrested for?"

"No."

"Assault and battery of a police officer with a deadly weapon. And I don't really give a shit if you answer any of my questions because we pretty much have your ass nailed. Do you know what the penalties are for assault and battery of a police officer with a deadly weapon?"

"No."

"Twenty years in prison and a $10,000 fine, Mr. Benjamin Rollins Tucker the fucking Third. Twenty years. I think the boys in Walpole are going to really like you with that long blond hair, pretty boy."

Shit. Twenty years. Goddamn. Deadly weapon. Motherfucker. Stone face. Name, rank, serial number. Shit. Goddamn. Motherfucker.

"And your bail is $1,000."

"OK." Shit. "So . . . when do I get my phone call?"

"Soon. We're not done here yet."

"Can I have a cigarette?"

"After your phone call."

The cop took his time filling out his forms, every once in awhile looking up at me with a sneer or a hateful smile, like he knew whatever bureaucratic bullshit he was writing down was just another way of getting at how fucked I was. The room was steamy hot and noisy and bright, with big bare lights hanging low and glaring over each desk. Other cops walked by and the desk cop would nod at me and tell them I was the sonuvabitch-cocksucker-asshole who hit Riley with the brick. They'd study me and look back at him and they'd exchange some knowing look about exactly what sort of lowlife scum I was. I tried not to look, not to let them play their game with my eyes, but also not to cower, keep my head up, my expression fixed.

When the desk cop finished filling out the forms, he told me to get up. He led me to another room, small and crowded, where he stood over me while another cop got my fingerprints, taking my hand firmly, pressing each finger down hard against a gooey pad of ink and then rolling it onto a form with two rows of fives squares like I used to check out in the display case at the New Bedford Post Office—next to a picture of some heinous criminal wanted for postal fraud or bank robbery.

Then he took me to another corner of the same room, where they handed me a number and put me up against a white wall to take a mug shot. The cops were making cracks the whole time, calling me a pretty boy, asking me if I needed a little hair spray before they took my picture. I didn't respond. I just stared into the camera like I was posing for a rock and roll poster. Stone face.

Fingerprints and a mug shot. I was officially a criminal.

"OK, pal, your fucking pictures are going to be beautiful," the desk cop said. "Now you can make your phone call. One call. Your dime."

The phone was in the hallway just outside the finger printing, mug shot room. It was full of people. The cop stood next to me as I reached for my dime.

Suddenly I realized I didn't know who to call. The Mountfort Street phone had been disconnected. I didn't know the number for the girls at 858. Cary didn't have a phone. The only phone numbers I knew were home in Illinois—sure as hell wasn't calling that—Sarah's home—shit, wouldn't that be a fun call; I could wish her father a happy birthday—and Sarah's phone booth in Philly. Of course, I couldn't call there on a dime and it wouldn't do me a hell of a lot of good to be calling Philadelphia. I wasn't quite ready to talk to her even if I could.

"Let's go," the cop said. "We ain't got all night."

Shit. The only thing I could think to do was to dial the BU exchange and four random numbers and hope that I got somebody who would help me. Shit.

I dialed 353—the beginning of all the numbers at BU—then a random 2517. It started ringing. I looked at the cop looking at me, wondering what he'd think if he knew what a shot in the dark I'd just taken.

A guy's voice answered, "Hello."

"Hello," I said. "Um…listen, this is kind of a crazy call, but please just listen for a second."

"Who is this?"

"My name is Ben Tucker. I'm a student at BU. I was arrested at a demonstration at Northeastern tonight. I'm calling from jail, and I need some help."

It was quiet for a second on the other end. Then I heard, "OK. Sure. Tell me more."

"Oh, man, thank you. I didn't know any other phone numbers so I just dialed a random BU number. Are you at BU?"

"Yeah."

"Where?"

"Myles Standish."

"Far out, man. What's your name?"

"Tim. Tim Sutton."

"I'm Ben Tucker. Guess I already told you that. Anyway, I have good friends in Myles Standish, some of them were with me tonight, so they may not be back there yet. Jerry Butler and his roommate Ronnie Spaulding—Ronnie wasn't there tonight. They're on the second floor—it's 219, I think, just like one door to the right from the top of the main stairway on the second floor."

"I don't know them but I could try to find them."

"Thanks, man. I've been arrested for assaulting a police officer. I'm at the Boston City Jail. I don't know the address or anything, but I'm sure they can find it. My bail is $1,000."

"OK."

"If you find Ronnie or Jerry, tell them what I told you and ask them to tell the people at Mountfort Street."

"OK."

"If they're not there, I've got to get word to my friends at Mountfort Street. It's not far from Myles."

"OK."

"From Kenmore Square, go up Beacon Street and Mountfort Street is just after the bridge over the turnpike on the right—there's a pizza joint on the corner. My building is right next to the pizza place—64 Mountfort Street. Apartment number 9. Whoever's there. Tell them what I told you. You got all that?"

"Yeah, I think so. Ben Tucker. You're in the Boston City Jail. You need $1,000 bail. Jerry and Ronnie on the second floor. 64 Mountfort Street. Number 9. I'll try to do what I can."

"Man, you don't know how glad I am that you're there and into helping me. Man, I can't tell you."

"It's all right. Take it easy, man."

"Thanks, brother. I mean really—thanks."

The incredible absurdity of that conversation and the reality that this completely random stranger at least said he was going to help me made me smile for a second as I hung up the phone and, with a new source of some strength, I drew a deep breath.

The cop saw me hang up and brusquely grabbed my arm and yanked me away from the phone: "Daddy coming to get you?"

I didn't say anything, but I stopped smiling.

"I'll show you to your accommodations. I hope you'll find them to your satisfaction, Master Benjamin."

"Can I have a cigarette, now?"

"I've got to put you in your cell now. I'll have somebody bring them to you in a little while."

We went through a locked door into an area filled with barred cells, one row of cells directly in front of us and rows going off to the left and to the right. I saw a couple of freaks in a cell just up ahead. Hoped maybe that's where I was going. But we turned left. No freaks in that direction. He put me in the fourth cell. By myself. To the right of me was a hobo-looking kind of guy who seemed to be sleeping off a drunk. Nobody was in the cell on the other side of me.

He rolled the cell door open and kind of shoved me in. Then he rolled it emphatically shut—the clanging metal ringing off the hard walls. He turned the key and smiled at me.

"I hope you enjoy your stay, you little worthless piece of shit."

"Would you please make sure that I get my cigarettes?"

"Sure thing, pal."

Fuck. His footsteps rang loud as he walked away and slammed the outer door behind him. I could hear the buzz of low voices in other parts of the jail, but it was quiet on my end except for the raspy snores of the drunk next to me. My cell was about four feet by eight feet. There was a metal bench in one corner and a piss hole in another. There wasn't really any place to sleep. The drunk was just curled up on the floor of his cell. I sat on the bench. Fuck, I wish I had a cigarette.

I felt myself really exhale for the first since the Red Squad cop grabbed me—or since I saw that girl go down in the quad, I guess.

I thought about my phone call. Tim. He could've been totally goofing on me or thought I was goofing on him. I didn't think so. Maybe he could tell by the tone of my voice that I was dead fucking serious. And he sounded like he was really going to do it. Shit. Had the stupid fucking dime. Just didn't have a fucking phone number. Where were they going to get a $1,000 anyway?

My brain was running amok. The here and now. This hard gray cell. These charges and the cluster bomb they would drop into my life. And songs. Whole long riffs of songs that roared over the frantic chatter of trying to make any sense of this. "Accidents" by Thunderclap Neuman, which was playing as we left the apartment, The Kinks' "Shangri-La," The Beatles' "Carry that Weight," "Down by the River" by Neil Young. Full-on blasting in my head—but my thoughts were louder.

Would anybody think to call Sarah? Shit, what a scene that would be at her house. Her father's birthday. What would she do? Was any chance we had gone now? Goddammit. I couldn't really blame her for packing it in now. I'd gone exactly where she didn't want to go, taken a leap to a ledge that there was no way back from, that forced a choice. I wasn't just some cute blond boy from Boston who played at radical politics anymore—I was a cop-assaulting criminal, all chances of cleaning up and becoming somebody mom and dad could learn to accept pretty much shot to hell now. What would she do? Fuck.

Deadly weapon? Why were the fucking cops talking about a brick? What was with the stop on the way to the jail? The two cops checking me out? Why'd they put me in a cell by myself?

My parents? Oh, man. I'd been arrested before, but this was something else. At sixteen, had to call my old man from the Champaign County jail. Busted for going ten miles over the speed limit, being out ten minutes after curfew, not having my driver's license (lost it), and having a rock and roll poster (for our show at the Homer Elementary School) in the back window of the car (obstructed vision). Had to call him at 1 o'clock in the morning. He was pissed. Then about a year later, six of us rock-and-rollers got arrested for disorderly conduct and riot because we had a little mock battle at a stop light after I had taunted a carload of guys from another band because I was going to see the Yardbirds and they couldn't because they had a gig. We were just goofing around but the Champaign cops flipped out. We sat in jail for about six hours—I didn't call my parents that time. We had a good time, all of us in jail together, because we knew it was bullshit. Except I missed the Yardbirds. This, though…this was different.

> *My eyes collide head-on with stuffed*
> *Graveyards, false gods, I scuff*
> *At pettiness which plays so rough*
> *Walk upside-down inside handcuffs*
> *Kick my legs to crash it off*

Say OK, I have had enough, what else can you show me?

And if my thought-dreams could be seen
They'd probably put my head in a guillotine
But it's alright, Ma, it's life, and life only

I sat on that cold, hard bench in my sweltering cell, drifting between being sharply tuned into the whispers and shouts and slamming cell doors—jail sounds that were as harshly bright as the oppressive lighting but also seemed far away from me—and slipping deep into my head, following the rushing streams of thoughts. For so long—shit, how long ago was it that the cop grabbed me? More than any specific number of minutes or hours, I knew that—I'd been focused only on not losing it in the next second. Now in the odd freedom of being locked in this cell unable to do a fucking thing except wait for that pig-ass cop to bring me my cigarettes and for my friends to raise the bail money, I let my mind go, knowing that I'd crossed some irreversible line. Everything would be different now. It had to be. Sarah, my parents, school, my friends. The fucking pigs and courts and lawyers were now part of a suddenly radically different future that would start when I got out of this place. I had no real idea what it would be, what I would do, what would happen to me, how others would react, but I knew this night had changed everything and I didn't really know how to even start thinking about it. My life had gone into some kind of suspended reality and I felt myself floating on that—or was it drowning? But, shit, man, I wished I had a cigarette.

My existential trance was broken by a swelling shrill echo of a herd of feet heading in my direction. Maybe somebody was bringing me my cigarettes. Or, maybe even, I'd been bailed out. But I quickly realized that the four TPF cops who now lined up along the outside of my cell, weren't there to make my stay any easier. From the neck down, they looked like they'd been carved from the same pattern. They were all big and beefy, their tight, deep blue uniforms showing the thickness of their arms and chests. They didn't wear hats, which somehow made their visit more intimate and personal. Beneath their marine-issue buzz cuts, I could see the individuality of their faces—a long crooked nose on one, dark, bushy eyebrows on another, a deep square forehead, oversized ears—but their eyes all bore in on me with the same contempt and loathing, like the look I'd seen across Huntington Avenue. And they seemed to speak with one voice.

"You little squirrelly ass cocksucker."

"You little piece of donkey shit."

"You fucking asshole."

"You cowardly son of a bitch."

"We just wanted to come and see the worthless piece of crap who thinks he's a tough guy with a brick in his hand in the middle of a crowd. You don't look so tough sitting here all by your pansy-ass self. You look like a fucking scared little maggot to me."

Don't say anything, I told myself over and over. These guys could kill me. Easy and quick. I looked for my stone face and picked a spot on the floor to stare at.

"Look at us, you little hippie shit." I didn't. I kept staring at the floor. "We all watched our brother Riley go down from the fucking brick you threw. Saw his face smashed and his mouth all busted up. And we're fucking pissed."

What the fuck were they talking about?

"We don't like it when chicken-shit punks like you hurt our brothers. We don't like it at all. I'd love five minutes alone you with you in this cell. Shit, I wouldn't need five minutes. I could fucking kick your ass to hell and back in one minute, you little snivelly faggot. But this place is crawling with lawyers. We don't like lawyers much either, but we don't want to give you an easy way out of this, fucking crying 'police brutality' like all the other babies who act tough until they're face to face with real men."

"We don't trust the fucking courts either—especially with spoiled rich college kids like you."

I looked up for just a second, looked quickly into their faces, and thanked whatever god there was that there were bars between me and them.

"That's right you little commie sissy scum, take a good look. Cause we're taking a good look at you, that pretty blond hair, those sweet blue eyes. And we're going to find you, cocksucker. Some day, you're going to be walking down the street minding your own business and we'll find you and you'll wish you were fucking dead. We'll fucking shave your pea head and cut your fucking balls off—if you have any to begin with—and you'll be sorry you ever set foot in this city. We'll fucking cut your whole little cock off and stuff it down your fucking throat. Try calling us 'pigs' then."

They all joined in a dark and violent laugh.

"That's not a threat, pal, that's a fucking solemn oath. You are a fucking marked man. We don't forget."

And the last guy to speak spit at me, the foamy white glob landing on my jeans just above my knee. I didn't react. Didn't look up. Didn't brush the spit off my pants.

"You fucking little pussy," the guy who'd done most of the talking said and his cohort joined in another sadistic laugh, and they filed away with the same barrage of insults they'd arrived with.

I let my breath out slow and wiped the spit off my jeans with my coat sleeve.

"Whoa man, what the hell did you do?" It was the guy next door, who'd been waken from his drunken slumber by the cops' little show. "Did you kill somebody?"

I was startled by his voice, which was thick and rusty.

"Um... no, no. I didn't kill anybody. I know that. But...you know...I don't know exactly what I did—or what they think I did."

"Man, those cops were pissed at you. They think they know what you did."

"Yeah, they do…but, you know, I have no idea what they were talking about."

"Well, bud, I'd tried to figure it out quick if I was you. Those cops weren't fooling around. They want to hurt you—bad."

"I know. I know," I said.

We talked for a while. He told me he didn't remember exactly when he'd been brought in. Last thing he remembered was the beginnings of an argument with some guy in a bar. He couldn't remember what it was about. He thought he was going to get out anytime now, but he figured the cops were so busy with all the demonstrators coming in that they'd forgotten about him. Turned out he'd grown up in Fall River, the next city over from New Bedford, but he was much older than me and we didn't know any of the same people, though we threw some names at each other.

A single set of footsteps came toward us and stopped in front of his cell. They were letting him out. I asked the cop if he could see about getting me my cigarettes. He said, "sure thing"—and I never saw him again.

Now, I got obsessed with time. What time was it? How long had I been here? Was I going to have to spend all fucking night in this cell? Maybe Tim just had a good laugh with his friends and lit up another joint. It was an outrageous request I had made. I heard people coming and going in other parts of jail, but it was dead quiet and still on my row. I gnawed at my fingernails until the tips of my fingers bled, playing with the little bits of nail I chewed off, guiding them with my tongue into the gaps in my teeth than forcing them through to the other side with streams of my spit. Shit. Goddamn. Motherfucker.

It seemed like a long time until they finally came and got me. It was a different cop than had booked me, but he was just as nasty. He shoved me in the back as I started to walk down the hall. Called me a maggot and a bunch of other names but nothing I hadn't been called many times already.

They took me to a room where they gave me the stuff that had been in my pockets. My fucking cigarettes weren't even there. Assholes. I had to sign some papers and then they led me down to the other end of the hallway I'd come in. I opened the door onto a large room, the public lobby of the station, big tall ceilings and high bright lights. Cops were shuffling around and little clusters of people talked in low tones that generated a steady buzz. Others stood, slumping or leaning against nearby walls, the awkward posture of waiting. As I walked through the door, all the eyes in the room looked to me for a second, with expectations and questions and, for all the cops, disgust. And there was Stu, coming away from the back wall toward me. He looked really tired but there was a twinkle of relief in his eyes. Suddenly I felt like I wanted to cry for the first time all night.

We met in the middle of the room and I gave him a big hug. "Thanks, man," I said quietly.

"How are you doing? Are you OK?" He had a soft smile and his eyes got big with concern.

"I'm OK, but I could sure use a fucking cigarette—I know you can't help me with that." Stu didn't smoke. "Those assholes took mine."

"We'll get you a cigarette. There's a lawyer over here who needs to talk to you, then we can get the hell out of here."

He led me to a bench along a wall where a guy with a loose fitting tie and thick glasses was sorting papers, making piles on the bench. He looked up as we approached. Stu spoke, "Russ, this is Ben Tucker."

He stood up and shook my hand. "Ben, I'm Russ Manley, I'm with the Lawyer's Guild. Sit down. How are you doing? Did they hit you or anything?"

"I'm OK. They didn't beat me but...a bunch of them, a bunch of the TPF cops, four of them, came and threatened me, said they'd get me on the street someday. Cut my balls off and shit like that. And they stole my damn cigarettes."

"Consider yourself lucky if that's the worst you got...for now at least."

"Yeah, I guess so." Just then Stu handed me a cigarette he'd scrounged from somebody. I dug my matches out of my pocket—they'd given them back to me—and lit it. I pulled long and hard on it, filling some deep emptiness in me. Man, that felt good, the gliding smoothness down my throat, the warm pressure in my lungs, and then the release…

I must have drifted away for a second cause all of a sudden I noticed Manley kind of smiling impatiently at me, like he was ready to move on but trying hard not to rush me.

"Sorry," I said and took another quick drag on the cigarette but kept my focus on him.

"It's OK. So Ben, you know you've been charged with assault and battery of a police officer with a deadly weapon."

"Yeah…but they kept talking about a brick. I didn't do anything with any brick."

"They did, huh?" the lawyer looked like he was trying to put something together. "It doesn't say anything about that here. But…" He was rubbing the back of his head. It must have been a long night for him, too. "They do seem especially upset about the cop they say you hit. They'll present their evidence tomorrow in court, and then we'll have a better idea what we're dealing with."

I looked at Stu, who shook his head. This was a whole other level of dealing with bullshit from the cops. And he didn't even know about the twenty years yet. I took another deep drag on the cigarette and looked back at Manley.

"So listen, Ben, you have to appear in court at 9:30 tomorrow to be arraigned. What that means is that the cops have to show there's some good reason to believe you committed this crime, reason enough to proceed to a trial, and you have to enter a plea. It's usually pretty brief and straightforward. I won't be there but we'll have somebody there to represent you. If it does go on to trial, you'll probably want to see about getting your own lawyer."

"Thanks, man. 9:30, Huh? Where do I have to go?"

"Roxbury District Court. The address and stuff is on your bail form. You should probably be there by 9:00. Look for our lawyer. I'm not sure who it will be, but he'll tell you everything you need to know. Do you have any other questions for me now?" He looked concerned, but also harried. There were other people waiting to talk to him.

"Nothing I can think of now. Thanks, man."

"Good luck, Ben." He stood up and shook my hand, smiled, and then was immediately shuffling papers again. I started to walk away and then stopped and turned back toward him.

"Hey, man, do I owe you something for this?"

"No," he said. Then he thought again. "Yeah…you do. You owe it to me to try to stay out of jail," he smiled bigger now. "Live to fight another day."

"Right on. Thanks, man."

Stu was kind of hanging back as I finished up with Manley. I caught his eye and he came up next to me. I must have looked confused because he nodded his head toward the doors as we started walking and asked, "Are you really OK, man?"

"Aside from being totally fucked, I'm fine," I laughed and Stu cracked a smile. Then I suddenly needed to reorient myself to what had been going on outside that jail. "How the hell did you get here? What time is it? How'd you come up with all that money? Did that cat from Myles find you guys? How's everybody else? Anybody else get arrested or hurt? Does Sarah know? Cary?"

"Shit, man," Stu laughed now. "Take another hit off your cigarette and then give 'em to me one at a time." I laughed and took a drag as we went through the big doors out into the brightly lit street. It didn't seem as cold as I remembered from before they'd thrown me in jail, and a little sleety rain was falling. It felt great.

"Brian gave me a ride," Stu said. "He couldn't find a legal place to park anywhere near here, so he was just going to kind of move around double-parking." He scanned the quiet street as we got to the bottom of the jailhouse steps. "There he is." I saw the little VW bug about half a block down, purring and releasing a steady stream of white smoke. "What were your other questions? Oh, yeah, time? Shit, I guess it's about two. We got down here a little after one, I think. The pigs weren't moving real fast to let you out. Mike would have come down, too, but he was afraid they might decide to bust him, too."

"That was probably smart. Did the guy from Myles find you?" We crossed the street toward Brian's car. "Man, I can't believe I didn't know a fucking phone number to call. Shit."

"Yeah, yeah," Stu said. "He was cool. He couldn't believe you just dialed a random number." He looked at me and chuckled. "You were pretty lucky. We would have found you eventually but..." We were at the car now. I finished my cigarette and tossed the butt into the gutter. Stu opened the passenger-side door for me and Brian held the seat forward so I could climb in the back.

I said hello to Brian. His thick eyebrows were all scrunched up as he checked me out: "Hey, man, how are you doing?"

"Oh, man..." I laughed. "I'm doing better all the time. So glad to be out of there. Thanks for coming."

"No problem, man. We all wanted to get you out of there as fast as we could."

"Thanks. You got a cigarette?" He handed me a cigarette and I lit it as he started moving down the street. "Where'd you guys come up with all that money?"

Stu looked at Brian. "Tucker's playing twenty question—that's about number three now." Both Brian and me laughed. "Lots of people gave us money. Mike and Brian and Little Eddie went to 858 and worked the phones—called a couple of our friendly marijuana suppliers. They came through—they don't want to lose your paper writing skills. Lenny and me and Jerry and Ronny and Mac and Wes—and Tim, the guy you talked to on the phone—went door to door in Myles Standish. Shit, almost everybody gave us something—a buck or two or five or ten, even a couple of joints. It was pretty far out. Most of them didn't even know you—wait, come to think of it maybe that's why they were into contributing." He looked at me with a winking smile.

I felt a little teary again. Took a long drag on my cigarette. We were going around Boston Common. The trees sparkled as the gentle rain frosted them with a shimmering coat. I'd been this way before in the dead time between night and morning, once riding a borrowed bike early in my freshman year. But then I felt as if I owned the silence of the streets, the emptiness of the Common paths: blank possibilities that I dared to fill with my own imaginings. On this night, the Common hung like a still life, a static landscape I watched drift by and disappear in a blur.

"How about Sarah? Does she know?" I asked as we turned on to Commonwealth Avenue.

"I think so," Stu said. "I think Leslie called her."

I took another drag and watched the stately brick buildings go by. I still couldn't imagine what was going through Sarah's mind, what it would mean. I wanted desperately to talk to her, but I had no idea what I would say. Maybe it was good that I couldn't talk to her yet. The car was silent for a while as I held an image of her in my head and tried to conjure how her eyes would react to the unintelligible sounds coming out of my mouth. All I could see was distance and doubt. But I just couldn't go too far down that road right then.

"Hey, how was the concert?" I asked. It was a relief to think about something else.

"It was great," they said together, also seeming relieved to break the silence with a topic other than my fucked condition. Stu said, "Alvin Lee's amazing ..." and he looked back over the seat at me, his eyes bright with the enthusiasm that a good rock and roll show lit in him. "Man, you should have been there." Then, realizing all that he just said, his expression dropped and our eyes met in an intimate and scary place.

Then I laughed. "Maybe, Stu. Maybe...."

CHAPTER TWENTY-EIGHT

January 30

THE ALARM SHOUTED AT ME.

The clock said 8 o'clock. Shit, I thought through my fuzzy brain, I can't possibly have to get up already. I could skip whatever class I had that morning. What day was it? Where was I supposed to be? I tried to remember. And then it all started creeping back into my head.

I sat up quickly, rubbing my face hard with my hands. The smell of jailhouse ink lingered on the tips of my fingers, still a smudgy black. Court. I have to be in court. By nine. Deadly weapon. Twenty years. Shit.

Mike had given me a sleeping pill when I got home. I don't think I could have slept without it, but it left me in a shell of fogginess that I was having a hard time cracking. I was in my bed, in my room, in my apartment, but I felt lost.

I crawled out of bed and grabbed a cigarette. My heart was speeding, but my brain just wouldn't engage as it stumbled through a maze of images from the night before. I searched through my pants, laying on the floor beside my bed, for a match. I lit the cigarette, inhaling deeply and then coughing it out, and looked around my room—piles of clothes and papers filling the floor, posters staring at me from the wall, the burlap curtains, hanging crooked over the tall windows onto the alley. I was looking for something, but I wasn't sure what.

Then I saw Mike standing in my doorway. He had a big brother kind of expression. "Glad to see you're up," he said. "You all right?"

"Yeah, I guess. That pill knocked me on my ass. I'm feeling a little spacy, now."

"You'll be all right. You probably need to get your shit together pretty quick. Stu told me you were supposed to be in court at nine." Stu had already gone to work.

"Yeah, I remember that." Then I looked around the room again. "Tavola. Where's Tavola? Have you seen her?"

"No, I ain't seen her in a couple of days. Listen, man, get dressed. Brian's going to give you a ride to the court. He thinks it will take about fifteen minutes. I don't think it would be smart for me to go. They might be looking for me. They'll have a lawyer there for you, right?"

"Yeah, that's what the lawyer last night said."

"Good, so get dressed now."

I looked at the pile of clothes on my floor. "What do I wear?"

"Wear that three piece suit you got hanging in your closet," he laughed. I didn't have a suit. Shit, I didn't have a closet. "It don't matter, man, just put on something sort of clean."

"Yeah, OK." I was still having a hard time doing anything. I looked at Mike. He almost filled the doorway. He could be cold and hard, mean even sometimes, but now that scary bulk and intensity, his piercing eyes, made me feel safe, protected. A surge of gratitude and sadness made my eyes start to water. "Mike, I think this could be pretty heavy."

"I know man, but don't worry, I'm with you. You got a lot of people with you. We won't let nothing happen to you. Count on that."

"I know. Thanks, man. I know that…it's just…I don't know…it just makes everything so different."

"I know. But don't worry about that right now. You just gotta get through this court thing today and then we'll figure out what we're going to do. OK, get dressed now." He started pulling himself out of the doorway.

"Mike," I said. "I really thought I was going to get away. I mean I wasn't running so much because I was scared. Really. It all happened so fast, I didn't have time to be scared. It just seemed like the right thing to do—to get away. I just needed somebody to slow him down a little more. Patrick tried, I know. But…"

"I know. Hey, man, I wished I would've seen him sooner. I would have slowed him down."

"I know you would have—I'm not saying anybody did anything wrong—just that I ran to get away, not just to run." I heard myself kind of pleading to him. He gave me a big smile.

"It's all right, man. It's all right, but you gotta get dressed."

"OK. OK. Just one more thing. Do you know what Sarah said to Leslie when she called her?"

"I don't know exactly but I think she was pretty freaked out," he said. "You can call her when you're done in court. Listen, man, you got to start moving."

"OK." I grabbed some sort of clean-looking jeans and pulled them on. Mike was heading back toward his room. "Did anybody get a hold of my sister?"

"I don't know. I don't think so," he yelled back. She didn't have a phone. I'd have to get over there sometime. I didn't want her to read about in the paper first—if this even made the papers.

"If you see Tavola," I yelled to Mike, "keep her in, OK?"

"Sure," he yelled from further away. He was in his room now.

I found a blue button-down shirt that wasn't too dirty or wrinkled and a light brown sweater to wear over it. I went into the bathroom and splashed my face a dozen times with cold water and brushed my hair back and gathered it into a ponytail. I cleared a hole in the film on the mirror so I could see myself. I looked strange. My face seemed leathery, worn. Red streaks filled the white surrounding my blue eyeballs. The ridges ran deeper and thicker across my forehead. A dull coating grayed my skin, making it looked filmy, like the uncleared parts of the mirror. I tried smiling, but it took the muscles in my face a direction that they just didn't want to go. I splashed another dose of cold water over it all, shook it off, and headed out the door.

Brian drove me to the courthouse. My head was going a mile a minute, replaying the scenes from the night before, imagining what Sarah was thinking—what that conversation would be like—wondering what I'd say when I called my parents. Brian talked nervously about the traffic and the weather—the sun was actually breaking though the gray haze and it looked like it might even be a nice day. I just kind of nodded and grunted. He seemed to know where he was going—good thing because, as I looked out the window, everything seemed unfamiliar.

He dropped me off in front of the building. He had to be someplace else soon. It didn't register with me exactly where he was going, but he told me someone would try to get back to the courthouse before it was over. And that, if nobody made it, it was easy to get the MTA back to Kenmore Square. I told him that was cool, but as he drove away, I felt startled to realize that I was alone again. I lit a cigarette before starting up the stone steps. Looked around. Lots of people in suits and uniforms were filing through the big doors at the top, chatting, holding coffee cups, going to work, I guess. Shit, man, where was I going?

The lobby outside the main courtroom was a chaotic scene. People shuffled in and out of a glassed-off office to the left. Groups of cops, drinking coffee and smoking, stood just to the side of the doors into the courtroom. Lawyers and their clients, and their families and friends, were gathered in small groups on the benches that lined the wall. The Movement lawyers were obvious—their hair was a little longer, their suits hadn't been pressed in a while, their briefcases were worn and floppy, and they were talking to freaks. I saw three of them and headed in their direction.

I introduced myself and the lawyers looked down their lists and one of them claimed me. "Hi, I'm John Kelly, I'll be representing you today." I thanked him and he ran down what I should expect. When the judge called my name, he and I would go stand in front of him. The judge would read the charges against me and ask for a plea. I'd say, "Not guilty."

When Kelly said that, I looked at him with a question in my eyes and started to try to say something. He stopped me. "I don't even want to know what happened. Right now, you want to plead not guilty, which will give you a chance to figure out the best strategy for a trial. You plead guilty today and you're looking at a possible twenty years in jail. I don't think you want to do that. OK?"

"Yeah, OK." I said.

Kelly told me that after I entered my plea, the judge would set bail. He said all the indications from the prosecutors were that they'd just go with the bail I'd put up the night before. He asked me if there was anything he should know about my background, criminal history and stuff like that.

I told him about my arrests in Illinois. He said those wouldn't show up since I was a minor when they happened. I told him about the injunction at BU and the charges I'd faced because of the occupation of the dean's office.

"That shouldn't matter. No criminal charges there. They probably don't even know about those. So," he said with a reassuring look, "that's it. Pretty straightforward. Once you're up there, it should be less than ten minutes and you'll be free to go. Then you'll need to think about who you want to represent you when you go to trial."

"OK. Yeah, I have a lawyer I've worked with before."

"Good. You all set? Any questions? You all right?" I nodded. "OK, you should go into the courtroom in about ten minutes. You've got time for a smoke if you want one."

"Thanks, man."

I found a spot of wall to lean against and lit a cigarette. If that's all there was to it, it was just as well that nobody else came. I could just take the MTA back home and maybe try to get a hold of Harry Stone. Try to call Sarah. Call my parents. Maybe go see Cary. What a day this would be. I saw a newspaper lying on one of the benches. "Riot Rocks Northeastern!" the headline read. I picked it up. It said the cops repulsed several attempts by demonstrators to storm the auditorium—that was bullshit—and that thirty-one people had been arrested—and printed our names—and fifteen cops and "several" demonstrators had been injured. Below the headline on the front page was a picture showing broken windows at the Northeastern auditorium and beside that was a picture of a black cop with his face bandaged. The caption said, "Patrolman Fletcher Riley had five teeth knocked out at Northeastern University riot."

Riley? Shit, that was the name the cops kept saying the night before. But there must be more than one Riley on the Boston police force. Had to be. Besides this guy was black. The guy I hit was white.

Just then Kelly motioned to me that it was time to go in the courtroom.

The courtroom was packed and buzzing. I found a seat toward the back, next to a couple of freaks. We nodded and smiled at each other. It turned out they'd been arrested at Northeastern, too, but for disorderly conduct. We talked a little bit about it and how what we'd seen in the newspaper was totally different from what actually happened. Then a gavel sounded and somebody with a deep official voice said, "All rise." The judge—Wilson was his name—swept into the courtroom and we all sat down.

The first few arraignments were on regular criminal charges, young black men charged with petty theft and burglaries. The judge dispatched them quickly, heard their not guilty pleas, and set their bail. They must have come right from the jail because they were escorted to the front of the room in handcuffs and when their arraignments were over, the cops took them to a room in the back of the courtroom, some kind of holding cell.

When the Northeastern cases started, they went just like Kelly had said. Name called. Plea entered. Bail continued. They started with the assault and battery cases. Nine of us faced those charges. I was the fifth one called.

"Benjamin R. Tucker the third," the clerk read.

I stood up and the freaks next to me smiled encouragingly.

I met Kelly at a little gate through the wooden railing that separated the spectators from the people involved in the trial. We took our places, standing behind a long table on the right side of the courtroom. I held my hands together at my waist. My heart pulsed up into my throat and my breathing got tight. The judge looked up from the pile of papers in front of him, and spoke in a matter-of-fact monotone.

"You are Benjamin R. Tucker the third?"

"Yes," I said. Kelly kind of nudged me with a look. "Um…your honor. Yes, your honor."

"You live at 64 Mountfort Street, Back Bay?"

"Yes, your honor."

"Do you know that you have been charged with assault and battery of a police officer with a deadly weapon?"

"Yes, your honor."

I could feel the blood rushing through the veins in my hands as I squeezed and rubbed them together.

"Have you been fully apprised of your rights to legal counsel."

"Yes, your honor."

"And you are represented by legal counsel today?"

"Yes, your honor."

Kelly spoke. "John Kelly representing the defense, your honor."

"Very well. Mr. Tucker, how do you plead to the charges the Commonwealth of Massachusetts has entered against you today."

"Not guilty, your honor."

"So noted. Let's see. You have posted bail in the amount of $1,000. Is the Commonwealth comfortable with this amount of bail for Mr. Tucker?" He looked at the prosecutor's table where two lawyers sat behind stacks of folders, lawyers who had done nothing but nod and say yes up to this point in the proceedings.

"No, your honor. We believe the nature of Mr. Tucker's actions at Northeastern last night and his history warrant a higher bail. We request bail of $3,000, your honor."

Fuck. Kelly looked a little confused but still calm. He picked up a folder and leafed through it.

"Your honor," Kelly finally spoke. "We see nothing that would justify treating Mr. Tucker any differently than the previous cases involving similar charges."

The judge asked the prosecutors why I should be treated any differently.

The prosecutor opened a folder on the lectern in front of him and cleared his throat. He was short and thin with black, greased-back hair and a neatly pressed gray suit.

"Your honor, Mr. Tucker is part of an extremist, violent group of radicals from Boston University, that in combination with radicals in other parts of the city, is waging a systematic campaign of disruption in the hopes of instigating a violent revolution in our society. Mr. Tucker and his group have been part of virtually every violent disturbance in the Boston area in the past two years, including disturbances on election day 1968 at the Boston Common, occupation of the dean's office at Boston University, a fight with students at Boston English High School, efforts to interfere with the work of laboratories at the Massachusetts Institute of Technology, a recent series of disruptions at Boston University in connection with the strike at the General Electric company, as well as the events last night at Northeastern. Mr. Tucker was named in disciplinary charges by the Boston University administration in connection with the dean's office occupation and is currently named in a restraining order at that institution because of his involvement in the recent violent disturbances related to the General Electric strike. Tucker and his group are known to associate with the Weathermen, the extremely violent communist group, and other extremist left-wing groups. He went with his group to Northeastern last night for the sole purpose of creating a violent disturbance. He had no other business being at Northeastern last night. As you know, your honor, that disturbance led to serious injuries to several police officers, including Patrolman Fletcher Riley, the officer injured by a brick thrown by Mr. Tucker."

This was a bad fucking movie. Who the hell was he talking about?

"I would like to bring Patrolman Riley before the court now, you honor."

"Very well," the judge said. Kelly stood there, looking busily through his folder.

A tall black man came to the front of the courtroom. It was, of course, the cop from the morning paper. He had a long square face that was accented by a straight stiff row of half-inch-high hair. A bandage covered his mouth and the lower half of the left side of his face. You could tell even with the bandage that his whole jaw and mouth area were swollen. I couldn't help staring at him, at the size and thickness of the bandage, but our eyes never met. He was fucked up, for sure, and I was horrified that he, that they, that the Commonwealth of Massachusetts believed I had done that to him. Or at least that's what they were about to say in this court of law.

"Your honor, because of his injuries, Patrolman Riley has difficulty speaking. So I will just ask him questions that he can respond to with a nod or a shake of his head, if that pleases the court."

"Yes, of course," the judge said.

"Patrolman Riley, You were injured last night during the disturbance at Northeastern University, is that right?"

Riley nodded.

"You were struck in your face by a brick?"

Riley nodded.

"This happened while you were on the steps of the Northeastern Auditorium, trying to prevent unlawful entry into that building, isn't that correct?"

Riley nodded.

"Am I correct in stating that you lost five teeth and had to have seventeen stitches in your mouth as a result of that injury?"

Riley nodded.

"It's a very painful injury, isn't it, Patrolman Riley?"

Riley nodded.

"And will prevent you from performing active duty as a police officer for some time, won't it?"

Riley nodded.

"Thank you very much Patrolman Riley, I know it was hard for you to come in here today."

Judge Wilson asked Kelly if he had any questions. Kelly said no. The judge spoke to Riley. "Thank you very much Patrolman Riley. I wish you a speedy recovery." He swept a glowering look at me and then said to the prosecutor. "Do you have anything more?"

Now I wanted to scream "Not guilty! Not guilty! Not guilty!" But I was so dumbstruck and dazed, all I could do was to squeeze one hand tightly in the other and look to Kelly for some reassurance. But he didn't have any to give.

"Yes, your honor," the prosecutor spoke. "I'd like to call Officer Michael Brogan before the court."

"Very well."

A cop with a bandage on the side of his forehead came forward. He looked familiar.

The prosecutor addressed him. "Officer Brogan, were you at Northeastern University last night?"

"Yes," he replied. Brogan looked over at me and I suddenly realized he was the cop who had checked me out at the first place we stopped in the paddy wagon. Man, this was a trip. My heart was pounding now and my brain racing, it all was starting to make sense, bizarre fucking unreal sense.

"Did you have occasion to observe the defendant, Benjamin Tucker, during the disturbance at Northeastern last night?"

"Yes I did," again he looked at me, his lip curled in a sneer.

Kelly found his voice, "Your honor we're not prepared to try this case right now. What's the Commonwealth's point?"

"Your honor, we're trying to establish why the bail should be raised for this defendant—both because of his history, which we've cited, and his specific actions last night."

"Yes, yes," Judge Wilson said. "Proceed."

"Tell us what you observed Mr. Tucker doing last night during this disturbance, Officer Brogan."

"I saw him stand up on a bench in the courtyard outside of Northeastern University's auditorium and throw a brick that struck Patrolman Riley."

"Where were you when you saw this?"

"I was standing on the steps outside the auditorium, right next to Patrolman Riley?"

"And you are sure it was the defendant you saw throw the brick?"

"Positive."

"How can you be so sure?"

"I saw him very clearly and went after him and apprehended him on Huntington Avenue just outside the courtyard."

"And you have no doubt it's this man now standing before the court?"

"Absolutely no doubt."

I looked at Kelly, shouting "he's a fucking liar" with my eyes, but Kelly was a passive spectator to this far-fetched drama and nothing in his folder was of any help.

"Thank you, Officer Brogan," the prosecutor said. The judge again asked Kelly if he had any questions and again Kelly said no.

"Your honor," the prosecutor said. "I believe given Mr. Tucker's history of stirring up violence all over this city and the severity of the injury he's accused of inflicting, bail of $3,000 is more than justified."

"What do you have to say, Mr. Kelly?" the judge asked.

Kelly gathered himself. "Your honor, the Commonwealth's argument is based on a claimed history for which it has provided no evidence. There was not one previous criminal charge cited against my client. And I would remind the court that the State has proved nothing concrete about my client's involvement in the injuries to Patrolman Riley. Your honor, I still see no reason to treat my client any differently from the other defendants you've seen today."

Judge Wilson spoke, "Well, I'm going to disagree with you there, counselor. I'm very disturbed by the fact that the defendant is a student at Boston University and not at Northeastern University. Apparently, he caused plenty of trouble at Boston University and he and his gang are looking for other places to cause trouble. From what I heard today, I think even $3,000 is too low a bail, so I'm setting his bail at $3,500. Maybe that will help him remember where he goes to school. Thank you, gentlemen. Next."

I looked at Kelly. I could tell he hadn't quite figured out what he was going to say to me.

"Ben, I'm sorry…" Just then a couple of cops came up and put handcuffs on me—leaving my arms in front this time—and started moving me toward the back of the courtroom. "We'll get you bail. Is there someone I can call."

Mike had given me the number at 858 just in case. I fished awkwardly into my pants and found the piece of paper and handed it to Kelly. But there was a good chance no one would even be home. The cops were pulling at my arms. I told him he could try calling Harry Stone. "He's a Movement lawyer, too. He's helped me out a few times," I said over my shoulder as the cops led me away.

They took me toward a barred door in the back of the courtroom, the holding cell. The cops tossed me in there. It was about six feet square with benches along three walls in a U-shape facing the door. Three black guys who had been arraigned at the start of the session were in there.

I took a seat on the bench to my left, opposite two of them. The third sat on the bench between us. One guy smiled at me as I sat down. He was probably around my age, eighteen or nineteen. I nodded back at him and then the others.

The first one spoke. "Shit, man, you fucked that cop up. Right on, brother," he smiled at me again. He had a raggedy Afro and a scar just below one eye. "But they're going to fuck you up now. Them cops don't like that shit."

"Yeah man, you are one dead motherfucker," the guy on the bench between us spoke. He was kind of fat and his face was soft and ripply. He was giving me a hard look. "Man, you fuck a cop up like that and they don't forget—ever. They gonna put you in jail for a long time. What kind of time you lookin' at?"

"Well," I said, kind of soft, "the maximum is twenty years."

"Well then you looking at twenty years, bro. They don't take this shit lightly man, fucking up a cop like that. You going to jail for twenty years, man. What the fuck did you do that shit for anyway?"

"I didn't do this," I mumbled. I was stunned and scared and these guys were not exactly making it easy for me to try to get my shit together.

"Sure, man." The guy with the scar said. He was laughing. "Hey, man, it's cool. There's no cops in here. The thing is, man, it don't matter whether you did or you didn't. The cops say you did, so you did. That's the way it works, man. You been in jail before?"

"Yeah, a couple of times, nothing like this, though." I let out a deep breath.

"Well you did it up right this time, brother," he laughed again. "What were you doing last night anyway that cops were getting so fucked up?"

"We were protesting a speech by this guy named Hayakawa, who did some pretty brutal repression of a student movement in San Francisco. Lot of people just kind of standing around and yelling and shit and the cops just attacked. They fucked a lot of kids up, too."

"I heard about that dude, man," it was the third guy who hadn't said anything yet. He was tall and tight, with a thin pointy beard. He leaned into the corner of the room and sprawled across the bench. He looked at me with kind of a sneer. "Bad motherfucker. So did you throw anything at Hayakawa?"

"No, never saw him. Never got close to him. It was mostly between the cops and kids outside of where he was speaking."

"Bunch of crazy motherfuckers," it was the first guy again. "At least the Panthers have guns when they go picking fights with cops. Though a brick seems like it can do some pretty serious damage, too."

"I don't know nothing about any brick," I said, but he'd somehow made me smile. "You guys been here before?" I asked him.

"Yeah, but we never done it either—just them fucking cops keep saying we did."

I laughed. "So what happens now?"

"Well, we stay here until they're done in court, and if you don't make bail—and I gotta tell you, it ain't looking too promising for us right now—they'll take us down to the jail and we stay there until we get bail or we go to trial."

"What kind of time are you looking at?"

"A year or two. Shit man, no big thing. Maybe get out of this with no time at all. Ain't nothing like you're looking at. Hey man you got a smoke?"

"Yeah, can we smoke here?"

They all laughed. "What the fuck they gonna do? Put us in jail?" the tall one said. I laughed, too, and reached into my pocket and pulled out my crumpled pack of cigarettes. I had five left. It was a clumsy little dance trying to pull one out with my hands locked together. But I managed to get one and then passed the pack around.

"Shit, man," the fat one said. "What did you do to them cigarettes? Looks like you assaulted them with a deadly weapon, too." They all laughed again as they each examined them closely.

"Hey, don't smoke 'em," I said. "You won't hurt my feelings."

Lighting a match was another challenge with hand-cuffs, but I managed it somehow and passed my lit cigarette around. It was quiet for the first time since I'd been led into this room. I leaned hard against the stiff back of the bench and took a deep drag. Shit, man, I wasn't looking forward to going back to the city jail. And where the hell were we going to get another $2,500? I wasn't sure how much I could count on Kelly, especially if he couldn't get a hold of anybody at 858. Even if he managed to find Harry, what could Harry do? Shit. And now I was down to one cigarette. I tried to listen to the goings-on in the courtroom and all the other cases were flying through, nobody else was coming back to our holding cell. I guess I was a fucking serious criminal.

The first black guy told me they always tried to wrap up the arraignment hearings before lunch and it seemed like we must be getting close to that as the courtroom was starting to empty. Then we heard a key in the door and we all kind of straightened up and looked in that direction—another criminal to join us?

A cop stuck his head in the doorway.

"Tucker, Benjamin Tucker," he said with a disgusted look as he surveyed the room.

"That's me," I said, allowing some hope to creep into my head.

"Looks like you made bail." He sounded pissed.

Far out, I thought, as I awkwardly got to my feet, though I didn't allow myself to smile as the cop glared at me and my three cellmates looked at me with a kind of distant disbelief.

"Good luck, you guys," I said, turning back as I reached the door the cop was holding open for me.

The guy with the scar mumbled something that might have been like, "yeah, you too, man," but he wasn't looking at me. I hesitated for a second or two, thinking there should be something more I should say, but they were all looking at the floor and the ceiling, so I stepped toward the guard and out the door.

The guard led me, still handcuffed, across the back of the nearly empty courtroom, then out a door that led to a hallway between offices, out of sight of the main lobby, then through another door, into an office that was buzzing with activity. He took me to a counter next to a window that looked out on the lobby that was jammed with people. A clerk put some papers in front of me. While she explained them to me, the guard took off my handcuffs. I looked out through the window, and saw tall Lenny standing out among the milling crowd. When he saw me, I could see him look down to his left, saying something, and then out from behind someone blocking her line of sight stepped Sarah.

She waved to me and I could see tears in her eyes.

As soon as I finished signing the papers and the clerk told me I was free to go, I started moving as fast as I could toward Sarah and Lenny. I could see they were moving toward me, too. Before I could get very far though, a man with stringy hair and a thin moustache put his hand in front of me and introduced himself as Theodore J. Frothingham, bail bondsman. He wore a dark shiny suit. He explained to me that Kelly, my lawyer, and Sarah had made arrangements with him to cover my bail. He was smiling and patting me on the back like he was my new best buddy as he explained how it worked. I couldn't really follow him. All I wanted in the whole world was to hold Sarah tighter than I'd ever held anything. I tried to keep moving, but with him on top of me it was like pulling an anchor. Somehow, Frothingham was telling me, they applied the bail I'd posted the night before and he guaranteed the rest for a ten percent fee. He was betting that I'd show up for my trial, which was set for late February. If he won he'd win $350. If he lost, he'd be out $2,500, but he was sure, he said with a threatening smile, I wouldn't do anything foolish. I nodded and agreed and thanked him, though paying as little attention to him as I possibly could.

"That girl of yours is something," he said with a nod toward Sarah who was now just a little more than an arm's length away. "She was determined to get you out of there. When she got here, she started lighting fires."

And she was there and his oily voice faded into the hum of the crowd as I looked into her wet eyes and saw a love that was stronger than anything the pigs had thrown at me in the past eighteen hours. And we filled each other's arms and squeezed as though the strength of our hug could somehow shelter us from it all, take us from this courthouse to that rich and colorful place where love is not ridiculous, where to not love, to not believe in love, to not fight for love, is insanity beyond belief. We squeezed and pressed our faces tight together, so tight her tears ran down my cheek.

"Are you OK?," she finally said.

"Yeah." I said "Yeah...I'm so glad you're here...so glad...and I'm sorry...."

"Hey, you guys need a room?" It was Frothingham. "I can help you with that, too."

We didn't respond, but we were pulled back into the reality that we were standing in the middle of the lobby of the Roxbury District Court. Sarah wiped her eyes and I reached up to give Lenny a hug.

"Thanks for coming, man."

"Sure thing, man. She was coming no matter what. I just thought someone should come with her. You OK?"

"I'm OK *now*, man," I said. But looking around, I saw we had become something of a spectacle for everyone in the lobby—the tall black guy, the long-haired criminal, the crying hippie chick, and the greasy bail bondsman. "Hey, let's get the hell out of here."

We said our goodbyes to Frothingham. I put my right arm around Sarah's shoulders and pulled her close to me. She put her left arm around my waist. Lenny walked beside us as we made our way through the crowd out of the lobby. When we opened the door, we were momentarily blinded by an unexpectedly bright day and then saw a posse of newspaper photographers and TV cameramen lined up along the bottom of the steps. We stopped for a second, dazed by this brilliant light and the media mob. But Lenny urged us forward. I lifted my coat in front of us to block the view of Sarah's and my face—like you always see criminals do on TV and in the movies. But Lenny had a better way to keep us off the front page and the evening news.

As we started down the steps, he moved in front of us, then raised both his hands in front of his face and emphatically extended his middle fingers: "Print that, motherfuckers," he said.

CHAPTER TWENTY-NINE

January 30 [aftermath]

AS WE RODE THE MTA HOME, I TOLD SARAH and Lenny the whole story and, even as I told it, it was like telling a dream, or a story about somebody else. Everything that had happened was as real to me as my skin but it was this really unfamiliar skin, like what you find when you peel off a scab, all oozy and raw and sore, not quite skin yet. Sarah held my hand tight in hers and listened, her eyes reacting with surprise, anger, concern, empathy. Not once did I see a flicker of doubt in those eyes.

She told me what had happened when Leslie had called her. They'd been out to dinner for her father's birthday and were hanging out at home, watching TV, the first time in a long time they'd all been together and mellow. She said when she got off the phone, she was hysterical, but her parents never said anything except to ask what was wrong and how they could help. She'd flown out on the first flight in the morning. Her father paid for her plane ticket.

"He was really good about it," she said. "I know he doesn't really like it…but he knows."

I knew, too, looking into the well of her eyes, knew that love is as complicated as it is real. That was the first time I could remember that she had mentioned her father that I didn't feel a surge of anger. And in the traffic jam of thoughts careening around my head I had this sudden clear memory of the poem we'd seen on the wall of the Philadelphia Art Museum: "Is it you or I who says/ Out of my love for you/ I will give you back to yourself."

The day was sunny and surprisingly warm as we walked from Kenmore Square to Mountfort Street, Sarah and I arm in arm, Lenny ambling beside us. It was the middle of the lunch hour, Friday afternoon, and the streets were full of people, looking bright and hopeful at this early tease of spring. Shaggy-haired students moving with a bounce into the weekend, young office workers in suits and skirts and sweaters strolling slowly around the square, construction workers sitting, leaning against the side of a brick building, black lunch buckets between them, hands waving in animated conversations.

A gusty wind swept around us as we crossed the bridge over the turnpike, where the traffic seemed denser and louder than usual. I pulled Sarah in tighter to me and gave her a searching smile. She smiled back at me, the breeze blowing her hair off and away from her face, exposing the full curl of her jaw into the soft whiteness of her neck. Why was I so lucky to have this beautiful girl beside me, smiling at me, ready to risk… ready to risk what? Ready to risk whatever it was? She'd already risked a lot just to be there on that bridge beside me. Risked a lot for me.

I looked past her and saw Lenny grinning, a voyeur's grin—someone watching love being made and digging it. I wondered if he remembered that he was beside us that first night we'd slept together in the dean's office. Me and Sarah between Lenny and Mike. What romance. I was thinking about saying something, recalling the innocence within all the militancy of that night, when, beyond Lenny, I saw a blue-and-white Boston police car, on the other side of the street, cruising toward Kenmore Square. And I flashed to the four visitors to my cell the night before. I felt a quick chill and ducked my head away from the street toward the cars speeding westward on the turnpike. Sarah moved her hand up my back and gently sheltered my head, which was now turned away from her. The cop car passed, but now we moved more purposely toward Mountfort Street.

When we went into our apartment, I could hear Hendrix coming from Mike's room, his great version of Dylan's "All Along The Watchtower."

Sarah shot me a quick smile. Jimi was not one of her favorites. It had come to be kind of a joke between us: I'd say something like "How 'bout some Hendrix?" and she'd always give me the same sour look. Today, she just smiled. Jimi sounded awful good to me just then.

My sister met us in the hallway. One of her roommates had seen my name in the newspaper, so Cary had come over. She gave me a big hug.

"How are you?" she said.

"I'm OK, I guess," I said as Mike and Little Eddie joined us.

"How did it go in court?" Mike asked.

"Man," I said to all of them. "You wouldn't believe it. You just wouldn't fucking believe it."

We all headed into my room, which was still a fucking mess. "Sorry, I didn't have time to clean it," I explained to Sarah. "I wasn't expecting you today."

As we went in, Mike pointed to Tavola who was curled up in a pile of clothes in a corner of my room. I picked her up and held her tight. She just looked annoyed that I'd woken her. Stu was still at work. Brian was still off wherever he had gone.

We all found spots on my mattresses and I tried to explain how crazy it was in court—they'd fucking accused me of hitting the wrong cop. I still couldn't quite believe it. In some ways that could be good. I was innocent. Absolutely. On the other hand, the cop I was accused of hitting was the headline cop-victim, hurt, I was pretty sure, much worse than the cop I actually did hit. The cops were claiming that him getting hit is what started the whole riot, justified their attack. And since the facts didn't really fit with the charges against me, the cops obviously weren't bashful about changing the facts. Hard to know what to make of it, but there was no doubt it was fucking crazy.

Cary hadn't talked to our parents yet. Shit, I knew I had to call them. I had aunts and uncles in the Boston area who read the papers, too. But I didn't want to call my mother or father at work, so I asked Sarah to remind me to call sometime in the early evening, when they'd be home.

There was probably something I should have been doing, but it felt so good just to sit in my room, talking quietly with Sarah and Mike and Cary and Lenny and Little Eddie. After we talked through the arrest and jail and court as much as we possibly could, Cary told stories about when I'd gotten in trouble as a little kid. "Terrible Terry," some people called me. Terry was my nickname, what everyone called me, because I had the same first name as my father and my parents had come up with Terry because it was close to the Latin word for "the third" or something like that. "Terrible" was added to it because I got in trouble a lot. It was mostly just small neighborhood stuff, didn't usually involve the police. Except once when all these free samples of this hockey-puck shaped laundry detergent called Salvo ended up on everybody's door in our neighborhood. Me and two friends swiped enough of the samples to fill up our paper-boy bags and then launched an attack on the house of these elderly sisters (named the Grumpfs, I swear to God), who always fed our baseballs that ended up in their yard to their mean, growling dogs. Their brown-shingled house spotted with puffs of white powder, they called the cops and a major negotiation took place over the fence that separated our two yards, between the Grumpfs and the cops and our parents. In the end, I think we agreed to clean it all up and they agreed not to press any charges.

Everyone laughed as I tried to justify the attack—we'd lost dozens of baseballs to them and it was payback time. But even Mike acted shocked at this revelation.

"Terrible Terry, eh?" he said. "I had no idea what a bad ass I've been hanging out with."

After a couple of hours of shooting the shit like that, Cary had to get back home. She told me to keep her tuned in and let her know what she could do to help. I walked her to the door and she gave me another big hug and had some tears in her eyes when she said good-bye.

Mike had gone back into his room. Lenny and Little Eddie took up the spots on their respective couches, Lenny looking to take a nap and Eddie devouring another book he'd borrowed from my stack.

When I went back into my room, Sarah was sitting on my mattress with her back against the wall and Tavola curled up in her lap. She gave me a weary smile. "Hey there, Terrible Terry," she said.

I sat beside her and stroked her hand as she pet Tavola. She lifted her eyes up to mine for a second, then looked back down at the cat. We just sat there quiet for awhile. Sarah ran her fingers slowly down the full length of Tavola's back and followed her tail to its tip.

"I'm so happy you came," I said. "When I saw you at the courthouse, it was like…God, I don't even know how to say it…It was like I stopped seeing or hearing or thinking about anything but you. Man, when I saw you…"

She looked up, her eyes suddenly sharp. "I wasn't going to leave that courthouse without you. I just had to get you out of there. I just had to. Your lawyer was kind of a space case and then they said they were going to take you back to the city jail if we didn't get you bailed out before court adjourned. I just couldn't have handled that. I would have freaked." She looked full at me now, a tear was trickling down her right cheek. "I just had to get you out of there, Ben."

"I'm so glad you did," I said. Sarah was looking straight down at Tavola, petting her intently. Tavola's purrs were almost a rumble. I watched Sarah pet her for a while, neither of us saying anything.

"What are you thinking?" I finally asked.

"I don't know Ben," she looked up. As I tried to read what was in her eyes, I was struck by how incredibly tired she looked. "What's going to happen now?" she asked.

"I don't know."

The cat's purrs were the only sound again.

"I'm sorry, Sarah." My eyes felt heavy and wet.

"You don't need to be sorry."

"But I am…sorry to yank you into the middle of this…and on your father's birthday."

"You didn't yank me anywhere. I'm here because I want to be."

She looked straight down again, slowly, deeply petting Tavola.

"I hope so," I said softly. I scanned from her long thin fingers moving along the cat's smooth black coat up to the shimmering curls of her chestnut brown hair, which hid her face from me. I took a long breath.

"It was weird when the prosecutor was reading the list of all the shit I'd done—shit we'd done—trying to get the judge to raise my bail. I mean, it sounded like this serious-ass revolutionary and I sat there—or stood there—stunned, thinking 'what a bunch of bullshit.' But it's true. Every word he said was true. The injunction, the disciplinary charges, Boston English, MIT—shit, there was a lot of good stuff he left out. I mean it's not true true. He didn't say that the disciplinary charges probably happened because you and me were goofing around instead of going to a meeting and posed for pictures and that the injunction was totally ridiculous, that it linked me with a bunch of straight PL commies. But it's true in some bigger sense. At the heart of everything, it's true. What I am, all that I am, whatever it is that I am—all that we are—is dangerous to them somehow."

She lifted her head and our eyes met.

"Shit, Sarah, I'm guilty. I'll fight like hell to stay out of jail, but right here between us we need to face the reality that I'm guilty. They've got their facts wrong but the facts don't really matter. They'll make up whatever facts they need. Shit, so will we. I'm guilty. And I don't think there's any going back, now—not for me, that's for sure. And it's just…I don't know…I just don't know that you were at that place yet…or wanna be. And I'm sorry that I kinda made this jump without you. Shit, Sarah, I don't know…"

She glared backed at me, eyes hard, kind of pissed, it seemed. "You don't know, Ben, really? You don't know?"

She pulled back, away from me. "What do think? What do you think I've been thinking since I got that phone call last night? Sometimes you talk to me like you think I don't know anything, or that I haven't thought about any of this stuff. I don't think about it as much as you or at least I don't talk about it as much as you. But give me some credit. Yeah, you're guilty. Well I'm guilty, too, and Mike's guilty and Stu's guilty and Leslie is guilty and all our friends are guilty. That's not exactly a startling revelation. I had to look at my father last night on his birthday and tell him my boy friend, who he really doesn't like all that well, was in jail having something to do with hitting a police officer and I needed to go to Boston to be with him so could he please give me some money. That was not his dream way to spend his birthday.

"I think I broke his heart, Ben." Her look softened. "Last night more than ever, because he knew…he knew from looking at me after that phone call that I was never going to give you up." Tears started coming down hard and she stopped, took a deep breath and wiped her face, and looked straight in on me. "I'm sorry Ben, I know you've been through a lot worse than me in the last day, but goddammit, would you get this into your thick blonde skull, I love you. I'm on your side. You're the only one who's ever doubted that."

She couldn't stop the tears that were flowing hard now. She wiped one cheek and then another, but never took her eyes off me. Her love was sure, but her eyes burned in on me with a thousand other questions.

"I'm sorry, Sarah." I said. I picked up her hand and held it softly in mine. "I knew when I saw you in the courthouse what it meant that you were there. The joy that I felt when I saw you was like…it was like I had to be dragged through all the shit in jail and in court to know that joy. Seeing you there made it all fit together. Like somehow I'd won, even though everything seemed to be going against me.

"I know I shouldn't doubt you, Sarah. Maybe I'm just talking to myself. Sitting in that jail cell, or in the courtroom, or in the little cell room with those three black guys, I had to get face to face with what I am, with who I am. What it means for me, for us.

"Lawyers and courts, thinking about dealing with prison or splitting. That's what happens now, I guess. Even as I'm saying that I still can't believe it. I'm just a kid. I never really wanted to hurt anybody. I just wanted somehow to stop all the hurting. Now they've got twenty years over my head. Scary and heavy, but…"

Sarah reached her arms around me and pulled me in close to her. "I know, Ben. But I just know that somehow things are going to work out. I don't know how, but I know they will."

"Yeah, I believe that." I pulled back from her, so I could look full into her eyes. I held both her hands in mine. "We started today—walking out of that courthouse with Lenny's fingers clearing our path. The two of us together. That's it. That's where it starts."

And I held her tight and I knew that in that embrace was the defense strategy that really mattered, this love that wouldn't let us give up on each other.

"They're really going to test us now," I said. "But the two of us surrounded by all our brothers and sisters, we can stand up to whatever they've got. I'm not saying I'm not scared, that this isn't seriously heavy shit, but our only chance is to keep fighting, keep believing, keep loving—otherwise they win no matter what the fucking court does."

Tavola, trapped between us, stood up and stretched and slinked out into an open spot on the mattress. We both followed her with our eyes, then looked at each other and laughed softly at her oblivious independence.

"Sarah, I love you so much," I said.

"Ben, I love you, too." And we kissed slow and soft. Love, love, love.

"I can't move to Boston, Ben, not now," she said between kisses.

"I know Sarah. It's OK, probably for the best given how heavy things are."

"I still have to move slow with my parents—this just confirms all their worst fears about you."

"I know—this confirms all my worst fears about me, too."

She laughed, but it was a muffled laugh, a tired laugh.

"It's OK," I said. "We'll figure all that out."

Music from Mike's room crept in.

Oh, yeah, all right, are you going to be in my dreams...tonight?

I guess it'd been on all along but I hadn't really noticed until then. Sarah and I held our interlocked hands up between us, letting them flow in a kind of circular dance.

Love you....Love you....Love you.... Love you....

Our eyes danced a slower, more penetrating dance. So much of what I needed lived behind her eyes.

And in the end...

CHAPTER THIRTY

February 2 [postscript]

I SLEPT LATE. I REALLY DIDN'T FEEL LIKE GOING to school and having to deal with all the questions and looks I was going to get from people because of the arrest. Or maybe I didn't want to face all the people who didn't know and didn't care—the world going on just as it had last Thursday morning, when I knew to my core that the world would never be like that again. I just lay in bed for awhile, smoking cigarettes and trying to figure some kind of plan for dealing with lawyers and all the details I was going to have to handle. Cary had heard that a photographer for the *Old Mole* had some pictures that showed that Fletcher Riley was still on the police lines when they were clearing Huntington Avenue, long after I supposedly hit him. So I was going to try to track down those photos. But I found myself drifting off, thinking about Sarah. She was coming back up in two weeks, the Kinks were going to be in town—it'd be kind of an early birthday celebration for me. I turned twenty in three weeks.

Before she left on Saturday, Sarah had bought me a blue stocking cap to push my hair up into so I wasn't quite as identifiable when I was out on the streets. I didn't go out alone if I could possibly avoid it. Mike was real good about looking out for me. Shit, I always felt safe when Mike was walking beside me. He'd checked with me before he headed out this morning, but I told him to go ahead, I was going to try to get my shit together, maybe I'd catch up with him at the Union at lunchtime. But it probably was getting close to noon, and I hadn't got my ass out of bed yet. I was just kind of digging laying there in the calm and the quiet.

There was a knock on the door. Shit. Cops? Who else would knock? Nobody else was home, so I pulled on some pants and moved cautiously toward the door. "Who is it?" I asked as I got close.

"It's your father," the voice on the other side of the door said.

I stopped, stunned. My father? Then I hurried to open the door, and there he was—my father.

"Hi…I just…" he stammered as he took in the sight of me, disheveled and only partly dressed.

"Dad," I said, suddenly feeling kind of choked up. "Dad." And I hugged him. Something we hadn't done much of for a long time. He still smelled like Mennen after-shave.

"I'm sorry to surprise you," he said. "I just couldn't sit in Illinois thinking about what was going on here. I had to come and see for myself. Your mother and I are just worried sick about you."

"I know, Dad. I'm sorry," we were still standing awkwardly in the doorway. "Hey, why don't you come in." I looked back over my shoulder and saw my apartment from a perspective I hadn't thought of before—my father's. "I'll warn you, it's pretty funky. But just come in while I get some clothes on and then we can go somewhere."

He smiled at me but I knew he was kind of uptight. It took a lot for him to come and just show up at my door. I'm sure he had no idea what to expect from the place, from me. As we walked past the wall collage, he slowed a little to check it out. A smile came over his face. "Some wall you got here," he said. "You'll have to get me the name of your interior decorator." He laughed. That was good.

He sat, gingerly, on the first couch—Lenny's—while I put on a shirt and socks and shoes. I think he was afraid of being swallowed by the cushions.

I couldn't believe my father was sitting on a couch in the hall at Mountfort Street.

"Are you doing OK?" he asked as I dressed.

"Yeah, Dad, I am," I said. "I really am."

"We have a lot to talk about."

"Yeah, you're right," I said as I came back in the hall and he managed to pull himself out of the couch and we headed for the door. "We really do."

Acknowledgments

THANKS TO MY WRITING GROUP, WHO ARE the god-parents of this work: Kathleen Holt, Ross West, Cheri Brooks, Beth Hege Piatote, Debra Gwartney, Brett Campbell, Kimber Williams, Mark Blaine, Harley Patrick, Tim Sheehan, Jen Kocher, Mark Yates. Special thanks to Kathleen, Ross, Debra, and Jeffrey Schier for their insightful comments on versions of the finished manuscript. Thanks to John Daniel for his kind assistance. Thanks to Tom Griffin for listening to the oral version on the PCT.

Special thanks to Bruce, Larry, Gary, Kevin, Tom C., my sister Gale Maynard, Jimmy T., Betsy, who helped me, as always, to keep it real.

I will always cherish the times with Momo, Herbie, Deacon, Kenny, Scott, Jimmy P., Alice, Linda and Wendy, Carol, Alan, Eric, Charlene, Michael, Suzy, Patty, Seymour, Punky, Jane, Harry, Gerard, Steve, Marty, Jim S., Bob, Keith, Nancy, Ron, Wendy, Joe, Artie, Michael, Willy, Kit, Tom, David, Professor Yarrington, Howard Price, and so many others. Hope you have kept the faith.

Heartfelt thanks to my sisters, Trish Martin, Phyllis Maynard, Val Maynard, and Gale, who have always spoiled me with their love; to Al and Judy Schwartz, who taught me the amazing tenacity of love; to Corey, for teaching me new dimensions of love—and for not doing to me what I did to my parents.

And eternal gratitude to my parents, Guy and Peggy Maynard, whose love shone through.

And, of course and always, to Shelley, who saved my life with her love.

Music References

CHAPTER 1

"Hey Jude" written by John Lennon and Paul McCartney, performed by the Beatles, © 1968 Sony/ATV Music Publishing LLC, 8 Music Square West, Nashville, TN 37203. All rights reserved. Used by permission.

"The End" written by John Lennon and Paul McCartney performed by The Beatles, © 1969 Sony/ATV Music Publishing LLC, 8 Music Square West, Nashville, TN 37203. All rights reserved. Used by permission.

CHAPTER 5

"It's All Too Much" written by George Harrison, performed by the Beatles © 1968 Sony/ATV Music Publishing LLC, 8 Music Square West, Nashville, TN 37203. All rights reserved. Used by permission.

"Eskimo Blue Day" written by Paul Kantner, performed by Jefferson Airplane © (1969). Permission requested.

CHAPTER 6

"Whipping Post" words and music by Gregg Allman performed by the Allman Brothers, © 1971 by Unichappell Music Inc. and Elijah Blue Music. Copyright renewed. International copyright secured. All rights reserved. Used by permission. Reprinted by permission of Hal Leonard Corporation.

CHAPTER 7

"Good Lovin'" words and music by Rudy Clark and Arthur Resnick, © 1965 by Alley Music Corp. and Bug Music-Trio Music Company. Copyright renewed. International copyright secured. All rights reserved. Used by permission. Reprinted by permission of Hal Leonard Corporation.

"Not Fade Away" words and music by Charles Hardin and Norman Petty, © 1957 (Renewed) MPL Music Publishing, Inc. and Wren Music Co. All rights reserved. Reprinted by permission of Hal Leonard Corporation.

CHAPTER 8

"Subterranean Homesick Blues," written and performed by Bob Dylan © 1965 by Warner Bros. Inc.; renewed 1993 by Special Rider Music. All rights reserved. International copyright secured. Used by permission.

About the Author

GUY MAYNARD LIVED IN New Bedford, Massachusetts, for his first thirteen years, spent his high school years in Urbana, Illinois, went to two years of college back in Boston, and has lived in Oregon since the early 1970s. He was lead singer in a teen rock and roll band, was active in the civil rights and anti–Vietnam War movements, lived on a commune in southern Oregon, worked as a carpenter, and was a member of a worker-owned construction company. After receiving his degree in journalism from the University of Oregon in 1984, he was editor of a small community newspaper and then worked on a number of trade magazines in such fields as liquid and gas chromatography and geographic information systems. He has been editor of *Oregon Quarterly,* the University of Oregon magazine, since 1995; he co-edited the 2003 collection, *Best Essays NW;* and his essays and articles have appeared in several Northwest regional publications. He lives with his wife Shelley in a 1930s-vintage house in the middle of Eugene, Oregon. They have a grown son, Corey. This is his first novel.

Visit *TheRiskofBeingRidiculous.com* and
The Risk of Being Ridiculous Facebook page.

Breinigsville, PA USA
15 December 2010
251483BV00001B/2/P